PRAISE FOR

T0029456

Gone Too Long

"Gripping, gut-wrenching thriller."

—*Publishers Weekly*

"A riveting mystery, brilliantly crafted and weighted with real-world resonance . . . A timely thriller that will stay with the reader long after the last page has been turned."

—*Kirkus Reviews* (starred review)

"This compelling, issue-oriented story by Edgar Award–winning author Roy is a creepy, eerie account of a young girl and a community held hostage by the Klan."

—*Library Journal* (starred review)

"Filled with a creeping, entangling sense of danger. It's the kind of writing you would expect from the Edgar-winning author, but it's made even more powerful here, filled with the purpose of exposing a hateful legacy and issuing a timely warning of its historical ebb and flow."

—*Booklist* (starred review)

"This electrifying novel . . . [is] a gripping mystery with a timely, unnerving message—you won't be able to look away."

—*People* (Book of the Week)

"A book so good you can't look away."

—*O, The Oprah Magazine* (Best Books of Summer)

The Disappearing

"Lori Roy is one of the most elegant and enchanting writers to cross my path in a long, long time. I was transfixed by *The Disappearing*. A story of buried secrets rising to the light, it unfolds with a hypnotic grip that won't let go until the last secrets are revealed on the final page. This is a deep, dark, and wonderful book."

—Michael Connelly, *New York Times* bestselling author

"Roy's new novel is impossible to put down or forget, a masterful show of suspense."

—CrimeReads (Most Anticipated Summer Reads)

"Gripping . . . [Roy is a] rising star."

—*O, The Oprah Magazine*

"As atmospheric as a summer's night."

—*Family Circle* (Summer's Best Books Reading List)

"An irresistibly propulsive mystery wrapped in the haunted atmosphere of Southern Gothic and inspired by real Florida crimes . . . her best book yet."

—*Tampa Bay Times*

"Lori Roy . . . is a remarkable writer, especially when she is tracking with a strange elegance a family steeped in death. What makes her prose lyrically different from most mysteries is her capacity to build her plot from shreds of horror."

—*Washington Times*

"[An] exceptional novel. Lori Roy's writing oozes atmosphere."

—*Star Tribune* (Summer Reading List)

"Beautifully written and expertly plotted, *The Disappearing* is a twisty, haunting, and utterly riveting thriller. Lori Roy just gets better and better."
—Alafair Burke, *New York Times* bestselling author

"Lori Roy has been on my must-read list since her debut. There's a reason she's already won two Edgar Awards—exemplary plotting, clever twists, and compelling characters—but for me it is her voice that holds the most power. She writes with an ingenious, whispering menace and a masterful understanding of the way the past works on the present, and on the human heart. *The Disappearing* is her finest work to date."
—Michael Koryta, *New York Times* bestselling author

"As dark and atmospheric as a Northern Florida summer night, *The Disappearing* is Lori Roy at the top of her game. Her simmering tale is, at the heart, a compelling mystery. But it's also a deep meditation on family and the secrets and lies that can twist through our lives like a strangler fig. The powerful sense of place and a haunting cast of characters linger long after the book is closed. If you haven't read Lori Roy, now is the time."
—Lisa Unger, *New York Times* bestselling author

"Lori Roy is an impeccable writer—original, fearless, and insightful. *The Disappearing*, with its dark secrets and damaged souls, is another triumph of Roy's skill: it's insidiously sinister, seamlessly plotted, and relentlessly haunting."
—Hank Phillippi Ryan, *USA Today* bestselling author

"This contemporary slow burner oozes with atmosphere, and Roy effortlessly weaves numerous plot threads together without sacrificing her characters, who are very flawed and all too human. Secrets and lies abound, and Lane's struggle to be a good mother while fighting her own considerable demons will resonate with readers, as will the chilling finale. A twisted Southern Gothic winner."
—*Kirkus Reviews*

"Roy has created a town with a frightening past that just keeps getting worse. You get the chills just reading her hypnotic tale, which makes this four in a row when it comes to fantastic books written by Lori Roy."

—*Suspense Magazine*

"Roy . . . delivers another creepily atmospheric, cunningly plotted suspense tale . . . excruciating tension throughout."

—*Booklist*

Let Me Die in His Footsteps

2016 Recipient of the Edgar Award for Best Novel

"This Depression-era story is a sad one, written in every shade of Gothic black. But its true colors emerge in the rich textures of the narrative, and in the music of that voice, as hypnotic as the scent coming off a field of lavender."

—*New York Times Book Review*

"Roy excels in depicting the menace lurking in the natural world."

—*Washington Post*

"As the mystery deepens, so, too, does the suspense and affection for each Kentuckian who pulls up a chair at the kitchen table."

—Associated Press

"Roy does wonderful work weaving her complementary narratives into a naturally cohesive novel, and the central mystery . . . unravels in a way that is simultaneously elegant and unexpected . . . Though this mystery provides its engine, the novel demonstrates an undeniable literary bent."

—*Los Angeles Times*

"[A] richly detailed, highly suspenseful Gothic novel filled with indelible imagery."

—*Huffington Post*

"[*Let Me Die in His Footsteps*] has elements of crime fiction but moves into a new genre for Roy: Southern Gothic. It teems with family feuds, forbidden love, second sight, and wronged innocents, all held together by Roy's taut style and gift for suspense."

—*Tampa Bay Times*

"*Let Me Die in His Footsteps* gracefully moves toward a stunning finale as Roy unfurls insightful character studies . . . [It] is a story about what links families and drives them apart."

—*Sun Sentinel*

"Reading Lori Roy is a sinuous, near-physical experience, her stories so rich and well told they twine into the reader in a manner both gentle and profoundly deep. I consider her writing a love sonnet to American letters. Simply lovely."

—John Hart, *New York Times* bestselling author

"Something to tide you over until Harper Lee's book release: This is an addictive Southern Gothic thriller . . ."

—*Elle Canada*

"This is a beautifully observed story whose details of time, place, and character are stunning little jewels sure to dazzle the eye on every page. Quite simply put, I loved this book."

—William Kent Krueger, *New York Times* bestselling author

"There are echoes of Flannery O'Connor here: poverty, violence, malevolence, and grace. Roy's writing is spell-like, using a simplicity of language, deft characterization, an understanding of the dark side of human nature, and relentless plotting in order to pull together every aspect of the conjuring necessary to create a masterpiece of Southern Noir."

—Historical Novel Society

"The scents of Lavender and regret are heavy in this suspenseful coming-of-age novel . . . This powerful story . . . should transfix readers right up to its stunning final twist."

—*Publishers Weekly* (starred review)

"Edgar-winner Roy's third novel is an atmospheric, vividly drawn tale that twists her trademark theme of family secrets with the crackling spark of the 'know-how' for a suspenseful, ghost-story feel."

—*Booklist* (starred review)

"Young love, Southern folklore, family feuds, and crimes of passion . . . Roy describes life on a lavender farm in rural Kentucky in vivid detail, and the mystery of what happened years ago will keep readers engaged until the end."

—*Library Journal*

"Roy (*Bent Road*, 2011, etc.) draws a Faulkner-ian tale of sex and violence from the Kentucky hills . . . [Her] characters live whole on the page, especially Annie, all gawky girl stumbling her way to womanhood through prejudice and inhibition."

—*Kirkus Reviews*

Until She Comes Home

2014 Edgar Award Finalist for Best Novel

"That's the simple, heartbreaking truth Lori Roy delivers, sotto voce, in *Until She Comes Home*, a quietly shocking account of the tiny tremors in the life of a city that warn of cataclysms to come."

—*New York Times Book Review*

"Roy adroitly captures the atmosphere of the time, when racial tensions were bubbling over and fear of integration was prevalent. The author slowly draws the reader in, as violence flares and dark secrets emerge; this is a superb, tense suspense tale that's one of the year's best crime novels."

—*Lansing State Journal*

"Roy's language pulses . . . Days after finishing [*Until She Comes Home*], the lives of these women still haunted me."

—*Milwaukee Journal Sentinel*

"Lori Roy mixes lyrical prose, a noir approach, and gothic undertones for an urban story set in 1958 about a community pulled apart by racism, fear, and image . . ."

—*Sun Sentinel*

"Beach Reads you won't want to put down . . . In this thriller set in 1950s Detroit, a group of seemingly genteel women grapple with racial tension, gender violence, and two murders that throw their tidy suburban neighborhood into a tailspin."

—*Ladies' Home Journal*

"Extraordinary. Compelling. And beautifully, quietly disturbing . . . These gorgeously drawn characters and their mysteries will haunt you long after you turn the last page. Lori Roy is an incredible talent."

—Hank Phillippi Ryan, *USA Today* bestselling author

"A suspenseful, atmospheric work of crime fiction as well as a clear-eyed look at relationships between the sexes and races in mid-twentieth-century America."

—*Tampa Bay Times*

"A beautifully written, at times lyrical, study of a disintegrating community. Roy, author of the Edgar Award–winning mystery *Bent Road*, tackles similar themes here with equally successful results."

—*Kirkus Reviews* (starred review)

"What seems to begin in the glowing warmth of a homey kitchen transforms into a probing emotional drama that speaks powerfully to women about family, prejudice, power . . . and secrets."

—*Booklist* (starred review)

"Rich . . . lyrical . . . Roy delivers a timeless story that gives shape to those secrets and tragedies from which some people never recover."

—McClatchy-Tribune News Service

"Lori Roy has entered the arena of great American authors shared by Williams, Faulkner, and Lee."

—Bookreporter

"A tour de force of mood and suspense."

—*BookPage*

Bent Road

2012 Recipient of the Edgar Award for Best First Novel

"Writing with a delicate touch but great strength of purpose, Roy creates stark studies of the prairie landscape and subtle portraits . . ."
—*New York Times*

"A remarkably assured debut novel. Rich and evocative, Lori Roy's voice is a welcome addition to American fiction."
—Dennis Lehane, *New York Times* bestselling author

"Dropping us in a world of seeming simplicity, in a time of seeming calm, Lori Roy transforms 1960s small-town Kansas into a haunting memory-scape. Bringing to mind the family horrors of Jane Smiley's *A Thousand Acres* and the dark emotional terrain of Tana French's *In the Woods*, *Bent Road* manages to be both psychologically acute and breathtakingly suspenseful, burrowing into your brain with a feverish power all its own."
—Megan Abbott, Edgar Award–winning novelist

"In her promising debut novel *Bent Road*, Lori Roy proves that dark secrets hide even in the most wide-open places. Set in the beautifully rendered Kansas plains, *Bent Road* is a family story with a suspenseful gothic core, one which shows that the past always has a price, whether you're running from it or back toward it. Crisp, evocative prose, full-blooded characters, and a haunting setting make this debut stand out."
—Michael Koryta, *New York Times* bestselling author

"Don't be fooled by the novel's apparent simplicity: what emerges from the surface is a tale of extraordinary emotional power, one of long-standing pain set against the pulsating drumbeat of social change."

—NPR

"Roy . . . proves herself to be a new talent to watch in the mystery genre. *Bent Road* is one of the best debuts of 2011."

—*Sun Sentinel*

"Roy's outstanding debut melds strong characters and an engrossing plot with an evocative sense of place . . . Roy couples a vivid view of the isolation and harshness of farm life with a perceptive look at the emotions that can rage beneath the surface. This Midwestern noir with gothic undertones is sure to make several 2011 must-read lists."

—*Publishers Weekly* (starred review)

"This tautly written, chilling piece of heartland noir is . . . an impressive debut. Roy takes a bucolic setting—rural Kansas—and makes it an effective stage for a suspenseful tale of tragedy and dread . . . *Bent Road* is rich in sensory details . . . that anchor the story in its place and time. Roy populates that world with a believable cast of characters, deftly marrying a story of domestic violence and familial love with a gothic mystery that is compelling at each turn of the page."

—*Tampa Bay Times*

"Even the simplest scenes crackle with suspense."

—*People*

"Roy's exceptional debut novel is full of tension, complex characters, and deftly gothic overtones. Readers of Tana French's *In the Woods* will find this dark and satisfying story a great read. Highly recommended."

—*Library Journal* (starred review)

LAKE COUNTY

ALSO BY LORI ROY

Bent Road

Let Me Die in His Footsteps

Until She Comes Home

The Disappearing

Gone Too Long

LAKE COUNTY

A NOVEL

LORI ROY

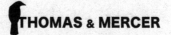
THOMAS & MERCER

Published by Thomas & Mercer, Seattle

www.apub.com

Amazon, the Amazon logo, and Thomas & Mercer are trademarks of Amazon.com, Inc., or its affiliates.

ISBN-13: 9781662519932 (hardcover)
ISBN-13: 9781662519949 (paperback)
ISBN-13: 9781662519925 (digital)

Cover design by Richard Ljoenes Design LLC
Cover image: © Lazyllama / Alamy; © Evelina Kremsdorf / ArcAngel

Printed in the United States of America
First edition

For Karina, a great writer and a great friend

AUTHOR'S NOTE

Lake County is a work of fiction. It is set in the fictional town of Hockta, which I have placed in Lake County, a real location in Central Florida. Many other real places are referenced throughout the novel. Though I have made every effort to accurately represent these locations as they would have been in the mid-1950s, I ultimately deferred to telling the best story I could. If history didn't support my story, I took liberties.

Lake County also features a few historical figures. They play parts both large and small. As I built these characters, I again made every effort to respect history, particularly those facts that are significant to understanding who these historical figures were and what they contributed to our culture.

However, once these characters stepped into my story, their lives took a new trajectory. It's a fictional path and one of my choosing. It's all about the story.

CHAPTER 1

Every April, the orange blossoms bloomed. Year after year, the whole of Lake County, Florida, would spend those weeks sucking in deep, full breaths and smiling at that sweet scent. They woke every morning hoping to smell those blossoms, and when they did, they felt good for a reason I never understood. They gathered on street corners, chatted longer, and laughed louder, and they kept on until the weight of the summer's humidity rolled in, sank the sweet smell, and sent them scurrying for shade.

The orange blossoms marked a new beginning for them, but not for me. Those blossoms, each and every one, were barbs on my cage. Starting when I was about ten years old, being trapped in Hockta, Florida, stung a bit more every April. One more year had come and gone, and I was still stuck.

But the orange blossom bloom in the spring of 1955 would be my last. Soon I'd be leaving it behind forever, because in two days, I'd turn eighteen. Then the day after, I'd step onto a train bound for Hollywood and then New York. It was supposed to be a six-week-long trip for Aunt Jean and me, a birthday gift from her. But for me, the trip was never going to end. I had dreams of being in the pictures, and once I left Hockta, I was never coming back.

Like we did every Friday when Aunt Jean was in town, she and I took Mama's sedan to do the shopping at the only grocery store in town.

"We should drive around back too," I said to Aunt Jean as she pulled in the parking lot. "Just in case."

There was no sign of a peacock blue sedan. That was good, but Siebert Rix could be a sneaky man, and a sneaky man might park behind the grocery store where we wouldn't see him. He might be watching us right now, peeking out from behind a tree or a bush.

As if she hadn't heard me, Aunt Jean eased into a space near the entrance, turned off the engine, and checked her face in the rearview mirror. She puckered her lips and smoothed her hair.

"Don't spoil our fun," she said, throwing open her door and smiling at me. Her smile was more persuasive than most, even on me. "It's a beautiful day, and you're sounding just like your mama."

"I promised her we'd be mindful," I said, trailing Aunt Jean toward the store. I wanted to grab her and slow her down. I needed time to spot what might be waiting for us just inside the door. "I promised Daddy too. Slow down, Aunt Jean. I just don't want any more trouble for you."

I didn't want trouble for me either. Trouble of any kind might cause Mama and Daddy to change their minds about my trip to Hollywood.

When Aunt Jean had stepped off the train almost two months ago, the same train she always rode in on when she came for a visit, Siebert Rix was with her. Mama recognized him right away. Mama was always happy to see Aunt Jean, no matter what shape Aunt Jean was in. She was not happy to see Siebert Rix.

Aunt Jean, Siebert, and Mama met as children because they all grew up in the Los Angeles area, each of them bouncing between orphanages and foster homes. Mama met Aunt Jean at an orphanage where together, they could look out one of the windows and see a water tower emblazoned with the RKO Studios logo. Eight years older than Aunt Jean, Mama was like her big sister. As Mama told it, Aunt Jean trembled to see the studio so close, and those days staring out at the RKO water tower first sparked Aunt Jean's dreams of stardom.

After that orphanage came another where they met a young Siebert Rix. He had a broken-down Vest Pocket Kodak camera, no doubt stolen, but it was enough to charm Aunt Jean. Even as a little girl, she loved to pose for pictures. That's how Siebert Rix first latched on to Aunt Jean, and he had been a problem ever since.

As we walked into Wilson's Market, I felt better, safer. The store was mostly empty, being as it was late on a Friday afternoon. I could keep track of every set of footsteps and hear if someone was sneaking up from around the next corner. Empty was easy to manage. But Mama's sedan was still out in the middle of the parking lot, announcing to anyone who might drive past that Aunt Jean and I were inside. We'd be quick about our shopping. I'd promised Mama, and it was the only reason she let us go without her.

Like always, Wilson's smelled of pine cleaner and bleach, a strong enough concoction to overpower the scent of the sugary orange blossoms that followed us inside. And the market had air-conditioning too. Sweet, glorious, life-giving air-conditioning.

Just inside the door, Aunt Jean and I paused, bathing in that cool air. We laid our heads back and exhaled, both of us at the same time. We locked eyes and giggled. Even as I scanned the aisles for a tall dark-haired man, I had to laugh. Aunt Jean was about the only person I ever laughed with. I'd reached the age where I felt she and I were more like sisters, and I wanted to be just like her. I wanted to check my lipstick in the rearview mirror and never worry about anything, but much as I wanted to, I couldn't live that way. I had to worry because Aunt Jean never did.

Every shop, café, and salon in Hockta grew larger when we started having to keep an eye out for Siebert Rix. Until he'd stepped off the train, I never knew how many corners there were in this town, spots that left a person blind to what was dead ahead. We had to keep watch everywhere we went, all of us. Me, Mama, Aunt Jean, even my five-year-old little brother, Urban. Siebert wasn't always trouble when we stumbled upon him or when he showed up at the house. But after he yanked Aunt Jean's arm from its socket and put her in a sling a few short weeks ago, Daddy said we were done extending the man any more chances. The next time, Siebert might kill Aunt Jean.

We couldn't let there be a next time.

With no customers to tend, the regular cashier, Donna Lee Foster, sat at the checkout counter, flipping through a magazine. Her surprising head of red hair flowed like melted pennies down her back, and her skin was like milk glass. But everything else about Donna Lee was tattered. The hem of her skirt. The laces on her shoes. Even her fingernails.

Donna Lee dreamed of being in the pictures too. Sometimes I think she piggybacked my dream, like not knowing what else to dream about, she hopped onto mine. Several times, she borrowed my copy of *An Actor Prepares,* and she would ask if I thought she was pretty enough to be famous. I always told her yes, because I truly thought she was, but at twenty-seven, Donna Lee still rode a bike to work. There wasn't much chance that bike was getting her out of Hockta.

Donna Lee glanced up from her magazine. Seeing me and knowing Aunt Jean was likely not far behind, she jumped to her feet. Spotting Aunt Jean as she drifted toward a bin of tomatoes, Donna Lee started to walk from behind her counter and then remembered she wasn't supposed to make a fuss when she saw Aunt Jean.

Lowering back onto her stool, Donna Lee picked up her magazine and flashed me the cover. It was Aunt Jean's face looking back at me.

I smiled so Donna Lee would know I wasn't upset but still motioned for her to hide the photo.

"Nobody else is here," she mouthed, clutching the latest *Movie Life* to her chest. She wanted me to know Aunt Jean wouldn't be disturbed. No pictures. No autographs. No one making a fuss.

But to me, no one in the store meant Siebert Rix wasn't in the store. More cause to stop worrying.

Siebert took real pictures of Aunt Jean now, not the pretend pictures he'd taken when she was a girl, and they had been published all over the world. For a time, I'd hoped he'd see his way to taking pictures of me too. I stopped hoping the night he yanked Aunt Jean's arm from its socket. The sound of her arm popping loose was like a cork popping loose of a bottle. Daddy had to pry Siebert off Aunt Jean. That was the night I realized Siebert Rix was nothing without her.

"A man who makes his living on the back of another person makes for a desperate and dangerous man," Mama said that night. "Never forget that."

I mouthed a "thank you" back to Donna Lee, and I thought it was safe to let Aunt Jean do the shopping on her own.

I was mistaken.

That was the moment when everything in the spring of 1955 started going wrong. If I hadn't left Aunt Jean, none of the rest would have happened.

But I did.

CHAPTER 2

Being away from home, if only at the grocery store, felt good. Me and Aunt Jean together, each of us soaking up that cold air, and no trouble in sight, was like getting a glimpse of the life waiting for me on the other end of a train trip. Even knowing it was the wrong thing to do, I let myself stop worrying and started dreaming instead.

Handing Aunt Jean the shopping list Mama wrote out for us, I lifted my chin and arched my back as if preparing for a director to call action. Aunt Jean knew just what I was doing. She struck a pose, too, but as she arched her back, she was pretending she had the director's big belly.

"Action," she said in the deepest voice she could muster.

I was ten years old when Aunt Jean first told me I had to practice if I wanted to be an actress like her.

"Anywhere you go, everything you do, it can be your stage. Work hard, even if no one else believes."

That's what she said on one of her visits to Hockta. By that time, she'd already been in two movies. Neither of them made it to Central Florida, but they were real. I had a poster from each, and since the day I taped the first one on my bedroom wall, I'd been doing what Aunt Jean said. I made everywhere I went my stage.

As I took long purposeful strides across the tile floor, my footsteps ringing out, I imagined the director was angry at me for being late to set. He shouted my name over and over: *Addie Anne Buckley to the stage.*

Where the hell is Addie Anne Buckley? The store's overhead lights flickered as if a camera crew were setting up for the next shot. I smoothed my hair and tucked my blouse neatly into my skirt. Once I reached the magazine rack near the back of the store, I glanced down to make sure I'd hit my imaginary mark.

Sometimes, I dreamed I was in one of Aunt Jean's movies and playing her part. I knew every line from every one of her films. She'd send me scripts so I could study them, not just her part but every part. But today, I was playing myself. The plot was simple: I was a seventeen-year-old girl, preparing to steal a magazine from her hometown grocery store.

My character was pretty, but only recently. For the first sixteen years of her life, she'd had long gangly arms and legs, big feet, and ordinary, drab hair—all the things that made a girl disappear. On the inside, she felt she still had all those things, so she was still awkward, still felt invisible. That was what came from never fitting in. My character was also smart. She had finished high school a year early and at the top of her class. She was shy too. Always had been. Except when she was playing a part. When she was playing a character, she knew exactly what to say and how to say it. Lastly, and most importantly, she was passionately in love with a slightly dangerous boy who was almost a man.

My character also knew better than to steal, which is what made doing it the most thrilling part of her life. Nothing else was thrilling when you lived in a tiny town, in the middle of an orange grove, at the end of a dusty road, with a grimy little brother who was forever in your belongings. And yet my character, same as me, didn't steal for the thrill of stealing. She stole to spare Aunt Jean's feelings.

But the most important thing about my character, which was to say the most important thing about me, was what I wanted for my life.

I wanted to break free of my hometown. I wanted to escape the dirt road that ran past my house and the sugary scent of orange blossoms that dripped in the air. I wanted to escape becoming a wife and a mother who was trapped like my mama. I loved my mama, loved her dearly, but loving her didn't mean I wanted to be like her. My mama stopped being a woman named Inez the day she got married. Instead, she became Harden Buckley's wife, and then Addie's mama and Urban's mama. And mostly I wanted to escape so I could be somebody and not the nobody I'd been all my life.

Understanding what a character wanted was of primary importance to any actress playing any part. That was another thing Aunt Jean taught me.

Still standing on my imaginary mark, I listened to all the ordinary sounds of the market. One aisle over, the refrigerated bins hummed. Up at the checkout counter, Donna Lee pecked on the register's keys, probably changing dollar bills for quarters, dimes, and nickels. And over by the vegetable bins, there was the *click, click, clicking* of Aunt Jean's high heels. It was a slow, lazy click as she strolled among the tomatoes and peppers.

Whenever Aunt Jean came to town, which was every year or two, she made a point of not hurrying. Not downstairs for supper. Not when someone needed in the bathroom. Not even when Mr. O'Dell, a simple man who loved her, was waiting for her in the living room, a bouquet of flowers in hand. She said once she stepped foot in Lake County, her hurrying was done because her entire life was nothing but hurrying from one thing to another. To me, that sounded like the most wonderful life ever.

Other than the clicking of Aunt Jean's heels, the store was quiet. Quiet was good. Quiet was safe.

But there, in aisle three, every can of cream of mushroom was gone, leaving an unsightly gap on the second shelf. That unsightly gap was trouble. Mrs. Harrington surely bought all the soup for the party she was hosting the next night. Cream of mushroom was a staple in most every appetizer Mrs. Harrington made. She and her husband threw the party each year, and the whole town was always invited. Given the time of year, it grew to be called the Orange Blossom Ball even though it was a plain old party in their living room. Mama and Daddy were going, same as they always did.

Mr. Wilson wouldn't put up with that gaping hole and would be back soon to fill it in with cream of something, meaning I didn't have much time. Standing squarely on my mark, I imagined the director shouting action. I was cautious but daring. Brave but humble. I wiggled my fingers, so they'd be nimble and quick, and cozied up to the wire magazine rack. The camera, if there was a camera, would have been focused on my eyes, so I used them to show my resolve, fear, determination. It's all in the eyes. That's where the inside shines out. That was another thing Aunt Jean taught me.

Easing closer to the magazine stand, I listened one last time to make sure Aunt Jean wasn't headed my way. I didn't want her to catch me stealing a magazine that had her face on the cover. She didn't mind other people looking at her picture on magazines and at her face up on a movie screen, but not me.

It would make her sad to see me staring at her picture. That's not me, she'd say. You know that, right? And sometimes when Aunt Jean got sad, it stuck for days.

Now was the time. I slid the latest *Movie Life* magazine from the black wire stand, and in one smooth motion, lifted my shirt, sucked in my gut, tucked the magazine in my waistband, and draped my shirt back in place.

A *LIFE* magazine was the first I ever stole. I was fourteen years old. Aunt Jean had been on the covers of other magazines, ones she mailed to me, but the April 7, 1952, edition of *LIFE* was the first to make it all the way to Hockta, Florida. The second I saw Aunt Jean smiling down on me from the rack, I had to have the magazine for myself. I had to hold it, feel and smell it. In the photo, slick and shiny under the grocery store's fluorescent lights, Aunt Jean wore a white dress that slouched off her shoulders, and silky waves of ivory hair framed her face. She looked sleepy and happy, like she was soaking up a sunny afternoon. She was the most beautiful woman I had ever seen. Mama was beautiful, too, but in a simple, scrubbed-clean way. Aunt Jean sparkled, like she floated above the whole world, a single star in a dark sky.

As I looked at that picture, the ache to live a bigger life, be a different person—any other person—grew stronger than it had ever been. It doubled me over as I clutched the magazine.

Since that first *LIFE* magazine, nine more with Aunt Jean on the cover had made it to Hockta, and I had them all. I only stole them when Aunt Jean was with me, and even then, it wasn't really stealing. I always dropped a quarter near the checkout stand on my way out.

Hugging my stomach, the cover slick and cool on my skin, I closed my eyes and imagined the camera had zoomed in for a close-up. The lights overhead warmed my face as it filled the entire screen. I felt more myself playing a part than I ever did living my regular life, even when I was playing myself. I knew what to say and how to feel. And then the imaginary director yelled cut, and I opened my eyes.

Straight ahead, the double doors that led to the store's back room swung in and out. In and out. Someone had pushed through them just as I was stuffing the magazine in my waistband. I'd been caught stealing, and Aunt Jean and I were no longer alone.

CHAPTER 3

The day Aunt Jean stepped off the train in Lake County almost two months ago, she told me about her idea for my birthday gift. We had been plotting our trip ever since. It took plenty of convincing, but Mama and Daddy finally agreed.

For my eighteenth birthday, Aunt Jean would take me on a trip to Hollywood, and from there, we'd travel to New York just in time for Aunt Jean's birthday and the premiere of *The Seven Year Itch*. I'd be her date, walk the red carpet, and smile as flashbulbs snapped in my face. No one, not even Aunt Jean, knew I wouldn't be coming back. No one except Truitt. He was the only person other than my family who I'd miss once I was gone. But I wouldn't miss him for long. When the time was right, he'd join me, and we'd be together forever.

But as those swinging doors took their last shallow swing, my hopes of boarding a train bound for California and then New York slipped away. My eyes darted side to side, this time for real. Not for the fictional camera.

I thought my only worry today was being caught stealing by Mr. Wilson. Mama and Daddy would cancel my trip if they found out I stole something. They'd been looking for a reason to cancel it ever since they'd agreed. Mama, I think, suspected if she let me go, I'd be gone for good.

But Mr. Wilson was no longer my biggest concern. If Siebert Rix had come in through the back door, I needed to get to Aunt Jean first and hustle her out the front. She was barely out of the sling Siebert put her in the last time he'd come to our house. I couldn't let that happen again. I ticked through all the things Daddy told me about keeping clear of Siebert Rix. Don't talk to him. He's slippery and will make you doubt your better judgment. Always expect him where you least expect him. And never let him catch you alone.

Still huddled up to the magazine stand, I listened hard, but there was no sound of black wing tips hitting the tile floor. Clutching the magazine to my stomach and trying not to breathe so I could hear more clearly, I took a few steps toward the end of the aisle, where I could get a better view. Once there, I looked left and right and then exhaled a quiet laugh.

Mr. Wilson hadn't pushed through the swinging doors, and neither had Siebert Rix. It was Truitt Holt. My Truitt. I missed him already.

Truitt stood next to the refrigerated bin filled with cellophane-wrapped cuts of meat, a small spiral notepad in hand, a pencil poised over it. He was never without that notepad.

"Guess I know what you're up to," Truitt said, his eyes squarely on me.

Other than when I was playing a part, being with Truitt was the only time I didn't feel at odds with myself. It was as if the whole world was walking in one direction, and Truitt and I, the other. For me, he was the first boy and the only boy.

Like it always did, his voice reached inside me, grabbed hold, and reeled me in. It was gravelly and lazy, especially on the vowels, and whenever I heard it, my body knew exactly what came next and prepared itself. My heart pounded. My breathing picked up. It was built in, my body's need for him. A reflex. Like breathing. I needed him to live.

Lots of girls liked Truitt. They liked that he was tall, had loose blond hair that hung in his eyes, and always had plenty of walking-around money. The hair and the height were nice, but I never cared about the money. What Truitt did to make his money was a crime, and no matter how good his intentions, he was still breaking the law.

Daddy never had an unkind word for anyone, but it only took Truitt making one phone call to our house for Daddy to say no. Absolutely not. Not my daughter. The money was why he didn't much care for Truitt. He understood why Truitt did what he did, but that didn't make it right. He thought the money meant Truitt was on a slippery slope to being just like his daddy. In the six months since that first call, Truitt and I had managed to keep what was between us a secret.

"Guess I know what you're up to too," I said, imagining myself as the character Aunt Jean played in *Gentlemen Prefer Blondes*. Cunning, confident, irresistible. And beautiful. "And it's not delivering those newspapers of yours."

Truitt had been delivering newspapers around Hockta for years. He still did, though he no longer did it for the money. He did it as cover. His mama and the sheriff insisted.

"Guess we're both lawbreakers, then," Truitt said, smiling and playing along as he swaggered toward me. Swaggered like my leading man.

Truitt knew all about my dreams and believed every one would come true. Sometimes, it seemed he believed more than I did.

Extending a hand, he nodded toward the swinging doors as he invited me into the back room. I glanced down the aisle. Sneaking off into back rooms with Truitt was one of the few bad things I did. Except it never felt bad.

I saw no sign of Aunt Jean, heard no sign either. The store was still quiet, and that made me think we were alone and that she was safe. I forgot everything Daddy said about not letting Siebert Rix catch us when we were alone.

Still clutching the magazine to my stomach with one hand, I took Truitt's with the other, and together we stumbled into the back room.

CHAPTER 4

Growing up, I was always the tallest, my muddy blonde hair hung in my face, and my clothes were too small or too big. Mama tried, but the moment a new skirt would come in the house, I'd shoot up, leaving the hemline too short and the waistline too big. The day a new white blouse would appear in my closet, I'd drip tomato sauce on it. The girls at school who had perfect smiles and crisp pleats rolled their eyes at my short, baggy clothes and ragged hair. They also didn't like me because I lived in a house built in the middle of an orange grove way outside of town. Outside of town was never good enough for inside of town.

But I didn't care that they laughed at me or turned a shoulder when I walked by. When I was twelve years old, Aunt Jean held my face in her hands, brushed my ratty hair from my eyes, and told me to remember it all. Remember what it feels like to have big feet and long stringy arms. Remember what it feels like when the girls don't talk to you and the boys poke fun. You'll grow into who you're meant to be, and you'll be a sight to behold. But remember all the rest, and use it. Your pain'll pave the way, not your beauty.

Aunt Jean was right about me outgrowing what Mama called my awkward stage. Even though Aunt Jean wasn't my aunt by blood, people began telling me I looked like her . . . you have her eyes, her easy smile. And Lord if you aren't getting her figure. I didn't have her shimmering blonde hair, but Aunt Jean said she didn't, either, until she found it in a beauty shop.

The girls still mostly turned a shoulder when I walked by, but the boys stopped poking fun. Instead, their eyes followed me, coming and going. There was a weight to their stare. Once I felt it, I didn't much like it.

Truitt was the only boy I cared about. He was from outside of town, too, and though he was a few years older, he had always been kind to me, even when my hair was ratty and my clothes didn't fit. The kissing and everything else, however, were new in the months leading up to the spring of 1955.

Standing in the back room, a storeroom filled with crates of dusty vegetables surrounding us and our time together short, Truitt and I dove in quick. As the two of us worked ourselves into a frenzy of hands, lips, and tongues, I forgot all about Siebert Rix and Aunt Jean. That's how it always went between Truitt and me, and yet something was different. We were more, somehow. Truitt couldn't make his way around my body quickly enough, like he wanted to stake a claim by covering every inch of me before I could get away.

After only a few minutes, we clawed our way back to the surface. Pushing off Truitt, I braced myself with one hand to his chest, and with the other, I cradled his neck. The edge of a scar peeked over his collar. I trailed a finger over the rough skin. Under his shirt, the scar spread down one side of his chest and across his shoulder. It was a reminder of the night, years ago, when his house burned down, and he and his mama almost died.

Truitt groaned at my touch and dropped his head, sad, pained at having to let me go. As my breathing slowed and my heart quieted, I touched his face to assure him I wasn't going far. Not yet. Sunday was my birthday, and we'd see each other then. We'd made plans to meet after I had cake and ice cream with my family. And my leaving with Aunt Jean was not the end of Truitt and me. I was going to write every day, share with him every wonderful thing I was seeing and doing.

Eventually, when I was settled in my new life and the time was right for Truitt, he'd join me wherever I was.

Having resurfaced in the real world, I realized Aunt Jean would probably be ready to check out by now. Not wanting her to go outside without me, I let my fingers slide from Truitt's face and reached for the swinging doors, but Truitt grabbed my hand.

"You still planning to go?" he asked, kneading each finger like he was committing every knuckle to memory.

"Of course I am," I said, peeking through the doors and seeing no sign of Aunt Jean or anyone else. "Monday. We already have our tickets. And I have new luggage, and Aunt Jean said . . ."

The worrying had snuck up on me again. The store had been quiet for too long. Aunt Jean didn't like to be alone, not because she was scared, but because being alone made her feel lonely. She should have come looking for me by now.

"You should stay," Truitt said, tugging me from the doors and wrapping me in his arms. "Marry me. We could live in my mama's house until I buy us something of our own. There's places in Tampa you could go to college, learn to be a teacher maybe."

I pulled back and tried looking in his eyes to see if he meant what he was saying, but he wouldn't let me. Shaking his head, he glanced off to the side and then at the floor, anywhere but at me.

"I can't," I said, resting a hand on his cheek so he had to look at me. "The tickets. The luggage."

I grabbed his hands and tried to draw him out of the storeroom and back into the store.

"Is this because of your daddy?" he said, not budging from his spot. "He'll come around. Your mama too. They'll see. I got money. I make plenty for us both."

"It's not about my daddy," I said. "You know I want something else. Something more. You know that."

"Jesus, Addie," he said, shaking his head.

He took a breath to say something more but pushed me away instead.

"Go on," I said. "Say it."

The words he wouldn't say hung between us, and I could see every one of them.

"You don't think I can do it." I said it for him.

For six months, I'd been wrong about Truitt. He'd been lying to me all along. He never believed I was as beautiful as Aunt Jean, never thought I was as talented. He had never, not once, really believed I could make my way to the pictures. And every time he said otherwise, it had been a lie.

"If you don't want to marry me," he said, "I got nothing else to say."

"Come with me," I whispered. It was the dying breath for the two of us. "Right now. Don't wait until later. Buy your own ticket. You have money. We can be married out there, wherever. On the train maybe, with Aunt—"

"You know I can't do that," he said, pushing past me to leave. "I got responsibilities. Can't live with my head in the clouds."

"And that's what you think I'm doing?" I said, stumbling around crates and boxes as I trailed him. "You think I got my head in the clouds?"

Truitt stopped at the back door leading to the alley. He turned to me, the littlest bit of light from the grocery store falling across his face. He reached out and swiped the hair from my eyes.

"Don't you, Addie? Don't you have your head in the clouds?"

"What if I do?" I said, my anger spilling out like water boiling over on the stove. "Where is your head? What are you doing with your life? Breaking your mama's heart every day. Making her worry some gangster's going to burn down your house again. Or worse, shoot you dead like he shot your daddy dead."

Every week, another headline ran about one gangster killing another in the streets of Tampa, all of it because of a game called bolita.

Anyone could play. Working men. Rich men. Ladies too. It took only a few cents to buy in. It was as simple as playing a number between one and one hundred by buying a bolita ticket. If, during a weekly drawing, your number was blindly pulled from a bag of one hundred numbered balls, you would win.

The mob made it easy for people to place their bets. They had taxi drivers on their payroll and men working the corner gas station and the local market. Anywhere there were people, there was someone to take their bet, hand them a ticket, and wish them luck. Games were run throughout Tampa, throughout the state, and everyone paid a share up to the mob. Everyone except Truitt.

Truitt ran his own game, top to bottom, and ran it only for the people of Lake County. He took the bets, held the money, and ran the drawing on his own front porch. He thought the mob would never bother with him and his small game that now reached into every town in the county. He thought he was smart enough to stay invisible. He thought he was smarter than every dead man who ended up in a headline.

"I'm sorry, Truitt," I said. "I shouldn't have said that about your daddy. I didn't mean—"

"Have a good life, Addie Anne," Truitt said, pulling free of me and leaving me alone as he ducked out the back door.

"Wait," I said, shouting after him as he jogged into the alley. "What about Sunday? My birthday? Will I see you?"

I stood in the doorway, watching him leave. When the scent of orange blossoms brushed past me, I took a backward step and let the door fall closed. I stood in the dark again, darker than before because the sudden burst of sunlight had blinded me.

Uncertain which way to go and waiting for the dark room to come back into focus, I heard someone call my name. It was faint, maybe just my imagination. Taking care as I wove through the boxes and crates, I made my way toward the swinging doors.

"Addie, where are you? Addie Anne."

It was louder. Yes, someone was calling out to me.

My walking turned to running as I stumbled through the dark storeroom. I'd forgotten all about leaving Aunt Jean alone. Just for a moment. Just while Truitt was breaking my heart.

"Addie Anne, come quick!" It was Donna Lee.

CHAPTER 5

Pushing through the swinging doors, I stumbled up the soup aisle toward the voice still calling out to me. Donna Lee appeared. Her face was red, and she waved for me to come on.

"It's your aunt," she said, flustered and out of breath.

I had thought Aunt Jean and I were safe on a Friday afternoon when no one else did their shopping. I had thought the store being empty was a good thing, and I stopped worrying and started dreaming. But I was wrong. In an empty store, I had no one to help me. I'd never be able to pry Siebert Rix off Aunt Jean the way Daddy had. I'd never be able to save her.

Still unsteady on my feet, I rounded the end of the aisle and ran in the direction Donna Lee pointed. I stopped short and braced myself, both hands on my knees when I saw Aunt Jean. She was safe. We were safe. That was my first thought. She stood near the greeting cards, talking with Mrs. Danielson. This situation was bad, but not Siebert Rix bad. Still, I knew why Donna Lee had come to find me.

Mrs. Danielson wrote a newspaper column called Hockta Happenings that ran every Saturday. She was almost as wide as she was tall and always wore a hat. That day, it was a dark-blue Juliet cap to match her dark-blue skirt. Some people said wearing a hat all the time was Mrs. Danielson's way of putting on airs. Plenty of the girls around Hockta thought I was putting on airs by going around town with Aunt

Jean. So, I tried not to think that way about Mrs. Danielson, but she'd caused Aunt Jean so much heartache over the years, I didn't try too hard.

At least once or twice, whenever Aunt Jean was in town, Mrs. Danielson called the house, asking if Aunt Jean had a comment for her latest article. Most recently, a few short weeks ago, she had called to ask if Aunt Jean had anything to say about the troublesome photo of her standing over a subway grate. That photo and all the ruckus it caused the year before was the reason Aunt Jean finally jumped on a train and headed to Florida. Aunt Jean said plenty to Mrs. Danielson about that photo, and when her comments ended up in the newspaper, Siebert Rix ended up in our driveway, aiming to teach Aunt Jean a lesson about loyalty. Instead, he yanked her arm out of its socket.

"We need to go," I said, resting a hand on Aunt Jean's shoulder and nodding hello to Mrs. Danielson.

When Aunt Jean didn't move, I grabbed the shopping cart and pushed it between the two of them, hoping a wedge would break up the conversation. I still wasn't steady on my feet. What happened with Truitt had left me feeling I'd woken from a bad dream that I couldn't shake off. But I couldn't give myself room to think about Truitt anymore. Aunt Jean and I were leaving in three days, and I didn't want anything getting in the way of that. Mrs. Danielson was a person who got in the way of things. Running into her was better than running into Siebert Rix, but whatever she and Aunt Jean were talking about could end up in print and set Siebert off again. I couldn't let that happen.

"Please, promise you won't print what I told you," Aunt Jean said, ignoring me and reaching past the cart to grab Mrs. Danielson's hands. "I shouldn't have said anything. I wasn't supposed to. Promise me, please."

Mrs. Danielson ripped her hands away. Pursing her lips like she was tasting something sour, she stared at Aunt Jean in a way people sometimes did. Mrs. Danielson was disgusted that Aunt Jean didn't look like the person she was supposed to, as if Aunt Jean owed Mrs. Danielson a show. But same as Aunt Jean left behind hurrying at the state line, she also left behind brushing her hair and ironing her clothes. She regularly left the house in a simple dress Mama might wear, a scarf tied over her hair, and only a smudge of lipstick for makeup.

"You should see your aunt home," Mrs. Danielson said to me. "Help her with a brush. Maybe take a little more care before she goes out in public. She's embarrassing herself."

Mrs. Danielson's top lip curled in a way that made me want to shove her clear of Aunt Jean. And given Truitt had left me standing all alone, smack-dab between the summer squash and the radishes, I wanted to shove her hard.

"But will you promise me?" Aunt Jean said, smoothing her hair and straightening her skirt as if sorry to have disappointed Mrs. Danielson. And then she slipped into the voice people wanted to hear. Sweet. Throaty. Helpless. "I know I'm just a fright. Not feeling myself at all. That's what it is. Won't you please just forget what I said?"

"Like you've told me so often, Marilyn, when I've called asking for a few words," Mrs. Danielson said, stepping back as if Aunt Jean had begun to rot on the shelves, "I'm afraid I have no comment."

As Mrs. Danielson walked away, adjusting her blue hat, Aunt Jean hugged herself and looked around to see if anyone heard Mrs. Danielson use her real name. Even though it wasn't Aunt Jean's real name. But it was the name the whole world knew her by.

In Hockta, it was an unspoken rule. She was Jean, not Marilyn. Never Marilyn. Aunt Jean had been my age when she first started coming to Hockta, wanting to be near Mama and my family. Her hair had still been brown, and she went by Jean. Marilyn Monroe didn't exist yet. And in Hockta, she still didn't. When Aunt Jean needed to tend her wounds, she came back to the one place where people were still willing to pretend she was just a girl named Jean.

"Let's go home," I said, meaning to leave the groceries behind and somehow explain to Mama why we had bought nothing at the store. "It'll all be fine."

As we walked toward the front doors, Donna Lee waved to me from the checkout counter. During all the commotion, she had taken our cart of groceries, totaled them up, and placed everything in two bags.

Cradling Aunt Jean with one arm, hoping the magazine didn't fall from my waistband, I handed money to Donna Lee.

"Add a quarter," I said as she made my change. "And thank you."

The last time Aunt Jean and Mrs. Danielson spoke, Aunt Jean saying things about the subway-grate photo that Siebert didn't like, he got even by putting her in a sling. But that wasn't all he got. Siebert got himself a beating. After hauling Siebert off Aunt Jean, Daddy gave him a beating so bad that he almost landed himself in jail. If it weren't for Mama, Daddy would have killed the man.

I was afraid that might be about ready to happen again.

CHAPTER 6

It was long past midnight when Truitt started for home. His head was swimming in warm beer and whiskey. He stretched his eyes, trying to bring the path ahead into focus. Rising off the seat of his bike, he used all his weight to drive his pedals faster and harder. His tires wobbled and creaked on the dirt road. The night air was soggy and thick and went down hard, clogging the back of his throat. His first rule of business was to get home before dark, especially on Friday nights, and he'd broken it.

Right this minute, his mama would be standing on the front porch and craning her neck as she hoped to catch a glimpse of him pedaling up the drive. She was probably near to tears. Dang it all, he hated worrying her. Sometimes it seemed the harder he tried to do right, the more he did wrong. First, he'd let down Addie, and now he'd let down his own mama. He was the man of the house, and worrying his mama and being hateful to his girlfriend were not things a man did.

Truitt was six years old when his daddy told him that he was the man of the house. It was one of the only things he remembered his daddy having said. The two of them had just pulled into their new driveway, his daddy driving, and Truitt riding shotgun. Truitt was still mending from the burns he got when their house in Tampa burned down. His daddy switched off the ignition, stepped out of the car, and the shot rang out. The last thing his daddy said to Truitt before dying right there in his own front yard . . . you're the man of the house now.

Even if today hadn't been the day Truitt lost Addie, getting home before dark was always tough on Fridays, because Friday was payday for most every fellow in town. Not only did the fellows have extra money in their pockets, but Truitt held his bolita drawing on Saturday nights. So come five o'clock on Friday, the fellows were looking for a shot of Jim Beam and their last chance to pick a number and buy a bolita ticket from Truitt. Payday for the fellows meant payday for Truitt, his biggest day, the day he sold the most bolita tickets, and everybody in Lake County knew it. With his own pocket full of money, he was a tempting target. That was why his first rule was to get home before dark.

Up ahead, a light appeared on the side of the road. He slowed. His hand went to his pocket. A reflex. The money was still there, a tightly rolled wad his mama would use to buy groceries for the week. He slapped his other pocket. His spiral notepad was right where it should be too. Having his money stolen would be bad. Having his notepad stolen would be worse. It held all the names and bets of every person he'd ever sold a ticket to, the date of every drawing he'd held, and the number he'd pulled each week from a bag of one hundred numbered balls.

A few more yards on his bike, and Truitt was sure. It was the headlights of a car pulled over on the road. He lowered onto his seat and coasted. He shifted his weight to the left, tipping his bike so it edged toward the opposite side of the road. His vision blurred. He blinked, stretched his lids wide again. He needed to be smart, careful.

He slowed more so his tires would quit kicking up gravel. If he was quiet enough, whoever was inside that car wouldn't hear or see him. But once he was past the car, the headlights would throw a smoky glow down the center of the road and give him away. That was when he'd have to stand and pedal like hell. Probably, the car belonged to some unlucky fellow with a flat tire, but maybe it belonged to someone who knew this was the way home for Truitt and that he had a wad of money in his pocket.

He slowed to a crawl and blew out long quiet breaths, trying to flush the whiskey that was swirling behind his eyes. He was close enough to see the trunk of a sedan. It stood open. He leaned over the handlebars, swallowed the urge to vomit, and positioned himself to drive his right foot down on the pedal. That would give him the fastest, strongest start. A few more feet. He sucked in a deep breath so he could explode. He drew almost even with the car, and a silhouette came into view.

A petite, curvy silhouette.

Even as he veered toward the person, Truitt was thinking . . . the harder I try to do right, the more I do wrong. He knew stopping to help was the right thing to do. He also knew it was going to turn out wrong. But before he could change course, his bike was at a full stop, and he had one foot planted on the ground.

"Is that you, Truitt Holt?"

It was a sweet voice, and the worries about this being a mistake melted. For one whiskey-soaked moment, he thought it was Addie. But it wasn't. The voice was sweet, but it was also small and meek. Addie was neither of those things. Before she grew up to become beautiful, she was lanky and scrawny and tripped over her own feet, but that didn't make her small or meek. She was shy, would rather stand at the back than the front, but only because she liked to study people. She also thought before she spoke, so when she said something, it was worth listening to. Damn it all, Truitt was going to miss her.

The voice wasn't Addie's, but he did recognize it. More reason not to worry. He was going to be even later getting home, but at least he'd have a good reason to give his mama. She'd be proud of him for stopping to help. That might tamp down some of her being mad he was late.

"Yes, ma'am. It's Truitt Holt," he said, keeping a polite distance.

As his eyes adjusted and the ground stopped tilting, he rolled his bike forward a few inches. In the dim lighting, he could make out that the car was bright blue.

"Is that Donna Lee Foster?" he said. "Just saw you at the grocery store today. What are you doing all the way out here?"

Everyone in Lake County knew Donna Lee Foster. She rang up their groceries and had golden red hair that could be spotted a block away. Donna Lee was the girl all the ladies smiled at and all the men eyed up and down, but once she passed, they'd shake their heads. Poor simple thing, they'd think. She didn't realize her life was as good as it would ever get, and the rest was a straight tumble downhill.

"It is Donna Lee Foster," she said, her voice as sugary as her perfume. The sound of one and the smell of the other were mixing up in Truitt's head and making him dizzy. "And aren't you precious for stopping like this."

Truitt eased his bike closer. The heavy perfume made it hard for him to think.

"Looks like you could use a hand," he said to Donna Lee. "Didn't even know you had a car."

A shadow slid up and settled behind Donna Lee. It was a man, a few inches taller than Truitt and almost twice as wide. He smelled of cigars and musty cologne. He rested a hand on Donna Lee's shoulder and leaned to get a look at Truitt.

Truitt stiffened. The man was familiar, but Truitt couldn't put a name to him. He resisted slapping his pocket again, not wanting to let on to this man that he had a pocketful of money.

"You much for changing a tire?" the man said and stuck out a hand. He smiled, a giant wide smile that showed a row of glistening white teeth.

"Yes, sir," Truitt said, giving the man's hand a solid squeeze and shaking it firm like his daddy taught him. That was another one of the few things Truitt remembered about his daddy. "I can change a tire just fine."

He was relieved the man and Donna Lee were on the side of the road because of a flat tire and not to steal his money, but he tried not to show it.

The man still smiled as he dipped his head in Donna Lee's direction as if to say . . . take a look at what I got, and Donna Lee took that as her cue to speak.

"And after he's fixed our tire, he can sell us a bolita ticket," Donna Lee said, her squeal surprising both Truitt and the man. "Won't you, Truitt? Won't you? Drawing ain't until tomorrow. We can still buy, can't we? Will you buy a few, Siebert? Will you, please?"

Siebert Rix. That's who the man was. The glistening white teeth should have given him away. He was a photographer from Hollywood, and everything about him screamed it. His pitch-black hair, his shiny shoes, his smooth shave. He had been taking pictures of Addie's aunt since before she was famous. The two had arrived together on the train, and Siebert had been bumping around Hockta ever since, stopping pretty girls on the street. He'd take their pictures and then promise to send them the photos in the mail.

"If I like what I see," he'd tell them, "I'll make you famous too."

As far as Truitt knew, the man lived out of his car and not a single girl ever got any pictures in the mail. But whatever Siebert was selling now, Donna Lee was buying.

"Lord, Donna Lee, does that mouth of yours ever stop?" Siebert said, the gravel crunching under his black wing tips as he walked toward the front of the car and waved for Truitt to follow. "The answer is no. She never fucking shuts up."

Donna Lee pinched her lips tight and lowered her eyes as if embarrassed. Truitt hustled past her, giving her a quick squeeze on the shoulder.

"We can talk about a few bolita tickets when I finish getting this tire changed," he said. "I think this might be your lucky night."

And he followed Siebert toward the front of the car.

Truitt got the idea to run a bolita game from the newspaper. Week after week, articles ran about the growing popularity of the game, the mobsters who were fighting in the streets to control it, and the money it brought in. He started small, taking bets from men who had been his father's friends before his father was killed. They played the numbers of their choosing. They gave Truitt their money, and he gave them hand-written tickets as proof of their bets. For the drawings, he used small pieces of scrap wood in the beginning instead of bolita balls. He carved numbers—one through one hundred—on them, chiseled them down to the same size as best he could, dumped them in a beat-up burlap bag, and held his first drawing.

His early customers surely bought in as charity, a way to help him and his mama. The men patted Truitt on the head and said good for you for taking care of your own but be careful, son. And then a few of those first fellows were lucky enough to bet on the winning number. They told others, and more men started to place bets with him. He was the seller and the bank, and he made enough money that he bought one hundred cork balls from the Sears catalog, painted numbers on them, and sewed a new burlap bag.

Now, every Saturday night at ten o'clock, he stood on his front porch in plain sight of anyone who wanted to watch. He invited the fellows to inspect the balls. No weighted balls in Truitt's burlap bag. No frozen ones either. Truitt didn't cheat. And then he'd pull a single bolita ball from the bag, call out the number to anyone watching, and write down the winner in his notepad.

Truitt's game, unlike many run out of the Ybor City bars and all over Tampa and the state of Florida, was run fair. He kept careful records of the bets placed with him, gave good odds, and made sure every man who played the winning number was paid by sundown on Sunday. He was well trusted, and not many fellows came to the drawing anymore, but by church on Sunday morning, everyone knew the results. Maybe this Sunday, Donna Lee could come out a winner.

When Truitt and Siebert reached the front of the car, Siebert stood back and motioned for Truitt to go on ahead. Not wanting to get too close, Truitt squatted at the side of the car where he could get a better look. Siebert had already jacked up the front end, or rather he'd tried to. He'd positioned the jack on the soft shoulder. If a handful of gravel gave way, the jack would slide out from under the car, and if Truitt was trying to pull the tire off when that happened, the car could come down on him.

"Tire's bald, that's for sure," Truitt said.

Seeing Siebert's face in better light, Truitt could make out the last signs of the beating Addie's dad had given him a few weeks earlier for putting Addie's aunt in a sling. Must have been about a month since it happened. Someone not looking for remnants of the bruising probably wouldn't notice.

"I know the damn tire's bald," Siebert said.

"Sure," Truitt said. "Sorry, sir. Just thinking out loud."

Donna Lee leaned into Truitt and whispered, "Ain't your fault. Lady from the newspaper told him there's news coming tomorrow he won't like, but she wouldn't tell him what it was. Then she asked what he planned to do when he couldn't be a famous photographer no more. Been drinking and carrying on ever since."

"Told you once, Donna Lee," Siebert said. "Shut your damn mouth. Or I'll shut it for you."

"All's I'm saying is you can take all the pictures of me you want," Donna Lee said and struck a pose like the ladies in magazines sometimes did, one hand behind her head, the other on her hip. "You don't need Jean . . . Marilyn. Don't matter what her big announcement is. You got me."

"Kind of worried about this soft shoulder," Truitt said, glancing down at the road and thinking it best to change the subject. "How about we let the jack down and roll the car to flatter ground?"

All three looked up when a set of headlights splashed across them. Siebert swayed, as if thrown off balance by the sudden brightness. Donna Lee was right about Siebert drinking whiskey, and it seemed he'd been drinking a good bit of it.

A car slowed, rolled past, and parked in front of Siebert's. Two doors flew open, and two men stepped out. Under the glare of Siebert's headlights, Truitt couldn't make out either one. But he saw enough to know they wore dark suits and hats.

He was back to worrying that stopping to help was a bad idea.

CHAPTER 7

Truitt had forgotten the time. It was simple as that. If he'd have been paying attention, he'd be home already. But he hadn't. He'd stood too long outside Terrance's Tavern, talking and drinking with the fellows. Usually, he only stayed for one drink. He could hide one from Mama. She didn't like it, any of it, but the drinking and talking were part of Truitt's business.

Sure, the long shot of winning a few bucks brought the fellows back week after week. They liked a little action in their lives, a bit of money to rub between their fingers. But they also came for the conversation. Truitt gave them hope, made them feel better about their lives. That was what Truitt was selling. Hope and action. And he was good at it. Though he was careful not to sell promises. That could have led to broken spirits for them and broken bones for Truitt.

His daddy had the same way with folks. Truitt had been only a child when he last saw his daddy, but he remembered how people wanted to be near him. Spencer Holt would walk down the street, his police uniform crisp, a gun on his hip, and people would cross the street just to say hello. They'd shake his hand, pump it hard, so Spencer Holt would remember their name.

Truitt liked that people flocked to him and his bolita game like they'd flocked to his daddy and his uniform. He felt he was carrying on a tradition that would have made his daddy proud.

But tonight, as the fellows kept offering to buy another round, Truitt forgot his rules and kept saying yes. The more he drank, the more it sank in that those few minutes with Addie in the back room of a grocery store were the last he'd ever have. And it was his fault, his prideful, jackass, stubborn fault. After the first few beers, he'd told himself there'd be plenty of other girls; a couple even walked past and gave him a smile. But a few more beers and that feeling was gone.

No other girl would ever be enough to take Addie's place. By the time he was shooting whiskey, he'd tumbled all the way to knowing he was nothing but a coward. Afraid to live on his own. Afraid to be without her. Afraid he'd never love anyone again. And so, in the back of the grocery store, he'd tried to strong-arm her into staying with meanness.

Now here he was on the side of the road, regretting what he'd done to Addie and regretting that he'd stopped to help.

Squinting into the glare of Siebert's headlights, Truitt tried to get a look at the license plate on the car that had just pulled to a stop, but he couldn't make it out. He was right about the two men wearing suits, and both wore their hats pulled low over their eyes. Something about those hats gave him pause.

"Looks like you could use a hand," one of the men said, walking straight into the glow coming off Siebert's headlights. He was the taller, rounder, and older of the two.

Truitt looked to Siebert, thinking that since it was his car, he should say if they needed help or not.

Balancing on one foot, a hand on his car's hood for balance, Siebert had one foot draped over the opposite knee and was buffing his wing tip. Under better lighting, Siebert's pants were frayed at the cuff, one of his soles was peeling loose at the heel, and his white shirt gaped where he was missing a button. Readjusting to buff the other shoe, he didn't answer the man.

"Much appreciated," Truitt said to the voice coming out of the glare. "Got ourselves a flat."

As the two men continued closer, the gravel crunching louder, Donna Lee slid up alongside Truitt and latched on to his arm. Still buffing that shoe, Siebert glanced up to see Donna Lee clinging to Truitt. The way Siebert was looking, he was thinking Donna Lee should have been clinging to him.

"Think we need to push the car off this shoulder," Truitt said, looking to Siebert and wishing he'd stop leaning on the car. His weight could be enough to send it sliding over the shoulder. "That okay with you, sir?"

Without Truitt's daddy around to teach him, his mama was always trying. Eye what's most fragile on a man, Mama always said, and then take care not to test it. On a man like Siebert Rix, his ego was most fragile. Truitt needed to be careful not to test it, and he wished Donna Lee would let go of his arm. Instead, she latched on tighter. She didn't sense the kind of trouble bearing down on her, but Truitt did. If Siebert's ego took a beating, Donna Lee would be next.

The two men were close enough now for Truitt to get a good look. He still didn't recognize either one. They smelled of strong, spicy cologne that stung Truitt's nose, which meant they weren't from around Hockta. Tampa maybe. They looked and smelled big city, not Lake County. It was one more thing that gave him pause. As quickly as he could, he wanted to roll the car to steadier ground, change the tire, and leave.

"We'll do the pushing," the older of the two men said, tipping his hat at Truitt and bending to get a look at the flat. Then he stood, and both men positioned themselves at the front of the car. "You say when and where. You're the boss."

Donna Lee squeezed Truitt's arm. "You hear that?" she whispered, her breath hot on Truitt's neck. "You're the boss."

Still standing with one foot propped in the air, Siebert studied the men.

"Don't recognize you two," he said. "Maybe it's best you move along."

The second man, the shorter, thinner, and younger of the two, glanced up to see Siebert still buffing his shoes.

"I got an idea about what's best," the shorter man said. He wasn't much older than Truitt and not at all worried about pampering Siebert's ego. "How about you make yourself useful. Get off the hood, hop in the car, and do the steering. Or should we have the lady do it?"

Trouble rumbled underfoot, drawing closer the longer they all stood out there in the dark. Siebert's ego was definitely taking a beating. Truitt shrugged Donna Lee away, squatted at the jack, and avoided looking at Siebert.

"Hey," Donna Lee said to the two men in suits as Truitt cranked the jack to lower it. Maybe sensing the same trouble as Truitt, she thought she'd distract them. She stepped into the headlights and posed with a hand to her hip.

The other thing that told Truitt the two men were big city—they only glanced at Donna Lee. As pretty as she was, as sweet as she smelled, they barely looked. They were used to seeing pretty women. Women who were prettier than Donna Lee.

"This is your lucky day, gentlemen," Donna Lee said and paused as if waiting for them to notice her. "We were just talking about what a lucky day it is."

Truitt sat back from the jack and reached for Donna Lee's skirt, but she was too far away. She needed to stop, not say another word, because Truitt knew what was coming next.

"If you play your cards right," Donna Lee said, not paying any attention to Truitt, who was scrambling toward her on his knees. "I'll bet this fine young man here will sell you a few bolita tickets. Ain't that right?"

The second rule of business, right after be home before dark . . . never take bets from anyone he didn't know, especially fellows from the city. Especially fellows from Tampa.

Donna Lee might have just outed Truitt to the Tampa Mafia.

CHAPTER 8

The first time anyone let on that a gangster killed his father, Truitt had been selling bolita tickets for only a few months. One Friday night, when the fellows were drinking whiskey and placing their bets, they got to telling Truitt the story. At first, he thought they were just trying to scare him. Everyone knew the Tampa Mafia ran bolita, and Truitt's customers didn't want him to end up like his daddy. But he kept hearing the same story in the months and years to come.

"Your daddy was a dirty cop," all the men would say. "Who ain't in Tampa? But your daddy, he made the wrong man angry. Got greedy, and that got him killed. It was the mob. They tried killing your daddy the first time when that house of yours in Tampa burned to the ground. Make no mistake. That fire was no accident. When that didn't work, they got him with a bullet. Shot in his own driveway. Says something about a man when he's killed in his own driveway."

After hearing the story several times, Truitt asked his mama if she knew who shot his daddy and why he was shot in their driveway.

"He's dead," she had told Truitt. "Don't matter who pulled the trigger or why. Knowing won't change what's done."

Not wanting to get himself shot by the Tampa Mafia like his daddy, Truitt tried to get Donna Lee's attention to make her stop talking. Still squatting at the side of the car, the jack in hand, he waved at her, but she was too busy posing for the men from Tampa to notice. Maybe Truitt was being too cautious, but too much caution scarcely got a man killed. He shuffled his feet until they were squarely under him, readying himself to take off running if the men turned out to be with the mob.

Easing the jack free, he squeezed its handle with both hands and flicked his eyes at the tail end of the car the men drove up in. Donna Lee blocked the glare coming off the headlights, and the license plate was in plain sight now. Yes, the men were from Tampa. Hillsborough County.

"Only a quarter a ticket," Donna Lee was saying. She wouldn't stop talking, but so far, she hadn't said Truitt's name. At least, he didn't think she had. "You fellows know about bolita? You just pick the numbers you want to play, pay your money, and get a ticket in return. Drawing's tomorrow night."

The jack was heavy as Truitt lifted it from the ground, taking all its weight in his hands. It was made of solid steel, and its base was six inches square. If he had to swing it, he'd lead with that end. Any one of its sharp corners could put a man back on his heels.

"You say bolita?" the older and bigger of the two men said. He dipped his head and looked out at Donna Lee from under the brim of his hat. "This boy here is running a bolita game?"

Truitt raised his eyes.

In tandem, the two men lifted their hands from the car's hood.

The younger man lunged. Truitt exploded to his feet and pulled back the jack, cocking it like a baseball bat. He swung, connecting with something. What, he didn't know. And ran.

The road's soft shoulder crumbled under his sudden movement. He dropped the jack and slid down the embankment, falling on his hind end at the bottom of the ditch. Pushing onto his feet, he dove for the cover of the pines.

After two years, Truitt made enough money off his bolita game for his mama to keep food on the table and the lights and water on. In fact, he'd started making so much he was afraid to tell his mama. He was also afraid of letting on to the mob how much he made, and the two fellows wearing suits and hats, they were definitely mob. No doubt. That was the only reason for them to care about Truitt selling bolita tickets. At the very least, these fellows would want Truitt to hand over their share of what he'd brought in over the past few years. Or more likely, they'd want Truitt's hide to make an example of him.

Weaving through the pines and oaks, chest already pumping, Truitt glanced over his shoulder. He dropped back to a jog when he didn't hear the men anymore. The ground was littered with slick pine needles, and the men would be struggling to keep up in their smooth-soled wing tips.

At a fork in the trees, a spot that opened to two separate paths, Truitt threw a few rocks into the wiry moss that hung from trees along one path and then ran down the other. He didn't know if men from the city would know enough to watch for swaying moss, but if they did, they'd take note and think Truitt went that way. They'd follow the path south. Donna Lee and Siebert would have time to get in their car, even if it meant driving on a flat tire. And Truitt would be able to circle back, grab his bike, and get home to Mama. If the men didn't know his name, they wouldn't be able to find him. At least, not quickly.

Truitt stopped short when he heard a scream. Ducking behind a palmetto scrub, he dropped to the ground. The damp air immediately settled around him. His shirt stuck to his back. His hair hung in his face. Burying his mouth in his forearm to quiet his breathing, he listened. Yes, it was a scream because he heard another. It was Donna Lee.

Rising to his knees, he watched the dark pines, squinting to catch a shadow or a rustling in the scrub. There was nothing. The men hadn't followed him.

Back on his feet, Truitt ran toward the road. The thing about men like Siebert—they only looked after themselves. He wouldn't help Donna Lee, and she'd need it. Those men would be wanting to know who Truitt was and where he lived. She might try not to tell them, but in the end, they'd make her.

When the sparkle of headlights appeared up ahead, Truitt slowed. His throat and chest burned from sucking in the damp, soggy night air.

He leaned forward, threw up a hot mixture of beer and whiskey, and braced his hands on his knees. The voices were clearer.

"Right fucking now."

Already Truitt recognized that voice. It was the same man who asked Donna Lee . . . this boy runs a bolita game? He was the older, taller man.

Slipping from one pine to the next, careful to step softly, Truitt made his way close enough to see the road. The headlights of both cars were still on, lighting up the whole scene. The man held Siebert by his collar, a gun pressed to his temple. Siebert was sobbing. There was no sign of Donna Lee and no more screaming.

"I told you, I don't know," Siebert was saying, his head hanging as he shook it side to side.

"Tell me his fucking name," the man shouted. His hat teetered on the back of his head. He looked from Siebert to the ground near his feet. "Christ, is he breathing?"

"She knows the kid's name," Siebert said, his head popping up. He stopped sobbing and pointed at the ground. "Donna Lee. She talked to him. When he first pulled up. Like they were old friends. Ask her. She knows. Not me."

Truitt strained to get a glimpse of Donna Lee, but he couldn't see her. Still, she was alive. That was something. That was everything.

The man in the suit cocked the gun still pointed at Siebert's head.

"Tell me the kid's name," he said, glancing at the ground again. He was talking to Donna Lee. "Tell me, or I pull this trigger."

When Donna Lee came into view, Truitt pushed off the pine tree and took a backward step. His mouth hung slack.

Donna Lee must have been down on hands and knees, but she was standing now and holding her two hands out in front of her. They were slick with something shiny. It could have been anything. But her pale-yellow dress was no doubt covered in blood. She wiped the back of one hand across her face and brushed her hair from her eyes, leaving a bloody smear on her forehead.

"He's dead." Her voice quivered as she looked at the ground and back at the man with the gun. "There ain't nothing I can do. I don't know nothing about—"

"This one's going to be dead too," the man said, his voice steady as he nodded at Siebert, "if you don't tell me the kid's fucking name."

Truitt continued backing away. The blood wasn't Donna Lee's. When Truitt swung that jack, he'd connected with something. He connected with one of the men in suits. He killed him.

"Jesus, Donna Lee," Siebert said. "Tell him. You said it when he first rode up on that bike of his. I remember you saying it. What's his fucking name?"

"Truitt," Donna Lee said, dropping back against the hood of the car, her hands still stretched out in front of her like she was reaching for help. "His name is Truitt."

Truitt knew what came next. The man was going to ask where Truitt lived, and then he would jump in his car and be on Truitt's porch, pointing his gun at Truitt's mama in less than ten minutes. Without his bike and a head start, there was no way Truitt could beat the man there. He took a step forward. He had no other choice. He couldn't let that man find Mama at home alone. He'd show himself, and the man would let Siebert and Donna Lee go. It was the only way he could protect them. It was the only way he could protect his mama.

"And you know where this Truitt lives?"

Truitt took another step closer. If any one of them had turned and looked into the pines, they'd have seen him. But they didn't. Truitt couldn't be sure the man would let Donna Lee go once he had Truitt, but at least he'd be trying to do the right thing. Still, the more he tried to do right, the more things went wrong.

"He lives south," Donna Lee said. Her voice was stronger. She'd stopped crying.

The man in the suit lowered the gun and shoved Siebert, who stumbled and fell to his knees.

Truitt slipped behind a pine and pressed tight against it. He didn't live south. He lived north.

"Go south of Hockta, like you're headed to Mount Dora," Donna Lee said, reaching to help Siebert, but he swatted her away. "You know that road?"

She paused, must have been waiting for the man to nod.

"Then you take a right at the Baptist church outside of town. Can't miss it. Next right'll land you at his place. It's a ways back in there, so just keep driving. But Truitt's a good boy. Just putting food in the cupboards, milk in the fridge."

Truitt knew the area Donna Lee was describing, and it was nowhere near his house. There was nothing out past the Baptist church but gravel roads winding back to the lake down there. Easy to get lost on those roads—that was what everyone in Hockta knew.

"What's your name?" the man shouted as he threw open his car door.

A silence followed. And then the click of a gun being cocked.

"Siebert Rix."

"Well, Siebert Rix. Don't try running. If I got to go looking for you, and I can't find you, you're going to be damn sorry when I do. Take my word for it."

An engine started. Up on the road, the man in the suit was gone. Siebert was on his feet again, standing as if a gun was still pressed to his head. And Donna Lee had melted to the ground.

Truitt had time now. Since the man was going the wrong way, Truitt could get to his house first, but what then? He couldn't really protect his mama. Not from a man like that and whoever he brought with him, because more men would come. Truitt's only mistake hadn't been running a bolita game. He'd also killed one of them. More men would come for sure.

Once Siebert Rix held the jack in hand and was staring down on the flat tire, surely wondering if he could change the thing himself, Truitt took off into the pines again. He wouldn't take his bike because that would mean sticking to the road and making himself an easy target. The sheriff's house was closer than Truitt's, and he would know what to do.

Wiley Bishop had been sheriff for as long as Truitt could remember, and he would do anything for Truitt and his mama. He'd been making that clear since the one-year anniversary of the death of Truitt's daddy.

Wiley was Truitt's best chance to see home, his mama, and Addie Anne one more time.

CHAPTER 9

By the time I went to bed, I had talked myself out of worrying about what happened at the grocery store. Before we'd even pulled out of the parking lot, Aunt Jean was smiling and laughing and talking about how much she loved the sweet smell of April in Lake County. Plenty of times, Aunt Jean had said too much to Mrs. Danielson, and plenty of times, Mrs. Danielson had written about Aunt Jean in the newspaper, but only once had it been something that enraged Siebert Rix. If Aunt Jean wasn't worried, I wouldn't worry. Instead, I started trying to figure how to strike out on my new life without Truitt by my side.

My bedroom was dark, and the house was quiet. Something had woken me. I blinked and stretched my eyes open. All night, I'd been drifting off only to wake with a start. Each time, confusion quickly gave way to remembering what had happened in the storeroom among the dusty boxes and crates of vegetables. Truitt had made me the fool. And then I pinched my eyes, buckled my toes, and clenched my fists, bracing, because I knew what came next.

All the times Truitt and I fumbled in the dark came crashing down, his hands roaming my body, the moaning, the heat, his breath, my breath, the fingers, the tongues, and me liking it. Me liking it all because I was fool enough to believe he really loved me. Now I was left wondering . . . how could I like doing all those things with a man who didn't love me? What did that make me?

Truitt thought proposing marriage was proof he loved me, but loving someone wasn't supposed to hinge on an ultimatum. He teased me with promises of a future, and then he unleashed his meanness when I said no to him. He thought I had my head in the clouds. He told me so and gave me a two-handed shove that sent me tumbling back to reality. If I wouldn't marry him, he didn't want me. That was reality, and that wasn't love.

But this time, something other than feeling the fool woke me.

Across the hall, my little brother Urban's bed squealed as he rolled over. A clock ticked. A fan whined as it rotated side to side. In the room next to mine, Daddy snored. The steady, deep grumble filled the house, making me think I was wrong about hearing something. Daddy would be the first up and out of bed if anything was amiss.

Sinking back into my pillow, I stared at the dresses draped over the chair at my desk. Two new suitcases lay open on my floor, half-full of all my delicates, laundered and fresh off the line. My train case sat on my desk, the special stationery I bought for writing letters to Truitt the only thing inside. But I wouldn't be writing him any letters. I would be leaving Hockta and starting my new life all alone. Even though Aunt Jean would be with me, and I'd meet countless new people, the trip still felt scarier and harder to face without Truitt. I'd heard Aunt Jean say she often felt loneliest in the biggest crowds. That's how I felt. Lonely.

A floorboard creaked, and I started to scramble out of bed. I settled back, pressing a hand to my chest as Aunt Jean swept into my room. She wore a shimmering white peignoir that floated and made her look like a ghost. Prancing to the side of my bed on her tiptoes, she settled on the mattress.

"You awake, Addie darlin'?" she said in a breathy whisper. She'd set pin curls in her hair and wore a sheer scarf over them.

I slid up in bed. "What is it? What's wrong?"

Aunt Jean smiled with just her mouth while her eyes cast off to the side. It was as if someone else were holding her smile in place. But it wasn't only the concocted smile that signaled trouble. Aunt Jean always slipped into that breathy voice when she was nervous or afraid. In every movie. In every interview. In every public moment. I used to wonder why Aunt Jean spoke in her normal voice to our family and in another to everyone else. Now, I was beginning to think Aunt Jean so often used that breathy voice because she was so often afraid. And Aunt Jean being afraid made me afraid, as afraid as I'd been when I first heard Donna Lee hollering for me in the grocery store to come quick.

Aunt Jean slipping into her breathy voice was usually only the beginning of her slipping into a whole different person. Other things followed. The way her shoulders dipped and swayed. The way her neck-lines plunged. The way she walked and stood and arched her back. That person did well for a while. She got through a movie, made people laugh during an interview, found herself a new husband. But once the job was done, she started a long downward slide. Sometimes, the slide lasted for weeks before she clawed her way back to normal. That slide was usually what brought her to Hockta.

Wanting to snap Aunt Jean out of using that voice, so I could also snap myself out of being afraid, I grabbed her hand and squeezed. I wanted to remind her she was in our house where she was just Aunt Jean. Aunt Jean, who helped Mama with the laundry and saw Mr. O'Dell almost every night and helped Urban with his reading. She was safe. She was ordinary.

"I need a favor," Aunt Jean said, still holding that smile. But the smile wasn't enough. She dipped her head, fluttered her lashes. She was slipping, this time right before my eyes.

"I'll go get Mama," I said.

Mama would know what to say to reel Aunt Jean back in. She always did.

"No," Aunt Jean said.

As if someone called cut, she fell silent. She closed her eyes and took a deep breath like she was preparing for another take. When she opened them, she popped another smile and dipped her head onto one shoulder.

"It's a simple thing, really," she said, whispering, her lips pouty. "Won't take any time at all."

"Is this because of what happened in the grocery store?" I said, wishing Aunt Jean were simpler like Mama. Mama never swept into my room in the middle of the night or slipped into being another person. "Did you say something to Mrs. Danielson you shouldn't have? Did you say something about Siebert Rix that's going to make him mad again?"

Still holding Aunt Jean's hands, I squeezed them, willing her to remember she was safe.

"Whatever happened," I said when Aunt Jean didn't answer me, "it's all right. I'll do whatever you want to make it better. Just tell me. Whatever you want."

I glanced at my clock. It was after midnight. That meant my birthday was tomorrow, and the day after, Aunt Jean and I would leave on our trip. After years of practicing, planning, dreaming, and preparing, my life would finally begin. If she'd said something Siebert Rix wasn't going to like, I'd beg Mrs. Danielson not to print it. I could do that. She wouldn't want to see Aunt Jean hurt.

But I'd have a harder time talking Aunt Jean out of her sadness. If it got hold of her like it sometimes did, we wouldn't be going anywhere for a long time. Maybe for forever. No matter how lonely I feared I might be when we left Hockta, I would be lonelier if I stayed. Without Truitt, I had nothing left except my escape. I'd have done anything Aunt Jean asked if it meant keeping her happy.

"It'll mean getting up real early tomorrow morning," Aunt Jean said. "And you can't tell. Not anyone."

She paused and looked up at the many pictures and posters that lined my walls. They were all photographs of Aunt Jean. She seemed lost for a minute, as if she didn't recognize the woman in all those pictures. Then her eyes dropped back to me.

"Can you do that for me? I fear my whole life depends on it."

I couldn't be certain, but I thought that dialogue came from one of Aunt Jean's movies.

"I'll do whatever you want me to do," I said.

I wanted to get as far away from Hockta and Truitt Holt as fast as I could.

CHAPTER 10

Siebert Rix clung to the steering wheel of his car, every rut in the road making him worry the spare he'd just put on would pop off. His hands and forearms were numb from holding so tight. Driving deeper into the trees that closed in tighter and thicker the farther he traveled, he didn't have a glimmer of moonlight to go by. The night was black except for the narrow hole his headlights cut in the road ahead. Donna Lee was slouched in the seat next to him, her head in her hands. She was crying as she swore again and again that this was the way she'd sent the man when she lied about where Truitt Holt lived.

Up ahead, a pair of taillights appeared.

"Sit up," Siebert shouted at Donna Lee. He grabbed her and hoisted her up in her seat. "When we get out of this car, you start talking. And by God, you talk fast."

Siebert knew not to lie to the wrong person. He'd been on enough movie sets and watched enough films to know how things went down. If you lied to the wrong person, the wrong gangster, the wrong gunslinger, you paid the price. Even good men paid the price if they got tangled up with the wrong woman, and Donna Lee was for certain the wrong woman. Not that Siebert had been the one to lie about where Truitt Holt lived, but he'd damn sure get the blame if he didn't set it right.

Flipping his headlights and honking his horn, Siebert pulled up alongside the other car, squinting hard at the road ahead and holding the steering wheel firm. He'd gotten a clear view of the license plate. It was definitely the man Donna Lee had sent on a wild-goose chase. Siebert shouted at Donna Lee to roll her window down and hollered for the man to pull over.

"It's me," Siebert shouted, waving and pointing at his own face. "You got to stop. You got to let me tell you where you're going."

The other car slowed. Siebert pulled in front of it, kicking up a cloud of dust that doused the other set of headlights. By the time Siebert threw his car in park, stepped out, and the dust cleared, the man from Tampa stood in the middle of the road, his gun pointed at Siebert.

"You're going the wrong way," Siebert said, both hands in the air, his heart pounding hard inside his chest. He didn't feel so good. "It was her. She lied. Gave you the wrong address. I got it out of her. Got it out of her for you."

"You telling me the middle of fucking nowhere ain't the way to that boy's house?" the man said, glancing around.

There wasn't a light anywhere. No houses. No other cars. Siebert was no fool. He'd seen *On the Waterfront*. Seen it more than once. He knew a thug when he saw one, and this man was a thug. His suit fit poorly through the shoulders, his shoes were scuffed, and his nails were unkempt. And here Siebert and Donna Lee were, stuck without a soul in sight to witness what might come next. This man could shoot him, and there wouldn't be one person to hear or see. Siebert read the newspaper. Men like this fellow, this thug, bought off cops and judges. They knew just where to bury a body.

Damn it all, Siebert should have dumped Donna Lee on the side of the road and left for California the second she told him she'd lied to the man about where that Truitt kid lived. But as the man had driven off, he'd warned Siebert not to run. Now, out here in the middle of nowhere, Siebert hoped the man realized Siebert was doing the stand-up thing and that if anyone had to suffer, it would be Donna Lee.

"Second she told me she lied, I came looking for you," Siebert said, his hands still in the air. He figured if he kept talking, the man wouldn't shoot. "Drove out here on a tire barely hanging on because I knew I had to find you. This is me, taking your word for it. I knew—"

"Get her out here," the man said, cutting Siebert off.

Siebert nodded and slapped the roof of his car.

"Come on out, Donna Lee," he said. "Tell this man I didn't have nothing to do with it. Tell him how you lied all on your own."

Donna Lee was slow in getting out of the car. Siebert had slapped her around good as soon as she told him she put one over on the man by sending him off into the darkest, roughest, most dead-end roads in Lake County.

"You lie to me about where that boy lives?" the man said, waving the tip of his gun so Donna Lee would walk into the glow of his head-lights where he could get a look at her.

Donna Lee stood in the middle of the road, hands clasped, head lowered. Her pale-yellow dress hung stiff around her legs, made rigid by the dried blood of the man's friend. The man should have seen all that blood and wanted to take the same from Donna Lee, but instead, he walked toward Donna Lee, his head tipped off to the side like he felt sorry for her. That was not a good sign.

If the man felt sorry for Donna Lee, that meant he blamed Siebert. Goddamn, this hadn't been a good night for Siebert. He should have paid closer attention when that gossip columnist told him Marilyn had made a big announcement. She said it would be running in the next day's paper and that Siebert wouldn't want to miss it. She teased him with the news but wouldn't give him any details. And then she landed the big question . . . what'll you do with yourself if you're no longer photographer to Marilyn Monroe?

Yes, Siebert should have listened. And he should have forced the woman to tell him exactly what would be running in the paper, and then he should have grabbed Marilyn and left town. He should have pried her out of the Buckley house and threw her in his car.

She was going to make a damn fool of him in the newspaper again, and what did he do? Nothing. He pretended there was no news that could possibly derail his career, went out drinking with Donna Lee, and spent the last of his goddamn money. He'd have never been out on that road, trying to fix a flat tire and ending up in the path of two gangsters, if he'd have stopped playing nice with Marilyn weeks ago. He was too easy on her—always had been. And now look where he was.

"Tell him you lied, Donna Lee," Siebert said, his arms going numb from being stuck up in the air so long.

"Shut your mouth," the man said, jabbing his gun at Siebert. Then to Donna Lee, he raised a hand to her left eye and drew a finger around it, all gentle and caring. Siebert had slapped her face so hard he'd knocked her to the ground, and it had already begun to swell. "He do this to you, sweetheart?"

Donna Lee nodded.

"Why'd he slap you?"

"I told you why," Siebert said, not liking the way things were going. Not liking it one bit. "Found out she lied. Doing your work for you."

"You can tell me," the man said, ignoring Siebert. "Why'd he hit you, sweetheart?"

"He hit me so I'd keep my mouth shut," she said. "Told me I'd better not let on what he was up to, or I'd get more of the same."

"That ain't true," Siebert said. Goddamn it, she was lying, right here in front of him. "I told her to tell you everything. That's why we tracked you down. Told her she better talk fast too."

"He didn't smack you because you lied to me?" the man said, squeezing Donna Lee's hand, treating her like he would his own daughter.

Donna Lee flicked her eyes at Siebert, and hand to God, she smiled. A small smile. One that said, this is for all the times you smacked me, not just tonight, but every other night. This is for all the promises you made that never came true. That smile was warning Siebert to hold tight, because she was getting ready to take her revenge.

She smiled because for once in her measly, pathetic life, someone cared what Donna Lee had to say.

CHAPTER 11

Standing in the middle of a dark road, not a single person within shouting distance, Siebert wanted to scream at Donna Lee to shut her lying mouth. She'd always been one to talk too damn much. Siebert started toward her, intending to grab her by the hair and fling her to the ground before she could do him any damage. That would shut her up. But the man stopped him by pointing a gun in Siebert's face.

"Siebert knows Truitt, same as I do," Donna Lee said, that smug look still on her face. "Been to his house, even. After you left, he told me he was glad I lied to you about where Truitt lived. Said it was smart thinking."

"That ain't true," Siebert said. "I ain't never—"

The man stopped Siebert with a look this time.

"Go on, sweetheart," he said.

"This is the whole of what happened," Donna Lee said, lifting tall, enjoying the attention the man was giving her. "Siebert didn't want you finding Truitt and shutting down his bolita game. Siebert bet big this week. He said he went all in, spent every dime he had buying bolita tickets from Truitt. Siebert's broke. Flat broke. And he's washed up too. If you don't believe me, you'll read about it in the newspaper tomorrow."

The man studied Donna Lee as if just noticing how pretty she could look in the right light. "I'll read it in the newspaper, huh?"

"That's how you know I'm telling the truth," Donna Lee said, giving Siebert another smile as if to say . . . get ready for this. "He's Marilyn Monroe's photographer. Or, rather, he was. Ain't going to be no more, and tomorrow's news will prove it. You know who that is, right? Marilyn Monroe. Siebert used to be somebody. Now he's going to be nobody. Going to have no career. I lied, that's true, and I'm real sorry for it. I'm real sorry for your friend too. But Siebert knew I was lying, and he didn't say nothing to let on."

"But that ain't true," Siebert said, clamping his mouth shut when he realized it was hanging open. "Why would I be here, right now, if I was covering for that Truitt kid?"

The man turned from Siebert to Donna Lee and cocked his brows, looking to her for an answer.

"After you left," Donna Lee said, "Siebert got worried that you'd figure out he was in on the lying and that you'd come find him. He thought he'd fast-talk you and blame it all on me. He smacked me around, saying I better go along with him or get more of the same. Said he could outsmart any old thug. That's what he called you. And now, here we are."

"Thought he'd outsmart me, huh?" the man said.

"I didn't say that," Siebert said. "Didn't say nothing about outsmarting nobody."

"Meaning I won't see nothing in the newspaper tomorrow?"

"It's just a gossip column," Siebert said. "Don't mean I'm washed up. I got plenty of money. Marilyn or no Marilyn, I got plenty. And I ain't played bolita a day in my life. That Truitt kid is nothing to me."

"And what's this news I'll see in tomorrow's paper?" the man asked Donna Lee, smoothing one of the sleeves of her dress.

"The woman, she wouldn't tell," Donna Lee said. "Just told Siebert not to dare miss tomorrow's column, because it was going to be big, and it was going to mean the end for him."

"You know who that boy killed?" the man said, nodding as if satisfied with Donna Lee's answer and lifting her face with a finger to her chin. His hand was the size of a ball glove next to her tiny head. "That was Santo Giordano's nephew. Kid's dumb as fuck, but blood don't care. Understand what I'm saying."

Siebert understood. Some people counted for more than others. Dumb or not, the dead man counted for more because he was the nephew of a mob boss.

"Like I was telling you," Donna Lee said, using her "first thing in the morning, we been screwing all night long" voice. "I'm real sorry about your friend getting killed. I know Truitt didn't mean it."

"Here's the thing," the man said, lowering his gun and glancing around like he was ready to be on his way. "I'm wasting time here with you two. Time I ain't got. Tell me, sweetheart, where do I find the boy's house?"

The man tucked his gun in his waistband as Donna Lee told him the real directions to Truitt's house. She said again that Truitt was a good boy. Siebert exhaled, maybe for the first time since he'd stepped from the car. He lowered his hands. The blood rushed to his fingers, making them tingle. Nothing had ever felt so good. That tingle meant this was almost over.

"If I go back to Tampa empty handed, I'll be taking the blame for Santo Giordano's nephew being dead," the man said, turning to go back to his car. His round, sweaty face glowed in his headlights. He reached in his jacket as if to pull out a kerchief. Something glimmered in the dusty light. "And that ain't happening. I'm hauling someone back with me, and if it ain't that kid, it's going to be you."

Siebert lifted a hand to shield his eyes and get a look at which one of them the man was talking to. Him or Donna Lee.

He was talking to Siebert.

"No," Siebert said, pointing at Donna Lee. "Don't take me. Her. She did it. If that kid gets away, it's her fault. Take her."

Siebert was going to fling her at the man and make him take her. He could take her right now, for all Siebert cared. But as Siebert made his move, the man moved too. His right arm swung around, smooth like he was reaching for Donna Lee's hand to give her a twirl on the dance floor, and there was another glimmer. Something caught the light. It was long and slender. Metal. Donna Lee let out a breath, no more than that, and sank to the ground.

"Like I told you before," the man said to Siebert, pausing as he waited for Donna Lee to stop convulsing at his feet. "Don't try to run."

When Donna Lee lay still, the man scooped her in his arms. Her mouth hung limp, pulsing like the mouth of a fish as she tried to get a breath of air. And a knife stuck out of her side, firm, stiff like the man had hit bone with it.

A man like this man, a thug, he was intentional with a knife. He drove this one deep into Donna Lee's body because he wanted to send Siebert a message. The man could do the same to Siebert, if need be.

Walking toward Siebert's car, Donna Lee cradled in his arms, her red hair nearly dragging in the dirt, her mouth still trying to squeeze out one last breath, the man nodded at Siebert's trunk.

"Open it," he said.

Siebert dug his keys from his pocket and, hands shaking, popped the trunk. He backed away as the man carefully laid Donna Lee down, tucked her skirt around her legs so she was covered, and brushed the coppery red hair from her face. Her empty eyes, the blue in them having turned to cloudy water, flicked from Siebert to the man. The trunk slammed closed.

Turning to leave and digging out his own keys, the man paused.

"Here's what you need to know . . . we got people all over the state, on every road, in every town. If you think about running before I find this Truitt kid, I'll find you, and it won't be a quick end for you like it's going to be for that pretty little redhead."

Damn it all, the whole mess was Donna Lee's fault. And Marilyn's. She was the reason he was in this godforsaken town. And what the hell was going to happen tomorrow when that man opened the newspaper and read an article making everyone think Siebert was on the brink of being a nobody? Siebert knew what would happen. Good Lord, that man would think Siebert was so desperate for money that he tried to protect Truitt and his damn bolita game. He'd think Siebert tried to outsmart him and fast-talk the mob. He wouldn't be happy just hauling Truitt back to Tampa. He'd come looking for Siebert too. Just out of pride. Just to prove Siebert wasn't man enough to fast-talk anyone.

"It's you or the kid," the man said. "One of you's going back to Tampa and accounting for killing Mr. Giordano's nephew. If you don't want it to be you, I suggest you make sure that boy finds his way home."

"I don't know where to find him," Siebert said. "Don't even know where to look."

Siebert barely remembered what the kid looked like, and the only one who could help him find the boy was dying in his trunk this very minute. Or maybe she was already dead.

"I'll be going directly to the boy's house," the man said. "Maybe I find him there, and your troubles'll be over. They'll be over, too, if you bring me the boy."

"Bring him where?" Siebert said. "I don't know him. Don't know anything about him."

"You heard where he lives same as I heard," the man said, brushing imaginary dust from his jacket. "Me or some other fellows like me will be at the boy's house until we flush him out or you bring him to us. And heaven help you if I don't like what I read in the paper tomorrow."

"It ain't like what Donna Lee told you," Siebert said. "Whatever's going to be in the paper, it ain't going to ruin me. Ain't nothing can ruin me. I'm famous practically. You ask anyone. Famous and got plenty of money. There ain't one damn reason I would try to fast-talk you or outsmart you. Not one damn reason."

The man let out a deep sigh and shrugged as if saying . . . we'll see.

"I'm thinking you should concern yourself with finding that boy," he said. "Because if he ain't at his house, and you don't bring him to me, real soon, I'll come find you."

And then the man was gone, and Siebert stood alone, not even sure how to get back to town. The road was darker with only Siebert's headlights. One wrong turn of the steering wheel and he could end up in the ditch, and then what?

He walked in a wide arc, keeping far from his trunk. Dear Lord, he hoped he didn't hear any crying or knocking around back there. He stopped, bent forward, and tried not to vomit because that was the sound of Donna Lee gasping for air.

The man had said to find this Truitt kid and bring him to his house soon, real soon, but Siebert forgot to ask how soon was soon. He couldn't do it. It was too hard. Siebert didn't know where to look or who to ask for help.

Siebert didn't do hard things. He wasn't built for that.

He'd find a way out of town. That was the best plan. A plan Siebert could manage. He had to find a way to run.

CHAPTER 12

Wiley Bishop stood in his front room, every light in the house switched off. With his shotgun in hand, he looked out the front window and scanned the porch and the dark drive beyond. He'd heard that thud before. Someone had jumped on his porch. Anyone who knew Wiley knew the steps leading to his front door weren't for shit, and they'd grab hold of the newel post and jump instead of risking it. But none of that meant the visitor was a friend. Everyone in Lake County knew all about Wiley Bishop, because everyone knew all about the sheriff.

The last time Wiley scrambled out of bed at hearing a thud like that, it had been a group of fellows dressed in hoods and robes. They'd been mostly out-of-towners, though he'd recognized a few. You can always recognize a man by the gun he carries and the shoes he wears. They'd been toting torches, and those damn fool robes glowed. They weren't sneaking up on anyone, but he guessed their goal wasn't to sneak. Their goal was to be seen.

But peeking out the window this time, Wiley didn't see the orange glow of torches, and no white robes fluttered in the wind. He saw nothing. A man coming at you with every intent to be seen had something to say. He also had every intent to leave you alive so you could pass his words along.

A man coming at you in the dark didn't plan on leaving you alive.

Cracking the door, he led with the shotgun's barrel. Now he was the damned fool because he'd been meaning to oil the hinges. He was sure not sneaking up on anyone.

"Wiley." It was a whisper.

Wiley opened the door enough to poke his head out.

"Wiley. It's me. Truitt."

Wiley Bishop was tall enough as men went but on the slender side. He was cautious, measured, and most folks would probably describe him as bookish. In short, he wasn't the big, bold, boisterous kind of man people might think of as a sheriff. Especially folks in Lake County. He wasn't even a good shot. Simply said, Wiley was a bad shot. Not once, in all his years of being sheriff, had he shot his gun other than to practice on his makeshift shooting range.

A quick mind was the reason Wiley kept getting elected. He could sort things faster and better than most anyone. That meant he could solve problems with little fuss, sometimes so fast that he headed off trouble before anyone knew it had been brewing. With Wiley Bishop as sheriff, folks lived a quiet life, and that's mostly how folks liked to live.

For example, hearing those four words . . . Wiley, it's me, Truitt . . . was all Wiley needed. He knew exactly what had happened and exactly what he'd be doing the rest of the night. He'd be headed straight for Ilene Holt's place. Truitt was in trouble, that trouble was looking for him, and it was about to find his mama, Ilene, alone at home, wondering where her boy was.

CHAPTER 13

I was up and out of bed early, just like Aunt Jean asked. Standing in my bedroom doorway, I glanced up and down the dark hallway. I crossed to Urban's room, where his door stood open. His small body was lost in a jumble of sheets and blankets. The door to Mama's and Daddy's room was closed. Daddy would sleep until Mama poked her head in the door to hustle him down to breakfast. Aunt Jean would usually still be sleeping, too, but she'd promised to get up with Mama and distract her while I slipped outside. That was the plan.

Reaching the bottom of the stairs, I took care to step over the grate in the floor. Urban kept his baseball cards and collection of pennies in the space under the iron grill. The two-foot-by-two-foot hollow space was his secret hiding place, and he thought no one would find his treasures there.

A few more steps, and I reached the entrance to the kitchen. I pressed against the wall where Mama couldn't see me.

As I tossed and turned all night, I'd teetered on the idea that I might not be brave enough to go on my trip now that Truitt and I weren't together. I worried that if I didn't have him here in Hockta, missing me and waiting for the perfect time to join me, I'd never have the courage to build a new life. Then I tried to appease myself by deciding I could go on the trip and when we reached the last leg—New York, where I'd walk the red carpet—I could decide what to do. Maybe once I was out in the world, I'd be brave enough. If not, I could always come home.

But then the look on Truitt's face as he'd told me I had my head in the clouds kicked me back to the side of leaving Hockta and never coming home again.

In the kitchen, the radio played, its volume turned low. Bacon sizzled on the stove. A fork tapped the bottom of the cast-iron skillet as Mama whisked eggs. And pages of a magazine flipped. That was Aunt Jean, sitting at the table and thumbing through one of her favorites. Up until that moment, a small part of me wondered if I'd dreamed the whole thing, but Aunt Jean was exactly where she said she'd be.

"You could wear something of mine," Aunt Jean said to Mama.

Without looking, I knew Mama was shaking her head and smiling. She fit just fine in Aunt Jean's dresses, but whenever she wore one, she was forever tugging at the neckline and trying to cover up what the dress wouldn't.

"They're too young for me," Mama said, still whipping the eggs.

"We're practically the same age," Aunt Jean said.

"Eight years makes a difference," Mama said. "Especially in a dress. And I'd like something new. Something special. We'll go into town. Take Addie with us. She seemed a bit down yesterday, don't you think?"

I hadn't told anyone about things ending with Truitt, because to them, there was no Truitt and me. I thought I had done well, playing the part all last evening of Jane Russell's character, Dorothy Shaw, in *Gentlemen Prefer Blondes*. I wore bright red lipstick and teased and sprayed my hair so it stood off my face. I couldn't change that my hair was muddy blonde while Jane Russell's was dark and shiny as black ink, but I performed as if I were confident, adventurous, and still believed in love. Just like Dorothy Shaw. And yet, Mama still noticed something was wrong, which meant maybe I wasn't as good an actress as I hoped.

Taking another step toward the back door, I leaned around the corner to look into the kitchen. Wearing a plain, ordinary cotton robe belted tight at her waist and a scarf tied over her hair, Mama stood at the stove. Steam rose from the coffee percolating on one of the burners, and toast popped in the toaster. Aunt Jean, still wearing the same silky dressing gown she wore into my room in the middle of the night, looked elegant, even with a scarf tied over her pin curls. Like I thought, she sat at the kitchen table where she flipped through a magazine.

Licking her thumb and pressing it to the next page, Aunt Jean flicked her eyes toward the doorway. She'd probably been looking since she first sat down, and finally seeing me startled her. She started to stand but thought better of it. Instead, she settled back onto her chair, struck a firm posture, and dared a quick look in Mama's direction. Seeing Mama still busy with her eggs, she waved me on with a frantic flick of her hand.

The back door was already open because Mama loved fresh air running through the house to clear the steam when she was cooking. I eased the hook free of its eye and pushed on the screen door. I slipped out, careful not to let the door slap closed.

Once outside, with only the light from the kitchen to go by, I scrambled around in the dark as I searched for the newspaper. Not finding it, I figured Truitt hadn't been by yet to deliver it. Sometimes, when I woke up early, I'd crack my window so I could hear his bike creaking as he rode up. The creak would be followed by a thud and rattle as he threw the rolled-up paper and landed it square at the foot of our screen door.

I hadn't heard him this morning, so that meant he was likely still headed this way. Not wanting to see him, not ever again, I crouched in the bushes just outside the back door to wait.

The sun had cracked the horizon, and the slender trunks of the pines across the drive glowed, the glow creeping higher as the sun rose higher. Somewhere out in the dark, cricket frogs clicked and chirped. The morning air was soggy, and a heavy fog clung to the gravel drive and dampened the smell of the orange blossoms. I drew my knees tight to my chest, wrapped my arms around them, and buried my face.

Eventually, I'd hear Truitt's bike kicking up gravel, and I would not let myself look. Seeing Truitt look at me once like I was pathetic, pitiful, and foolish was enough. I didn't want to see that look again. Ever.

I braced, waiting for the creak. My eyes were pinched tight, my jaw clenched until it ached. I squeezed my knees. Dorothy Shaw would never do what I was doing.

Directly above where I was crouched behind the bushes, Aunt Jean's voice drifted through an open window. She was going on about some unflattering pictures of herself that she'd come across, and a clatter coming from inside meant Mama was taking plates from the cupboard. Soon she'd be setting the table and calling everyone to breakfast. I couldn't wait much longer, or I'd be explaining to Mama why I was huddled in the dark, waiting for the newspaper. And the truth was, I really didn't know, though I figured it had something to do with what Aunt Jean had told Mrs. Danielson at the grocery store. Whatever it was, it was going to be in today's newspaper, and Aunt Jean didn't want Mama or Daddy to see it.

Usually, Aunt Jean's trouble began and ended with Siebert Rix. Ever since he'd yanked her arm right out of its socket, he'd been dishing out one apology after another. For the last month, Siebert had been showing up at church, trying to make Aunt Jean, Mama, and Daddy think he'd prayed his way to being a better man. Aunt Jean was more inclined to believe him than Mama or Daddy.

Whatever was in that newspaper, I sure hoped it didn't bring Siebert back to our doorstep.

I sat tall when a set of headlights splashed across me, making me squint. I'd been waiting for Truitt's bike to come rattling up the drive. Instead, it was a truck. The gate on its bed knocked about as the truck slowed. Lifting high enough to see over the bush, I peeked out. It was Mr. Olsen's truck. He was Truitt's boss and had only done the delivering one other time. Truitt, like me, had come down with the chicken pox, and he missed doing his deliveries for almost a whole week. I knew Truitt wasn't sick this time. More likely, he told Mr. Olsen he couldn't deliver to the Buckley house anymore, and Mr. Olsen was doing him a favor. Truitt didn't ever want to see me again either.

A folded newspaper sailed out of the truck's open window, landing just shy of the back door, and the truck rattled past. When the glow of the headlights was gone, and the drive fell dark again, I hurried out to grab the paper. Knowing Truitt couldn't even be bothered to wobble past on his beat-up old bike to deliver our newspaper was another dose of humiliation. After knowing him since we were just kids and us being together the last six months, he had totally pried himself loose of my life.

As I watched the taillights of Mr. Olsen's truck fade, my pain was worse than it was in the grocery store. In the back room, my body still sweaty where Truitt and I had been pressed together, shock had dulled the pain. But the shock had passed, and my pain was left uncovered, raw to the touch.

Running across the drive, my mouth clamped tight because I would not let myself cry, I reared back and threw the paper into the scrub of pines and palmettos where Daddy would never find it. That was something Dorothy Shaw would do.

CHAPTER 14

Truitt had killed a man who worked for Santo Giordano. He knew that because every man in the Tampa mob in one way or another worked for Santo Giordano. Truitt had swung a steel car jack and split the man's head open, and his blood ended up all over Donna Lee's dress. That was it in a nutshell.

Every time a new headline hit the papers about mob murders in nearby Tampa, folks around Hockta warned Truitt. "You're messing with a kind of trouble you ain't never seen, young man," they'd say. "Mob killed your daddy for getting greedy. Imagine what they'll do to you for taking money right out of their pockets. Take care, or you'll find yourself shot in your own driveway or stuffed in the bottom of a barrel."

It was an oil drum, actually, and it sat outside the Trinidad Café in Ybor City, a vibrant community just northeast of downtown Tampa. Ybor was known for cigars, nightclubs, and bolita. One of its most famous nightclubs was the Trinidad Café. The newspapers called it a swanky establishment, owned by reputed mob boss Santo Giordano. The story went that Santo Giordano's only brother was inside the oil drum, put there by Santo himself. When the two brothers went to war over who would run bolita in the state of Florida, the younger brother ended up in the oil drum. And the war was over. Truitt had never been to Ybor City to see it, but he'd heard about it. That drum was all Truitt could think about as he sat at Wiley Bishop's kitchen table and waited.

The chair Truitt sat in had one leg that was shorter than the others. Every time he drew in a deep breath, trying his best to stay calm, the chair wobbled. It was as if the chair kept shaking him awake, but he was nowhere near sleep.

Before Wiley hightailed it to Truitt's house to get his mama out of there, he sat Truitt down in this chair at the kitchen table, held him by one shoulder, and jabbed a finger in his chest.

"Unless someone that ain't me walks through that door," he said, hardly letting Truitt explain what happened, "don't you fucking move."

And Truitt hadn't. His legs were numb, the spot between his eyes pounded, and his mouth was so dry he struggled to swallow. He didn't even dare get up to get a glass of water. When he noticed the dark windows were growing lighter, his breath stuck in his throat. A gasp, because seeing dawn break was a surefire sign Wiley had been gone too long. Truitt pressed his hands flat to the table as if he were holding on, just hoping his world didn't tip him upside down.

It took a few minutes of working up his courage, and then Truitt glanced at the clock over Wiley's old green sofa. Time had never passed so quickly and so slowly all at once. Many times, Wiley had sat Truitt down on that very sofa under that very clock and tried to talk some sense into him. Wiley had started having those talks when Truitt's mama started being afraid Truitt was becoming like his father.

"I'm only going to tell you things your own daddy would have told you," Wiley said those times. "And I know, because I knew the man longer than you did."

When Truitt was younger, he hadn't wanted to listen, and he sure didn't want to believe Wiley Bishop knew anything about his father. But as Truitt got older, the memory of seeing his own daddy stretched out dead on the ground became proof of what his daddy had been, and Wiley's words began to stick. The ones that stuck best . . . I love your mama, Truitt. That means I love you too.

Truitt looked at that clock again and again, but no matter how many times he looked, it only got worse. He'd been waiting for hours, and every warning he'd heard over the years was screaming in his face.

Truitt should have made Wiley slow down and listen. He should have told Wiley the men weren't looking for Truitt only because of his bolita game. They were looking for him because he'd killed one of them. Wiley was always telling Truitt that a man had to be certain he had thorough information if he was going to make good choices in his life. Never barrel ahead, only knowing half of what counts. Truitt should have made Wiley listen, but Wiley loved Truitt's mama. He was out the door and on his way to her before Truitt could tell him how deep his troubles ran.

The longer Truitt sat at the table and waited, the more certain he was. Something had gone very wrong for Truitt's mama and Wiley.

CHAPTER 15

The house still smelled of freshly brewed coffee and bacon frying in a skillet when Daddy opened the hall closet and grabbed his gun. I knew the sound of him patting the top shelf until he felt the box that held his revolver. He did the same every weekend, meaning he didn't have to call for me to come downstairs, but he did.

Saturday mornings, in addition to being the day Daddy slept in, though he was still up with the sun, was also the day he and I practiced shooting. He'd started me out when I was about Urban's age, and I was a good shot. Slapping me on the back and shaking his head like he couldn't quite believe it, he told me so all the time.

"You got a steady hand," he said the first time I hit three bottles in a row. They exploded, one after another, the glass shards glittering in the morning sun. "Same as me. Got nothing to do with being a man or a woman. Has to do with being able to rein in your nerves. Person can think better when their nerves are in check. It'll serve you well, staying calm when trouble's barreling down."

Hustling outside, I met him as he walked across the drive toward the side yard. The tips of his dark hair were still damp from his shower, and he smelled of spicy cologne and a T-shirt fresh off the clothesline. He rested a hand on my shoulder but was distracted. Scanning the ground ahead and to each side, he was still looking for the newspaper. Coming up alongside him, I stretched my stride to match his and hoped he wouldn't see something in my face that told him I was the reason he still couldn't find it.

I liked my Saturday mornings, shooting with Daddy. I liked the quiet, peaceful part of the morning, when everything I'd do that day lay ahead. Everything I'd do for the rest of my life lay ahead. I liked the feel of drawing in one deep breath and my heartbeat slowing to a trickle. My stance steady, my shoulders relaxed, I'd exhale long and slow and pull the trigger. The loud bang and the kick in my arms that followed were all the anger and frustration of being trapped and not fitting in exploding out of my body in one single shot.

Once I left Hockta, I doubted I'd shoot another gun, but my being a good shot made Daddy proud. As I stood, waiting for Daddy to set out a row of tin cans and bottles on three separate crates, I realized this would be my last Saturday having this time with him. I'd miss making him proud when I was gone.

We went about our practice the same that morning as every other morning. Daddy had me load the revolver, unload it, and load it again. My fingers were stiff, and I twice dropped the bullets. When I squared up to begin shooting, he stood behind to watch. The first crack always startled me, but every shot startled me that morning. The gun was heavy in my hands, and my shoulders ached as I tried to hold it steady. My shots drifted low, and no matter how I shuffled my feet, I couldn't find stable footing.

Daddy wasn't focused either. Instead of watching my shots and asking what I might do to correct that drift, all he did was fuss at me.

"You're not concentrating," he said. "Got a decent wind out of the southwest. Do something about it. And your shot's falling short."

Guilt was throwing me off. That's what was troubling me, and it got heavier with every sigh and headshake Daddy gave. Somehow, he knew all the secrets I was hiding, and the longer I kept them, the more his disappointment grew.

After missing six straight shots, I turned the gun, handing it to him handle first. I had to tell him I'd been seeing Truitt even though he'd forbade it, starting with the first time Truitt called the house for me. I'd been sneaking and hiding and carrying that secret for months. I had to tell Daddy even though Truitt and I were over. I wanted him to know so I could also tell him how much I loved Truitt and how badly it hurt that instead of doing the hard work of loving me back, Truitt had taken the easy route of an ultimatum. I didn't know much about love, but I knew it didn't teeter on demands and threats. I needed to tell someone how bad Truitt hurt me. I needed help carrying that load.

But mostly, I needed to tell Daddy I was the reason he couldn't find his newspaper. I was covering up for Aunt Jean, so I could leave here, this house, him, Mama, everything, and never come back. I had to tell him, because if I didn't, Siebert Rix might put Aunt Jean in a sling again or worse.

I was the first one outside the last time Siebert Rix came to our house, drawn by something he'd seen in the newspaper. It had been near midnight, and through my open window, I heard the crackle of tires rolling across our gravel drive. I hurried downstairs because I thought it was Truitt driving up in his mama's car. We did that sometimes, snuck out while everyone else was sleeping so we could be together. Drawing my robe around me, I pushed through the door, my breath already coming faster, my body already preparing. But it wasn't Truitt.

Throwing open his car door, his headlights still on, Siebert Rix fell out onto the ground. Not seeing me on the porch stairs, he started hollering up at Aunt Jean's window. He looked nothing like he looked most days. His hair stuck to his sweaty face, his shirt hung loose over his trousers, and his jacket was rumpled. He smelled too. It was a mixture of stale cigar smoke and whiskey.

"You're nothing but a whore," he shouted. On hands and knees, he tilted his head toward the upstairs window. "You whore yourself out for a picture and a headline. Nothing but a whore."

Siebert was angry about the things he'd read in the newspaper. That everyone had read in the newspaper. Mrs. Danielson had called the house to ask if Aunt Jean was sad that her choice to take a lurid picture that featured her skirt blowing up and over her waist had led to her second divorce. Aunt Jean didn't answer that question. Instead, in a sweet, sticky voice, she talked about the wonderful photographer who took the picture, and it was not Siebert Rix. She talked about what a dear friend the man was and that he wasn't capable of taking a picture that could possibly be considered lurid. His work was true art. But mostly, she said he was the greatest, most talented photographer she'd ever worked with.

Siebert did not like reading that Aunt Jean said another man was the greatest photographer.

Pushing himself off the ground, he had looked up to see me standing on the porch stairs, almost close enough to touch. I wrapped my arms around my waist, holding my robe closed. My feet were heavy, and my legs were numb. I thought about the times Daddy told me I had a steady hand because I could rein in my nerves. I tried to do that, to rein in my nerves. I inhaled and took one backward step.

"You're just like her, ain't you?" Siebert said, stumbling as he reached for me. "Do you know all the things I could do for you?"

Aunt Jean was next through the door. She grabbed my arm, pulled me backward, and ran down the steps toward Siebert. She tried to push him away, but instead, he got hold of one arm, slapped her across the face, and dragged her toward his car.

Aunt Jean screamed when her arm popped out of its socket, causing Siebert to startle and let go. He stumbled, regained his footing, and reached to grab her again. But before he could, Daddy sent Siebert flying backward with one shove. Daddy knocked him to the ground, planted a knee in his chest, and punched him in the face. He didn't stop until Mama wrapped her arms around Daddy's neck and pulled him off.

His chest pounding, his face sweaty, Daddy stood over Siebert, pointed down on him, and said, "Don't you ever fucking come to this house again."

If Mama hadn't screamed for Daddy to stop, and if Daddy hadn't loved Mama enough to do as she asked, he would have killed Siebert Rix right there in our driveway.

I had to tell Daddy that I was worried Aunt Jean had done it again, said something she shouldn't have that Siebert was going to read about in the paper. I had a terrible feeling what was coming if it happened a second time.

Thinking Daddy already knew all my secrets, and that was why he was being short with me, I opened my mouth to confess everything. My trip wasn't going to happen. I would never leave Hockta. I would never have a different life, but I'd have told the truth.

But before I could speak, Daddy did.

"You know, Addie Anne," he said as I handed him the gun, "sometimes, something is shiny for a reason. It's covering the rot beneath. You understand? The shiny part is to distract you, trick you into playing along."

"Yes, sir," I said, though I didn't understand. Instead, I felt anxious.

Daddy's life lessons were usually things like how to change the oil or reglaze a leaky window. But he was homing in on a different kind of life lesson that morning.

"You're going to see a whole lot of shine when you go off with your aunt Jean," he said. "Shine like none of us can even imagine. Promise me this. You got just one life to lead. Before you make any decisions, see to it you buff off the shine and take note of what's hiding underneath."

I told Daddy again that I understood and instead of telling him all the things I was going to tell him, I tucked away every confession I had almost made. I only had to choke them down for two more days. I wouldn't think about what might go wrong or what might happen. I would choke that down too. I wasn't only running toward a new life anymore. I was also running away from Truitt. I was so close to getting out, I could carry the weight a little longer.

I'd always thought Mama was the one who suspected once I left, I'd never come back. But after that, I knew Daddy worried most.

CHAPTER 16

Wiley sat on Truitt's front porch. Truitt's mama, Ilene, sat next to him. The sun was up. For a long while, it seemed it would never rise, but now the damp, sandy scrub leading up to the house glittered under the bright light. The day was drying out and warming up, but on the shaded porch, the air was still damp. Wiley rested a hand on Ilene's knee and gave it a slight squeeze, a reminder that he was here and that he loved her.

Wiley and Ilene each rocked steadily but slowly in a rocking chair. The rocking kept them warm, and the steady whine of the chairs was a timer, ticking down the seconds. Wiley hoped after enough seconds passed, the men hiding inside the house would give up and go home. Truitt was just a kid running a small-time bolita game. At least, Wiley assumed that's all the kid had been doing. And a small-time bolita game wasn't enough of a slight to keep these men in town for long. They'd soon lose interest, figure they'd done their best, and head back to Tampa.

People didn't have patience anymore. That's something Wiley had learned being sheriff. But Wiley did. It was his greatest weapon. He could wait out anyone. Even shivering here on the porch for several hours, Wiley was nowhere near done being patient. He'd made the first move by suggesting to the men that they use Wiley and Ilene as bait to draw Truitt home, something he'd offered because he knew nothing would draw Truitt home. Truitt was back at Wiley's house, where he was sitting and waiting for Wiley to return. And since Wiley made the first move, the next move had to come from the men inside. Wiley could wait as long as he had to and then some.

When Wiley first arrived at Truitt's and Ilene's house, he'd found a large sedan parked out front and a man standing on the porch, his gun to Ilene's head.

"The fuck you doing here in the middle of the night," the man said as Wiley slowly approached, his hands lifted to show he was no threat.

"She don't let me come until the boy's asleep," he said, the lie spilling out because it was partly true. In a situation like this, sticking as close to the truth as possible was best.

"Well," the man said. "You can turn yourself right around. This ain't your business."

Wiley crept closer. When he smelled smoke, he figured he was close enough. Before Ilene and Truitt lived here in Hockta, they'd lived in Tampa. That was back when her husband was still alive. The house in Tampa burned down, Ilene and Truitt nearly dying in the process. Soon after, they all three moved back to this house and to Ilene's hometown. Even though this house wasn't the one that caught fire, it still smelled of smoke. It must have seeped into the chairs that set on the porch and all the other furniture they'd managed to save and move to Hockta. Or maybe it was only Wiley's imagination. Not a day passed that he didn't think about how differently that house fire could have turned out.

Standing on the porch next to the man with a gun pressed to her head, Ilene looked small, but she didn't shrink from him. Instead, Wiley worried she might try something foolish like giving the man a solid kick in his groin.

"I'm guessing you being here means the boy ain't, and you're looking for him," Wiley said, giving Ilene a stare to warn her off trying anything foolish. "Told that kid a hundred times to close up shop on that damn bolita game. Hardly makes a buck from it."

"Ain't saying it again," the man said. "Time for you to go."

"Got me all wrong," Wiley said. "I don't want any trouble. And I don't want any for the boy's mama. I can see you're in charge here, and I'm happy to make it simple on you."

The man dipped his head at Wiley, making Wiley think he might have overdone it by telling the man he was in charge. But confidence was key to any negotiation, so he plowed ahead.

"Let me and his mama sit here on the porch. It's what we always do when the boy's late getting home. Give us a couple cups of coffee and a blanket for Ilene's lap. Boy'll see us sitting here like usual and walk right in the front door. Then you can have words with him."

An hour or so later, a second sedan pulled up carrying four more men. As they moved their cars out back where they'd be out of sight and made themselves comfortable inside the house, Wiley managed to whisper two words to Ilene. Truitt's safe, he'd said to her. In the hours since, Tyler Olsen had driven up in his old truck and tossed them the newspaper, not noticing Truitt and Ilene on the porch, or he'd have asked where the hell was Truitt and why wasn't he making his deliveries.

Other than that, Wiley and Ilene had sat in silence, each of them rocking in their chair and shivering in the damp air as they pretended to wait for Truitt to come walking up the drive.

"Where the hell is he?" a voice said from inside, startling both Wiley and Ilene.

It was the man who had been holding a gun to Ilene's head when Wiley first got to the house. He was about Wiley's height but thicker through the middle. The men who arrived in the second car called him Tony. He'd told the others what to do and had been the only one to speak to Wiley, making him most likely the one in charge.

The man, Tony, finally speaking up after several hours of silence was the move Wiley had been waiting for.

Wiley turned in his seat as if to answer, testing to see if Tony would respond like Wiley figured he would. Tracking down a kid running a measly bolita game couldn't be a high priority, so Wiley was dealing with the benchwarmers out of Tampa, not the standout guys. Chances were high he could finagle them some and send them on their way by noon.

"Don't fucking turn around," Tony said.

Wiley stifled a smile. There was only one reason Tony would order Wiley not to turn around. Tony, still hoping Truitt would come home on his own, was worried that Truitt would see Wiley talking to the front window, realize someone was hiding inside, and get scared off.

After all this time, Tony and his men hadn't come up with plan B. But Wiley had. He'd waited through all these hours to convince the men he was trustworthy. He'd also waited because now the men would be tired enough, hungry enough, and desperate enough to give a new plan a try.

"I got an idea for you fellows," Wiley said.

Ilene stopped rocking and sat taller in her chair. Her long brown hair was pulled over one shoulder and woven into a braid, same as it always was. Same as it had been for as long as Wiley had known her, which was all his life. He'd loved her since he was a boy, even after she married another man and moved off to Tampa for a time. When the fire brought her back to Hockta, her husband was soon after shot dead in this very driveway. Truitt was there when it happened, though he doesn't seem to remember much.

Lord knows, Wiley didn't celebrate when Ilene's husband died, but he thanked the same Lord every night that he lived long enough to be her second love. Almost fifteen years they'd been together. He wasn't ready for that to end.

"The fuck you talking about?" It was Tony again. He sounded tired and irritable. "What idea do you have?"

"The boy never stays out all night," Wiley said. "Never seen him do it. Not once. Might come home late, but he's never stayed out all night. It's out of character for him, is what I'm saying. Ain't that right, Ilene?"

"That's right," Ilene said, dipping her chin to look out from under her brow. She was warning Wiley to be careful what he suggested when it came to her son.

"Something has happened to keep him from coming home," Wiley said. "That's what I'm saying. And I figure a new plan is in order. Wait as long as you like, but the boy ain't going to show up here."

And dear God, Wiley hoped that held true. He hoped like hell Truitt stayed exactly where Wiley told him to.

CHAPTER 17

Rocking slowly in his chair and feigning a sip from his empty coffee cup, Wiley flicked his eyes in Ilene's direction, a reminder he had told her Truitt was safe.

"What do you mean something happened to him?" Tony said. "Something like what?"

Wiley felt a comfortable rhythm settling in between the two of them. Tony had no choice but to trust Wiley.

"Something like I don't know. Something like maybe he knew he was in deep trouble with you fellows and is already long gone. Jumped a train. Stole a car. Who knows? But I could look into that. Could look into any reports of stolen vehicles. Or something like maybe someone else from your outfit already got hold of him. I'm assuming you fellows ain't the only ones looking for him."

"Keep talking."

"Let me go do some looking," Wiley said, setting the hook. Now, he had to be careful not to jerk too hard.

"Looking for what?"

"The boy," Wiley said, straining to keep frustration out of his voice. And then, knowing how to impress men who were short on brains and made to lean on brawn, he shifted course ever so slightly. "This is my fucking town. My fucking county. Or did you all not know? I'm the sheriff, and I'm not going to have some jackass of a kid putting my county in danger. No offense, but I'd just as soon not have you fellows meandering my streets. If that means giving you the kid to get rid of you, well, fine by me. His own damn fault he was running that game."

He made sure not to look at Ilene as he said those things.

"We'll meander your damn streets as long as we want. Don't give a shit if it works for you or not."

Wiley raised a hand in apology.

"All I'm saying is I'm tired of sitting out here in the cold, and I'm hungry as hell," Wiley said. "If he was coming home, he'd be here already. Let me go round him up. In fact, let's all go. I can see how you all have no reason to trust me, so join me. I'll take the lead. He won't hide if he sees me coming. And you five'll be right there to grab him when he stumbles out of wherever he's holed up. He won't stand a chance of slipping past you five. Unless, of course, the boy's already long gone."

"And if he's already gone?"

"Like I said, I can look into stolen vehicles, train tickets, bus tickets. I can point you in the right direction. If it comes to that."

Wiley would haul these five all over Hockta. All over Lake County. He'd fake a few calls to check on stolen vehicles, bus tickets, and the like. Then after an hour or so, he'd take the men past Stacy's Café. They'd smell her sausage and eggs—and by God, there was nothing as fine as Stacy's sausage and eggs—and they'd decide Truitt was long gone. Wiley had already planted the idea twice. Another thing being sheriff had taught Wiley . . . a hungry man was a pliable man.

"I like the first plan better."

A new voice floated through the dark screen in the window, a voice Wiley hadn't heard, and he'd done his best to keep track. It was deep and round. One of the fellows who'd showed up in the second car was a head taller than the rest, thick around the middle, and barrel chested. It was probably him.

This was not what Wiley expected.

"The first plan?" Wiley said, trouble sizzling in the air. "What do you mean by that?"

Next to him, Ilene stiffened. She felt the sizzle too. Her face went gray, and her eyes stopped blinking. She held her tiny hands in her lap. Her two bare feet peeked out from under the blanket draped across her legs. She lifted her eyes to Wiley. The soft morning light hit them, making their blue centers glisten. Slowly, she shook her head.

"Don't," she whispered. "Don't you dare."

As good as Wiley was at figuring things, Ilene was better. She'd already figured what Wiley hadn't.

Wiley wanted to ask her . . . don't what?

"What I mean is," the booming voice said from inside before Wiley could ask Ilene anything. "You go round the boy up. You. Alone. We'll stay here, and your lady there can cook us some breakfast. Because you're right. I'm hungry as hell. Bring him back, and we'll be on our way. Don't bring him back, well, you tell him he don't have a mama no more."

Wiley thought he'd waited them out long enough to know what and who he was dealing with, but he'd been wrong. The booming voice had been waiting *him* out.

Next to Wiley, Ilene stood, the blanket sliding from her lap. The button-down shirt she wore hung nearly to her knees, and her jeans were rolled up to keep her from tripping on them. She lifted her chest and shoulders, squared up to Wiley. The screen door flew open. One of the men, a younger one, grabbed her as the blanket pooled at her feet. Wiley jumped up and reached for her as she started to scream.

"Don't you bring him here," she shouted. "Don't you do it. Don't you do it, Wiley Bishop. You make him run."

The younger man dragged her into the house as she continued to shout.

"If you ever loved me," Ilene shouted, "you won't bring Truitt to this house."

Once she was out of sight, the shouting trailed off, replaced by muffled sobs. Then the sobs fell silent.

The barrel-chested man walked from the house, his footsteps rattling the floorboards. He pulled on a narrow-brimmed fedora, tucked in his white collared shirt, and buttoned his coat. He had a fleshy nose and red splotches on his cheeks. He was an unhealthy man, too much alcohol from the looks of it, and that was likely why he'd been sent on such a menial job. But the man still had pride.

"So, you'll go now," he said, looking down on Wiley and talking in slow, measured tones. Wiley hadn't remembered the man being so tall. "We'll give you until, say, suppertime."

"You kill her and then what?" Wiley said. "You got nothing. No leverage. And all over a small-time bolita game?"

He was flailing, spitting out words without putting an ounce of thought behind them. He was afraid, and being afraid was the worst place to be. A man couldn't think when he was afraid. He couldn't move, couldn't talk, couldn't make sense of anything.

"Game's not as small as you think," the man said, drawing a kerchief across his brow and hollering inside to ask if the coffee was about ready. "But the game is also the least of the boy's problems. And you're right about us being left with nothing to show for it if we kill his mama. But you leave that worry to me."

"Suppertime, what's that mean?" Wiley said, not knowing what to do next but knowing time was his only asset. "What if the kid's left town? What if I have to track him down and haul him back? That could be hours each way."

The silence coming from the house throbbed in his ears and broke up every thought he tried to piece together.

"Fair point," the man said, shying away from the sun and shedding his coat. "I'll give you midnight, how's that? You don't come back with him by then, don't bother. We'll come find you."

"What else did the boy do?" Wiley said. "Besides running the game?"

"You just see him home," the man said. "That's plenty enough for you to worry about."

Wiley backed away, straining to see something on the other side of the dark windows. A shadow. A silhouette. A glimpse of Ilene.

"Nobody touches her," he said, his eyes rolling from the windows to the barrel-chested man and settling on his face. "You understand. Nobody."

"Not sure you're in much of a position to tell me anything," the man said, blotting his face with the limp kerchief. "But all right. You do your part. I'll do mine. One more thing before you get going. You know a man named Siebert Rix?"

"I do."

"We'd take him too," the man said. "The boy comes first, mind you, but if you stumble upon this Mr. Rix, we'd be interested to talk with him."

CHAPTER 18

Daddy asked me to put the gun away when we were done with shooting practice, and as he passed it off, he held my hand and squeezed. I thought I was the only one who knew that was our last time spending a Saturday morning together. But I think he knew too.

Back in the house, I cleaned up and changed into a dress to wear into town. Mama wanted to do some shopping. She didn't like going into Tampa, which is where Aunt Jean took me to buy a dress for our trip. Instead, we'd be going into Hockta.

Seeing me in my room, combing out my hair as she passed down the hallway, Aunt Jean waved for me to join her. I smiled, though I still didn't feel much like smiling, and followed her.

Since the moment Aunt Jean told me about a trip to Hollywood being my birthday present, I'd been lying to Mama and Daddy. And now, knowing when I kissed them goodbye in two days that it would be forever had finally caught up to me. Add to that my covering up for Aunt Jean, and I was exhausted.

Shooting with Daddy this morning was the first of all the last things I would do. I would have the last breakfast here in this house, a last supper, a last time waking up here. So many last things were coming, and I was struggling to stand up under the weight of it all. Sure, I'd come back on occasion to visit like Aunt Jean came to visit, but I was still lying to my parents every time I said . . . it's only for six weeks.

The drapes in Aunt Jean's room were thrown open, and morning sunlight spilled into the room, filling it with a warm glow. Her window got the best of the early-day sunlight, almost like the sun itself was drawn to her.

Taking a seat on the tufted bench at Aunt Jean's dressing table, I thought about what Daddy had said that morning. I wondered if the lipsticks, compacts, and crystal perfume bottles spread out before me that shimmered like jewels were part of the shine Daddy warned me about.

Ever since Aunt Jean first started coming to our house, I'd loved being in her room. I loved the shimmering dresses, the elegant shoes, the glamorous jewelry. All of it was a glimpse of what waited for me out in the real world. Even now, when I was far too old for it, I still found myself pretending I was Aunt Jean when I sat at this table. But that morning, I wasn't pretending to be Aunt Jean. I was just myself, and that left me awkward and uncertain.

I touched one of the crystal perfume bottles, rubbed my thumb on it, but nothing was hiding beneath the shine.

Standing behind me, Aunt Jean rested her hands on my shoulders. She wore a crisp white dress that hugged every curve and nipped snugly at her waist. Having removed all her pin curls, she'd combed out her blonde hair, creating soft waves that framed her eyes. She'd also put on a full face of makeup, something she didn't often do when she came to Hockta. She must have decided dress shopping in town with me and Mama was a special occasion.

Leaning down so she could smile at my reflection in the mirror, she tucked her chin in the curve where my neck met my shoulder. She smelled like vanilla and soap, clean and fresh. Her panic from the night before when she'd crept into my room was gone. She was already packed for our trip, which meant she'd been busy this morning. Two suitcases sat near her bedroom door, her closet was mostly empty, and her train case sat on her makeup table, open and ready for her to toss everything in.

Sliding around to the side of me, Aunt Jean knelt next to the bench. I turned my head, so I could look at her straight on. Reaching out, she cupped my face in her hand. Her fingers were like feathers under my chin. She leaned close, puckered her mouth so I would do the same, and drew the red tip of a lipstick over my lips.

"Not too much," I said, rubbing my lips together and smoothing the lipstick. "Mama won't like it."

Turning back to the mirror, I considered my new look. The soft shade, much softer than what I wore yesterday as I conjured Dorothy Shaw, made my lips shimmer like Aunt Jean's.

"Not just anyone can wear this shade," Aunt Jean said, waving off my warning. She drew my face toward her again and pulled back to study her work. "It suits you. Always know what suits you and insist on it. Other people will tell you they know better, but they don't. You know what's best. Remember that."

A silence settled in as Aunt Jean continued to toy with my face. With every swipe of a brush or a sponge or the tip of Aunt Jean's pinky, my face softened, brightened, grew more beautiful.

"Why'd you have me do it, Aunt Jean?" I whispered, hoping the question would find a soft landing and that her secret had nothing to do with Siebert Rix.

Instead of looking at the real Aunt Jean, I watched her reflection as my question sunk in. In one hand, she held a makeup brush, but instead of cupping my chin so she could swipe the brush across my forehead and cheeks, she lowered it. Her eyes drifted, and her shoulders drooped.

So often, whether staring at a magazine, combing her hair, or dabbing silky powder on my face, Aunt Jean got a faraway look like all her thoughts had turned inward. As if consumed by trying to make sense of what was going on inside, she forgot that on the outside, the rest of the world was still going on. Sometimes, the look came and went in an instant. Other times, it lasted for days.

When I was young and Aunt Jean slipped into that faraway place, I shied away, thinking she had the flu or a stomach bug. Mama would sit at her bedside, brush the hair from her face, and drape cool washcloths over her forehead. Somewhere along the way of my growing up, I realized it wasn't the sniffles that sent Aunt Jean to bed. Though I still didn't understand why it happened, I knew it wasn't catching, and I began helping Mama tend to her.

One day shy of turning eighteen, studying Aunt Jean's face in the mirror, I finally understood. That faraway look was the crack in Aunt Jean's perfect life. It was the rot under all the shine. Sometimes that crack was no bigger than a sliver. Other times, it was a crater so big she disappeared inside it for days. I hoped it never grew so big that she disappeared forever. The crack in Aunt Jean's perfect life was loneliness.

"Aunt Jean?" I said when she still didn't tell me why she'd had me throw Daddy's paper in the pines.

Aunt Jean's eyes snapped back into focus. The faraway look was gone, and I was relieved. We could make it until Monday as long as Aunt Jean didn't fall back into her sadness.

"Do what, darlin'?" She wiped a smear of lipstick from my bottom lip.

"You know," I said, flicking my eyes toward her open doorway to make sure no one was listening.

"No, sweetheart, I don't know," she said, resting her hands on my thighs and tilting her head as if worried about me. "What is it you're asking me?"

"The newspaper," I said, a bitter taste creeping up the back of my throat. I had been hoping Aunt Jean's secret wasn't all that bad. It was the only hope I had left to hold onto. But I worried the bitter taste in my mouth was her secret. And it was bad. "You asked me to throw away the newspaper. This morning. So Daddy couldn't read it."

"What on earth are you talking about?" Aunt Jean said, tapping a round fluffy brush into a small tub of loose powder. She blew lightly on the bristles, the excess powder sparkling as it flew into the air.

"You came into my room last night," I said, staring at her reflection and not mine. "Asked me to sneak outside while you kept Mama busy."

"I think you must have been dreaming," she said. It was the perfect delivery. Subtle. Understated. Convincing.

She sat back on her knees to take one last look at me, fluffing her dress as she did. It cascaded around her in a perfect circle. Everywhere Aunt Jean went, a spotlight seemed to follow, even in her small bedroom on a Saturday morning in little bitty Hockta, Florida.

"I'll keep your secret," I said, trying a new way to coax the truth from her. If I knew what Aunt Jean was hiding, I could keep her safe, and Mama said knowing she was safe was what Aunt Jean needed most. "I promise. Even if it's about Mr. Rix, I'll keep your secret."

When Mama and Daddy argued with Aunt Jean, it always stemmed from Siebert Rix. Mama was constantly telling Aunt Jean that she didn't owe him a thing. He brought nothing but trouble into her life. Any debt Aunt Jean might have felt she owed him from the photos he took of her early in her career had long since been paid. Daddy took a more direct approach. After Siebert put Aunt Jean in a sling, he said he didn't care about debts or what was owed who. That man was not to come near his family again, and his family included Aunt Jean.

"Mr. Rix is off on his own," Aunt Jean said, pushing to her feet. "Got himself a new girl, even. He has nothing to do with me anymore or me with him. It was that Mrs. Danielson's fault. She's always after me to give a comment, tell her something exciting. She talks as if I've fallen off the edge of the earth."

"It wasn't something about Mr. Rix then?" I asked, relieved because no other secret could be as bad as one that involved Siebert Rix. "Or something that might make him angry?"

I could see it again, my bright, shiny new world as it rolled past the windows of the train that carried me and Aunt Jean out of Florida. I felt steady again, like I had the energy to keep going. The next two days would unfold exactly as planned. Mama and Daddy would go to the Harringtons' party. We'd celebrate my birthday tomorrow. And Monday morning, Aunt Jean and I would board a train. I could choke down all my secrets until then. It was really going to happen.

Aunt Jean and I both turned toward her open window at the sound of a rattling car engine. We'd heard it before, usually late at night, not early in the morning. Gravel crunched as the tires rolled to a stop, but the engine kept rattling. It was Siebert Rix's car.

Directly under Aunt Jean's window, the screen door flew open and slapped against the side of the house.

It was Daddy. He knew it was Siebert's car too.

CHAPTER 19

Rolling up to the Buckley house and hoping like hell Marilyn was inside, Siebert put his car in park but didn't shut off the engine. He was trying to be smart by thinking back on every movie he'd ever seen. First off, he needed to stay calm, be polite, and remember to call her Jean. It was a damn fool thing she insisted on, but he needed her to be happy. He needed her to remember the old days and how good they'd had it all these years. He needed her to miss home and the life she had back in California.

He also had to be ready to drive off at the first sign of another car rolling down the road, because that might mean the mob was coming for him. If that happened, he'd hit the gas hard, kick up a good bit of gravel, and disappear in a cloud of dust. Just like in the movies. However and whenever he drove off, he damn well hoped Marilyn . . . Jean . . . would be with him.

He'd spent the whole night parked in a low spot down in the cypress trees and oaks over near Mount Dora, a stretch of swampy, stagnant water nearby. He kept his windows rolled up the whole time to keep out the swarm of bugs that buzzed all night. He got out only once, and that was to drag Donna Lee from the trunk of his car. If he could dump her in that swampy water, he wouldn't have to ever think about her again.

Popping open the trunk, he had kept his eyes closed and prayed he heard nothing. No wheezing as Donna Lee tried to take a breath, no tears, no gurgling of blood as it bubbled up in her lungs. There was silence, so he looked.

Donna Lee's legs twisted one way and her shoulders the other, like she'd just stepped onto a dance floor. Red, sticky blood soaked her yellow dress, making it cling to her chest and neck. And dear Lord, her eyes were still open. He couldn't lift her without touching all that blood. Even if he could have brought himself to do it, he didn't have clean clothes to change into and for sure had no money to buy new ones. So, he'd slammed the trunk shut and climbed back in the front seat.

Every time a set of headlights passed by on the main road, he'd ducked. He dozed off a time or two, but he did his best to stay awake so no one could sneak up on him. And the whole night through, he kept reminding himself to breathe through his mouth. He didn't know when a body would start to smell, but he knew it would. Eventually. He damn sure didn't want to get a whiff of Donna Lee, because that was the kind of thing a man would never forget.

After spending the whole night fending off mosquitoes, when the sun finally broke the horizon, he figured the counter at the train station would be open. He thought about driving back to Hollywood, but there were only a few roads out of this godforsaken state, and he'd have been an easy target. That fellow from Tampa was clear about that. You try to run, we'll find you.

A train had seemed the perfect answer. Safer. Faster. They'd never expect that when he had a perfectly good car. With the money he found in Donna Lee's purse, he hoped to have enough to buy himself a ticket. Then he'd hide out in the men's room until it was time to board and leave his car in the parking lot. Wouldn't even care he was losing all the money he'd spent to buy it when he and Jean got to Florida. Parked out in the Florida sun, the car would no doubt start smelling in a day or two. Someone would find Donna Lee in his trunk, but by then, he'd be long gone.

That had been the plan, and it was a good one. Might even have made a good script. But when he pulled up to the train station, a black sedan sat in the parking lot. Two fellows were in the front seat, both wearing suits and hats, just like the two who'd stopped to help with his flat tire. They were thick through the chest and had square jaws. They were fellows who were looking for Siebert. That might mean they hadn't found the kid and were wanting to take Siebert in his place. Or it might mean they'd seen today's newspaper and thought it was proof he had tried to cover up for Truitt by lying to one of them. At some point, Siebert needed to find that paper and learn what was inside. Either way, seeing those men wasn't good for Siebert.

Every half hour since Siebert first drove by the train station to see that big black sedan waiting for him, he had driven by again, hoping the car would be gone. But every time, it was still there. Once eight o'clock rolled around, he decided the hour was decent enough for a casual visit to the Buckleys' house. Breakfast would be done, the dishes washed and put away. He couldn't walk into the train station and buy a ticket on the first train out of town, but Marilyn . . . Jean . . . could. She could buy two, one for each of them. He'd figure out later how to board the train without being seen.

But first, he needed the tickets, and that meant he needed Marilyn. She'd have money too. The sooner the better. He couldn't drive around with Donna Lee in the trunk forever. Eventually those men would find him.

The moment Siebert put his car in park outside the Buckleys' house, he knew he had an uphill climb ahead of him. The screen door flew open before he could open his car door, and Harden Buckley came barreling out.

"Put it right back in drive," he hollered, pointing at Siebert. "Don't think you're setting foot outside that car."

The thing about Siebert . . . he'd spent too many years being pampered. The whole town of Los Angeles knew he was the quickest way to Marilyn Monroe, and everyone wanted a way in. There was a time a man like Harden Buckley wouldn't dare raise his voice to Siebert. Siebert was a good bit taller, but he was also a good bit rounder in the middle, which made him slow and unsteady on his feet. There was no denying that. Harden, on the other hand, was average as height went, but he was full through the chest and shoulders, probably because he grew up around orange groves. Probably doing things like toting crates and hauling ladders and what all, Siebert would have no idea.

Even though today Harden made his living with a pencil and a pad of paper for figuring, he still had that solid build. If a machine broke or needed to be invented, Harden was the man to do it, though he still hauled the occasional crate. Siebert had seen it with his own eyes.

Harden had also lived in this house since the day he was born, walked these same roads, known all the same people. This was Harden's home field, and that gave him an edge on Siebert. Siebert couldn't feel bad about that. But good Christ almighty, what had happened to Siebert? He used to have that strong build too.

Easing back into his seat but leaving the door ajar, Siebert raised his hands in surrender.

"Not here to cause you any trouble, Harden," Siebert said. "Sober as can be and have been for weeks. Thought I'd come around first thing, so you'd know I was in shape enough to be up bright and early."

"Don't know anything of the sort," Harden said, glancing back to see Inez in the doorway.

Harden dipped his head, a signal for Inez to get herself back inside, but she didn't move. Instead, she leaned in the threshold and crossed her arms. She was making a point to both Siebert and Harden. She wanted Harden to know he didn't tell her what to do and for Siebert to think she wasn't afraid of him.

Siebert had known Inez since they were kids. Same with Marilyn. All of them had grown up in the same part of Los Angeles and been shuffled around all the same orphanages. Inez was several years older than Marilyn and a few older than Siebert and had always been Marilyn's protector. Never Siebert's, which never made a damn bit of sense to him. Inez started pampering Marilyn when she was a little girl, her own real mama in a hospital for being crazy. She latched on to Marilyn back then and hadn't let go since.

Most days, Siebert didn't give Inez much thought, except to tell her to shut her damn mouth when she said he wasn't good enough for Marilyn and that he should be ashamed for not making his own way in the world. But today, he couldn't help smiling at her, even though she was glaring at him.

Inez was sturdy because she worked around the house from sunup to sundown. She had soft brown hair that hung loose to her shoulders, and the color in her cheeks and the shine in her eyes were from the sun, not a makeup brush. Inez was pretty in a simple, natural sort of way, just like Marilyn used to be. But hadn't been in a long time.

"You're looking real lovely this morning, Inez," Siebert said, easing the rest of the way out of the car, his hands in clear view for Harden to see.

"My shotgun'll be the next thing out of the house if you take another step," Harden said.

Siebert could jump in his car, be halfway down the drive, and Harden would still be able to put a bullet square in the back of his head. Everyone knew Harden Buckley was the best shot in Lake County. Good thing he's one of the good guys, people would say.

The screen door creaked open again, and this time Addie Anne appeared. Not knowing if Harden already had a gun on him, Siebert moved slowly as he tipped his hat to Addie.

"Addie," Siebert said. Tipping his hat was a good move. Respectful. Dignified. "Good to see you this morning. You're looking real lovely too. And who's that you got with you?"

The youngest one, the boy with a name Siebert could never remember, slipped out from behind Addie's skirt. Clinging to her leg, he buried his head in her side. He had blond hair, and every time Siebert had seen the boy, he'd been cowering in some lady's skirt.

"Urban," Inez said, peeling the boy off Addie's leg. "Go on inside. Up to your room. I'll be in shortly."

The screen door opened again, this time barely making a sound, and Marilyn appeared. She paused in the doorway, ruffling the boy's hair as he passed inside, and then joined Addie. Like the boy, Marilyn clung to Addie, wrapping both hands around her arm. Siebert took a deep breath, tasting the change in the air. It grew lighter, crisper. Even the sun shined brighter. He clamped his jaw firm to stop his mouth from falling open.

Siebert was only getting one chance. He had to play this just right.

CHAPTER 20

No matter how many times Siebert saw Marilyn, and he'd seen her plenty—through a camera lens, on a movie screen, in the early morning and the wee hours—she still surprised him. This morning, she wore a white dress that turned her body into a sculpture, a perfectly formed figurine that glided out the door and into the morning light. Her hair shimmered. Her skin glowed. As much as Siebert knew she was an ordinary woman, with all the same parts and pieces, she hovered while all the others lumbered. But he couldn't let on that she was special. He couldn't let on that she still stunned him. No, it had never done him any good to give a woman the idea she was special, and he'd known plenty of women.

"You look lovely, Jean. You're well, I trust," he said, and then he took off his hat and nodded in Harden's direction. "Not here to cause trouble. I'll say that right up front."

Another nice touch. Another sign of respect. He was doing well not to let panic control him. Yes, he'd been hoping Harden wouldn't be home, but he was, so now Siebert had to win him over first.

Harden took another few steps toward Siebert. He wore a white undershirt, dark trousers, and black work boots. He had likely been headed to the groves to check on the blossoms or some such nonsense.

"Don't let me stop you," Siebert said, because it was worth a shot. "Looks like you're headed off to work."

"Don't suppose I'll let you do anything," Harden said.

Darn it all, if Siebert had waited a few more minutes, he might have missed Harden altogether. And darn it all, that white undershirt of Harden's hugged his upper arms because they were still strong and thick. Siebert pulled his jacket closed and buttoned it, trying to hide that the button barely reached.

"Let's get back to why you're here," Harden said, leaning into Siebert with a hard stare.

"Just saying my goodbyes," Siebert said, forcing himself to maintain eye contact with Harden.

Harden was a dog protecting his pack, and Siebert couldn't give him reason to rear up. Hard as it was to admit, a man had to know when to use his head because his brawn wasn't going to get the job done.

"You're leaving?" It was Marilyn . . . Jean. "That's why you're here? To tell us you're leaving? That's all?"

"Were you expecting him to come for another reason?" Inez said to Marilyn.

Once Inez asked the question, Siebert wondered the same. It was an odd thing Marilyn had said. Maybe she'd been hoping Siebert would come for her. Damn it all, that was the answer. Maybe whatever nonsense she had told the gossip columnist was a cry for help. Marilyn thought he'd see the paper and rush to her side. He'd done it before. Plenty of times, he'd saved Marilyn from herself. He'd stopped her from destroying her entire career. She never came right out and asked for help. Being late to set. Drinking too much. Taking those damn pills. Talking to a reporter when she damn well knew better. Every one of those was a cry for Siebert to come and save her. Lucky for her, Siebert had come to do just that—he'd come to whisk her away.

"No, I wasn't expecting anything," Marilyn said, but it was a soft no, a wishy-washy no. "Just making idle conversation."

"Never mind all that," Harden said, giving Inez a look as if to ask her to please let him handle it. "If it's goodbye you're here to say, then fine. Goodbye."

The next move was Siebert's most daring. He was going to take a giant step off the cliff and hope like hell someone grabbed his shirttail before he fell. But Marilyn's wishy-washy no gave him confidence.

"All right, then," he said and tipped his hat again to Harden. "I'll be off. Best to you all."

"Just like that, you're leaving? Alone?" Marilyn said. Her lips quivered as if a camera were drawing in for a close-up. And her eyes shimmered. She always could cry on demand.

Siebert bit the inside of his lip so he wouldn't smile. Marilyn was practically begging him to save her from this town and these people. Inez must have sensed the same because she shouldered her way in front of Marilyn. Addie, the daughter, mirrored her mama.

"Like Harden said, if you're saying goodbye, then goodbye," Inez said.

Siebert didn't know how Harden did it, putting up with a wife that stepped all over him like that. Siebert had to dip his head and bite his lip even harder to stop from telling her to shut her fucking mouth. When he looked up again, he had manufactured a fitting smile, and Marilyn floated out from behind the two women acting as her shield.

"You're going back to California, then?" Marilyn said. "To Los Angeles?"

"Saturday's always a good day for driving," Siebert said. "Care to join me? Even thought about taking the train. You always did like the train, didn't you?"

It slipped out. Siebert didn't mean to ask so quickly, but it was out there now, and he couldn't take it back. He shrugged as if he didn't really care what the answer was. That was the best he could do.

"No, she does not care to join you." It was Inez again.

Harden slid up next to Inez and wrapped an arm around her, a clever way of reining her in.

"You've said what you came to say," he said, "so we'll let you go."

"Looks to me like you're thinking about it, Jean," Siebert said, happy he'd remembered to use the right name. It always felt awkward on his tongue, but he'd done good. Marilyn noticed too. She dipped her head and gave him the slightest smile. "Am I right? You must miss it. You're so loved out there in California. Everybody wants you. I get calls all the time. You thinking you might like to join me?"

Inez ducked out from under Harden's arm and took Marilyn by the hand.

"She is thinking no such thing," Inez said.

"Pretty sure I'm not talking to you, Inez," Siebert said, having had just about enough of Inez and her mouth. "In fact, I'm damn sure. Jean, you coming?"

Harden was on Siebert in two long steps. Siebert scrambled back to his car, raising one hand in apology. Harden slapped the hand away and grabbed hold of Siebert's lapel. Damn it all, Siebert had let his temper get the better of him again.

"Stop." This time it was Addie Anne, the young one. Though if Siebert remembered right, she was about to turn eighteen. "Tell him, Aunt Jean. Tell him you don't want to go with him. You can't go with him. Tell him about my birthday and our trip."

Harden held on to Siebert's jacket for a long beat and then gave a shove. Siebert fell into the side of his car, got his footing, and smoothed his jacket. He was confused now. He didn't know what trip the girl was talking about, but there was still something in Marilyn's eyes that was telling Siebert she wanted to jump in that car with him.

"Addie's right," Marilyn said, pulling Addie into a hug, her perfectly sculpted body turning to go back inside the house. "Addie and I have plans. Special plans. Good luck to you, Siebert. Now, please go."

Harden grabbed the driver's door and yanked it all the way open, giving Siebert all the clearance he needed. He could have kept on, telling Marilyn everything she'd be missing if she stayed in this dump of a town, but Harden would have made sure that didn't end well for Siebert. Still, he had to do something, anything.

There was no way Siebert was getting out of town without Marilyn. He needed her to buy the train tickets, and he needed her for money. He needed her even if he drove the car, because cars needed gas, and gas meant money. That was the toughest nut to swallow. He was broke, with not a dollar to his name except what he'd taken from Donna Lee's purse. And that wasn't much. He had no other choice. He had no idea where to find that Truitt kid. Even if he could turn him over, those gangsters might still think Siebert had tried to pull a fast one on them. Siebert either found a way out of this town or he very well might end up dead like Donna Lee.

"Didn't mean for it to go this way," Siebert said, his mind spinning and coming up with one small idea. "Just wanted to wish you all well. This town, it ain't for me. I can see it suits you though, Jean. I can see you're happy. If you ever make it back to California, give me a shout."

Siebert had made a misstep or two, but he'd recovered well. He'd just made it so everyone would think he was on his way out of town right now. They would relax. Let down their guard. Hell, Harden would even stow his guns.

But Siebert wasn't going anywhere. He'd grab something to eat, finally pick up the newspaper to read Marilyn's cry for help, and go back to the low-lying spot among the cypress trees and oaks. He'd roll up his windows, wait for dark, and hope like hell Donna Lee didn't start stinking before he figured out what to do next.

Something would come to him. It always did. And whatever plan he came up with, he'd have an easy time of pulling it off now that no one would be on the lookout for him. He needed Marilyn, he knew that. Not just for train tickets and money. He needed her so he could go on making a living. The best thing a man could do for himself was to be truthful about who he was and who he wasn't.

Without Marilyn, Siebert was nobody.

Yes, he needed her. But as long as Harden Buckley was in that house, Siebert wasn't getting her.

That's what Siebert had to do. He had to figure a way to get rid of Harden Buckley.

CHAPTER 21

Truitt had done exactly what Wiley told him to do. Sitting at the table in Wiley's kitchen, Truitt still hadn't moved from his chair. Not even now that the sun was full in the sky. He passed the time taking in all the pictures Wiley had put up around his place, pictures of Truitt's mama and Truitt himself. He never realized there were so many.

Doing what Wiley told him to do meant doing what was best for his mama, because Wiley loved Truitt's mama. Truitt knew it. He'd known it all along, but sometimes he put on like he didn't. He hadn't always been good to Wiley, didn't always listen, could have a smart mouth. Still, Wiley had been a daddy to Truitt longer than his real daddy had. Difference was, beyond one being blood and the other not, Wiley was on the right side of the law. His daddy had been on the wrong side.

Truitt wasn't sure if his real daddy had always done right by his mama either. He'd sometimes hear echoes of his mama crying, chairs being toppled, his daddy yelling, the slap of an open hand against a face. They were memories, he figured, that were forcing themselves to the surface. They were the sounds of his daddy beating Mama.

But as for Wiley, well, Wiley would die a painful death if it meant saving Truitt's mama. That's why Truitt did exactly what Wiley said and didn't move until he heard tires rolling up the gravel drive.

At the first crackle, Truitt lunged for the front windows, his chair tipping over behind him. His knees buckled because his legs were numb. He fell. Scrambling across the hard pine floors, he knocked over a lamp and the tray where Wiley ate all his meals. At the window, he crouched and peeked just over the sill. It was Wiley's truck, and Wiley sat in the front seat. Alone.

Switching off the engine, Wiley didn't move. His hands stayed on the steering wheel. After a few moments, he hunched over and buried his face in his arms. When he lifted his head, he looked down the road and then up at the house.

Truitt's thoughts began to disappear. One after another, they fizzled and vanished like thin smoke from a candle. No more wondering what had happened to Donna Lee. No more remembering the sound of the jack when it connected with that fellow's head. Truitt's mind became a hollowed-out hole with no light and no air. He could form only a single thought, one simple thing he knew for sure . . . Wiley was alone because Truitt's mama was already dead.

The front door opened. Footsteps crossed the pine floors, stopped, and started up again. Something grabbed Truitt and hoisted him to his feet. He was shivering like he was cold, but not an ordinary kind of cold. It was the coldest he'd ever been. Two hands held his arms and gave him a shake.

"Truitt." It was Wiley. He was whispering and jostling Truitt as if trying to wake him up. "You got to listen to me, son. Your mama's fine. You hear me? Truitt, you hear me?"

Truitt was walking in a haze. Something from behind guided him. It must have been Wiley, because his voice was in Truitt's ear, telling him over and over his mama was fine. But that wasn't true. Something wasn't right.

A light switched on, and they were in Wiley's bedroom. Truitt stretched his eyes, trying to see what was in front of him. A simple bed came into view. Wiley sat Truitt on the edge of the mattress and then drew the shade on the room's only window. At his closet, Wiley riffled through his clothes. He tossed shirts, pants, jackets, and hats on the bed.

"Tell me really," Truitt said, catching the clothes that landed near him.

"Don't have time right now," Wiley said, sorting through the clothes and pulling out the ones that suited him. "You're going to do exactly as I say, and once we get through that part, I'll tell you whatever you want to know."

Wiley handed Truitt a pair of dark blue pants and a shirt.

"Put them on," Wiley said and started pulling on a fresh shirt himself.

Truitt began to strip off the shirt he'd been wearing since yesterday, but before he could untangle both arms from it and pull it over his head, Wiley grabbed the fabric.

"Jesus," he said, and then again. "Jesus, how did I miss this?"

Truitt looked down to see a faint splatter of blood near the collar of his white shirt. Wiley stared, shaking his head, then dropped the handful of fabric he'd grabbed and hurried Truitt along.

Truitt yanked off yesterday's shirt, glad to be rid of it, and slipped on the stiff button-down Wiley had handed him. It was one of Wiley's uniforms, the same type of shirt Wiley was pulling on.

"Fits you good," Wiley said, putting a hat on Truitt's head and tugging the brim low on his forehead. "We want it down close to your eyes."

Leaving the clothes scattered across his bed, Wiley took Truitt by the arm and led him from the room. Truitt's mind was lighting up again, and instead of every thought trailing off in a puff of smoke, some were sticking. Wiley had dressed the two of them alike.

At the back door, Wiley pushed aside the curtain and looked outside. The only thing back there was a stand-alone garage in the middle of a barren field.

"I walk faster than you do," Wiley said, sliding over to a window and taking another look out on the backyard. "When you walk from the house to the garage, pick up the pace. Don't hunch, like you're trying to hide, but walk like you got somewhere to be."

"Why am I going to the garage?" Truitt asked, squirming in the shirt and wanting to know why Wiley dressed him up and was shoving him out the door.

While Truitt didn't know what was happening, his heart had already figured it out. It started pounding, sending blood to his arms and legs, getting him ready. Truitt had killed the nephew of Santo Giordano. Whatever plan Wiley had concocted, it was meant to keep Truitt alive.

"First, you're going to stop all that fidgeting," Wiley said.

And then he told Truitt exactly what to do, and just like Truitt had sat in the chair until he was numb because Wiley told him to, he'd do the same now. He'd do exactly what Wiley told him to.

At the back door, his hand on the knob, Truitt took in a few deep breaths and blew them out like he was getting up the courage to jump off the high dive. He gave his hat another tug, making sure it was on good and tight. He started to look behind him at Wiley, who was pressed against the cabinets where no one on the outside would see him but thought better of it.

"Once you start," Wiley had said, "you can't hesitate. You need to hustle, because I would hustle. But don't run. And for the love of God, don't trip. All you're doing is walking to the garage and going in through the side door. You done the same a thousand times."

Truitt nodded and opened the door. The moment he breathed in the soggy morning air, he felt eyes on him, the heavy, steady pressure of eyes.

"Be sure you close the door behind you," Wiley said in a whisper. "And make like you're locking up."

Standing in the threshold, Truitt nodded, but he couldn't take that first step. Maybe someone was out there, watching, or maybe not. But the pressure he felt turned the ground to mud, and he couldn't lift his foot.

"Go," Wiley said. It was a hiss. He meant go right damn now. "Truitt, you got to go now."

Truitt took one step and then another. His movements were stiff, as if his hands and feet were icy cold. He closed the door behind him. With nothing in hand, he pretended to lock it and rattled the doorknob as if double-checking that it was locked. Then he hustled down the stairs but didn't take them two at a time like he always did when he and his mama came to Wiley's house.

When he hit the gravel walkway that led to the garage, he walked fast, just like Wiley said. He thought to stop and pick a few of the dollarweed springing up between the bricks. That's what Wiley would have done, but Truitt didn't. He kept walking, not feeling his legs beneath him, and the garage kept drawing closer.

He couldn't help that he squinted, barely able to keep his eyes open. He was bracing for the sound of a gunshot. He couldn't stop imagining a pump-action pointed at the back of his head. He'd read all the stories in the newspapers of one mobster killing another, sometimes in their own driveway, and always with a 12-gauge pump-action shotgun. A Smith & Wesson .357 had killed his father, but the shotgun was the favorite now. Blood runs deep in the streets of Tampa; that's what the newspapers said.

At the garage, Truitt walked directly to the door Wiley told him to use. Having made it, the feeling in his hands returned, and he could hear the gravel underfoot again. A few deep breaths calmed him. He'd been to this garage countless times, just like Wiley said. Maybe he'd been getting a tool for Wiley, pulling out the hedge trimmers, or grabbing the pump to put air in his bike's tires.

"Chances are no one's watching," Wiley had said as he explained the plan. "It's a precaution, right?"

Truitt turned the knob and pushed, because he knew the door opened in, but the knob didn't turn. His heart started running away on him again, pounded so loud in his ears he couldn't hear anything. Seconds passed as he stood there, his hand on the door. The door was locked.

Wiley would have the key. He'd have a whole ring of keys. Any man who had just left his house would have a set of keys. But Truitt didn't. He had nothing.

Truitt would get one chance at making this look normal. He slapped his pockets, as if looking for keys, pulled an imaginary set from his right pants's pocket, and pretended to drop them near his right foot. Most of the time when Mama or Wiley sent Truitt out to the garage, it was to get rid of him for a few minutes. He didn't know that when he was a kid, but he knew it now. Use the spare key, Wiley or Mama would say.

Bending down, favoring his left knee like Wiley always did, Truitt nudged the flat river rock with his toe, and as he picked up his imaginary keys, he picked up the real spare.

He unlocked the door, slipped into the dark garage, opened the back door of Wiley's patrol car just enough to crawl inside, and dropped down flat on the floorboards.

By the time the door opened again, and sunlight spilled into the dark garage, Truitt had stopped crying. He pushed to his knees and wiped at his eyes quick so Wiley wouldn't see.

"You all right back there?" Wiley said, sitting in the driver's seat and tossing a thermos in the back.

The hope was that anyone watching would see Truitt walk to the garage and assume it was Wiley. Inside the house, Wiley would wait a few minutes, and then make the trip himself, except he'd be carrying something. Anyone who might have been watching would hopefully assume they'd missed Wiley double back for his forgotten thermos. So far, it had worked because no bullets had come their way.

"Sorry about the door being locked," Wiley said, reaching over the back seat and motioning for Truitt to get down. "We don't have far to go."

CHAPTER 22

After Siebert said his goodbyes and drove away, I found Aunt Jean in the kitchen, struggling to clamp the meat grinder on the countertop. Four layers of a three-egg cake cooled near the open window, the beginnings of my birthday cake and the cake Mama would take to the Harringtons' party. Mama made both every year and would finish them with caramel frosting.

I sat at the table, picked up a magazine as if interested in it, and started planning what to say to Aunt Jean. The rest of the house had settled into a normal Saturday since Siebert left, but I didn't feel certain he was gone for good. Siebert never came and went so easily. He was a talker, as if he had learned that enough talking eventually got him what he wanted. But he didn't do that this morning. He left, all by himself, off to California, even though he was nothing without Aunt Jean.

"Do you know how to get this thing to clamp on tight?" Aunt Jean asked, brushing the hair from her eyes and frowning at the meat grinder. "It's about to wear me out."

The heat in the kitchen had given Aunt Jean's face a light sheen. She still wore the same white dress, but the makeup she'd carefully applied had faded. Mama didn't want to go dress shopping anymore, not since Siebert Rix came and went, so there was no reason for Aunt Jean to reapply.

Not wanting to see her beautiful dress stained, I grabbed an apron from the closet and draped it over Aunt Jean's head. Then I grabbed a tea towel, laid it over the counter's edge, slid the grinder on, and clamped it down tight. Aunt Jean followed along, quietly saying each step aloud as if committing them to memory. Lastly, I grabbed a plate from the upper cabinets, tucked it under the spout to catch the ground meat, and sat back at the table.

Tying the apron around her waist, Aunt Jean tossed a few cubes of beef in the grinder's funnel and cranked the handle. After a few cranks, she let out a giggle as ground meat spilled out the other end.

"I'm making Mr. O'Dell a meat loaf for supper tonight," Aunt Jean said, enthralled as more ground meat spilled from the grinder. "He'll like it, don't you think?"

I glanced out the kitchen window. Mama was clipping sheets to the clothesline. Urban sat on the ground at her feet, tearing apart a motor from Daddy's old mower. He'd tear it apart and put it back together a half dozen times before the day was done. Urban was slow to reading and not much for counting, but Mama liked to say he came home from the hospital being able to rewire a lamp.

Mama stopped pinning laundry on the line when Daddy walked up behind her, wrapped his arms around her waist, and pressed his cheek to hers. Mama closed her eyes and shook her head slowly like she did when she was relieved about something. They were talking about Siebert Rix and were both glad he was gone. I was sure of it. No more late-night phone calls. No more of him standing in the drive and hollering at Aunt Jean. No more trips to the doctor in the middle of the night. No more chance Daddy might kill him.

He was gone. Mama and Daddy knew it and believed it, so I should believe it too. But I couldn't shake the feeling that we'd only seen his first act. If I said something to Mama, she'd say I'd read too many of Aunt Jean's scripts.

"Real life isn't like a movie," Mama once said. "You never know when you're in the middle or when you're near the end. And you never get a second take."

"Did you know Mr. Rix was coming this morning?" I asked Aunt Jean.

"Look how it's working," she said, ignoring my question as she dropped a few more chunks of beef in the grinder. "Isn't it amazing?"

"You got all dressed up," I said, staring at Aunt Jean's back. "Did your hair, your makeup. Was that because you were expecting him?"

Still Aunt Jean didn't answer my questions. And then I remembered her luggage, and I was certain.

"Your luggage," I said. "You're already packed. Everything but your makeup. You were going to leave with him."

"How on earth would I have known Siebert was going to pick today to leave for California?" Aunt Jean said, leaning into the crank as if her arm were getting tired. "I promised your daddy I wouldn't talk to him again, and I've kept that promise."

"You knew he'd see the newspaper," I said as the grinder continued to whine. "Didn't you? Whatever's in there, you thought he'd see it and come here to the house. You knew he'd want to take you away."

Aunt Jean said nothing, just kept rotating the crank on the grinder.

"Aunt Jean," I said. "Were you going to leave with Mr. Rix and not go on our trip? Were you going to miss my birthday?"

"You're the reason I stayed," she said, leaning on the counter, her posture collapsing as she decided to confess. "It was that Wilma Danielson at the grocer yesterday. She begged me for some news to print. Said if I didn't have any, everyone would forget about me."

She let go of the meat grinder's handle and turned to me.

"Mr. O'Dell and I," she said, slipping into the voice that was so recognizable. Like honey dripping from her tongue, it was a sweet whisper you had to lean in to hear. "We're engaged. We agreed to keep it quiet for a while, seeing as how I only just got divorced. People wouldn't approve of me taking up with a new man so soon. Siebert wouldn't have liked it either. He was always on me to leave here and get back to work."

"You're getting married?" I said. "You're going to marry Mr. O'Dell and stay here in Hockta? Are you really going to give up everything?"

Just like that, Aunt Jean yanked my future out from under me and stranded me in a life like Mama's.

"I didn't really think about leaving or staying," Aunt Jean said. "Leland gave me the sweetest ring. I just couldn't say no."

"But saying yes means you're going to stay here in Hockta," I said. "Mr. O'Dell isn't moving to Hollywood. He has a job here. He wants a house and children. You tell me that all the time. If you're his wife, he'll want you to live here."

Aunt Jean smiled and went back to turning the crank on the meat grinder.

"Aunt Jean," I said, thinking Aunt Jean couldn't be so cruel, and yet I had to say it. "You shouldn't have told Mr. O'Dell you're going to marry him if you're not going to."

"Of course I'll marry him," Aunt Jean said, not looking at me but instead watching the meat as it spilled from the grinder.

For the first time ever, I was angry at Aunt Jean. Nothing she was saying made sense. Sometimes the movie magazines wrote about her being difficult, being late to set, forgetting her lines. I never reread those articles. The woman they wrote about wasn't the person I knew, but now I thought maybe Aunt Jean was that woman.

Mr. O'Dell was a kind man, and Aunt Jean had left him before. Mama and Daddy put him back together every time only so he could go back to waiting every day for Aunt Jean to return. Now it was worse. She'd said yes to marrying him.

She didn't care one bit about me either. Not only had she been planning to run off and leave Mr. O'Dell, but she had also been planning to run off and leave me. It seemed she didn't even remember we were supposed to go on our trip, though we'd been washing, ironing, and packing for days. A hundred times or more, she'd told me I was special. I could do what she did. I could do it better.

"You'll never believe how glorious it is to feel the lights snap on and hear the camera roll," she'd said. "You can actually feel your eyelashes sparkle, your skin glow. Ah, Addie Anne, you'll have a wonderful, beautiful life."

It had all been a lie. Aunt Jean never believed in me either.

"I thought it would be better for everyone if I left with Siebert," Aunt Jean said, picking at the clumps of raw meat between her fingers. She looked like a child being scolded. "The second I told Wilma Danielson about Leland and me, she asked if that meant I was staying in Hockta and what would Siebert do if he wasn't taking pictures of me anymore. She asked didn't I feel badly, stripping a man of his livelihood, and I knew I'd made a terrible mistake. I knew he'd see the paper and come here in a fit. After the last time, when he caused so much trouble, I thought it would be best if I just left with him. Safer for everyone. But I changed my mind. You changed my mind."

Aunt Jean glanced out the window as if checking that Mama and Daddy were still out of earshot.

"Your mama and daddy, they'd have been angry with me for running my mouth," she said. "I'd promised never to bring that kind of trouble to this doorstep again, and I didn't mean to. But I decided to stay for you. So we could go on our trip."

"And what about Mr. O'Dell? We can't go on our trip if you're getting married," I said, finding more reason to be angry because Aunt Jean was still pretending we could go. "Now that you're engaged, Mr. O'Dell will expect you to stay here with him. He must have told you as much."

"It's only for six weeks," Aunt Jean said, because she, like everyone else, thought I was coming back home. She really thought six weeks was all I wanted. "Of course, we're going on your trip. And Mr. O'Dell will be right there waiting at the station when we come back."

After Aunt Jean and I visited Hollywood for a month, we were going to travel to New York to celebrate her birthday and attend the premiere of *The Seven Year Itch*. A week later, she was supposed to put me on a train back to Hockta. But I wasn't going to go. By then, she'd know I was ready. She would let me live with her, take me on photo shoots and to movie sets. I was going to build a brand-new life, but if she came back to Hockta to marry Mr. O'Dell, none of that would happen. I would have to come back too.

I could have struck out on my new life without Truitt, but I couldn't do it without Aunt Jean. She was going to take me out into the world just long enough to give me a glimpse of an extraordinary life. I'd see it, taste it, feel my eyelashes sparkle and my skin glow, and then I'd have to return to Hockta with her so she could marry Leland O'Dell. And I'd spend the rest of my days in the dark, soggy shadow of the glorious life I should have had.

"We'll have a wonderful time," Aunt Jean said, leaving the plate of meat on the counter and stepping up to the window to look outside again. "Don't you worry about that."

Mama and Daddy were still out there, standing together under the white sheets billowing in the breeze. Aunt Jean stared at them and sighed like she was wishing she was out there, and someone had his arms around her.

"You know Mama and Daddy will hear about your engagement at the party tonight," I said, putting the meat in the refrigerator and soaping up the grinder in the sink. "They'll figure out you were planning to leave with Mr. Rix and break Mr. O'Dell's heart. Again. They'll know you invited trouble to our house."

"Maybe," Aunt Jean said, turning to face me, "but now it really doesn't matter what I said or what I was going to do. Siebert is gone. He can't cause us any trouble, no matter what the newspaper says."

I couldn't do it. I couldn't go on our trip, see everything the world had to offer, and come back to live in a soggy shadow. I couldn't live seeing Aunt Jean here every day in this tiny town. I couldn't live in the aftermath of her giving it all up. I'd let her take me on our trip. I'd let her believe I was coming back with her to watch her marry Leland O'Dell. But I wouldn't.

I was going to do it all by myself. Once I left this town, I was never coming back, because coming back would hurt too much. I felt the same about Truitt. I loved him once, but I would never do it again, because doing it again would hurt too much.

"Do you really think Mr. Rix is gone?" I asked, wanting to wad up the two cake layers that would eventually be my birthday cake and throw them out the window.

"You heard him same as me," Aunt Jean said, still leaning in the window and sounding sad when I thought she should have sounded relieved. "Siebert is well on his way to California by now."

If I'd have told Mama and Daddy about the newspaper article, they wouldn't have gone to the Harringtons' party. They'd have known, same as me, that Aunt Jean getting married to a man who lived in this tiny town, was, to Siebert, the end of his career. They'd have stayed home, just in case, because Siebert was nothing without Aunt Jean, and he never left that easy.

But I didn't tell. I kept Aunt Jean's secret. My wanting too much of something that was too shiny tricked me into making a terrible decision.

CHAPTER 23

Once Wiley had Truitt safely hidden on the back floorboard of his patrol car, he did what he did every morning. He drove from his house to the sheriff's office in town. That's where he had phone numbers to call on things like train tickets and stolen cars.

Taking care not to glance over his shoulder and give away that Truitt was lying in the back seat, he took the corners too fast and rolled through a stop sign. He didn't usually do that, but to any of those men from Tampa who might be watching, it would be expected. He was working against a deadline, after all. He had until midnight to deliver Truitt to five members of the Giordano family without actually delivering him. And he had to hope like hell they let Ilene live.

By the time Wiley reached town, he was sorting through ideas as fast as they came to him, tossing out the bad ones, tucking away the good ones to think more on later. He couldn't let himself think about Ilene or the sound of her shouts going silent, because that silence was the loudest thing he'd ever heard. It pounded in his head still. If he stopped to think about what might have been happening to Ilene back at her house, he'd make another mistake, the first being the blood on Truitt's shirt that he hadn't seen straightaway. If Wiley made a second mistake, Ilene would end up dead for sure, as would Truitt, as would Wiley. If the first happened, if Ilene died, Wiley would just as soon be dead anyway.

The sun was full in the sky, and the summer humidity had snuck up on the town between yesterday and today. Folks were out and about early, knowing from experience that if they wanted to get it done, they needed to do it before the heat drove them inside. That was good. He needed people out on the streets so he could talk to as many as he could as quickly as he could.

When Wiley reached the part of town where folks could get themselves a haircut, stock up at the drugstore, or pick out a new dress, the shop owners were already sweeping sidewalks and turning closed signs to open. Others were cleaning fingerprints from their display windows. As Wiley passed, a few stepped out onto the curb to give him a wave.

Normally, Wiley would stop and check in on folks. That was his favorite part of the job, but he didn't have time for checking in just yet. He was busy sorting ideas, and every so often, he almost choked on the question he'd had to swallow since he dragged Truitt off his living room floor and threw him in an old uniform . . . what the hell had Truitt done besides running that damn bolita game to make those sorts of men so intent on finding him? What had he done to get that blood on his shirt? He'd eventually get his chance to ask Truitt. Once he had the boy safe, he'd find out exactly what Truitt had done and exactly what Wiley was up against.

Keeping his eyes straight ahead, Wiley passed by all the onlookers, knowing that soon enough, every one of them would know why he'd been too distracted to give a polite wave. Wiley would make sure of it. He'd make sure the entire town knew Truitt Holt had run afoul of the law, was on the run, and that Wiley Bishop was doing everything possible, including crossing lines he'd never crossed before, to find him.

He slowed at the sheriff's department, a redbrick single story situated on a hillside. It had an office for Wiley and a holding cell big enough for two, though Wiley had stuffed as many as ten in there before. But the thing about the sheriff's department most folks didn't know was that it had a basement. He'd never used it himself and had only been down there a few times. The remnants of what once happened there were plentiful. He'd thought to strip them all out when he took over, but that felt like stripping out history, like he was saying what happened down there never happened. Wiley hadn't been willing to do that.

He pulled into the garage around back, shut off the car, and pulled the garage door closed. Then he banged on the roof, signaling Truitt he could come out.

"I killed one of them," Truitt said, standing at the side of Wiley's car. His face was red and wet. He looked like a kid again, narrow shoulders, head hanging, like he did when Wiley first started helping Ilene with things around the house.

"I figured as much," Wiley said, not looking the boy in the eye.

It wasn't what he wanted to hear, but Wiley had known it since the barrel-chested man told Wiley the bolita game was the least of the kid's problems. Truitt had killed one of Santo Giordano's men.

"I'm sorry, Wiley," Truitt said, his voice cracking. "Wiley, why won't you look at me? I'm sorry."

Wiley couldn't look at him. Even though he knew it was the kinder thing to do. He didn't trust what the boy might see if Wiley locked eyes with him. He didn't want to be angry at the kid, but he was. He'd told Truitt he didn't need to run that damn game. It was trouble waiting to happen. Wiley had been trying to marry Ilene for years. He wanted to take care of her and for her to take care of him. But she couldn't stand the idea of another man she was married to being shot dead in her driveway or anywhere else.

Wiley gently, very gently, reminded her that in the end, Ilene did not love her husband. He also pointed out that married or not, Ilene did love Wiley, and he loved her. Would him getting shot hurt any less with no marriage certificate between them? She responded by warning Wiley not to try forcing common sense on her.

Despite having no official title to bind Wiley to the family, he had long ago told Truitt that if he or his mama ever needed anything, Wiley would provide. He wanted to provide. He ached to bring things into

Ilene's home and set them on her counter. A bag of potatoes. A carton of eggs. A bouquet of flowers now and again. But the kid was proud, said his daddy taught him to be proud, which was a goddamn lie. Truitt's daddy didn't know one damn thing about being proud.

"I didn't mean to hurt anyone," Truitt said, his voice breaking as he finished telling Wiley the whole story of changing a tire and killing a man. "Donna Lee, she talked about my game. The guy came at me. I didn't—"

"No time for this now," Wiley said, grabbing a box filled with files and hauling it toward the side door that led to the main building. "I'm going to go back and forth with these boxes, carry them inside like I need them."

"Need them for what?"

"It don't fucking matter," Wiley said, immediately sorry for lashing out at the kid. "Just listen, would you? I'm going to go back and forth a few times, hauling another box in with me each time. When I come back the third time, you're going to carry the next box in. I'll wait a few minutes and follow with another. You understand?"

Truitt nodded. They were doing the reverse of what they'd done at the house. Wiley motioned for Truitt to tuck in his shirt, so it hung more like Wiley's. Then he yanked the kid's hat down low and told him to brush the dust from his pants that he'd picked up when lying on the floorboards.

"I'm ready," Truitt said.

By the time four dusty boxes filled with files sat in Wiley's office, both he and Truitt were safely inside. Wiley had probably been too careful, but he had never once in his life regretted being too careful.

Pulling all the blinds, he sat Truitt down in a chair pushed up against a wall and rang Stacy at the café to order his breakfast. He did the same every morning. When he saw her crossing the street, a box and cup of coffee in hand, he met her at the door.

"Sure do appreciate this," he said. "Going to be a long day. A real goddamn long day."

Stacy was a talker, and a talker was what Wiley needed. Before the breakfast rush was over, she'd tell every person who sat at one of her tables that Wiley Bishop was in a mood, and something was giving him fits. Best stay clear of him today.

Back in the office, the boxed breakfast and coffee in hand, Wiley stuffed a flashlight in his pocket and waved at Truitt to follow him. On his way through the main office, he grabbed two blankets, draped them over his shoulder, and glanced at the clock. His deputy would come in soon to open the building, so Wiley needed to get a move on. Twice Truitt started to ask what was happening, but Wiley quieted him with no more than a look.

In the building's only bathroom, Wiley opened the door with his foot, his hands being full, and motioned for Truitt to go inside.

"If you got to go," Wiley said, "go now."

In the corner of the bathroom was another, smaller door, two-thirds the height of a normal door. It led down to the basement.

"Lock's not closed," Wiley said, nodding at the keyed lock dangling from the small door. He handed Truitt the cup of coffee so they'd each have a free hand. "Watch your head and keep hold of the banister. Stairs are steep."

"Stairs?" Truitt said. "Stairs going to what?"

Wiley didn't answer and instead nodded for Truitt to get a move on. Ducking to clear the threshold, Truitt took the stairs slowly and held the banister tight like Wiley suggested. Wiley followed, careful not to crowd Truitt. At the bottom, shoulders hunched to keep from hitting his head on the ceiling, Wiley fished the flashlight from his pocket and snapped it on.

"Wiley," Truitt said, whispering as he glanced around the dark space. "You got to tell me what we're doing."

The walls were made of thick stacked stone, ground down by age. They glistened where the flashlight hit them as if they were wet. This place was a grave for more than one man, and Wiley didn't believe in stepping on a man's grave. He never touched the chains that hung from the rafters or the lashing rings drilled into the wall. When Truitt reached for a chain dangling overhead, Wiley stopped him.

"Don't," Wiley said. He nodded toward a spot near the stairs and dropped the blankets. "Best you sit here and stay put. Try not to use the flashlight unless you have to. I'll try to come back when I can so you can stretch your legs, go to the john, get some lunch."

Wiley couldn't bring himself to look at the kid, because what he most wanted to do was throw him in a car, drive him out to his house, and trade him for Ilene. That was fear talking in Wiley's head. Panic. Still, he was afraid if he looked, that's what he'd do.

"You're locking me down here?" Truitt said.

"Have to."

"You don't have to do shit," Truitt said, puffing out his chest and knocking his head on a wooden beam. He shrunk back down and grabbed the back of his head.

"You're going to watch that mouth," Wiley said, "and be happy I tell you anything. You understand?"

Hearing no response, Wiley swung the flashlight up to Truitt's face.

He felt like smacking the kid, more fear and panic bubbling up, but he was glad he chose a stream of light instead. Light in the kid's eyes wouldn't get Wiley in hot water with Ilene.

"Yes," Truitt said, squinting and turning away. "Yes, I understand."

"There are five men at your house," Wiley said.

He figured if he stuck to the simple facts, he'd likely not end up doing or saying anything Ilene wouldn't approve of. The air shifted as Truitt's body went stiff. Wiley lowered the flashlight and kept on talking.

"There was one there when I arrived, a gun to your mama's head. You hear me. A goddamn gun. Four more came. I tried to get them to follow me around town to prove you were nowhere to be found, but they wouldn't go for it. Likely because running bolita wasn't the worst of your problems. They said for me to find you, bring you back, or they'd kill your mama."

The flashlight still dangled in Wiley's hand and threw a single spot of light on the floor at his and Truitt's feet. The glow crept up their calves and then the rest of them disappeared in the dark. Truitt's deep long breaths rattled in his chest.

"Then take me there now," Truitt said, his voice flat and not sounding like a kid's anymore. "To my house."

"I would in a second," Wiley said, sorry even as he said it. But goddamn it all, he was scared. "But your mama made me promise I wouldn't. So, I won't."

"I don't care what Mama wants. You take me there. Problem solved."

Truitt took a step toward the stairs. Wiley grabbed him, yanked him back, and dumped him on the spot where he dropped the two blankets.

"You don't get a say anymore," Wiley said, his fear of losing Ilene turning him into someone he didn't recognize. "You're going to stay here while I fix this mess. And don't you ever say you don't care what your mama wants. Make no mistake, your mama is the only reason you're alive. What she wants is the only damn thing that matters."

Wiley dropped the box of food in Truitt's lap, took the stairs two at a time, and once he was back in the bathroom, he snapped closed the padlock on the door, locking Truitt in the basement. Now, at least Wiley could be assured Truitt didn't go anywhere.

CHAPTER 24

Double-checking the lock on the basement door, Wiley turned off all the lights in the small building, made sure every other door was locked, and managed to leave well before his deputy showed up. He wasn't ready yet to answer questions about why he was in the office on a Saturday.

His deputy, Billy Pyke, was a good kid. Hopefully, if he intended to stay in law enforcement, he'd fill out some in the next few years. At least enough to hold up his trousers. But still, he was good at his job. Thorough. Eager. All-around good attitude. He'd no doubt show up at the office on time. Soon after, the phones would start ringing, something Wiley was going to make sure happened, and Billy would take painstaking notes about every call he received. He'd learn quick enough that Truitt Holt was on the run and be eager to join the hunt.

Billy was always looking for an adventure. They didn't get many in Lake County, not good adventures anyway, and when he couldn't find one in the real world, he found plenty in the stories he read. When Wiley returned later in the day, he'd give Billy a mission and send him off on an adventure all his own. He'd be so willing and so eager, he wouldn't stop to wonder why Wiley was trying to get rid of him.

Wiley's first stop was at Merle Gaffney's place. He lived on the main road into town, so as Wiley parked his patrol in Merle's drive, he and his car were plenty visible to everyone driving into and out of town.

The surroundings at Merle's place were sparse. In the distance, a thick line of oaks sprung up around the river that ran along the eastern side of town. In the years since Merle's wife died, the place had mostly been left to the wire grass. Dry, windy weather was hell on Merle because of all the dust that found its way inside his house. Walking onto Merle's porch, Wiley thought it might be time for him to send Billy out to replace a few pieces of the lapboard siding and shore up the railings.

At the front door, Wiley did his best to shut down the images of Ilene back at her house that kept springing up in his mind. He winced every time one appeared, each of them feeling like a wooden bat to his gut. She was a strong woman and had been through plenty, but strong and resilient weren't necessarily going to help with the situation she was in. They could make things worse.

Ilene had never been one to bite her tongue. She'd also made Wiley's task nearly impossible by insisting he not give up Truitt to a gang of thugs. Not that Wiley wanted to hand the boy over. Not when he was thinking clearly. The harder task was to keep the boy from giving himself up to save his mama. Hence, locking him in the basement. If Truitt somehow found his way back home and gave himself up to those men, Ilene would blame Wiley. And just like she wasn't one to bite her tongue, she also wasn't one to let bygones be bygones.

Wiley's challenge, as he saw it, was finding a solution that would get Ilene safely out of that house while also keeping the boy alive.

"Merle, it's Wiley Bishop," he said, knocking loudly. "Here about the report you called in the other day."

As he waited, Wiley counted the cars that passed by Merle's house. Four drove by, and two slowed. Seeing Wiley's patrol car in Merle's driveway would immediately raise concern. Everyone knew Merle was on his own out here and not so good at getting around anymore. The whole town would soon be wondering what was going on at Merle's place and hoping the old boy was all right.

"Well, good Lord," Merle said, opening the door and looking as if he just woke up. "I didn't expect the sheriff himself. I thought you'd send that boy of yours."

Merle's white hair stuck out at all angles, and his clothes were rumpled. Without a missus in the house, he wasn't bothering to change his clothes too often.

"Figured this was one I should see to myself," Wiley said, stepping back and motioning for Merle to join him on the porch.

"Why don't you come in," Merle said, stuffing his shirttail in his waistband as he pushed open the screened door. "Have some coffee. Sure didn't mean for you to drive all the way out here."

"Appreciate it, Merle," Wiley said. "But I've had my share of coffee this morning. Let's go on out to the garage and have a look right quick at what happened."

Wiley gave Merle an arm to steady himself on as he climbed down the steps, and he tried not to hurry the man along as they walked toward the stand-alone garage out back. Since the moment he left Ilene, Wiley had been fighting gravity. He was stumbling downhill, out of control, but he still wasn't getting where he needed to fast enough. He clenched his jaw and gut, curled his toes in his boots, all to force himself to slow down.

"Help me push open these doors?" Merle said as they neared the garage's rolling doors. "Hard for me to get them moving these days."

"Your old Ford still parked in there?" Wiley said.

"Sure. Don't drive it no more, though."

"No sense opening the whole thing," Wiley said. "Let's just go in through the side door."

As they walked around the side of the garage, dry weeds crunching underfoot, Wiley made a show of pulling out a pad of paper and pencil. He hung back when Merle shuffled into the dark garage to point out the spot where his lawn mower used to sit, an empty spot Wiley had seen on several other occasions.

This was the fifth time Merle had reported his push mower stolen. Each time, either Wiley or Billy found it abandoned somewhere on his property. As they pushed it back to his garage, Merle would remember having gotten a taste for lunch or a glass of something cool while he was last doing his mowing. Sorry for the trouble, he said each time it happened. This time, Wiley didn't suggest they look around the property. He needed a stolen car, and Merle's misplaced mower was as close as he was going to get.

Scribbling in his notepad, Wiley walked around the garage as if inspecting for broken windows or other signs of a break-in. There were only two windows in the garage, and Merle had painted over the glass in both after the third time he thought his mower was stolen. Another lucky break because no one would be able to look in to see the Ford right where it belonged. This was more of Wiley being overly cautious.

As he worked his way around the garage a second time, he counted six more cars passing by on their way into town. Folks would first worry about Merle. Maybe he'd taken a fall. Maybe it was his heart. And then a few would report having seen Wiley snooping around the garage. Only one thing of value in Merle's garage. His old Ford. Once Wiley got back into town and started asking around about Truitt, the town gossips would do the rest. The Truitt boy was missing and so was Merle Gaffney's old Ford. If Wiley was going to convince those fellows from Tampa that Truitt had made off for Georgia or beyond, he'd first have to convince the whole town.

By the time Wiley had walked around the garage a second time, squatting below each window to look at the ground, Merle realized Wiley didn't follow him into the garage.

"What you doing out here?" Merle said, stepping out of the garage and squinting in the sudden brightness.

"You lock that?" Wiley said of the side door Merle had used.

One more precaution. He didn't want anyone opening the door to look inside the garage.

Merle rattled the knob. "Yep. But what do you think about my mower? Hate to lose it. Still did a real fine job of mowing. You're looking around like you think someone broke in through the windows. Ain't got no broken windows."

Wiley gave a nod for Merle to head back to the house. At the porch, he gave him another hand getting up the steps.

"I'm guessing it's not gone for good," Wiley said, making a note to come back later and track down the mower. "I'll send Billy out in the next few days and have him take a look too."

After he left Merle's place, Wiley spent the next hour walking up and down Main Street, stopping in at the grocery store, the hardware store, the barber shop, and the beauty parlor, asking everyone he came across if he or she had seen Truitt Holt recently. He'd had an argument with his mama, Wiley told folks, and she was worried he'd taken off on her.

"I'm sure the boy's fine," he said, not wanting to send up too loud an alarm. "Not as if he can get too far without a car."

After an hour of asking around and no one having seen Truitt since midnight the night before, when he was drinking outside Terrance's Tavern, the manager at Wilson's Market said to him . . . heard you were out at Merle's place and that his old Ford is missing.

"Sounds like something, don't it?" the manager said. "That old Ford going missing at the same time Truitt Holt goes missing. That apple didn't drop out of the sky, you know. Came from a tree."

This was another fact that would help Wiley convince folks Truitt had run off. His father had been no good in the eyes of most in town. Thinking the same of Truitt was a natural next step.

CHAPTER 25

Giving the manager at Wilson's a nod as if Wiley thought the same about Truitt's lineage, he excused himself and headed back to the sheriff's office. It was nearly time for Billy to show up for work, and Wiley wanted to catch him as soon as he got in. Wiley had done what he needed to do around town. He'd planted the story, and it would continue to spin and grow all day long. Now he needed to move on to the next thing on his list.

Eventually, someone would see Merle out in his front yard, stop to chat, and discover the Ford wasn't really missing. But Merle wasn't much for getting out these days, especially after Wiley tired him out by walking him to his garage and back, so Wiley had some time.

The front door of the sheriff's office was unlocked when Wiley returned. Billy sat at his desk, his knees bumping the underside. A *Science Fiction Quarterly* lay open in front of him, and he was talking with someone on the phone. Wiley was always after Billy to get himself a haircut and maybe bathe a bit more often, and while Billy wasn't much for keeping himself clean and tidy, Wiley's office had never been in better order.

Holding the receiver in one hand and taking notes with the other, Billy was hunched over the desk. He squinted for listening so hard to the caller on the other end. At the sound of Wiley's boot hitting the entry, Billy looked up. Relieved, he exhaled, and his bony shoulders slumped. He ended the call and set down his pen.

"You won't believe the calls I'm getting," he said after hanging up. "Just now walked in, and that's my third. Haven't even put on the coffee yet. And sounds to me like we got a rat stuck in the gutters again. All kinds of rattling out back, but ain't had a second to check on it."

"What are folks calling about?" Wiley said, resisting the urge to look toward the back of the office. The rattling was likely Truitt. He needed to get Billy on his way before Truitt realized they were out here and started yelling.

"Calling about Truitt and Merle Gaffney's missing Ford," Billy said, standing and pacing. "Sounds to me like Truitt Holt might have stole it and headed out of town. Makes sense, you know? I'm guessing he headed north. No sense in going south."

Just like the characters in the stories Billy was always reading, he was cataloging clues, flushing out motives, planning how best to track down his subject and the vehicle he'd made off in.

Every week, Billy had another story to tell Wiley. He had a whole stack of magazines he brought with him to the office every day, their covers wrinkled and worn from so much reading. Every few months, he got a new one in the mail, always *Science Fiction Quarterly*, and his stack grew taller.

His most recent favorite had been about the miracle of hypnosis. He had already sent off for a kit that promised to teach him how to hypnotize the truth out of people. Best of all, it came with a money-back guarantee, proof positive to Billy that the kit was legitimate. Most days, Wiley thought Billy read too many of those stories of his, but today, Wiley was going to make the most of Billy's appetite for adventure.

"We should talk to his mama," Billy said, still pacing, his long strides carrying him across the room in a few steps. "'Course you probably already did. And you already been to Merle's, too, so that's good. Seems to me, Truitt hasn't been seen since around midnight last night."

Wiley nodded. He'd found it was best to let people make their own way to an idea. They tended to be far more accommodating of their own ideas than they were of someone else's. But waiting was hard, because

Wiley was still straining against his insides that were aching to move as fast as possible.

"What do you suppose that means?" Wiley said, moving with an awkward stiffness as he forced himself to lean against Billy's desk and drape one leg over the other like he was just passing time.

Billy took a few more long strides and paused.

"I'd say it means Truitt could have been on the road since midnight. Probably had to sleep some, but that's still a good six hours of driving, at least. And as many as ten. We know he's got money, all that bolita money, for gas, food, even a place to stay the night."

"Six hours would easily carry him to Tallahassee or Jacksonville," Wiley said. "Because you're right about him going north. Even as far as Georgia."

"Nothing we can do in Tallahassee or Jacksonville," Billy said, hoisting up his pants that were forever sagging on his hips. "Don't have jurisdiction up there."

Wiley considered telling Billy the truth, telling him about the dead man Truitt left on the side of the road, the mobsters holed up at Ilene's place, the fact that Truitt was locked down in the basement. But Billy was still young and believed following the rules would always favor the good guys. Wiley had learned the hard way that wasn't always true. He also liked Billy and didn't want to see the kid get hurt. Telling him anything other than the story Wiley had already planted could have led Billy straight into trouble he didn't need or deserve.

"But you know, Truitt's one of our own," Wiley said, glancing out the window as if struggling with his conscience. "Like a son to me. Maybe we could find him and bring him back. We put Merle's car back in his garage. We get Truitt home to his mama. No need to make a fuss or even pull out a badge."

Billy raised his brows, letting Wiley know he wasn't sure about doing a favor for some kid who stole a car.

"Guess there'd be no harm in one of us driving up to Lake City," Billy said, slowly nodding. "No matter if he went west or east or north into Georgia, he'd pass through there. Long as I just went as one fellow doing a favor for another fellow."

"That's a good idea," Wiley said, hearing the rattle Billy had mentioned. It was time to get Billy on the road. "You suppose you could do that for me? I'll cover your gas. Truitt knows you. He'll listen to you. I think you're just the man for the job."

"Why, sure, I can do that. Make good time too."

Wiley scribbled a phone number on a piece of paper.

"I want you to call me at this number," Wiley said. "At eight o'clock sharp, you understand? That's Ilene Holt's phone number. I'll be there at her house, with her, in case Truitt calls home. You should be into Georgia by then. Find yourself a sheriff's office. Tell them who you are and that you just need a favor. They'll let you use their phone, no questions. Eight o'clock on the button."

It would be getting dark by eight o'clock. It would make sense for Wiley to stop searching after dark. The men back at the house with Ilene would see it that way too. The dark would make them tired; it would mark the end of the day.

"Eight o'clock," Billy said. "Got it."

"And take good notes," Wiley said, knowing Billy would even without being asked. "You know what Merle's old Ford looks like. But Truitt's a crafty one. Might have changed the license plate, maybe even taken a can of paint to the old beast. Take note of everything. If it's close, write down the license plate and note which way the car was headed."

"Probably I should look at every driver too," Billy said, his eyes snapping side to side as he thought through the problem ahead. "Could be that if Truitt would steal one car, he'd steal another."

"That's good, Billy," Wiley said. "Real good thinking."

Billy would see old Merle's Ford in every car he passed and Truitt in every driver wearing a hat or slouching low in his seat. That was how hungry Billy was for a little adventure. By the time he called Wiley to report in, he'd be certain he saw Truitt a half dozen times, already headed deep into Georgia.

Billy grabbed his hat and keys and was gone before Wiley could dig the gas money from his pockets. The same rattling rose out of the back room again. Wiley locked the front door behind Billy, put out the **BE BACK SOON** sign, and headed toward the basement door.

CHAPTER 26

Siebert hadn't had a bit to eat since last night, but he'd still planned to wait until he was closer to Mount Dora before stopping for some breakfast. But when he'd been at the Buckley house, he smelled fried bacon and eggs, and that sure did make him hungry. Inez was a good cook, he'd give her that. When he did eventually stop, he'd have to be smart. Those fellows in the big black sedan he kept seeing at the train station might be out looking for him.

Rolling into Hockta's only grocery, Siebert parked where he was surrounded by cars on each side. Anyone passing by would never notice his car tucked in among all the others. Before getting out, he pulled on his hat and took off his jacket. He'd been wearing his jacket each time the man in the black sedan had seen him. He would be less recognizable in only a shirt. Better yet, he unbuttoned his cuffs and rolled up his sleeves. Now he looked like someone who might work alongside Harden Buckley over at the groves. Siebert scoffed at the thought. Him, a working man.

Inside the store, a burst of cool air ruffled his hair. He shivered and drew in a crisp breath. Once he got a little food in his stomach and maybe a few hours of sleep, he'd figure a way of getting out of town. He had no hope of finding that kid, Truitt, so leaving was his only option. Driving was too much of a risk, and taking the train meant he needed Marilyn and her money. And getting hold of Marilyn meant getting rid of Harden.

Several aisles stretched before him, each of them crowded with women pushing carts, their heels clicking as they scurried about. He'd never been inside the store before, preferring to eat his meals out, and he didn't know where to find anything. He wasn't even sure what he wanted or needed. This was already an obstacle he hadn't planned for. The longer he stayed in this store, in Hockta, for that matter, the more likely it was someone would recognize him.

A woman pushing a cart headed toward Siebert. As if knowing her way around, she moved quickly. She was about Inez's age, and women that age liked Siebert. They liked his height, his wide smile, and his charming ways. But darn it all, he didn't have his jacket on. Still, he gave it a try.

"Do you mind?" he said as the woman passed him by.

She stopped, glanced at Siebert, and then looked again.

"Mr. Rix?" she said. Her eyes widened and a smile broke across her heavily powdered face. "Why yes, it is you."

Already, Siebert had been recognized.

"You remembered?" he said, making a quick adjustment and dropping his voice to a whisper in hopes the woman would follow suit. He didn't want to draw attention.

The woman had a plump face and ordinary brown hair done in a style Marilyn had made popular. But the soft curls that were elegant on Marilyn looked childlike on this woman.

"We're still checking the mail every day for your photos," she said, easing her cart closer to Siebert.

The woman's high-pitched voice cut through the clatter of the carts rolling past. Siebert resisted the urge to reach out and cover her mouth.

"Indeed," he said, glancing around and hoping the woman's shrill voice had attracted no attention.

"I'm Tillie Harrington," the woman said, nearly screeching. "My daughter, you took pictures of her down at the lake one Sunday a month or so back."

"And that's exactly why I stopped you," Siebert said, thankful he had always been quick on his feet. He forced a smile and used both hands to gently signal that the woman should quiet down. "But I'd rather no one else take notice. You're aware, I'm sure . . . so many mothers mistakenly think their daughters are as lovely as yours. I do so hate having to disappoint them."

The woman pressed a finger to her lips. "Certainly. You must be forever fending off requests for your services."

"But your pictures, they're on their way as we speak," Siebert said, ready to be done with the pleasantries. He only wanted a few groceries and the directions to find them. "If only I'd have known I'd be seeing you today."

"Were they really good then?" the woman asked.

"We'll talk, you and I, once you've seen them. But I wonder, in the meantime, I'm looking for bread and jam and maybe a newspaper. Could you point me in the right direction?"

The woman directed him down a center aisle and pointed out a stack of newspapers near the counter where another woman was totaling groceries and taking money. Siebert stared at the woman, realizing this was likely the store where Donna Lee worked before . . . well, before.

"Perhaps they'll come today," the woman said as Siebert nodded his thanks. "The pictures. And perhaps I'll see you this evening, and we can talk more then."

Siebert took a few unsteady steps, eager to get away from the woman before she noticed how poorly he suddenly felt. Lord, what if Donna Lee had bragged to any of her customers that she knew Siebert Rix? Once people realized she was missing, they'd start wondering who she'd been running around with, and someone might mention Siebert's name. He really needed to buy his things and be on his way. But the woman had said something he didn't understand. He stopped and backed up.

"This evening?" he said. "What is that you said about seeing me this evening?"

"I certainly hope I will," the woman said, and then she dropped to a whisper again. "At our party, mine and Mr. Harrington's. It's a tradition around here. The Orange Blossom Ball, some people call it. Practically the whole town is invited. Not that everyone comes. But . . . well, I just assumed . . . hoped you might join us."

Now that he knew where to find his bread and jam, Siebert had grown tired of the woman. He saw no sense in continuing the conversation, but he'd always done well in life by trafficking in information. He'd hear one thing from one person and turn around and make a profit from it, maybe in money or maybe in the form of a favor. The woman was offering information, and Siebert's instincts reared up and told him to grab hold of it.

"You thought I'd be at a party?" he said. "Your party, you say?"

"I thought you might be Jean's guest and that I'd see you there. Although perhaps she isn't going. She often doesn't attend local events." The woman's voice trailed off as she pressed a hand over her mouth. "Oh, dear. Of course. I only saw the news this morning. Of course, you won't be her guest. Please, accept my apologies."

"And why, I wonder," Siebert said, "would I not be Mar . . . Jean's guest?"

Luckily, Siebert was a strong man, because it took all his strength to tamp down his disdain for this small-town shrew. But she had mentioned having seen the news and that meant she'd read the newspaper Siebert had yet to get ahold of. He needed to know what she knew.

"I'd expect Jean to bring her newly minted fiancé," the woman said. "That's all I meant to say. The announcement, as I'm sure you know, was in today's newspaper. It must be a disappointment to see her settle here in Hockta. But perhaps you'll have more time for taking pictures of others, yes?"

Siebert knew how to weather tough situations, and this was a tough one. Another marriage for Marilyn, but no one knew her like he did.

She'd sooner grow horns than settle down in this backwoods town. This piece of news was an annoyance, yes, but it could be worse. It was all in how he played it. Bad news could be good, if you knew how to give it a spin.

"You needn't apologize," Siebert said, leading with his chest to ensure a firm, solid posture. "I couldn't be more thrilled for the happy couple. You wouldn't know because you're not in the business . . . yet . . . but this engagement is good news for me, good news for all of us. Why, the happier Marilyn . . . Jean is, the more successful we all are."

The woman caught Siebert's subtle reference, implying her daughter would one day be in the business just like Marilyn Monroe. She smiled and gave him a wink, letting on that she understood. God, people were easy. If Siebert kept this up, he'd be out of this mess in no time.

"Tell everyone I said so," Siebert said, spinning a tale he hoped would quickly make its way around town. "Tell them the news in the paper is good news for Siebert Rix."

Siebert's story might never reach those men from Tampa, but if it did, they'd understand how powerful Siebert was and that he had no reason to protect a low-life criminal running a low-life game of bolita. Hearing that Marilyn's engagement meant more success for Siebert, those thugs would soon realize Donna Lee had been telling a lie, trying to save her own hide.

"Well, I surely will tell everyone," the woman said. "It's a thrill to have a famous photographer living right here in our little town. And it's a thrill to hear Jean's good fortune is yours, as well. Perhaps our little girl will have some good fortune too."

CHAPTER 27

Back in his car, Siebert dropped his bread and jam on the seat next to him. No sign of a black sedan creeping up on him. No men in dark suits and hats watching his car. He wished he'd picked a color other than peacock blue when he bought this car. Tilting his head back, he drew in a deep breath because putting up with the small-town riffraff always took it out of him. He deserved a little rest. But on the tail end of that deep breath, he coughed, almost gagged. The car was definitely musty. He hoped that's all he smelled. He rolled down his window and sucked in the fresh outside air.

Unfolding the newspaper, he flipped through the flimsy pages, skipping the announcements about a fence being under repair or the yard sale scheduled for the following day. He'd played it just right inside the grocery store, even dangled a bit of gossip to bolster his reputation. But he still wanted to see the news for himself. He stopped when he saw Marilyn's picture followed by the headline STARLET TO WED AGAIN.

The short article announced Marilyn's engagement to Leland O'Dell. The man was an accountant at the groves where Harden Buckley worked. He was tall—too tall if you asked Siebert—and scrawny. The article ended with . . . The couple plans to make their home in Hockta and hopes to start a family soon, signaling the end to two extraordinary careers. Mr. Siebert Rix, longtime photographer to Miss Monroe, had no comment.

Two extraordinary careers over. Siebert's career was the second.

The news was worse than he'd expected. That Wilma Danielson had come right out and declared Siebert a has-been. He wasn't so sure anymore that the story he'd spun would be enough to put the gangsters off his scent.

The one thing Siebert could always count on was Marilyn finding a way to fuck up his life.

He slouched at the sound of footsteps. Glancing over his shoulder, he saw the same woman he'd just managed to escape in the store. A boy walked with her, carrying two bags in his arms. At the car next to Siebert's, the woman opened her trunk, and the boy set the groceries inside.

"Did you hear this, Mr. Rix?" the woman called out.

Siebert slid up in his seat, slapped on a smile, and turned as the woman—what was her name?—leaned in his open window.

"Do you know the young man Truitt Holt?" she said, her eyes darting around the car. She scowled like she was smelling something bad.

"Truitt who?" Siebert said, smiling as if he smelled nothing at all. "Afraid not. Not much for socializing with the folks around here."

"He's missing is why I mention it," the woman said. Harrington, that was her last name. "And Merle Gaffney's Ford, it's missing too. Seems the boy stole the car and run off, left town. That's what the bag boy just told me. The boy comes from bad seed, so it's no wonder. Can you imagine?"

"I most certainly can imagine," Siebert said, because he'd been afraid of this very thing since that man from Tampa dumped Donna Lee in his trunk.

"I just wanted to make you aware," the woman said. "It's a shame, isn't it? Right here in our own town. Take care with your belongings."

"I really must be going," Siebert said, overwhelmed again by that unwell feeling he'd had when he saw the cashier who replaced Donna Lee.

"Of course," the woman said and then stretched an arm across Siebert and pointed. "Why, right there it is. The invitation to our party.

You see it there in your newspaper? Everything you need to know is right there if you decide you'd like to attend. I do so hope you will."

Siebert stared down on the paper as the woman drove off. He steadied himself with both hands on the steering wheel. He shouldn't be surprised the boy ran off, leaving Siebert here to take the blame for what he did. So long as those men from Tampa were hungry for revenge, Siebert was the only thing left on the menu. Donna Lee was rotting in the trunk, and the boy was gone—stole a car and was God only knew how far away.

Just below the story of Marilyn's impending wedding, a large advertisement announced the annual Orange Blossom Ball. Yes, that was what the woman called it. It was an open invitation for any and all to come to the Harringtons' house at 231 Cypress Lane. As usual, Mrs. Harrington would be preparing her good cooking in appreciation for everyone coming out to help celebrate this special occasion. Mrs. Hazel Brandenburg would be bringing her beloved upside-down pineapple cake; Mrs. Maggie Phares, her famed lane cake; and Mrs. Inez Buckley, her always popular three-egg cake with a caramel frosting.

The more Siebert learned, the better. That had always been his motto, and here again, it had served him well.

Tossing the paper in the back seat, Siebert pulled out and started toward Mount Dora where he'd park down in his low-lying spot among the cypress trees and oaks. He'd stay there until dark and then go back to the Buckleys', because now he would have no trouble getting Marilyn and her money out of that house. Harden and Inez both would be at the Harringtons' party. It said as much, right there in the newspaper.

Thank the Lord above for the Harringtons and their ridiculous Orange Blossom Ball.

CHAPTER 28

Truitt had no idea how long he'd been stuck down in the basement. With no light to go by and no watch to check, he could only guess. Both fists hurt from banging on the door. He'd taken to kicking it instead and, every so often, rattling the doorknob. He'd been making so much racket, he didn't hear Wiley coming. Wiley was always trying to teach Truitt to talk less and listen more. You'll get further in life by listening.

The door swung open, flooding the dark stairwell with daylight and blinding Truitt. He stumbled on the top step, nearly lost his balance. Wiley grabbed him and then planted a hand in the middle of Truitt's chest.

"You got five minutes," he said, holding Truitt in place and making sure he was settled. Then he backed away and gave Truitt some space. "Do whatever you got to do because I won't be back for a good long while. Brought you more food. Plenty of water. A bucket, for, well . . . I can't be seen coming and going, or someone'll get suspicious."

"You got to tell me what's going on," Truitt said, squinting and blinking in the bright light. He wasn't past being angry at Wiley, but he knew anger wasn't going to get him out of that basement or get him any answers. "Please. Tell me. What's happening with my mama?"

"I'm seeing to it she's safe," Wiley said.

"That's supposed to be enough?" Truitt asked, biting a lip in place of saying what he really wanted to say. "Would it be enough for you?"

He needed to keep Wiley talking so he could keep thinking. His first plan of escape had been to fight Wiley. He'd punch and kick and do whatever he had to and then make his way back to his house as quickly as possible. Once there, he'd trade himself for his mama. She'd be safe, and whatever happened to Truitt didn't matter. Wiley wasn't much bigger than Truitt, but he was a good bit stronger, something Truitt was reminded of when Wiley had planted a hand on his chest. Trying to move past Wiley had been like trying to move through a rock wall.

Knowing he needed a new plan and fast, Truitt took in everything in the bathroom during those few minutes he was allowed to do his business. That was another thing Wiley was always trying to teach Truitt.

"Notice what's around you," Wiley would say. "Most folks spend too much time thinking about themselves and not enough noticing the goings-on right outside their front door."

The lock on the basement door was a keyed padlock. That was the first thing Truitt noticed. It hung loose from the latch, the key still in it. The lock was old, rusted, and Wiley hadn't bothered to work the key loose. That meant he didn't keep the key on a key ring. That meant he might snap the lock closed and leave the key in the lock when he left. That was something.

There was a window in the bathroom too. It was closed, but it could be opened, wasn't painted shut. That was something else.

And there was a stack of *Science Fiction Quarterlies* on the counter.

That was everything, even if Truitt hadn't yet figured out why.

"Guess you ain't got no choice but to believe me," Wiley said, hustling Truitt back toward the basement door. "But here's the thing you got to know. You have it in your head you can go back to your house, and those fellows will let your mama go. I'm telling you, that ain't what'll happen. Before they go back home, they'll want to scrape this mess off their shoes, and that'll mean doing away with you. And once they done that, they'll do away with your mama and me because we know what they done. Going back there is not the answer, and it damn sure won't make a hero of you."

"Then what the hell is the answer, Wiley?" Truitt said, hoping like hell he didn't cry again. If he was able to figure a way out of the basement, going back home had been his only play. The only way to save his mama. Now Wiley was telling him that plan was no good. Truitt didn't have any other ideas, and not knowing what else to do was making his insides feel like they were about to explode.

"The answer is making them believe you are long gone," Wiley said, softening his voice as if he knew Truitt was about to burst right out of his skin. "The man I talked to out there at your house, he was reasonable. If I can convince him you're gone, he'll decide it ain't worth his time to be chasing you all over the country. Your mama is only leverage if you're around to know they have her. And if she ain't leverage, they have no need of her. Understand? She ain't seen nothing she shouldn't have. Can't do them any real damage. Neither can I. Everything I done for them, I offered up."

Truitt nodded. He understood. Wiley's plan was to make Truitt hide in the basement like a coward, again a coward, and hope some mobster would decide he wasn't worth the trouble and let his mama go. Problem was, all that hinged on Wiley being right about the level-headedness of the man holding his mama right this minute. Sounded to Truitt like Wiley's idea was no good either.

Truitt needed a new plan. He scanned the room, his eyes darting around furiously as he tried to latch on to something that would give rise to a new idea, and he again landed on the stack of *Science Fiction Quarterlies*.

The moment he first saw them, he had known they were important, but he hadn't been sure why. Now he knew.

"Where's Billy?" Truitt asked. At the sink, he splashed cool water on his face and tried to sound like he was ready to play along and behave. "He's usually here on Saturdays, ain't he? What's he think about you keeping me locked up?"

Truitt needed the cold water to calm himself. The moment he realized what the magazines meant, his breath started coming fast, and his heart pounded in his ears. He didn't want Wiley to see either of those things and figure out what Truitt was up to.

"Far as Billy's concerned, you stole Merle Gaffney's Ford and are halfway to Georgia by now," Wiley said, hustling Truitt into the stairwell after he'd toweled off. Cautioning Truitt to stay put, Wiley set a box of food, a bucket, and a gallon of water on the top step. "I just now sent him off to track you down. He's hoping to catch you before you reach the state line. Whole town thinks you're long gone, so just sit tight and trust me. I'll swing by again by the end of the day."

Back in the basement, Truitt moved the food and water down the stairs and pushed them into a dark corner where they couldn't be seen. Then he went back to the top stair and sat. He'd been so busy banging on the door, he hadn't heard Wiley coming the first time. Well, Truitt had learned his lesson. He wouldn't make that mistake again.

With an ear pressed to the door, sitting as quiet and still as he could, he listened and waited.

With nothing else to do, Truitt found his thoughts going back and forth between his mama and Addie. Five men were sitting in his mama's kitchen, drinking her coffee, and doing God knows what else. Good Christ almighty, every time that thought pushed its way to the front, it was a punch in Truitt's gut. Anything and everything that happened to his mama was Truitt's fault.

And then there was Addie. He'd been late going home last night because he'd been tending his wounds. He was drinking, smoking, eyeing girls who weren't Addie, because he'd pushed her away with good old-fashioned meanness. Since the first time Addie shared her dreams of moving off to California to be like her aunt Jean, he'd known he could never go with her. Not today. Not ever. And not just because of his mama, but because he belonged in Hockta. He fit. Every step he took landed exactly where he knew it would. He liked that. He needed that.

Hearing Addie talk for the last six months about her dreams always made him uneasy. Every time she started up talking about studios, casting agents, and dying her hair golden blonde, he'd grab on to something and hold tight. He worried if he didn't, her dreams would knock him over the edge of everything he'd ever known, and he'd land smack-dab in the middle of her world.

Addie's world was too wide and too deep for Truitt. It was too full of things that glittered and shined. He wasn't ready for that. He wasn't strong enough for it. He guessed that made him a coward. That was why he lied to her, told her she could do anything she dreamed of, all the while hoping she'd one day stop dreaming and decide he was enough. Now, he might never see her or his mama again, and he would never be able to make right all that he'd done wrong.

The first sound Truitt heard was faint. He straightened and flattened both hands and an ear to the door. It was a rattle and a click. Then he glanced down at the floor and inhaled. A faint wave of fresh outside air leaked into the basement. Someone had opened the front door. He slid down, sat on the top step, and closed his eyes as if that would help him listen harder.

Somewhere out in the office, a floorboard creaked. Then another. The second creak was louder than the first. Someone was walking this way, getting closer.

He held his breath. He had to be smart, because he'd only get one chance. A switch flipped on. The sliver of light under the door grew brighter. When the first footstep crossed into the bathroom, he began to bang on the door, and he didn't plan on stopping until it opened.

"Hello," he shouted. "Anybody out there?"

He shouted it like he didn't already know who was on the other side, standing in the bathroom. But he did know. At least he hoped he did, and he hoped it wasn't Wiley again, back with yet another round of supplies. He grabbed the doorknob and shook it.

"Hello, it's Truitt Holt. Whoever you are, can you help me? Can you let me out?"

CHAPTER 29

Huddled on the top stair, Truitt stopped banging and rattling and listened. The light shining under the basement door shifted, the shadow thrown by someone walking up to the door.

"Help me, please," Truitt said, dropping his voice to a whisper. "I think there's something down here with me."

"Truitt?"

Truitt smiled and dropped his head in his hands. It was Billy Pyke, just like he knew it would be. Billy, who couldn't resist a mystery.

Still crouched on the top of the stairwell, Truitt stood and backed down a few steps when the lock on the basement door rattled. Billy was working the key back and forth. Just as Truitt hoped, Wiley had left the rusted key in the lock after he snapped it shut.

The lock popped. Truitt held his breath and listened. No sound of Billy working the key out of the lock. He left it in too. Truitt didn't know if he'd need the key or not, but it was good knowing it was there.

The door eased open. Truitt squinted into the light. Then, just as he'd planned, he glanced over his shoulder as if afraid of something at the bottom of the stairs.

"Lord am I glad to see you, Billy," Truitt said, standing still so as to not startle Billy.

"Mighty surprised to see you, Truitt," Billy said, leaning to look down into the dark basement. "Thought I'd be finding you up in Georgia. The hell you doing here?"

The stack of *Science Fiction Quarterlies* that Truitt had spotted when Wiley was letting him do his business meant one thing: Billy had been into the sheriff's department that morning. And then, Wiley told Truitt as much. Wiley said he'd sent Billy north in search of Truitt. First, Truitt had to hope Billy might run a few errands before leaving town. Gas up the car. Pick up a few groceries. Go home to change out of his uniform since he'd be crossing out of the county.

During all that running around, Truitt had hoped like hell Billy would realize he'd forgotten his magazines back at the office. Billy took them everywhere. Back and forth between home and work, to the café, even to church on Sundays. He certainly never left them lying around for someone else to make off with.

Truitt would have only given one hundred–to-one odds that Billy would come back to the sheriff's office before leaving town, but it was the only bet he could make. And he'd come out on top.

"I'll tell you everything you want to know, Billy," Truitt said, taking another backward glance, "but can I come out first?"

Truitt jumped like he saw something down in the dark.

"What are you seeing down there?" Billy said, stepping aside and motioning for Truitt to come on up. He cradled his stack of *Science Fiction Quarterlies* under one arm.

Truitt slid past Billy, and once in the small bathroom, he braced himself with his hands to his knees. He needed Billy to believe he was unsteady, weak, no threat. For the moment, he was all those things because the sudden fresh air, bright light, and the long odds that had gone his way made him lightheaded.

"You mind getting away from the door?" Truitt said, his head hanging as he waited out the dizzy feeling.

"You got to start talking," Billy said, striking a formal tone and setting aside his magazines. He must have remembered he was a deputy and not sitting across from Truitt in history class. "Tell me what you're doing here?"

"Found myself in some trouble, and I'd come to see Wiley," Truitt said, slowly standing and feeling steady again. "Front door was open. Came back here looking for him, and that basement door, cellar, whatever it is, was open too. Never even noticed it before. I called out, thinking maybe Wiley was down there. And I'm telling you, hand to God, Wiley answered me."

"The hell you mean Wiley answered you?" Billy said. "You telling me he's down in the basement? Right now?"

"I can tell you with absolute certainty he is not," Truitt said, blowing out a mouthful of air as if he still couldn't believe what had happened to him.

He'd thought long and hard about what story to tell Billy. It would have to be something Billy couldn't resist. Truitt settled on one that resembled a story Billy had read aloud from one of his magazines the last time Truitt was at the office, helping to paint this very bathroom. It was about a space alien who mirrored people's voices in order to lure their loved ones to certain death. It was titled "The Mirror."

"I kept calling for Wiley to come on out, even walked down a few steps and kept calling to him," Truitt said, shaking his head like he couldn't believe it himself. "I thought he was hurt maybe. And damn it all, he kept calling back to me."

"How do you know it ain't him?" Billy crept closer to the open door and tipped to look down the dark stairwell.

"Got about four steps down," Truitt said, crossing his arms and backing up against the far wall, "and that door slammed shut and locked on me."

Billy looked down on the keyed lock hanging from the door. "Someone locked you in?"

"Someone or some*thing*," Truitt said, leaving a long stretch of silence so Billy would grasp what Truitt was saying. Something, like something from another world. "I mean, you know more about things like this than me, but the second that door slammed shut, whatever was calling out to me stopped sounding like Wiley."

"What'd it sound like?"

"I don't even want to say. And then I saw eyes. Two red eyes, glowing like fire, staring up at me from out of the dark. Don't even want to think about it."

"Right down there?" Billy said, sliding closer to the dark doorway and straining to see the basement below. "Well, that don't sound human."

Truitt shrugged. "Like I said, you know more than me. Know more than just about anybody, right? Call out like I did. You know, call Wiley's name."

Billy held tight to the threshold, leaned into the stairwell, and called out Wiley's name.

"You hear anything?" Truitt said, clinging to the sink so he wouldn't accidentally make his move too quickly. He had to give Billy space. He had to be patient.

"Don't hear nothing. Don't see nothing either."

"I walked down a few steps, but I don't think you should do that."

Billy glanced back, eyed Truitt, and lifted his chin as if to remind Truitt who the deputy was. "How many you go down?"

"Four, I figure," Truitt said.

"You just wait right there, you hear? Wiley's going to want to talk to you."

"Yeah, sure. Couldn't move if I wanted to."

Truitt's fingers ached from holding on to the sink.

Still clinging to the threshold, Billy inched down the first two steps. When he stretched for the third, he had to let go of the doorframe.

Truitt lunged. He slammed the door, dropped the lock in the eye, and snapped it closed.

He was gone before Billy had a chance to yell his name.

CHAPTER 30

I stood in the kitchen window and watched as Daddy escorted Mama toward the car. Dusk was already closing in. The light had faded from white at the height of the afternoon to yellow as the sun dipped to a dusty purple as it hovered on the horizon.

Unaccustomed to high heels and the red dress Aunt Jean had talked her into wearing, Mama shuffled in the dry dirt and gravel. Aunt Jean and Mr. O'Dell waved goodbye from the porch. After the glamorous dress she'd put on early in the day for Siebert Rix, Aunt Jean had changed into one made of simple tan-and-white cotton. Urban sat on the floor near my feet. He'd found a chip in the kitchen table's laminate top and was picking at it.

Urban could be like that, finding one thing and picking at it or counting it or sorting it until Mama took it away. The doctor told Mama that Urban would outgrow his peculiar habits and not to worry. But she did worry. Earlier in the day, when Aunt Jean and I were helping Mama choose a dress from Aunt Jean's closet, I promised her I'd keep a close eye on Urban while she and Daddy went to dinner and the Harringtons' party.

"You sure Mr. Rix is gone?" Urban said, looking up at me from the floor like he'd done a dozen times already. When he got a worry in his head, he'd chew on it for days.

His blond hair hung across his forehead. He still had a toddler's round face and soft skin. He blinked. I brushed his hair from his eyes.

"He's gone for good. Said so himself."

"Are you sure Mr. Rix is gone?" Urban said, scratching at the laminate and seeming not to have heard anything I said.

"Remember last year?" I asked, hoping to shake him loose of thinking only about Siebert Rix. "The cookies Mama brought us? Think they'll do that again? I sure hope so."

Every year, April unfolded the same way. The orange blossoms came first. Then the Harringtons' party. And the month ended with my birthday followed by Urban's. Mama liked to say April was her favorite month. Some years, after they finished their dinner at the Lakeside Inn, they'd stop home on their way to the Harringtons' house to drop off dessert for Urban and me. They'd call it an early birthday surprise.

"Do you think Mr. Rix is gone for good?" Urban said again, thinking for a moment about cookies from the Lakeside Inn before falling right back into his worries.

Waiting as Daddy opened the door for her, Mama tugged on her neckline and lowered herself into the passenger seat. Daddy made sure her hemline was tucked in before closing the door, and then he leaned as if taking a peek down Mama's dress. Even from inside, I heard her squeal. I smiled but didn't say why when Urban asked what I was smiling about.

Mama and Daddy had been loving each other since Mama was my age. Daddy had traveled by train to California to talk to citrus growers out there about adding zinc and other things to the ground so they could grow more oranges. When he traveled back home, he brought Mama with him.

Watching them out the window, I realized something. If I didn't have gumption enough to stay in New York when Aunt Jean returned to Hockta to marry Leland O'Dell, that scene out in the driveway was going to be my life. If I didn't have gumption enough, I was never going to see a movie set or drink champagne from crystal glasses or see my picture on the cover of a magazine. I'd live in a small house at the end of a dirt road. I'd wear belted cotton dresses, go for a nice supper once a year, and have children. If I didn't have gumption enough, all that was left to figure out . . . who would lend me a hand as I teetered across the drive in high heels? Because it was not going to be Truitt Holt.

Walking around the front of the car, Daddy knocked on the hood and waved to me up in the kitchen window. He looked handsome in his dark jacket and crisp white shirt. That was my last chance to stop him, to run out the back door and ask him and Mama to stay, but I didn't. Instead, I nudged Urban to wave goodbye and watched until the car disappeared.

I let myself believe Aunt Jean was right about Siebert being gone, because believing was easier. It let me pretend we were safe, let me protect my dream of escaping Hockta. But like Urban, I couldn't stop worrying that my believing Aunt Jean was a mistake.

CHAPTER 31

After we finished supper—overdone meatloaf and mashed potatoes—
Mr. O'Dell helped me clear the table. He was a slender man and a good
foot taller than Aunt Jean. He wore dark slacks and a white shirt most
every day and was forever tapping his glasses back into place. Working
at the groves with Daddy, Mr. O'Dell took care of all the accounting.
Twice already, Aunt Jean had left him without even a goodbye to go
back to her life in Hollywood, and each time she returned, he'd been
waiting as if she'd never left.

Mr. O'Dell had been all smiles as he ate every bit of the dry meatloaf, surely because he was happy about his engagement to Aunt Jean.
He'd had to tamp down his smiles until Mama and Daddy left, because
they still didn't know. Seeing as how Aunt Jean must have asked him not
to let on, I still worried that, somehow, someway, she might be gearing
up to break his heart again.

When the kitchen was clean and the leftovers put away, I sat Urban
in the landing at the bottom of the stairs. I pulled up the grate in the
floor and leaned it against the wall. Urban scooted close to the hole I'd
uncovered, tipped his head toward me, and gave me a stare. I turned my
back, pretending I didn't already know what was hidden down there.
When I still didn't hear him reach into the hole, I tipped my face in
his direction to prove my eyes were closed. Then I heard a rattle as he
pulled out his box and began to stack and count his penny collection.
He'd sit there all night, counting and stacking.

Aunt Jean and Mr. O'Dell sat in the living room, cuddled up on the couch as they watched the television. With their heads pressed together, they gazed at the ring Aunt Jean had slipped on after Mama and Daddy left. The sun having nearly set, the flicker of the television danced over them like candlelight. Aunt Jean nuzzled into Mr. O'Dell's side, her head on his shoulder, looking as if she never wanted to leave that spot. Every place was a stage for Aunt Jean. There was no telling which was true . . . was she gearing up to break Mr. O'Dell's heart by leaving Hockta? Or was she gearing up to break mine by staying?

I wandered into the kitchen, where I could keep an eye on Urban. The evening breeze swept through the back door. Outside, the last bit of daylight was melting away. The cicadas whined. The brittle pine needles rustled. I sat in the chair nearest the telephone, like I had done all day. I had been hoping Truitt would call and somehow unwind every nasty thing he'd said to me, but he hadn't. I had heard not one thing from him since he left me in the storeroom at Wilson's Market.

Closing my eyes, I tipped my face toward the open window. Even at night, in my own home, the sugary orange blossoms clogged my throat. I stood to close the window, to slam it as hard as I could because I was stumbling and staggering and had lost so much, when the sound of tires rolling down our gravel drive rose out of the darkness.

From the landing at the bottom of the stairs, I heard Aunt Jean tell Urban to put away his pennies. He whined that he didn't want to, then I heard a clatter as Aunt Jean swept them all into their box and put the grate back in place. Urban was still squealing for her to stop when Mr. O'Dell appeared. He walked past the kitchen and directly to the back door, closed it, and locked it, but not before a car door slammed closed.

Seeing me in the kitchen, standing at the open window, he motioned for me to get Urban and take him upstairs. He pressed a finger to his lips when I started to speak. I wanted to ask what was happening, but I already knew.

"Go on, now," Mr. O'Dell whispered, smiling as he crinkled his nose and tapped his glasses into place. "Take Urban upstairs. Stay put until we call you back down."

Footsteps on the dry gravel grew louder and stopped outside the kitchen window. Slipping past Mr. O'Dell, I took Urban's hand and quieted him because he was still fussing about his pennies. I reached for Aunt Jean's hand too.

"Come with us," I whispered.

I jumped when the back door rattled in its frame. Three sharp knocks.

Aunt Jean smiled and dipped her chin into one shoulder like she so often did in the movies.

"See that Urban stays quiet. We'll let you know when Mr. Rix is gone."

"Tell him you're not marrying Mr. O'Dell," I said, the words popping out before I could think them through. "Tell him the newspaper was wrong. Tell him, Aunt Jean. It'll make him go away."

I'd known Siebert would be back when he drove away from our house this morning, saying his goodbyes and claiming he was off to California. He'd proven himself a predictable man in the short few months he'd been in Hockta. Knowing he'd come back for Aunt Jean was low-hanging fruit, but still I tried to wish it away.

Three more knocks rattled the back door.

"Jean." It was Siebert Rix. "Come on, darlin'. I know you're in there."

Mr. O'Dell motioned again for me to get going. I gave Aunt Jean one last look, pleading with her to come with us. When she turned a shoulder to me, I led Urban up the stairs. Near the top, I looked back in time to see Aunt Jean slip off her ring and tuck it in her pocket. Mr. O'Dell straightened his glasses, made sure his shirt was neatly tucked, sent Aunt Jean into the living room, and turned to face the back door.

"You go on, now, Siebert," Mr. O'Dell shouted.

Upstairs, even though a few bedroom doors were open, the beginnings of moonlight spilling through the thresholds, the hallway was still dark. Holding Urban's hand, I led him to Mama's and Daddy's room. The closer we got, the slower his feet went, like he already knew I was going to leave him there alone.

At the door, we both jumped when we heard more rattling, Siebert banging on the back door again. I squatted and held my hands over Urban's ears. I pressed our faces together, nose to nose. He held his lips in a hard line, trapping inside the sobs that made his tiny body quiver. There was more banging, and Mr. O'Dell continued to shout at Siebert to stop and go home.

The knocks were coming in threes, louder each time. After each round, I relaxed for one breath before bracing for the next. And then they stopped.

Still holding my hands over Urban's ears, I looked down the hallway to the funnel of light shining up the stairwell. Mr. O'Dell had stopped shouting too. Then there was a quiet tapping, the sound of Aunt Jean's high-heeled shoes as she crept from the front room toward the back door. I stood and wrapped my arms around Urban. His head was hot, and his hair stuck to the sides of his face. I stroked his head, whispering to him.

"It's all over," I said. "He's gone. That wasn't so bad, was it?"

I turned to take Urban to his own room. The house was quiet, except for the whine of the cicadas. All the windows were open to let in the cool night air. It made for better sleeping.

I stopped when I realized what I hadn't heard. My body tensed, bracing again because this wasn't over.

There had been no sound of a car door. No sound of an engine starting up. No tires crunching over gravel as Siebert Rix drove away.

Leading Urban into Mama's and Daddy's room, I switched off the one lamp that had been left on and sat Urban on the side of the bed.

"I'll be right back," I whispered, moving toward the door before he had time to grab on to me or cry out. "Count to twenty. I'll be back before you're done."

Siebert had shown up at the house plenty of times in the last few months, and when he'd finally leave, it was never easy. He always had one more thing to say, one more question to ask, one more point to make. He'd never listen the first time Daddy asked him to go, and he'd smile through Mama telling him he wasn't welcome.

This time, the house had fallen quiet, but I didn't believe Siebert was gone. I knew he had one more thing to say.

CHAPTER 32

Truitt had no idea where he was and no way of knowing how long he'd been running and walking. The mosquitoes were gnawing the backs of his legs, he hadn't eaten for hours, and he wished he'd brought the jug of water Wiley left on the basement stairs.

Every so often, he saw a sign for Tampa. That was enough to let him know he was at least headed the right way. Keeping to the cover of the pines had slowed him down. Every time a car neared, he ran off the road into the trees but stayed close enough to check the plates and the drivers inside. He'd seen some Tampa plates, but so far, he'd seen no one he thought he should flag down. He also saw no sign of Wiley's patrol car or his truck. Eventually, Wiley would find Billy locked in the basement and come looking for Truitt.

With every car that passed, Truitt had been hoping to see a big black sedan and men wearing dark suits and dark hats like he'd seen last night. His plan was to flag them down, tell them who he was, and insist they take him straight to Santo Giordano himself. But so far, he hadn't seen that car. He'd seen men wearing short-sleeved shirts, families headed to the beach, farmers driving pickup trucks. He'd shied away from all those cars, but he couldn't shy away anymore. The sun had set some time ago, and though he didn't know exactly where he was, he knew he was a long way from Ybor City. He knew he didn't have much more time.

Wiley said the men at Truitt's house had given Wiley until midnight to bring Truitt back, but Truitt didn't have until midnight. It would take him some time to figure out where to go in Ybor City and then more time to talk his way into a deal that might save his mama. He couldn't wait for the right car any longer.

Finding a spot in the trees where he could get a breeze to cool off, Truitt smoothed his hair and tucked in his shirt. It was dark enough for people to switch on headlights, and that would make them less likely to stop. If he looked presentable enough, maybe he wouldn't have to point a gun to get someone to pull over for him.

Standing still for the first time since he'd left the sheriff's office, Truitt felt the ache in his knees. His mouth and throat were dry. And the skin on his nose, cheeks, and ears was crisp from too much sun. He was exhausted, and he thought about just leaving. Wiley had spent all day convincing folks Truitt had already run off, so what was the harm? It would mean never seeing his mama again, but she'd live. That's all that mattered. And she'd have Wiley to look after her. It'd also mean never seeing Addie again, but that was already going to happen because Addie was leaving Hockta with her aunt.

Maybe that was the smart thing to do. Start over. Take a new name. Live in a new place. But what if Wiley was wrong about the levelheaded man holding Truitt's mama? He might kill her just because, and Truitt would be the coward who ran away and let it happen. He'd live, and his mama would be dead. That was the very worst of outcomes. Truitt might fail, but he wasn't going to fail by being a coward.

When the ground at Truitt's feet lit up, Truitt ran into the road, raised the handgun he'd taken from the sheriff's office, and pointed it into the oncoming headlights.

CHAPTER 33

The longer the silence echoed through the house, the more certain I was Siebert Rix wasn't really gone.

Outside Mama's and Daddy's bedroom, I glanced up and down the hallway. At one end, the light from downstairs glowed in the stairwell. At the other end, the bathroom door stood closed. On tiptoes, I ran for the bathroom. I opened the door, crossed the small room, my bare feet padding across the cool penny tile, climbed onto the commode, and looked out the window onto the front yard below.

I scanned the entire property, my eyes darting from one side of the house to the other. A figure emerged from a clump of overgrown fire bush and moved toward the porch. As it neared the house and I got a closer look, the figure turned into Siebert. Before I could run back into the hallway to call out a warning, he had taken the stairs two at a time, disappeared under the covered porch, and begun pounding on the front door.

"Marilyn, darlin'," Siebert shouted. "Open the door. I ain't got much time. Come on and let me in. Can see the both of you in there."

The worst thing about hearing Siebert banging on the door was remembering what happened the night he yanked Aunt Jean's arm from its socket. It was bad, seeing him drag Aunt Jean toward his car. It was bad hearing her cry for him to stop and hearing Mama yell at Siebert to take his hands off Aunt Jean. But the scariest thing had been how quickly Daddy turned into someone none of us had ever seen.

Everything that made him my father fell away, and something deep seated and raw was left behind. Even Mama had stumbled backward when Daddy lunged for Siebert. She stood frozen, not seeming to recognize Daddy as he drove a fist into Siebert's face again and again.

Other than the grunts as air left Siebert's lungs, it was a silent affair. As if we were in church, we were all afraid to interrupt the hush. None of us could move, not even Mama, but then, something woke her. She screamed, and that woke the rest of us. I grabbed Urban and Aunt Jean, and we ran for the house. And Mama grabbed hold of Daddy's shoulders and screamed for him to stop.

"Stop," she said. "You're going to kill him. My God, Harden, you're going to kill him. You promised me. Never again."

Nothing would have stopped Daddy that night except for Mama. Like she woke the rest of us with her voice, she woke Daddy too. Still straddling Siebert, Daddy slowly lowered his fist, his chest pumping, his face dripping sweat. Through the kitchen window, clinging to Urban and covering his ears, I saw Daddy come back. His shoulders softened, his fists unclenched, and he slowly stood.

If not for Mama, Daddy would have killed Siebert that night. That's when I had truly understood just how bad Siebert Rix was. It also set off something I'd silently chewed on ever since. Mama had said . . . you promised me. Never again.

It sounded like Mama was saying Daddy had killed someone before and had promised never to do it again.

Pushing away from the bathroom window, I ran back to Urban. He'd reached twenty already. I could tell because he was repeating it—twenty, twenty, twenty—when I grabbed him from the side of the mattress and led him to the closet. His little head bobbed as he continued to repeat it. Twenty. Twenty. Twenty.

"I'm here, right?" I said. "I didn't lie. I came back."

I pushed aside Mama's dresses and motioned for Urban to climb in. He didn't move. I took his two small shoulders to guide him, but he looked up at me, a deep frown on his face, his chin quivering.

"It'll be fine," I said. "You crawl back in there and wait until I come for you. You know Daddy told Mr. Rix he's not allowed here. He'll go. Mr. O'Dell will make him go."

Urban stood still, not moving and no longer chanting twenty.

"Call them," he whispered, smiling up at me. Then he pointed at the telephone on Daddy's nightstand. "Call Mama and Daddy. Make them come home."

The orange grove had installed the second line the year before because Daddy often got called in the middle of the night, sometimes because a machine broke down, sometimes because the trees needed watering to save the oranges from freezing. We were the only house in all of Hockta to have two telephones.

"Yes, I will," I said, trying to speak calmly and evenly because that's what Mama did when she was trying to calm Urban. I lifted him and set him inside the closet. "But I have to call from downstairs. Mama left the numbers in the kitchen. You understand that, right? We have to know the number now. We have to know what to dial."

Urban crawled back in the closet, squatted, and wrapped his arms around his legs.

"Count the holes in Daddy's shoes," I said. "Where the shoestrings go. Count how many in all."

I slipped back into the hallway. The pounding was steady, no longer coming in sets of three.

"Stop that banging, Siebert." It was Aunt Jean, screaming at Siebert to stop.

It had to be Aunt Jean, though I didn't recognize the voice—not from the movies, not from the interviews I'd watched her give on the television, not from anywhere.

I ran to the top of the stairs, tucked under my skirt, and dropped onto the top step. My heart fluttered, and my breath was getting away from me. I clung to the stair beneath me and slid to the one below.

"Don't break that door." It was Mr. O'Dell. His voice was different too. It cracked, was pitched higher. "Don't you do it."

I continued to slide down the stairs one at a time. Halfway down, the wall opened up to the living room. I could see Aunt Jean's back. She stood behind Mr. O'Dell, clinging to his shoulders. I cringed and closed my eyes with each bang at the front door. Siebert had to be kicking it. Over and over.

"Siebert," Aunt Jean screamed.

The doorframe splintered, and the front door flew open. I scrambled backward, hugging my knees tight.

With my hands pressed over my mouth, I glanced toward the top of the stairs to make sure Urban hadn't followed me. When I looked down below again, Siebert stood in the middle of the living room.

CHAPTER 34

Siebert was glad he was sober when he took his first step inside the Buckleys' house. If he'd had a drink, kicking down their door wouldn't have felt so good. He was smart, not wasting money on a bottle of scotch.

Sitting in his hot car all day, windows rolled up to keep out the mosquitoes, he'd wished more than once he'd bought himself a bottle. Every time a car passed on the road above, he'd been afraid it might be the black sedan he'd seen parked outside the train station, and he wished for a bottle. And when he got a sniff of what had to be Donna Lee's body baking under the Florida sun, he'd damn sure wished for a bottle. He didn't think the smell of something could soak in so deep so quick. The smell of sweet rot.

But that smell was wiped clean the moment he stepped inside the Buckley house. It smelled of supper—meatloaf, buttery potatoes, fresh baked rolls. His stomach rumbled, and he thought he'd ask for a plate while Marilyn got her bags together. He'd done good, staying out of sight, sticking to his plan. Now, he could relax, fill his stomach, maybe even have that drink he'd been wanting since dawn. If those men couldn't find him in the light of day, they sure weren't going to find him now, out here in the middle of this grove. And once he had Marilyn on his arm, he'd have a built-in distraction. He'd be able to slip onto the train unseen. Not even men tasked with hunting him down would notice him when Marilyn Monroe was on duty.

Across the room, Leland O'Dell stared at Siebert, trying his best not to let on he was afraid. The man looked scrawny, tender even, under the soft lighting. Siebert had seen Leland plenty of times before, at church mostly. For a time, Siebert went almost every Sunday, but it didn't do one thing to make Harden and Inez soften to him. They were always right alongside Leland, though, patting him on the back, shaking his hand, inviting him to Sunday lunch.

"I guess I should say congratulations to the happy couple," Siebert said, buttoning his suit coat.

Before getting out of the car and knocking on the Buckleys' door, he'd put on his coat, and he was glad of it. It was a nice touch, classy, and would remind Marilyn of the difference between Siebert and Leland O'Dell. Siebert took up space, had a presence about him. People noticed when he entered a room, so long as Marilyn wasn't at his side. No one noticed Leland O'Dell.

Wrapping an arm around Marilyn, Leland lifted his chin and shoulders. He was trying to make himself a match for Siebert. Marilyn tugged at her cotton dress as if she were uncomfortable wearing it. It was too simple, too ordinary. It was the type of dress Inez would wear.

Or maybe she was uncomfortable with Leland O'Dell's touch.

"We don't need the well-wishes of the likes of you," Leland said.

Instead of leaning into Leland, Marilyn shrugged away. Siebert stifled a laugh. Good Lord, she was easy to read. Easy like she was written for a first grader.

"Leland's right," Marilyn said, sweeping through the room, picking up framed pictures Siebert had knocked to the floor when he broke in. "Just go on and leave us."

"Harden and Inez here?" Siebert asked, though he knew they weren't. He'd have been dealing with Harden if they were. But Inez and Harden were well on their way to a party tonight because they believed Siebert was well on his way to California.

"I think you know they aren't," Marilyn said, squatting to pick up shards of glass from another broken frame. "Good heavens, Siebert. You've broken some of these. Inez'll be just heartbroken."

"You'll have to see to fixing that door," Leland said, helping Marilyn to her feet.

"Supposing you better think twice, talking to me like that," Siebert said, wrenching Marilyn away from Leland.

Marilyn yanked free of Siebert, but instead of spiraling into one of her episodes, crying and wailing and carrying on, she smiled. Marilyn's many personalities were like a stack of playing cards. She could turn over whichever she wanted with a flick of her wrist. She turned her smile on poor Leland, who didn't have near enough experience to know what was coming. But Siebert did. This was the sincere version of Marilyn.

"I think I know why Siebert is here," she said, pressing Leland's hand to her lips.

Amused, Siebert leaned against the broken threshold and draped one foot over the other. He was never bored by what came out of Marilyn's mouth.

"Yes, I saw the newspaper," Siebert said, knowing Marilyn thought jealousy had brought him here.

"Jean didn't intend for you to find out that way, Siebert," Leland said, cupping Marilyn's face. "She's far too kind. Too thoughtful."

"That's true," Marilyn said, swinging around to Siebert. "It was that Wilma Danielson . . . she's the trouble."

"Was she pestering you for some news worth printing?" Siebert said, knowing exactly what happened. Wilma Danielson was smart like Siebert and knew exactly how to work Marilyn. "Did she ask if it was hard for you, living out here in the middle of nowhere? Did you feel you'd lost yourself?"

Marilyn drifted toward Siebert, her hand falling from Leland's.

"She said if I had nothing to share," Marilyn said, "then maybe I was just like everyone else. Maybe I was ordinary."

Siebert took Marilyn's hand and cupped it in both of his.

"I understand, darlin'," Siebert said. "I know you didn't mean no harm."

"Of course, she meant no harm," Leland said, staring at Siebert's and Marilyn's hands, their fingers tangled together. "But she means to marry me."

"You don't really believe that, do you, Leland?" Siebert asked, letting Marilyn's hands float back to her sides and motioning for her to head upstairs. "You knew she'd never stay. You couldn't possibly have thought you were enough."

"Well, that ain't true," Leland said. "We have plans. Tell him, Jeannie. A house, children, a nice garden maybe."

Marilyn flipped another card, turning over another version of herself. She clasped her hands, lowered her head. She was a little girl, shuffling her feet, afraid to confess the truth.

"Please don't call me Jeannie," she said in little more than a whisper.

If Siebert had been a betting man, he'd have pulled his chips from the table, taken his money, and gone home, because he'd just won the jackpot. That comment was her breaking ranks with Leland O'Dell and coming over to Siebert's side. She was his—always had been, always would be.

"Marilyn, darlin'," Siebert said, putting himself between Marilyn and Leland. The man was no longer an issue, though he didn't realize that yet. "I'm sorry about the door. I got some trouble brewing, through no fault of my own, and I have to leave town. Should have been honest from the get-go. If not for this trouble, I'd have waited for you until the end of time. I'm sorry to put this on you, but I need to leave, tonight, now, and I need your help to do it."

"She's already told you no," Leland said, trying to shoulder his way back to Marilyn. "Come with me, Jean. Come on and let's call Harden. You know Siebert isn't allowed in the house."

"I can't," Marilyn whispered.

Siebert watched her eyes, trying to decipher who that comment was meant for—him or Leland. He buckled his hands into fists. His temper started to simmer, working its way into his chest and arms and hands.

"Can't what, darlin'?" Siebert said, dipping his head and looking out from under his brow.

Marilyn lifted her eyes, and they slid to Leland. Siebert bit his bottom lip to keep from smiling and let his fingers soften.

"I can't stay here, Leland," she said. "I'm sorry. I thought I could. But I can't breathe here. If you knew me at all, you'd know that. I can't breathe thinking about living Inez's life, day in and day out. I can't care for children. I don't want children. They want and they need something every minute of the day. I hate it here. Sometimes, I really hate it."

"I wouldn't expect you to understand," Siebert said to Leland, thinking he might leave the man with some dignity. "Marilyn was hoping an engagement to you would lock her down. She thought putting it in the newspaper would cement it, silence her cravings to move on. Or maybe she put it there for me to see, a call for help, so I'd come and save her. Maybe she was just wanting some attention. Or maybe, a little of all three. Much as she surely hoped a ring would be enough to stifle her need to fly, it ain't enough. It ain't nearly enough. She needs to fly. Ain't even a choice. And she needs me to do it."

"Jeannie . . . Jean," Leland said. He glanced around the room as if looking for a weapon or maybe a way out. "I'll call Harden all on my own. Call him right now."

"Suit yourself," Siebert said. "Just trying to make the point that it ain't about you. It's who she is, and that ain't never going to change. Now, you go on and pack, darlin'. I'll grab your purse and pull the car up to the back door."

Siebert escorted Marilyn toward the stairs with a hand to her lower back. It fit there so perfectly. Once they were on the train, she'd be Marilyn again. She'd scribble autographs and smile for the cameras. That's when she came alive. With every flash of a bulb, she soared higher. Everything would be fine, once they were on the train. The men from Tampa would fall farther behind with every mile they traveled north.

Siebert would be safe, and his future secured.

As Marilyn drifted up the first stair, Siebert grabbed her purse from the newel post and walked toward the back door. Once he knew how much money she had, he could put together a budget and start planning.

"She don't need you carrying her bags no more," Leland shouted.

Siebert stopped and slowly turned.

"You heard me," Leland said. His sunken chest lifted. He buckled his dainty hands. "That's all you're fit for. Carrying her purse."

Siebert was on him in three steps. Leland was no Harden Buckley, that's for sure. Siebert wrapped the man's neck up with one hand. He'd heard it all before. That Siebert Rix sure has a sweet deal. Wonder why she stays with him? And how many people had whispered in Marilyn's ear . . . you really should have a professional at your side. Your career will suffer. He isn't good for you. He isn't good for your image. He really should be ashamed, riding the coattails of a woman.

Leland's eyes were stretched wide, and his mouth hung open as he gasped, trying to breathe though Siebert was crushing his windpipe. Marilyn was screaming and beating on Siebert's back, but he only squeezed tighter. Nothing had ever felt so good as to watch those wide-open eyes slowly close.

When Siebert finally opened his hand, Leland crumpled to the floor. Dead.

Siebert stepped back, and with a forearm, he forced Marilyn off. She knelt at Leland's side, staring at him like she wasn't sure what to make of his lifeless body. Siebert reached down and stroked the top of her head. Marilyn looked up at him, her perfect lips parted.

"Are the kids in the house?" Siebert asked.

In the movies, the killer always took care of witnesses. But Christ, two kids. Siebert wasn't sure about that. He'd find out what they'd seen and scare them into keeping quiet about it. That should be easy enough.

"Ain't asking again," Siebert said, but he already knew the answer.

"No," Marilyn whispered. "They're not home."

But that wasn't true.

Marilyn could lie about most anything. She was convincing. But Siebert always knew the truth. This time, he saw the truth in the blank expression that fell over her face. It was fear. Usually, when that emptiness filled her eyes, she was suffering the fear of being found out. The fear everyone would think she wasn't a good actress, that she couldn't remember her lines, that she wasn't really Marilyn Monroe. She was just plain old Norma Jean.

This time she was afraid for Addie and Urban.

"I'll ask you one more time," Siebert said, towering over her. "The kids. Where are they?"

CHAPTER 35

Starting about noon, Wiley had known for certain he was being followed. The fellow wasn't even sly about it. He damn near rear-ended Wiley at a stop sign, and after the screech of his brakes faded, the man stuck a hand out his window and hollered sorry.

For hours, Wiley had driven from one end of Lake County to the other, the fellow in a black Lincoln trailing him. They'd been to Umatilla, Groveland, and Mount Dora and every little town between. Four times, they'd stopped for gas. Wiley crawled under back porches, peeked in barns and garages, climbed up under bridges, all to put on that he was looking anywhere and everywhere for Truitt. The long game was something most people didn't understand. It was also Wiley's only choice.

Every time he'd rolled through Hockta, he stopped at the gas station across the street from the sheriff's department and checked the building. He didn't know what he thought he might see, but the blinds in the windows were still, the parking lot was empty, and the CLOSED sign still hung in the front door. He'd left Truitt enough food and water to get him through dinner and a bucket to handle the rest. That wasn't pleasant, and Truitt surely wasn't happy about it, but Wiley would count it part of the lesson he hoped Truitt would learn from all this.

When 7:15 p.m. rolled around, Wiley decided he'd stop in at the office. It would be his first time since this morning. He'd stay only long enough to let Truitt use the bathroom and check how much food and water he had left.

"Just stopping in to make sure it's all locked up," Wiley had hollered to the fellow parked out on the street, one hand hanging out the window as he watched Wiley walk toward the department's front door. "Then we'll head out to the house. Got one of my men calling in a report to me out there."

The fellow flipped his headlights to let Wiley know he'd heard.

Nearing the main entrance, Wiley could see down the side of the building to the alley behind. A car was parked back there, and right away, he knew Truitt was gone.

He tried to be quiet when he opened the door and walked toward the back of the office, and he didn't turn on any lights, but Billy heard him. The pounding and hollering started right away. In the bathroom, Wiley shut the door, hoping to muffle the noise so the man outside didn't hear and come looking into what was going on.

"It's Wiley," Wiley said, pressing against the basement door. "For the love of God, Billy, stop all that ruckus."

"Let me out, Wiley," Billy said, sounding like he'd lost his voice from hollering so much for so long. "Been in here all damn day."

Wiley stared down on the rusted lock, even put a hand on it to twist the key and pop it open, but he decided against it.

"I can't let you out, Billy. And I need you to not say another word. Don't do no more pounding or carrying on. You're going to have to trust me."

"Trust you, like hell," Billy said. "You know how dark it is down here?"

"You still got food, water?" Wiley said, and once Billy had said he did, Wiley started doling out instructions again, not giving Billy a chance to complain. "I don't have time to talk you through it now, but you know me. You trust me. I will be back, and I will be back before sunrise. I'll let you out, even feed you a hot breakfast. But for now, not another peep."

And then, knowing this could be the adventure Billy had always wanted, Wiley added, "Lives depend on you staying quiet, Billy. I depend on it."

Back outside, Wiley gave a wave to the fellow waiting in his car. He couldn't help that he was sweating. Once in his own car, he mopped his face with a shirtsleeve. Truitt had been gone for hours. That's what Billy said once he calmed down. Wiley would have heard by now if Truitt had gone home to try to trade himself for his mama. The fellow following Wiley used the pay phone every time they stopped for gas, surely calling Ilene's house, checking in, giving and getting updates.

So, where the hell was Truitt, and what was he doing?

By the time Wiley got to Ilene's and Truitt's place, it was still a few minutes to eight o'clock. Ilene was banging about in the kitchen, frying chops for the five men who'd been sitting around her house all day. Ilene was wearing the same clothes she'd been wearing when he left her. Her hair was neatly done. She had no bruising on her face. No fat lip. He also noticed the scent of pine. She'd been cleaning. Surrounded by these men, waiting for her son to come home, she'd been scrubbing floors.

Wiley had only a few minutes to decide what to say to these men when the phone didn't ring at eight o'clock like it was supposed to. There was going to be no phone call from Billy, because Billy was locked in the basement. Maybe Wiley'd made a mistake. He could have let Billy out, set him down at his desk, explained what was happening, and had him make the same call. He could have pretended to be calling from North Florida. That's what Wiley should have put in motion. He wasn't thinking clearly, hadn't been since that man told Wiley he had to leave Ilene behind when he went to find Truitt.

Damn, Wiley had made a bad mistake.

CHAPTER 36

Dead came with a certain kind of silence. It was heavier, deeper, cloudier than any I had ever heard. That kind of silence throbbed like a heartbeat, and it knew I was on the stairs. I felt it coming for me in the pit of my stomach, in the shiver that rolled up my back, and in the tingle at the base of my skull. It crept across the living room, snaked under the banister, and rolled up the stairs where I was already scrambling toward the hallway above.

Mr. O'Dell was dead, and Siebert Rix killed him.

Crouched against a wall where no one could see me from downstairs, I drew my knees in tight, buried my face, and made myself as small as I could.

I'd been making my way down the stairs, trying to get to the kitchen so I could call Daddy. Mama left the phone numbers on the table. One was for the Lakeside Inn, where Mama and Daddy always went to dinner before the party. The other, for the Harringtons' house. I could have made it all the way. I could have called for help, but I stopped partway down when I heard Aunt Jean say she didn't want to stay here anymore. She said she couldn't breathe, that she never wanted children of her own, that she hated it here in our home.

Being near Aunt Jean made people happy. They saw a beautiful woman wearing beautiful clothes, walking on the arms of handsome men, and they bent to her happiness like flowers to the sun. She was special in that way. Powerful. Her hatred was equally potent, and it stunned me.

She said she didn't need us, couldn't breathe when she was near us. Just like Truitt unearthed all his lies, Aunt Jean had done the same. She never believed in me. Never loved any of us. She used us to make herself well again. Now she was well and would use Siebert to help her escape.

I had stopped on the stairs and didn't call Daddy, because Aunt Jean was going to pack a bag, and she and Siebert were going to leave together. We would have been safe, but then Mr. O'Dell shouted out. Now he was dead.

"Siebert." It was Aunt Jean, sounding nothing like I'd ever heard. "Stop. They're not here. The kids aren't here."

She sounded like her voice was trapped under something. She was screaming, and yet barely a sound came out.

Something tipped over. The coffee table, perhaps. Glass shattered. Aunt Jean cried out, and someone's footsteps hit the bottom stair. I dove across the hall and into my room. Closing the door and pressing against it, I knew I'd made a mistake. I should have gone to Mama's and Daddy's room. Urban was in there, hiding in the closet.

Knowing I couldn't leave him there alone, I reached to open the door so I could slip into the hallway and join him, but a footstep landed just outside my room. I yanked my hand from the knob and slowly lowered to the ground. Digging my feet into the floor, I pressed my back against the door. I wouldn't stop Siebert, but I might slow him down.

Across my room, moonlight spilled through a window. As the footsteps continued down the hall, I scrambled across my room on hands and knees and looked down on the road leading to our house. A field of orange trees grew between our house and the main road. Headlights sparkled in the distance, but they were coming from the wrong direction. They couldn't be from Mama's and Daddy's car. The first blush of relief quickly faded.

Outside my bedroom door, the pine floors creaked under Siebert, his footsteps heavy and slow. Aunt Jean scrambled after him, her footsteps light and quick as she begged him to stop.

At the window, I stood to get a better view and checked the clock on my nightstand. Mama and Daddy would have left dinner by now and been on their way to the party, if they weren't already there. Sometimes, after leaving the restaurant, they stopped by the house to drop off dessert before going on with their night. One year, it was bread pudding with a crispy meringue. Another, a triple-layer yellow cake with chocolate frosting. Last year, cookies. Mama didn't say if they'd be stopping tonight or not. Some years they brought home leftover hors d'oeuvres from the party instead.

"Let's just leave," Aunt Jean said from down the hallway, her voice still struggling to find its way. "You want me to go with you, I'll go. Right now. Wherever you want."

I held my breath, watching the road where Mama's and Daddy's headlights would appear. Beyond the tops of the orange trees, the dirt road was dark.

Siebert had reached the end of the hall. A door flew open. It was Aunt Jean's.

"Addie Anne," he said in a singsongy voice. "You in here, darlin'? How about you, Urban? It's your Uncle Siebert."

Another door flew open. The bathroom at the end of the hall.

"This is bad, Siebert." It was Aunt Jean again. She was crying now. Pleading with him. "This is real bad. You should go. I won't tell what happened to Leland. I'll say it was a stranger. A man who broke in."

Still looking out the windows, I lifted onto my tiptoes and squinted, straining to see farther down the dark road. Whether or not Mama and Daddy stopped to drop off dessert, they had to pass by our house on the way to the party.

Another door flew open. Urban's. Mama's and Daddy's room was next. Siebert would find Urban there, crouched in the closet, probably thinking I lied to him every time I said Siebert was gone.

My room came last in the line of rooms.

I pushed off the window, lunged for the light switch just inside my door, and began flipping it on and off. I closed my eyes, held my breath, and flipped as fast as I could, hoping Mama and Daddy would drive by and see it. Hoping anyone would drive by and see it. The whole town knew the Buckleys lived smack-dab in the middle of a grove.

In the room next to mine, Mama's and Daddy's door flew open and bounced against the wall.

"Siebert, stop." This time, Aunt Jean's voice broke free, and she screamed.

Heavy footsteps rattled the house as Siebert crossed into Mama's and Daddy's room. And then Urban, with his tiny, sweet voice, screamed.

I clamped a hand over my mouth, my shoulders twitching with the sobs I was muffling. I pinched my eyes harder and kept flipping the switch. My forearm burned. My wrist ached. The flashing light through my closed lids made me dizzy.

The footsteps were back in the hallway. Aunt Jean was cooing to Urban, telling him he'd be all right, everything would be all right. Hearing her voice, so sweet and soft, made me cry harder. I kept flipping the switch and began chanting, please, please, please.

When something clamped down on my wrist, I stopped chanting and opened my eyes.

Siebert stood just inside my door, his hand on my arm, smiling down at me. But it wasn't a real smile. It was flat, painted on. It was one that made my stomach swirl, and I thought I might vomit. His dark hair was damp on the ends and clung to his forehead. His suit coat hung open. Underneath, his white shirt was soggy and hugged his large stomach. His chest rose and fell as he stared at me, waiting for me to say something or do something.

"How about we all go downstairs?" he said. He pulled my hand from the light switch and made a looping gesture, inviting me to go first.

Aunt Jean swept into the room, the air she stirred fluffing her full skirt as if she were dancing. She led Urban by his wrist, and with her free hand, she grabbed hold of me. Urban trailed her, his head sagging, his body shivering as he sobbed. The soft waves Aunt Jean had so carefully combed into her hair before Mr. O'Dell arrived had fallen, and the sash she'd carefully tied at her waist had come loose. Dark smudges framed her eyes, and her red lipstick was smeared. She looked like no version of Aunt Jean I'd ever seen, not in real life or on a movie screen.

"The kids didn't see anything," Aunt Jean said, backing into my room and drawing me and Urban with her. She wrapped an arm around us and pinned us to her sides.

Siebert said nothing as he took a few steps into my room. He was distracted, looking at something on my nightstand. I followed his eyes, wanting to stop him from seeing any of the things that mattered most to me. I didn't want him in my house or near Urban and Aunt Jean. Whatever he was looking at, I wanted to grab it and hide it.

"I thought that kid looked familiar," Siebert said.

He was looking at a picture of Truitt. I hid it in a drawer every morning so Daddy and Mama wouldn't see it, and every night, I pulled it out and set it on my nightstand. Siebert crossed the room, sending Aunt Jean scurrying out of the way and drawing me and Urban with her.

Siebert was no longer between us and the door.

At my nightstand, Siebert picked up the picture and sat on the edge of my bed. Running his fingers through his hair, clearing it from his eyes, Siebert studied the photograph. It was a picture of Truitt sitting on the steps of his back porch, cranking an ice cream maker. He had been smiling at someone off camera. It was my favorite picture of him. By the time Siebert looked up again, I had taken a few more steps toward the door, bringing Aunt Jean and Urban along with me.

"Where is he?" Siebert said.

The three of us stopped. Urban buried his face in Aunt Jean's skirt.

"You," he said, looking at me. "I'm talking to you. This is your boyfriend, yes?"

I nodded but said nothing. I didn't tell him Truitt used to be but wasn't anymore. A new fear had begun knotting itself up in my throat, making it difficult to swallow. Difficult to breathe. I didn't know why or how, but Truitt was in some kind of trouble, and it was bad.

"Then I'll ask again." Siebert stood and walked toward me. "Where the hell is he?"

He was so much bigger than I remembered. His arms strained the sleeves of his coat. His neck spilled over the collar of his shirt. And as he got close, he bent down to look me straight on, his hot breath making my lashes flutter.

"I don't know," I said, turning away so I didn't inhale what he exhaled. I was confused by the question when really, it was a simple one. "At home, I guess. It's Saturday. Bolita night. He'll be at home to do his drawing."

But somehow, I knew that wasn't true. He hadn't delivered the paper this morning. I thought he didn't because he never wanted to see me again, but that wasn't the reason. Something had happened. Something bad.

"He's not at home," Siebert said. "Try again."

I shook my head and looked to Aunt Jean.

"She answered you," Aunt Jean said, lifting tall and tugging her dress so it fell properly. "She doesn't know where he is."

"He's run off," Siebert said, and ignoring Aunt Jean, he touched a finger to my chin and turned my face so I had to look at him. "He stole a car, run off, and left me holding the bag. Now, you're going to tell me where he went."

My mouth hung open, but nothing came out.

"Siebert, you asked, she answered," Aunt Jean said. She was back to sounding like the Aunt Jean I knew. "Why would she know where he ran off to? If this is the trouble you were talking about, then let's just go. Leave. I'll go with you. I have money. You know I do. All that you could possibly need."

As if he hadn't heard a thing Aunt Jean said, Siebert straightened to his full height and grabbed my arm. I struggled to keep up as he dragged me into the hallway and down the stairs. He mumbled to himself, something about being a damn fool for having not run off like the kid did. I tried to gather the bits and pieces of what Siebert was saying so I could make sense of them. It seemed that Truitt had run off, and Siebert had been left behind to account for whatever Truitt was running from.

At the bottom of the stairs, Siebert stepped squarely on the grate in the floor. It rattled. I glanced back at Urban, hoping he didn't hear it. It was a rule in our house. No one stepped on Urban's grate. Still clinging to Aunt Jean as the two of them followed me and Siebert down the stairs, Urban gave no sign he noticed or cared. He didn't even notice when Aunt Jean caught a heel in the grate and nearly fell.

In the kitchen, Siebert flung me toward the table and motioned for Aunt Jean to join me. She limped across the room, her ankle sore from having tripped on the grate. I helped her to sit, and she pulled Urban into her lap.

"I think someone's going to make a phone call," Siebert said and pointed at me. "You. You're going to make a call."

CHAPTER 37

Truitt said nothing when the car he was riding in rolled to a stop. The street sign outside the window read **7TH AVENUE**. That's the only thing Truitt knew about the Trinidad Café.

After stopping the car by standing in the middle of the road, his gun pointed at the driver, he had climbed into the back seat. With his gun pressed to the man's head, he'd told him to drive to Seventh Avenue in Ybor City, and nobody'd get hurt. He felt silly after he'd said it, like he was spitting out a line from a bad movie, but it worked. He was here.

Staring at the street sign, Truitt considered telling the man to turn around and take him back home. But that would be one more cowardly thing, and he couldn't stomach another. He forced himself to open the car door and stepped out, almost forgetting the gun he'd set on the seat next to him. Reaching back in, he grabbed it, stuffed it in his waistband, and muttered a thank you. The man who was driving didn't answer. The woman sitting next to him, a tiny brunette who was about the same age as Truitt, buried her head in the man's shoulder. They were probably newlyweds. Before Truitt delivered that bad line from a bad movie, they'd had that happily-ever-after glow about them.

As he began to shut the door, Truitt leaned in one last time. "You know which way to the Trinidad?"

The man shook his head and pulled away, the back door dangling open. A block up, he made a hard right turn, the door flying out and then slamming shut. They probably wanted to wipe Truitt from their rearview mirror as quickly as possible.

Standing on the corner, jostled by the crowd passing both ways on the sidewalk, Truitt looked toward one end of the street and then the other. This was Seventh Avenue. It had rained recently, a short burst that emptied out the damp night air, leaving behind crisp breezes and a dark sky. The paved street, lined with parking meters and tightly parked cars, glistened under the streetlights. Red-and-yellow marquees glowed up and down the avenue, marking the entries to redbrick buildings, some larger than any Truitt had ever seen. Letting the weight of the crowd choose his direction, he blew out a long breath and began to walk.

Dodging the people that flowed in and out of the doorways lit by flickering signs, Truitt struggled to keep up with reading each as he passed. There were many, and the bright green lights of one would distract him, or the yellow flickering lights of another. And on it went, up and down the street for as far as he could see. He was looking for one that read Trinidad Café. The papers often reported that Santo Giordano frequented the place.

As he passed from block to block, Truitt glanced down the adjoining streets and the alleys that emptied onto them. Some storefronts were dark. People drifted in and out of others, music spilling onto the street as their doors opened. Every so often, a cheer went up, coming from where, he couldn't tell. Overhead, wrought iron balconies dangled over the sidewalks. Women wearing slender dresses and high heels stood up there. Some were draped over the iron railings so they could wave to passersby on the street below. The orange tips of their cigarettes bounced like fireflies against the dark sky.

Truitt walked three blocks one way before turning around, retracing his path, and walking another three the other way. He'd started out nervous, everything around him a blur, and the cars, horns, music, and cheers all muffled like he was hearing them from far away. But after fifteen minutes of walking, and as he neared the end of Seventh Avenue where the crowds and lights thinned, his nerves softened. Truth is, he started to think he'd never find the Trinidad Café. He started to think he'd instead find a way to call Wiley. He'd come here and help Truitt find the place. He'd help him do everything he had to do.

A small red-and-white sign stopped him midstep. It hung over the entrance to a one-story brick building with black ironwork and green-and-white awnings. Two men stood at the small building's door. One wore a dark suit and a hat, just like the men who'd stopped to help with the flat tire. The other wore a white suit and straw hat. He was the older of the two. He threw his head back and let out a loud laugh, and as he did, Truitt got his first look at the oil drum. He'd found the Trinidad Café.

He might have swung around and run if that man in the white suit hadn't turned his way. As the man's laughter trailed off, his eyes settled on Truitt. Probably Truitt standing on the sidewalk and staring had set off an alarm. The man in the white suit nudged the other man, and a smile broke out on his face.

"I'll be goddamned," the man in the white suit said, waving Truitt to come closer. "If I didn't know better, I'd say I was looking at a ghost. You're a Holt, ain't you? I'd know that head of blond hair anywhere."

Truitt stepped into the street, pulling back as a car flew past, its horn blasting. When the street cleared, the man in the white suit was walking his way and still waving for Truitt to come closer. Once he reached the sidewalk, Truitt forced himself to keep moving. He felt he'd stepped into one of Billy Pyke's stories. This was a world he'd only read about in the newspaper or heard about from men drinking whiskey outside Terrance's Tavern back in Hockta.

He felt himself shrink as the man in the white suit wrapped an arm around him. The man was talking and laughing again, but Truitt didn't know what he was saying because as they walked toward the front door of the Trinidad Café, they were also walking toward the oil drum. Right there, just where all his customers said it would be. They'd been right about everything. Truitt should have closed up his bolita game long ago.

At the front door, the other man held up a hand, stopping Truitt.

"Hands up," he said.

Truitt raise both arms, and the man ran his hands around Truitt's waist. First, he pulled out Truitt's notepad. He glanced at it and handed it back. Then he pulled out the gun. Finding it empty, the man shook his head like he was sorry for what was about to happen to Truitt and waved him on.

As the man in the white suit led Truitt inside, he slapped the top of the oil drum and said, "How you doing in there?"

He let out another loud laugh as the door fell closed behind them.

CHAPTER 38

Inside Ilene's house, feeling small because of the five men crammed inside with him, Wiley sat on the chair nearest the telephone. He figured that's what he'd do if he truly expected it to ring. But he really chose the seat because he could see Ilene from here.

The last drizzle of daylight had disappeared since he first arrived, and the house was dark except for the light coming out of Ilene's kitchen. Wiley ached to turn on a few lamps, because in the dark house, the fear he'd made a bad mistake wouldn't stop sneaking closer. With a little more light, he might think better.

All five men sat in the living room. One slept under the hat resting on his face. Another flipped through a book he couldn't possibly read in this bad lighting, and two more stared at the ceiling. When Ilene called out that a couple of chops were ready, the two staring at the ceiling went to the table. The fifth man, the largest of the five and the one Wiley now understood was in charge, sat on the sofa where he was near the phone too.

"You say he's calling at eight o'clock sharp?" the man said, glancing over Wiley's shoulder at the clock on the wall.

"I'm sure of it," Wiley said, hoping he sounded convincing. "Told him to call me here. Wanted you all to hear whatever I heard, firsthand. I've spent the day combing this county. Been under every bridge, inside every barn, knocked on every door. And you already know we had a stolen car reported."

Wiley was talking too much. He knew that, but he couldn't stop. He was always so good at heading off a problem before it took root. But not this time. Every time he tried to sort his choices and make sense of where each choice would lead him, they all came tumbling down. Not one sorted thought in the bunch.

There would be no call, because Billy was locked in the basement. Wiley'd had to make a quick decision. He couldn't risk Billy getting out and saying the wrong thing to the wrong person. But that also left Wiley without anyone to make his eight o'clock call. His entire day had been leading up to this moment. His only plan had been to wait the men out and leave them with only one assumption: Truitt Holt was long gone. And then he'd receive a phone call, telling him as much. Now, his one and only plan had gone to shit because Wiley made the wrong choice by leaving Billy locked up.

The man shifted on the sofa, tugged on his pants as if they were too tight around his gut, and settled back in with a loud sigh. "To be clear, we're expecting this deputy of yours to tell us he's found the kid? Is that it? And you're thinking Georgia, yes?"

Wiley grabbed a quick look at his watch. One minute to eight. He glanced in the kitchen. Jabbing a pork chop with a fork, Ilene slid up alongside one of the men she'd called to the table, and as she dropped it on his plate, she lifted her eyes to Wiley and shook her head. It was a slight movement, one Wiley might have imagined. At the next plate, she did the same.

"Can't say he'll have found the boy," Wiley said, uncertain what Ilene was trying to tell him. "But maybe my deputy will have spotted the car or talked to someone who did. Maybe he has a sense of which way Truitt was headed. Because one thing's for sure, I've looked over every inch of this county, and he ain't here."

"Darlin'," the man said, talking over his shoulder to Ilene in the kitchen. "How we doing in there?"

"Will have another two fried up in just a few," she said, returning to the stove to fry another batch of pork chops.

"There we are," the large man said, tapping his watch. "Eight o'clock. Don't hear no phone ringing."

The man smoothed both hands over his head, and as he pushed to his feet, so did Wiley. The man's size triggered a backward step from Wiley.

"Guess my deputy could have had car trouble," Wiley said. "Or is trying to find his way to a phone."

Wiley said as little as possible because he was still thinking about Ilene shaking her head at him. Don't do it. That's what she was signaling. But don't do what?

The only thing he could figure . . . Ilene was telling him that he shouldn't do it. He shouldn't do whatever he was planning.

"We don't know where your deputy is," the man said, straightening up his shirt and tie before sitting at Ilene's table. "Correct? And we don't know where Truitt Holt is."

"That's about right."

Wiley thought to pick up the phone and call the sheriff's department, though he'd make like he was calling North Florida. The phone would ring and ring, and then he'd pretend Billy picked up. He would fake the whole thing, and when he hung up, he'd tell these fellows that Truitt was last seen headed for Georgia.

It was risky, and he'd have to step away where none of these men would hear the other side of the conversation. But it was his only play.

"You talk to your deputy since he went up north?" the man said, nodding his thanks as Ilene dropped a pork chop and spoonful of butter beans on his plate. "Maybe he spotted Truitt. Maybe told you something like that."

"Can't say that, no," Wiley said, glancing down on the phone and then over at Ilene again. "Only know I been everywhere I can think of and ain't found the kid yet."

From behind the man's back, Ilene smiled at Wiley and cocked her brows, a signal meant to tell him to keep on like that. He was on the right track. Stick to what was true.

Though Wiley wasn't yet sure why, it was a lucky break there would be no call from Billy Pyke, because Wiley had had every intention of turning that call into one big lie.

"Well, that's good," the man said, sawing into the pork chop. "Because your Truitt Holt appears to have made his way to Ybor City. I'd have been plenty disappointed if that phone rang, and you told me otherwise."

"Ybor City?" Wiley said.

Good Lord, he hadn't seen that coming.

"Glad you didn't lie to me, Wiley," the man said, chewing and smiling at Ilene for sharing her good cooking. "Already got that Siebert Rix to contend with. Have to say, I've had enough of this place. Wouldn't you say so, ma'am?"

"I would say this place has had enough of you, yes," Ilene said, a smile on her face like she was teasing the man.

He let out a laugh and went on eating.

"We'll be on our way soon as I've finished," the man said. "But mind you both stay here in town. Save us all the trouble of me having to deal with either of you again."

There was only one reason Truitt would go to Ybor City. He had gone to find Santo Giordano so he could make amends for killing one of Giordano's men. A phone call must have come to the house before Wiley got there, another of Giordano's men, calling to say they had Truitt. That's why Ilene had raised her brows and signaled Wiley to stick to the truth. She knew they already had her boy.

Truitt had made it all the way to the Trinidad Café and had found Santo Giordano. Now, Wiley had to figure what to do next.

CHAPTER 39

I sat across from Aunt Jean at the kitchen table as she inspected Urban for bumps and bruises. She was worried he'd been hurt when Siebert forced us all down the stairs.

When she was done making sure Urban was unharmed, she knelt in front of me and checked me over too. Her hands were warm as they brushed over my face and across my shoulders. She worked quickly, like Mama would have worked to make sure we were safe. I felt like we were all falling, and I wanted to grab her hands and hold on. As I reached for her, Siebert shouted at her to sit down. She cupped my chin. Her lower lip quivered as if she were about to cry.

"Are you all right?" she whispered.

I nodded, and she sat, pulling Urban into her lap. She stretched an arm across the table, and we touched fingers. Aunt Jean knew me better than anyone. She knew about me wanting something so bad that the fear my dreams would never come true made my insides ache every minute of every day. But right then, she knew me best because she and I were both afraid.

Siebert banged about, opening and slamming cupboard doors. Out in the living room, Mr. O'Dell's body lay motionless. I tried not to look, but I had to. Maybe I was wrong about him being dead. Maybe we could help him, get a doctor, take him to town. Aunt Jean wrapped her hand around the tips of my fingers, squeezed, and slowly shook her head. She knew what I was hoping, but she also knew he was gone.

"What are you looking for, Siebert?" Aunt Jean said. "Let me help you."

Keeping her eyes on me as she talked, Aunt Jean continued to shake her head like she was still thinking about Mr. O'Dell, but her voice was cheery. Seeing one thing and hearing another, the two parts not fitting, rattled me. I didn't know which to believe.

Giving Urban a kiss on top of his head, Aunt Jean sat him on the chair next to her, popped a smile into place, lifted tall, and swung around to Siebert.

"Are you hungry?" she said in her familiar breathy whisper. Walking to Siebert's side, she led with a shoulder. Her spine swayed, sending her opposite hip wide. This was Aunt Jean from the movies. "Can I get you something to eat?"

Siebert yanked a bottle of Daddy's whiskey from over the refrigerator, poured some in a glass, and waved the tip of the bottle toward the living room.

"That wouldn't have happened if he'd've kept his mouth shut," he said, draining the glass and pouring another.

"Yes, Siebert," Aunt Jean said. She flicked her eyes in my direction and winked at me. This was her plan. Keep Siebert happy. "You're right."

"Poor dope," Siebert said. "Probably believed you when you said yes to him."

Seeing Urban begin to squirm, I gathered him from the chair and pulled him into my lap. I felt better holding him in my arms, like maybe everything would be all right. He smelled like the peanut butter Aunt Jean let him have at supper. I wiped a smudge of it from his cheek. Keeping Siebert happy might work, at least until Mama and Daddy got home.

"You're the dope," Urban said in a loud voice, and that good feeling disappeared. "My daddy says so."

"Better watch your mouth, little man," Siebert said, jabbing the whiskey bottle at Urban.

"I was wrong to lead Leland on like I did," Aunt Jean said, easing the bottle from Siebert, pouring another drink, and pressing this one to her own lips. "I'm ready to go back to California. I have been for ages. But now's the time. We'll be long gone before Inez and Harden get home. And whatever trouble you're in, we'll fix it. Just you and me."

"How much do you have?" Siebert said, his eyes flicking over Aunt Jean's body as she arched her back to straighten the sash at her waist. "Money. How much?"

"I can call the bank on Monday." Aunt Jean wagged a playful finger at Siebert for looking, a reminder we had no other plan than to keep him happy.

"There is no Monday," Siebert said, turning from Aunt Jean to me. "Now. How much do you have?"

I shifted in my chair, holding tight to Urban. What I already thought was bad got instantly worse. I didn't like Siebert turning his attention to Urban and me, and I realized what Aunt Jean was doing made her brave. She was trying to take all his attention on her shoulders. I couldn't do the same. I wasn't strong enough.

"Harden thought the money would be . . . ," Aunt Jean said but stopped herself. "I thought the money would be safer in a bank. I did."

She looked past Siebert to see me and Urban. She tilted her head, smiled. She wanted us to know she was trying. Doing her best.

"Harden thought it'd be safer in a bank, you mean," Siebert said. "Safer from me."

"It's still my money," she said. "Can take it all out if I want."

Aunt Jean clung to Siebert, and I shifted in my seat. We both felt the knot tighten. If Siebert couldn't get money, he'd be one step further from getting himself out of whatever trouble he was in. I held Urban closer. His body was hot and damp against mine, and his hair stuck to his face. He squirmed, like he was trying to crawl inside me to safety. He sensed it too. Things were about to get worse.

"Answer my goddamn question," Siebert said again. "How much do you have in the house? Right here. Right now."

Though I tried to look anywhere but at Siebert, my skin sizzled, warning me his eyes were still on me.

"A few dollars in my purse," Aunt Jean said, pressing tighter against him, still trying to draw him back to her and away from me and Urban. Still trying to take all that weight on herself. "But Monday, I can get—"

Siebert threw the whiskey bottle across the kitchen. I ducked, turning a shoulder and pinning Urban to the wall. The bottle shattered on the doorframe behind us. Whiskey splattered on my head and shoulders, and glass scattered across the floor.

"I don't have until Monday," Siebert said.

Flinging Aunt Jean back into her seat, Siebert grabbed me and yanked me to my feet.

"You," he said to me. "Make the call. Right now."

I passed off Urban to Aunt Jean. He kicked and cried and reached for me as Siebert dragged me from the table. I wanted to tell Urban I was sorry I left him in Mama's and Daddy's bedroom, sorry all of this was happening. I wanted to tell him it would all be over soon, but I couldn't lie to him again.

"What call?" I said, wincing from the pain of Siebert's fingers digging into my arm as I tried to sidestep the shards of glass.

"You call that boy's house," Siebert said, shoving me at the phone. He paced a few steps and turned back. He was thinking, pounding a fist against his forehead. "Tell his mama you're worried about Truitt and only want to know where he's gone."

"What if she won't tell me? Or doesn't know?"

"You better hope like hell she does," Siebert said.

"Siebert," Aunt Jean said, still trying to calm Urban as she searched the floor for chunks of glass. "You have to tell me what's happening. Tell me so I can help you. How do you even know Truitt's gone?"

"Whole goddamn town knows he skipped out," Siebert said. "Stole a damn car and took off."

"Why?" I said, my chest so heavy the words barely squeezed out. "Why would he do that?"

"Because he killed one of Santo Giordano's men, that's why," Siebert said, grabbing me by the neck and forcing me to the telephone. "Killed his goddamn nephew. You know Santo Giordano? You read the paper, yes? And I was there. That's what happened. I saw it. That's my only crime. But they good as told me that if they can't find Truitt, they're going to settle for me. Now, make the fucking call because we're finding that kid."

With Siebert's hand still clamped on the back of my neck, I dialed, trying to think with every number that rolled past what I could say to help Truitt and his mama. When I reached the last number, I had nothing. I would say hello, and then I had nothing. The only thing I knew . . . Truitt would never run from danger if it meant abandoning his mama. He'd take her with him, or he'd have stayed and faced his troubles. If he was missing, then something bad had happened to him. I should have told him yes in that dark back room. I should have said yes, I'll marry you. If I had, he'd be home right now.

The line was silent as the call traveled through the overhead wires all the way to Truitt's house, but before it could ring on the other end, Siebert yanked the phone from my hand, hung it up, and stumbled backward. He stared at it as if it were a snake that might still strike.

"Siebert," Aunt Jean said, pulling me clear of him. "What was that?"

"That was a bad idea," he said, his eyes wide, his chest pumping. "I don't know who's there. Don't know who might answer."

"That's fine," Aunt Jean said, nodding so I'd nod along with her. "We don't have to call anyone."

"I need something bigger," Siebert said, tipping his head off to the side until he could look past Aunt Jean and see me straight on. "Insurance, that's what I need. A phone call ain't enough. A little information ain't enough. It's better I give you to them in person."

CHAPTER 40

Feeling as if the kitchen were spinning, and I was about to get thrown, I clung to Aunt Jean. I was trying to decipher what Siebert meant when he said that he planned to give me to someone in person. I assumed he meant he'd give me to the men looking for Truitt. I didn't know if I should be most afraid of staying here or being taken away. I didn't know what was on the other end of either possibility.

"You're not taking this girl anywhere," Aunt Jean said, pushing me behind her, putting herself between me and Siebert.

"You got a rope?" Siebert said, ignoring Aunt Jean and rummaging through the cupboards again.

"Absolutely not," Aunt Jean said. Instead of her words floating like they usually did, they were solid and landed with a thud. I wanted to duck and hide behind them. "What on earth could you want with a rope?"

Siebert closed on Aunt Jean in two long, heavy steps. She and I both stumbled backward.

"I'll tell you what I want with it," he said, spitting the words at Aunt Jean. "I'm going to use it to tie Addie to a tree, somewhere out near that kid's house. She'll show me the way, am I right? And if I need her, I'll trade her."

Aunt Jean shrunk at hearing Siebert's words. I clung to her shoulders, wanting to lift her up again. When she finally spoke, she whispered as if she had to ask the question but was afraid of the answer. I closed my eyes, wishing she wouldn't, because once Siebert responded, we'd never stop whatever was coming.

"Trade her for what?" Aunt Jean said.

"I'm leaving," Siebert said, lifting Aunt Jean's chin so she had to look him in the eye. "Flat out driving out of this godforsaken place. And if any of those fellows track me down, I'll tell them where they can find this little girl. She's the girlfriend, I'll tell them. The perfect bait for the boy they really want. I'll be proving I'm on their side, never fast-talked no one."

"And if they don't track you down?" Another whisper from Aunt Jean.

"Then I keep driving, and I'll be in California before you know it. Maybe Harden will find the girl before she rots. Maybe not."

There it was. He'd said it, and now it was going to happen. My eyes slid side to side, trying to latch on to something that would stop me from being dragged from the kitchen and strapped like raw meat to a tree.

"Take me instead," Aunt Jean said. "I know Truitt. I'll be the bait."

"What about you? Urban, right? That's your name?" Siebert said, laughing off Aunt Jean's suggestion. "You know where your daddy keeps rope?"

Urban puckered his lips and looked to me. He latched on and stopped me from spinning. He wanted my permission to give an answer. I had to nod, because if he didn't answer, Siebert would find a way to make him.

"In the garage," Urban said.

"What about a gun?" Siebert said, still using a softer tone meant for Urban. When Urban shrugged and went back to picking at the chip in the laminate table he'd found earlier in the evening, Siebert moved Aunt Jean aside with a straight arm and looked down on me. "Where's your daddy keep his gun?"

"The hall closet," I said, thinking I had to answer for the same reason Urban had to. If I didn't, Siebert would find a way to make me.

But really, I answered because I didn't have the strength to refuse. "Top shelf."

Taking hold of my arm, Siebert dragged me from the kitchen, grabbed the handgun from the top shelf, shoved it in his waistband, and pulled me out the back door.

As I stumbled down the stairs to the drive, I felt I was being dragged through water. Everything moved slowly, and the sounds were muted. Following behind, Aunt Jean burst out the door, Urban screaming in her arms, but I could barely hear him. Part of me was already gone, lashed to a tree, waiting to be found before I rotted under the Florida sun.

"Siebert, stop," Aunt Jean said, setting Urban on the ground and running after us. "There's not a place on this earth you can hide from Harden if you take Addie from this house. You know better than to cross him."

As Siebert hauled me toward the car, my head bouncing off to the side, I stared at Urban. He sank to the ground, drew his knees to his chest, and covered his ears. I thought I could see him chanting . . . twenty, twenty, twenty. When all this first started, I'd told him Siebert was gone and then left him alone in Mama's and Daddy's bedroom. He was still waiting for me to come back.

"Harden is the least of my problems," Siebert said, shoving me in the back seat of his car. "By the time he gets home, I'll be long gone."

"I won't tell about Leland," Aunt Jean said, grabbing his hand. "I won't tell anyone. We'll hide him. We'll say—"

"This ain't none of it about Leland O'Dell," Siebert shouted. "Santo Giordano's nephew is dead, and if I can't give him that Truitt kid, then I'm dead too. Those mob fellows got to have their patsy, their fall guy. Do you not understand that? If it ain't Truitt, then it's me."

Aunt Jean stared up at him. At first, her eyes were flat. She seemed in shock from what she'd heard. And then slowly, without her uttering a word, a cold cloudy gray emptied from her eyes, and a warm shimmer swelled in its place.

"No, I don't understand," Aunt Jean said, her voice dripping like honey again. She looked past him to lock eyes with me in the back seat. Telling me to get ready. "Tell me, Siebert. Explain it to me. Let me help you."

Siebert leaned against the car as if he was tired. He dropped his head in his hands and shook it side to side.

Keeping my eyes on Siebert, I slid sideways on the back seat until I could reach the door handle. I was getting ready, because that's what Aunt Jean wanted me to do. But if I opened the door, what then?

"This is all Donna Lee's fault," Siebert said, his voice slurring from all the whiskey. "She made those thugs think I tried to put one over on them. She made them think I was covering for that damn kid."

Aunt Jean stood in front of him, petting his neck and shoulders, keeping his back to me.

"I'm real sorry about that, Siebert," Aunt Jean said, cupping his face and pulling him closer. "She shouldn't have done that to you. I'll tell her so myself. Give her a piece of my mind."

Siebert buried his head in Aunt Jean's hair and wrapped his arms around her.

With one finger, I pulled on the handle. The door clicked. Before I could push it open, Siebert shoved Aunt Jean away, swung around, and pounded on the car's hood.

"Don't even try it," he said, pointing at me through the window. "Or that brother of yours comes too. And I'll do more than tie him to a tree."

Aunt Jean ran around the car and yanked open the door as I tried to close it.

"I'll go with you, Siebert," she said, trying to drag me from the car. "Take me instead. I'll tell them I know where Truitt is. I can make them believe."

In a half dozen long steps, Siebert stood over Urban, grabbed him, and lifted him in the air. Urban dangled limp, not making a sound. Not kicking or thrashing about. I pushed Aunt Jean away, pulled the door closed, and slid back into the middle of the seat.

"Make him put Urban down," I screamed.

When I saw Siebert drop Urban, I buried my face in my hands. Every muscle was coiled, ready to launch me from that car. I clung to the seat in front of me so I wouldn't try to run. Siebert would have thrown Urban in the car and tied us both to a tree. I couldn't let Urban be hurt like that. Truitt felt the same about his mama.

Truitt's mama never liked him running his own bolita game. You're asking for trouble, she'd always say. We can do fine without. But Truitt never wanted to do without, and he never wanted his mama to do without either. To him, the Mafia bosses making millions from bolita and the shootings in the streets of Tampa were just stories in the newspaper. He didn't believe any of that would ever reach him in Lake County. But it had, and it had ended with Truitt killing Santo Giordano's nephew. Siebert didn't let me call Truitt's house because he knew the men looking for Truitt were there. They were making bait of Truitt's mama like Siebert wanted to make bait of me. But they didn't know Truitt like I did.

There was only one reason Truitt wasn't already home, having traded himself for his mama. He was dead. And I started wishing I were dead too.

Aunt Jean pressed her hands to the car window. Her small, perfect mouth hung open. Her eyes, smudged and teary, stared at me, saying how sorry she was.

"You can't go," Aunt Jean shouted, pushing away from the window, excitement flushing the sorrow from her eyes. "Siebert, look. You can't go."

She stumbled toward the front of the car, pointing down at the tire.

"It's flat," she said, waving frantically. "Come look. This tire is flat."

CHAPTER 41

Clinging to the back seat of Siebert's car, I slid away from the door as Aunt Jean opened it. She reached for me and coaxed me to take her hand, but I was still afraid to get out. As I scooted just beyond her reach, I watched Siebert out the windshield, not wanting to let him out of my sight. He crossed the front of the car, leaning on it to keep his balance, and bent to look down on what Aunt Jean had been pointing to.

"Goddamn," Siebert shouted.

Now I understood. The front tire on the passenger side was flat, and the car was going nowhere on a flat tire. That meant I was going nowhere.

As Siebert kept shouting about the damn spare being no good, Aunt Jean leaned into the car again and extended a hand to me, a lifeline pulling me away from the edge.

"Come on," she whispered. "Now. Quickly."

I climbed out and followed as Aunt Jean led me around the back of the car, keeping us far from Siebert. She walked quickly, teetering in her high heels, her hips popping side to side, and I struggled to keep up.

"No one's going anywhere," Siebert said, walking his hands along the hood of the car to steady himself as he tried to follow us. "You two. Get the jack out of the trunk."

Aunt Jean and I stopped, and my hopes of going nowhere disappeared. Straight ahead of us, Urban was still balled up on the ground where Siebert dropped him. I wanted to scoop him up and run and never stop.

"I don't know anything about—" Aunt Jean began.

"Get in the damn trunk and get the jack," Siebert shouted. "You, Addie, help her."

Siebert pulled out a set of keys and tossed them at me. They fell short, landing in the soft dirt. I called to Urban to get up and come with me, but he didn't move. It was as if he'd sunk into a hole and couldn't see or hear any of us.

Picking up the keys and shaking the dirt from them, I met Aunt Jean at the back of the car. My fingers were stiff, and my hands trembled as I tried to open the lock. Aunt Jean rested her hand on mine and squeezed. Her way of telling me everything would be all right. Easing the keys from me, she popped the lock. The trunk opened. A sour rot washed over us. I sucked in a sharp breath to cry out, and Aunt Jean slapped a hand over my mouth.

"Don't say a word," she whispered.

I closed my eyes, but I hadn't been quick enough. I knew who I'd seen lying in the trunk of Siebert's car. It was Donna Lee, and she was dead. She was a hollowed-out, died-a-painful-death dead. Before I was able to close my eyes, I saw flashes of dark red and brown and torn skin and bloody nails. I saw her eyes, barely open, looking back at me.

Aunt Jean pulled me behind the cover of the open trunk, and with her hand still over my mouth, she whispered to be still, be quiet.

"You find it?" Siebert shouted.

"I got it," Aunt Jean said, her voice easy, almost cheerful.

She slid her hand from my mouth, watching my face to make sure I wasn't going to scream or cry out.

I nodded that I was all right and looked down on Donna Lee. There it was again, the heavy, deep, cloudy silence that rolled in behind death. Donna Lee was one of the only girls in town who would talk to me, though Mama didn't much like it when she did. Donna Lee was older, smoked cigarettes, and ran around with grown men. On Fridays, at the grocery store, we'd sometimes talk about our favorite movies, the newest magazine we'd found, the leading men we'd so love to work with. I gave her a picture of Aunt Jean once that I signed as if Aunt Jean had signed it. Donna Lee dreamed of leaving Hockta just like I did. Now, she was covered in blood, and a knife stuck out of her gut. The heavy silence that draped over the spot where her life used to be had already stranded her in Hockta forever.

"Well, bring it here," Siebert shouted. "You know, that's how Truitt killed the man. Swung that jack like a bat and cracked his head clean open."

Aunt Jean grabbed the jack that was wedged between Donna Lee and the car and motioned for me to step back. She stretched to close the trunk, but before she did, she leaned in so she could whisper to me.

"He doesn't have a spare," she said, flicking her eyes toward the back of the car where a spare tire should be.

I nodded, though I wasn't sure why she'd said it or why it mattered. I was still thinking about Donna Lee and her wafer-thin life. Her dreams on one half, her beating heart on the other. The whole snapped in two so easily. With no one to cling to, all the dreams she had would eventually disappear. I was the only one who knew about them, and even I knew they'd never come true. Truitt must have felt the same about me. Maybe he did love me, for a time, but he knew my dreams were wafer thin, and he wasn't going to waste his life waiting around while I kept trying to make them come true.

"Put it back," Siebert said to Aunt Jean. He was kneeling on the ground and staring at the flat tire.

"This isn't what you asked for?" Aunt Jean said, holding out the jack to Siebert and nodding for me to head toward the house. "I told you, I don't know much about these things."

"This is the spare," Siebert said, dropping back on his hind end. "Put in on myself not a day ago."

"And it's flat already?" Aunt Jean said, turning around. "Isn't that a shame. Do you have another?"

Waving at me to hurry up, Aunt Jean put the jack back in the trunk and slammed it closed. Donna Lee was dead, and Mr. O'Dell was dead, and the silence around them both was closing in. I felt as if it were chasing me. As quickly as I could without breaking into a run, I walked toward the house. When I reached Urban, I coaxed him to stand, but he still wouldn't move. I threaded two arms around him, strained to lift him, and carried him toward the house.

"Nobody's going inside," Siebert shouted. "We're not done here."

"Well, of course we're going inside," Aunt Jean said, hurrying toward Urban and me. "Without a tire, that car does us no good at all."

Aunt Jean's hair still hung in her face, and her makeup had all worn off, but she walked tall, shoulders back, chin up, and leading the way, just like I imagined she did when she walked onto a movie set.

Siebert pushed off the hood of the car and stumbled after us. "You get back here right now, the all of you."

"We're going inside to wait for Harden and Inez. Harden'll get us a spare, and then we'll tell them both we're leaving." Continuing toward me and talking over her shoulder, Aunt Jean broke character long enough to wink at me. "Been thinking about all the times they tried to keep us apart. Inez, especially. Ever since we were all kids. She never did like you. You remember that? Always wagging her finger at you. You were, what, ten or eleven years old, and she was wagging that finger at you. It's high time I give her a piece of my mind. Harden too. I'll be telling them I'm done with this life and that I'm leaving forever. Once and for all."

CHAPTER 42

Inside the Trinidad Café, Truitt sat at a table pushed up against a wall. From there, he could see the front door. That was important. Every time Wiley took him and Mama out to dinner, they sat where Wiley could face the front door. Being sheriff meant Wiley was always on duty. Either he was keeping an eye out for trouble or keeping a target off his back. Truitt understood that now, because he felt a heavy weight in his chest and at the back of his head, just like when he'd walked from Wiley's house to his garage, dressed in Wiley's uniform. Truitt was a target.

A dozen or more tables filled the small space, all of them taken by men in dark suits and ladies wearing tight skirts and hats. Waitresses teetered past on high heels, holding trays overhead. When one asked what she could bring Truitt, he shook his head but said nothing. Near the front, a small band had set up but wasn't playing. The five men wore matching tan jackets, white shirts, and dark ties. Truitt wished he were sitting closer to those men. They seemed like men Wiley and his mama would know.

Thinking Wiley would be nonstop scanning the place for signs of trouble, Truitt tried to do the same. When his eyes landed on the man in the white suit walking toward his table, another man trailing him, Truitt sat up tall and nearly tipped his chair. The man in the white suit was pointing at Truitt and waving at the other man to hurry up. Truitt had run through every possibility of how this meeting might unfold, but he hadn't considered that he'd be recognized before even walking in the door.

"Here he is," the man in the white suit said. "Just like I said. Go on, kid, tell him. Tell him your name. This is the darnedest thing. Go on."

The man's booming voice made people sitting nearby shift in their seats to get a better look at what was happening. They gave Truitt the same look the man at the door had given him. Heads tilted, brows raised, heavy eyelids, all of them were thinking they were glad they weren't Truitt.

"Name's Truitt Holt."

The man in the white suit slapped his thigh and nudged the other man.

"What did I tell you?" the man in the white suit said. "He's a Holt. In the flesh. Knew it the second I saw him. Spitting image of Spencer Holt. You remember him?"

As the man in the white suit spoke, the other man closed his eyes and cringed, like he knew once the man started talking, he wouldn't stop.

"Remember him getting what he deserved," the other man said. He had dark eyes and a large head. Nudging his coat open, he rested a hand on the gun stuffed in his waistband and nodded toward the man wearing the white suit. "Want to tell this gentleman why you're here to see him?"

"This gentleman?" Truitt said, looking between the two of them. He'd seen pictures of Santo Giordano in the newspaper, and the man wearing a white suit was not Santo Giordano. "No, I'm not here to see you, sir. Sounds like you knew my daddy, but I don't know you."

"Kid doesn't know who I am," the man in the white suit said. He plucked a drink from the tray of a passing waitress and nudged a man at the next table. "Hey, you want to tell this kid who I am?"

The man at the next table and the woman hanging from his arm let out sighs as if they'd already heard plenty from the man in the white suit too.

"That right there is Charlie Wall," the man at the table said, tipping his chair back and talking directly to Truitt. "Everybody knows Mr. Wall. Now you do too. He's pleased to make your acquaintance."

Truitt knew the name from the newspapers. Before Santo Giordano was the Tampa boss, Charlie Wall held the title. The newspapers still liked to write about him because he came from a wealthy local family. He was the first to harness all the money to be made by running illegal bolita games, and he did it by controlling every politician, judge, and policeman in Tampa.

Several years after Santo forced Charlie from power, Charlie came out of retirement, went in front of Congress, and sang like a bird. That's how the newspapers put it. The government called him to testify, and he told them about all the illegal bolita games and the people who ran them and made money off them. Nearly five years after he shared his secrets, he was still alive. That was the most surprising thing about Charlie Wall.

"The name Charlie Wall mean anything to you, son?" Charlie Wall said. "Because it should. Every person in this place knows the name Charlie Wall."

"Yes, sir. I know the name, but I still ain't here to see you."

Tipping his head back and draining his glass, Charlie studied Truitt. Seeming to be satisfied Truitt was telling the truth, Charlie signaled the waitress for another drink. He unbuttoned his jacket, and as he sat across from Truitt, he removed his hat and set it carefully on the chair next to him. Smoothing his thinning hair, he smiled when the waitress approached. As she set a drink on the table, Charlie swept up her hand and kissed it.

"You see how I did that?" he said as he watched the woman walk away. "That's a gentleman's move. Kissing a hand like that. No one's a gentleman anymore. You a gentleman, Truitt Holt?"

"Yes, sir," he said. "I guess I am. Don't think none of these ladies want me kissing their hands, though. I'm guessing they're more interested in how much money's in my pocket."

This made Charlie Wall lay his head back and laugh again. Each time was louder than the last. Charlie scooted his chair closer to Truitt as if already knowing he was going to have a hard time hearing their conversation.

"I like you, Truitt Holt," he said. "And I like you more now that I know you aren't here to see me. I'm too old for that sort of trouble. Can I take your word that you ain't here to see me?"

Truitt had no idea why Charlie Wall would think Truitt had come to see him, but he guessed there was no risk in being truthful. The man seemed harmless too. Up close, Truitt got a good sense of his age. He was old. His jowls sagged, his small eyes were set deep in his head, and his neck hung in folds over his tight collar.

"If a man's word is useless," Truitt said, "so is the man. And I ain't useless."

He started to say that was what his father always said, but that wasn't true. It was what Wiley always said.

"All right then," Charlie Wall said, leaning back in his chair as if to enjoy the music.

"I came here hoping to talk to Mr. Giordano," Truitt said, because it seemed Charlie Wall was settling in for a night of the two of them sitting together, drinking, and listening. "The newspapers say he likes it here. I think he might want to talk to me too. Might be looking for me."

Another man in a dark suit walked up to the table. He was a small man—wiry, Truitt's mama would have called him—and he was mostly bald. He was also older than the other men Truitt had seen. This meant he was likely the brains, because he didn't look like the brawn. Wiley'd taught Truitt that too. Man's got to work with what he's got. If he ain't got brains, he better hope he's got brawn. The man rested a hand on Charlie Wall's shoulder and whispered in his ear.

"Sure, I'll leave you to the kid," Charlie said, picking up his hat and pushing to his feet. He had a harder time getting up than he did sitting down. "No skin off my back. You know who this kid is? Darnedest thing, after all this time."

"You'll wait here," the wiry man with the brains said to Truitt once Charlie Wall had stumbled off to the next table. "You understand? That means you don't move."

Truitt nodded and tried not to look at anyone sitting nearby, because the looks on their faces showed pity, and that made him worry this was not going well. Santo Giordano might just as soon shoot Truitt as talk to him. It was also possible no one had told Mr. Giordano his nephew was dead, and Truitt would be delivering the news. That might lead right back to getting shot. Mr. Giordano might also refuse to talk to Truitt, and he'd find himself back on the sidewalk. He'd be left with no other choice. He'd make his way home to Hockta, hopefully before midnight, show up at his house, and hope the men there spared his mama.

At some point as Truitt waited, avoiding eye contact with anyone, a waitress set a soda in front of him. The sweaty glass had dripped water, forming a puddle on the table. The ice had melted, and Truitt wondered how long he'd been sitting alone, the drink untouched. Pretty soon, another girl came along and swept the table dry with a towel.

"Why didn't you drink it, sweetie?" the girl said, setting another one in front of Truitt. She smelled sugary sweet like Donna Lee.

Truitt had already vomited once in the past twenty-four hours. He didn't want to do it a second time, but that sugary smell swept him back to the side of the road and the sound of the jack as it connected with another man's head. His hands stung when he'd landed the blow and then there had been the wet thud as the jack's sharp corner split the man's head open.

Swallowing sour bile, Truitt shook his head at the girl and mumbled something about not being thirsty. Wiley always talked about keeping control of a situation. Stay calm and have an exit plan. Truitt didn't have either anymore. His head swirled. He struggled to get a full breath. The band was still playing, and the tables around him were more crowded. All of it made the room feel smaller, like a trap closing in on him. The breathing got harder, and the room swirled faster.

Charlie Wall's voice cut through the clatter of silverware, voices, laughter.

"Can you believe it?" Charlie Wall was saying. "Lord, that takes me back. Thought he come here packing a bullet with my name on it."

Truitt pushed to his feet, trying to keep his eyes on the front door. He was starting to get an idea of why Charlie Wall knew his father, and he needed to get out. Needed to think it through. Needed to clear his head and start again. Pushing aside his chair, he stopped. A hand landed square on his shoulder. He dropped back down in his seat.

"This is Mr. Giordano, son," said the same wiry man, the brains, who had made Charlie Wall leave the table. "Just as you requested."

"So," the man standing over Truitt said, "this is the boy who brought my sister to tears."

CHAPTER 43

Back in the kitchen, Aunt Jean hugged me. I still held Urban, and he was wedged between us. She held on a long time, so long Urban wiggled for more room. When she pulled back, she wiped the hair from my face and Urban's. She smiled. Not her plastic smile that left out her eyes. This was a real smile, and when Aunt Jean gave a real smile, she swept up everything in her path, breathed light into it, and made things right again.

"Don't say a thing about that girl in the trunk," she whispered as Siebert pushed through the back door. "We wait for your dad. Do nothing."

She cocked her brows as if to ask . . . do you understand? And I did. I understood.

Straining with Urban's extra weight in my arms, I started to sit in a chair, but Urban squealed and kicked the table, knocking several things to the floor. Siebert had already sat in one of the other chairs, which was too close for Urban.

Whispering to Urban that I wasn't going anywhere, I nudged the chair out of the way with a hip and started to sit on the floor, but Aunt Jean stopped me. Grabbing Mama's broom, she swept up the rest of the broken liquor bottle. When she was done, I sat on the floor, still damp from the whiskey.

Keeping one arm wrapped tightly around Urban, I tried to gather up the things he'd knocked to the floor, but he squealed again, so I left them.

Resting his forearms on the table, his head in his hands, Siebert mumbled about me needing to keep Urban quiet so he could think. After putting away the broom, Aunt Jean pulled a chair up to the refrigerator, reached into the top cabinet, and pulled down another bottle of Daddy's whiskey.

Trying not to think about Donna Lee lying in all that blood in the back of Siebert's car, I peeled Urban's arms from around my neck, but he only squealed louder. He was heavy on my chest. There wasn't enough air, and I couldn't inhale. And I couldn't stop seeing that blank stare looking up at me from the trunk, the only thing left of Donna Lee's dreams.

"I say we get these kids out of here," Aunt Jean said as she pulled two fresh glasses from a cupboard and poured whiskey in both. She handed one to Siebert and smoothed a hand over his damp hair. "What do you say? Before Inez and Harden get home. Let's have some time, just us two? A little privacy."

Her voice was light and cheerful, out of sync with Siebert, who was rubbing his forehead as if it ached. Siebert heard it, too, because as he took the glass from her, he studied her with a puzzled look on his face. Keeping his eyes on her, he drained the whiskey and handed back the glass for another.

"When was the last time we were alone? Just us two?" Aunt Jean said, pouring another two fingers. "Isn't that something, me not remembering? Must have been on the train on our way here."

Urban shifted in my arms, and the breeze blowing through the back door chilled the damp skin where our bodies had been pressed together. The small movement was enough. I had room to inhale. I took a deep breath, grateful for the fresh air. As Siebert took another long drink, I slid backward a few inches, closer to the breeze sweeping through the screen door and out the front door Siebert had kicked down.

At first, it was only so I could cool down, breathe, and get rid of the visions of Donna Lee staring up at me. But then, I felt how close the back door was.

Seeing my movement toward the door, Aunt Jean slipped behind Siebert where he couldn't see her and shook her head, barely, but enough. She wanted me to stop. I readjusted Urban in my lap so his head rested on my other shoulder, his face tipped away from the living room. I didn't want him to see Mr. O'Dell's body. Then I scooted another few inches toward the back door.

I'd have to convince Urban to let go. That was going to be the hardest part. Once outside, he'd have to run on his own. As much as I wished I could, I wouldn't be able to carry him. My arms already ached, and we'd be faster apart. Plus, we were sober. Siebert wasn't. We also knew where to run and where to hide. We wouldn't have to get far before we'd disappear in the orange trees. Once there, I'd hide Urban and run. I'd run until I found help to take back to the house.

Again, Aunt Jean pinched her lips and shook her head at me as she continued to run a hand lightly over Siebert's head, but the cool air was too tempting. Outside was right there, and Siebert's eyes were closed as he leaned into Aunt Jean's touch.

Draping an arm around Siebert's thick shoulders, Aunt Jean knelt at his side.

"Let me send the kids upstairs," she whispered. It was a husky whisper that made Siebert groan. She pressed a cheek to his, but her eyes were squarely on me. Again, the sound of her voice didn't dovetail with the look on her face. She was being one person for Siebert and another for me. "Please, let me be a little selfish. I want you all to myself."

I waited, watched Siebert's face. He cupped Aunt Jean's cheek. I planted my feet to scoot another inch, nudging aside the papers Urban knocked from the table. They were this month's bills, Mama's shopping list, and her notepad. I leaned forward as if hugging Urban tighter and squinted. The top page of Mama's notepad had writing on it—the phone numbers for the restaurant and the Harringtons' house. And I remembered the phone in Mama's and Daddy's room. It had been there all along.

Urban wasn't going to let go of me. The last time he did, I left him in Mama's and Daddy's room and Siebert found him. And I wouldn't be able to run and carry him at the same time. I doubted I could even stand up with him still clinging to me. But with the phone number to the Harringtons', if Siebert let us go upstairs, I could make a call from Mama's and Daddy's room. I could call Truitt's house. I could call any number. I could call and keep calling until I got someone. I could get help for us.

I looked up to see Aunt Jean still whispering in Siebert's ear. She flicked her eyes at the notepad, having seen the same as me, and smiled.

The upstairs telephone was our way out. Siebert didn't know about it. At least I didn't think he did. I should have made a call the first time Urban mentioned it. I could have called anyone, any number. But I didn't because I never imagined life could take such a bad twist.

The silence that had settled in behind Mr. O'Dell and Donna Lee had turned thick like putty. It took the shape of them, a placeholder for who they had once been. If Truitt was dead, I thought I'd feel that same silence taking the shape of him, but I felt nothing. I hoped that meant I was wrong and that he was still alive.

Readjusting myself, I leaned against the wall, shifted Urban's body to one side, stretched out my legs, planted a heel on the notepad where Mama had written the phone numbers, and pulled it within reach. I shifted Urban to the other side and readjusted myself. As if trying to get comfortable, I covered the paper with my hip.

Aunt Jean nodded. I'd done my part. Now she would do hers.

"We have time, Siebert. Inez and Harden won't be home for a while," Aunt Jean said, Siebert shivering as she whispered in his ear. "Let's take a little time for ourselves. It's been so long. Please, Siebert, let me send the kids upstairs."

CHAPTER 44

Wiley threw the car in drive and pulled away from Truitt's and Ilene's place slowly, watching out his rearview mirror in case Ilene changed her mind. He tried explaining to her that the men who just left her house could come back. He wanted to take her somewhere she'd be hidden, safe, but she refused to leave. She told Wiley that unless he agreed to take her to Ybor City with him, she wasn't going anywhere. She was staying in her house until her boy came home.

At the end of the drive, Wiley checked one last time. Every light was on in Ilene's small house, but the front door remained closed. Ilene had never been one to change her mind.

Wiley was only a few minutes from Harden Buckley's house and from there, another forty-five minutes to Ybor City. If Ilene wouldn't let Wiley take her somewhere safe, and if Wiley couldn't be there to protect Ilene himself, Harden Buckley was the only man Wiley trusted to do it instead.

Harden was a solid man. He wasn't the richest in town, didn't talk the loudest or have the firmest handshake. His roots ran deeper than that. He'd been tested his whole life. He grew up poor, the kind of poor he had to scratch his way out of, and when he did, he came out knowing what mattered most to him. His wife. His children. And if his family mattered most, so did everyone else's. Wiley thought the same, though he didn't have a wife or a child yet. But he had Ilene and Truitt. To him, they were family, with or without the I-dos.

Wiley and Harden weren't exactly friends, but they were friendly. Around town, they'd say their hellos and catch up. The history they shared was painful. If they spent too long around each other, the past had a way of forcing itself to the surface, and neither one of them wanted to revisit it.

Harden's house was in sight, its lights peeking out from deep inside the grove. Wiley slowed, flipped on his blinker, though the road behind him was dark, and then thought otherwise. Harden and Inez, like most everyone in town, would be at the Harringtons'. He checked his watch. Yes, the party would be gearing up by now, going strong. He accelerated past the turn to the Buckleys' house and headed for town.

Slowing outside the Harringtons' place, Wiley parked in the middle of the street because the shoulder was already full of parked cars. Music drifted through the open front door, and white lights sparkled in the oaks that lined the drive. As he walked toward the house, Wiley felt himself slowing down. He wasn't sure what to tell Harden and what not to tell him. He deserved to know enough to understand what he was getting into. Figuring the truth was usually the best route, that's what Wiley settled on. He'd tell Harden the truth.

At the front door, he reached out to knock, but before he could, the door flew open. Tillie Harrington, wearing an orange dress covered with tiny white polka dots, the one she wore every year, greeted him with a smile, a tray of mushroom caps, and a drink.

"Thank you, no," Wiley said, waving off the highball glass and wishing he'd changed his clothes. Folks were sure to talk more and assume the worst, seeing him in his uniform. He'd be sure to change before leaving for Ybor City. "Would you mind hustling Harden out here? Nothing serious. No trouble. Just need a word."

Inez Buckley was first to the door, which was no surprise to Wiley. Although the way she was dressed surprised him. He guessed the dress she wore was borrowed. She carried the bright red beautifully, but she wasn't comfortable wearing it. She held one hand to her chest and crossed the other arm over her waist, covering herself as best she could.

Wiley had found over his years of being sheriff that mothers were much like him, at least when it came to their children. They were always on guard, always looking to sniff out trouble and stamp it out quick.

"Wiley?" she said, stepping onto the front porch and letting the screen door close behind her. "What is it? Is everything all right?"

"Everything's fine," Wiley said, tipping his hat. "It's nothing like that. Look real lovely, Inez. I hate to disturb. I just need a quick word with Harden."

"We only just got here," Inez said, as if she already knew Wiley would be taking Harden away from the party.

Wiley was right about mothers sniffing out trouble. Even as the music played on, the white lights twinkled, and the smell of stuffed mushrooms lingered in the air, Inez sniffed out Wiley. He was the trouble that was brewing, and she knew it. She did not want Wiley drawing her husband into something else they'd all spend the rest of their lives trying to forget.

Harden sensed it, too, though not as quickly. He was smiling as he appeared in the open doorway. He'd still been saying his hellos to everyone at the party and had barely touched the drink he held, the ice unmelted even.

Pushing through the screen door and still smiling, Harden reached out a hand to Wiley. But his smile quickly disappeared. He gave Inez a kiss on the cheek and whispered something to her. As she listened silently to what Harden was saying, Inez stared at Wiley. She didn't do it to keep tabs on him. She did it so he would see the warning she had for him.

If it'll hurt my husband, don't ask it of him. That was her warning.

"I need to go to Ybor City," Wiley told Harden once Inez had gone. "Truitt is there, and I need to bring him home. If I don't, his mama will likely never see him again. I can't have that. I'd like you to go to Ilene's place, keep an eye on things. Keep an eye on her."

Harden studied Wiley's face. Given Harden and Inez had only just arrived at the party, they likely hadn't yet heard the gossip Wiley had planted about Truitt. But Harden didn't need gossip to figure what had happened. Everyone knew that as long as Truitt ran his bolita game, he'd eventually end up in trouble with the wrong kind of men. Harden knew trouble had finally found Truitt.

"You mind having someone run you home?" Harden said to Inez when she returned to his side.

"He'll be home for breakfast," Wiley said. "I promise."

CHAPTER 45

Sitting on the kitchen floor, the back door only a few feet away, I held Urban tightly, our heads pressed together, hoping he would stay quiet. When he started to squirm, I bounced him like Mama bounced him when he was a baby. The outside air had cooled us both. I felt better. Stronger.

As I waited for Siebert to send Urban and me upstairs, I slid a hand along my hip to feel that Mama's notepad with the phone numbers was still there, but otherwise, I didn't move. Between Aunt Jean's husky whisper and all the whiskey, Siebert was hovering near sleep, and I didn't want to wake him from his stupor. He mumbled about spending all night in his car and the terrible smell and where were they going to get a spare. Aunt Jean continued whispering that they'd be all right. The two of them together would find a way. She cooed to him about all the fun they'd had as children, how he'd been the only family she ever knew. Mama had been part of that makeshift family, three children with no parents, but Aunt Jean had so far steered clear of using Mama's name.

"I'd be nowhere without you, Siebert," Aunt Jean said. "If not for you, I'd have never found my way. I need you. I need us to go back to California and to be together."

After what felt like an hour, Siebert flicked his fingers in my direction. It was the signal I'd been waiting for. The signal to get out.

I planted a hand on the ground as if to push myself up, crumpled the top page of the notepad, and peeled it loose.

Aunt Jean cupped Siebert's face and stroked his brows with her thumbs, continuing to murmur to him about the old days and all the fun they'd had. Once I was on my feet, the piece of paper crumbled up in my fist, I moved slowly, not wanting to break the trance Aunt Jean had created. My shoulders burned from carrying Urban's weight. My elbows were stiff.

Sliding my feet to be as quiet as I could, I turned to walk from the kitchen. Once I reached the landing at the bottom of the staircase, I'd have to force myself to keep the same stride. If I ran or tried to take the stairs two at a time, Siebert would know there was something upstairs that I wanted, and he'd stop us for sure. Then he'd figure out we had a telephone in Mama's and Daddy's room, and our escape would be ruined.

Stepping out into the narrow hallway, I paused, remembering the grate in the floor. If I'd have stepped on it, Urban might have cried out, another thing that could have broken the trance and ruined my plan. I jostled Urban so he sat more securely on my hip and readied myself to take one extra-long step that would carry me over the grate and to the first stair. Instead, I swung around, nearly falling, when the screen on the back door flew open.

I braced myself for Siebert. He'd heard something, seen something. I pressed Urban's head into my chest, held a hand over his face so he wouldn't see whatever was about to happen. But instead of Siebert grabbing hold, the arms that wrapped around us were Mama's.

The three of us stumbled backward as Mama pulled us into the kitchen, looking over her shoulder as she moved. Urban screamed when he realized it was Mama. He wiggled out of my arms and into hers.

"Is that Leland?" she said, kissing the top of Urban's head and checking me over for any bumps or bruises. "What happened? I saw Siebert's car out there. What are . . ."

And then she saw Siebert. Instead of sitting at the table, being seduced by Aunt Jean's stories of the old days, he leaned against the kitchen counter, Daddy's gun hanging at his side. He held his head high and his shoulders square. The trance was broken. When Mama's eyes landed on him, he smiled.

"Good to have you home, Inez," he said. "Didn't hear you drive up. Harden on his way in?"

"Jean?" Mama said. "Jean, what's happening? Why is Siebert here?"

"Asked you a question, Inez," Siebert said, glancing out the kitchen window. "Where's Harden?"

"He's not with me," Mama said. "And that's a good thing for you. Might behoove you to be on your way while you still can."

Mama talked in a slow, drawn-out way as if to give herself time to think. She was taking in the kitchen and what she'd seen in the living room and trying to decipher what would happen next. She kissed the top of Urban's head again and whispered something in his ear as she handed him off to me.

"Might behoove me, huh?"

"Yes," Mama said. "Harden will be along shortly."

"How about you have a seat then," Siebert said. "We were just having a drink and talking about old times. Something to do while we wait."

"Jean?" Mama said again. "What has happened here?"

Aunt Jean stood between Mama and Siebert. As if embarrassed to have Mama see her like this, she smoothed her hair and dress, slipped her shoes back on, and set down her drink.

"Everything is fine, Inez," she said, her everyday ordinary voice replacing the husky whisper.

"Everything is most certainly not fine," Mama said. "What has happened to Leland? We need to get him help. Right now."

"Nothing's going to help Leland O'Dell," Siebert said, still smiling at Mama. I followed his eyes, wanting to see what he was smiling at.

Mama was wearing one of Aunt Jean's dresses. It was a bright, rich red, something Mama would not usually wear. The neckline dipped too low for her taste, and when she'd left the house with Daddy, she kept tugging at it.

As if Mama figured the same thing as me at the exact same time, she raised a hand to her chest and pressed it there, covering herself. She glanced into the living room again, seeming to understand that Mr. O'Dell was dead.

"I'll ask you to leave my house then, right this instant," Mama said in a smooth, even voice.

That was the first time in my life I looked at my mama and saw the rest of who she was. Though, to be fair, that was my wrongdoing. She'd always been a strong person, determined, ambitious. It just hadn't looked like I thought it would.

"That Marilyn's dress you're wearing, Inez?" Siebert asked Mama, ignoring her demands. He leaned to look past Aunt Jean, who still stood between him and Mama. His eyes moved over Mama's body, studying her.

I didn't like the way he kept saying Mama's name. Every time he did, it was like he was planting a stake in her, claiming her.

"The kids were just going upstairs," Aunt Jean said, slapping on a smile like everything was all right and reaching for Siebert's hand.

But same as I didn't like Siebert staring at Mama and repeating her name, Aunt Jean didn't either. She fidgeted, shifting side to side and bending and straightening her fingers as if Siebert doing those things to Mama made her itch all over.

"Dress looks real nice, is all I'm saying," Siebert said, ignoring the hand Aunt Jean offered him.

"You kids go on," Aunt Jean said, waving at me to leave the kitchen. "Go on upstairs. We'll all talk, the three of us."

Still holding Urban, I shuffled him off to one side and grabbed Mama.

"You come too," I said.

Mama shook her head but kept her eyes on Siebert.

"Go on," she said, peeling my hand from her forearm. "Take Urban upstairs. We'll be fine."

I wanted to tell Mama about the phone numbers wadded up in my other hand. I wanted her to know I could call for help. I didn't know where Daddy was or why he wasn't with her, but I could still call the Harringtons' and tell them we needed the sheriff. I wanted her to know so she didn't do anything to make Siebert angry.

"You go, too, Marilyn," Siebert said.

The kitchen grew brighter. The outside air on my damp skin was like salt in a raw wound. I bolted upright. Urban no longer felt heavy in my arms. I no longer struggled to breathe. I looked to Mama, wanting to grab her and run. Her face was unchanged. She still stood tall, her eyes straight ahead.

"No," Aunt Jean said, shaking her head and grabbing for Siebert's hands. "No, I'll stay too. We can make you something to eat. You're hungry, yes. I have meatloaf from supper. I could warm it in the oven in no time. I'll stay and—"

"If it weren't for Inez, here," Siebert said, pushing Aunt Jean away with a straight arm, "we'd already be on our way to California. Isn't that right, Marilyn? Isn't that what you said? You said Inez was so happy seeing you and Leland together. Said he was better for you than me. Said she was all the time bad-mouthing me."

"That's not true," Aunt Jean said, her eyes bouncing between Mama and me. "It's not her fault, Siebert. I could have left if I wanted to. It's my fault."

"Inez has been bad-mouthing me since we were kids," Siebert said. "You said that, too, didn't you?"

"No," Aunt Jean said, pressing a hand to her mouth, her chin buckling as she began to cry. "I'll stay. I'll cook you something nice."

"Go," Mama said. "You, too, Jean. I'll be fine. Take the children, please. Harden will be home just anytime now. Whatever Siebert thinks is going to happen, he's mistaken."

I wanted to grab hold of Mama and run out the door. I was angry I'd ever wanted to leave Hockta and thought this was what I got for thinking Mama's life wasn't enough for me. Because it was more than enough. Maybe it was too much. Standing there in Aunt Jean's red dress, her back tall and straight, her head held high, Mama was the biggest person with the biggest life I'd ever seen. She had cemented herself to that spot to protect the rest of us, and nothing on this earth was going to make her move. Not me or Aunt Jean. And certainly not Siebert Rix.

"Don't do this, Siebert," Aunt Jean said, clinging to Siebert's hands. She dropped to her knees, begging him. "Please, don't do this to Inez. I know about the woman in your trunk. Where are you going to go? You don't have a car. They're going to know you killed that girl, and Leland O'Dell too. Whatever trouble you got in with Truitt, that's only the beginning for you. You need to leave, now, before Harden gets home. Just run. Run as far and as fast as you can."

Mama jabbed a finger at me, sending me from the room. I backed away, my mouth buried in Urban's head. He was limp in my arms, trusting me to keep him safe and never leave him again. I lifted my eyes to Mama's. She nodded like she knew I could do it, like I was as strong as she was, like she wasn't worried at all.

I backed away another step. One more, and I couldn't see her or Aunt Jean or Siebert anymore. One more, and I stepped on the grate at the base of the stairs, rattling it.

"You're right about one thing, Marilyn darlin'," I heard Siebert say. "I got nowhere to go, no money to get there, but I got so many troubles, one more ain't going to tip the scales. Besides, I think being here when Harden gets home is going to be the best part. Now, you go on upstairs with the kids and leave me and Inez to our business."

CHAPTER 46

The Trinidad Café had grown louder since Truitt first arrived. He wanted to cover his ears, thinking he might make better sense of the man standing in front of him if there weren't so much noise. But all he could do was try not to stare.

When the man was first introduced as Santo Giordano, Truitt almost asked . . . you sure? He'd read about the mob boss and heard plenty of stories, too, mostly from customers warning him to close up shop on his bolita game. He'd even seen a few pictures of him in the newspaper. Santo Giordano had been at the head of the Tampa Mafia for ten years or more, and he was smart. That's mostly what people said. He'd never spent a day in jail and probably never would.

Truitt had envisioned a large man with broad shoulders, monstrous hands, a squared-off jaw, and a stomach that hung over his belt. Instead, this man was slender and about Truitt's height. He wore a crisp white shirt under his jacket. He was clean shaven, and his thinning hair was neatly trimmed. Santo Giordano looked like a man who carried a briefcase, not a shotgun.

The wiry man pulled out a chair and motioned for Truitt to get up and move. Mr. Giordano took the seat Truitt had been sitting in. Now, Mr. Giordano was facing the front door, and Truitt was not. Right away, he was off to a bad start.

"Yes, sir," Truitt said, not remembering exactly what Mr. Giordano had asked. "I'm Truitt Holt."

"Truitt Holt who runs a bolita game in Lake County, I hear," he said. Getting a pained look on his face, he lifted a finger, and the band's volume instantly dropped. "You were saying?"

"Yes, sir," Truitt said, reminding himself to talk less and listen more. He couldn't do anything about not facing the front door, but he could mind what he said.

"Yes, sir, what?" Another flick of his finger, and a drink appeared on the table.

"I run a game," he said. "It helps pay the bills. It's just my mama and me."

Mr. Giordano started to speak, but an outburst from a few tables away silenced him. It was Charlie Wall's voice leading the sudden bout of laughter. Mr. Giordano removed a neatly folded kerchief from his jacket pocket and blotted his head as he waited for the ruckus to quiet.

"I understand you're Spencer Holt's son," he said.

This time, Mr. Giordano lifted a finger to silence Truitt while he whispered something to the wiry, brainy man. When the man walked away, Mr. Giordano gave Truitt a nod, the all clear to continue.

"That's right, sir," Truitt said. "He died when I was six years old."

"Shot in your driveway, yes?" Mr. Giordano said. "That how you remember it?"

"Yes, sir," Truitt said. "Shot as we were getting out of the car, him and me."

"Shot right in front of you, huh?" Mr. Giordano said, making a face like Truitt being right there when it happened was news to him.

Having left Mr. Giordano's side, the wiry, brainy man navigated through the crowd, people scooting forward in their chairs to make way for him. When the man reached Charlie Wall's table, he leaned in and whispered in Charlie's ear. Charlie shook his head and flared up like he was angry, but he quickly calmed down, stood, picked up his drink, and wandered off to another table.

"Yes to all of that, sir," Truitt said.

Mr. Giordano nodded like he was chewing on what Truitt said.

"So," Mr. Giordano said, settling back in as if finally able to relax. "I've been told you were changing a tire when the young woman you were helping made the mistake of telling my men you ran your own game. That also correct?"

"That's right, sir, I stopped to help with a flat tire," Truitt said, taking stock of every word before he spoke it and aiming to use as few as possible. He took a sip of his watered-down soda, the ice in this one having melted too. "On my way home. Truth be told, I'd drank too much, and it was long past dark. I'm always home before dark, especially on Friday nights. It's my biggest night. I shouldn't have stopped. I knew I shouldn't. But I did, and it was to help folks with a flat. And then the rest happened, just like you said."

A waitress arrived and set a steak in front of Mr. Giordano. She draped a napkin in his lap and gave him a damp washcloth. He cleaned his hands with it and handed it back. Truitt couldn't help that his stomach growled.

"Bring the same for Mr. Holt," Mr. Giordano said.

The woman had long dark hair that hung over one shoulder and was tied off with a bow. When she smiled, her white teeth glistened against her warm olive skin.

"Right away, Mr. Giordano," she said.

"I think you left out a few things," Mr. Giordano said, sawing off a chunk of his steak. The juices ran bloody red, and Truitt wasn't so hungry anymore. "See, I don't know how the rest went."

"The man," Truitt said. Less is more, he reminded himself. He was nervous, and he rambled when he got nervous. "Your nephew. He lunged at me when the woman told about my bolita game. I was scared. I held a jack in my hand, like a jack for fixing a flat tire."

Mr. Giordano held up his hand, silencing Truitt again, and got that same pained look on his face. The sound of Charlie Wall's laugh reached them all the way from a table up near the band. Once it quieted, Mr. Giordano signaled Truitt to continue.

"I swung it and ran," Truitt said. "I didn't know I'd hit him. I mean, I knew I hit something. But I sure didn't know I'd killed him. Sure didn't mean to."

"And that's the truth," Mr. Giordano said, taking a break from cutting his meat to dry his forehead with that same kerchief. "Home late because you were drinking too much and stopped to help with a flat tire. Didn't go looking for men from Tampa. Didn't see them and think it was your chance to get some payback? Settle a score?"

The same waitress returned and set a steak in front of Truitt, but she didn't drape the napkin in his lap or give him a damp washcloth. He mumbled thank you and started to worry. He was nearing the end of his story, and it seemed that Mr. Giordano thought Truitt's apology was going to end the conversation. But Truitt had a deal to strike. None of what had happened so far would assure him his mama was safe from now until always.

"Payback, sir?" Truitt said. "I don't know what that means. I'm guessing it has to do with my daddy being dead, seeing as how you all knew me before I knew you. But I was a kid when he was . . . when he died. I don't know anything about that day. Nothing."

Truitt shook out his napkin and laid it in his lap, liking the feeling of doing something that would make his mama proud. For a moment, he could breathe, and he felt he might be all right.

"Can I ask you, sir," Truitt said. "My daddy was shot in our driveway. Is that for a reason? I mean, I heard there's a reason a man gets shot in front of his own home."

"Could be," Mr. Giordano said. "But someone who knew your daddy a whole lot better than me would have made that call."

Mr. Giordano was telling Truitt something without saying it right out loud. Truitt stared down on his steak, red juices seeping across his plate. He wanted to push it away, but he knew that would be rude, and he wasn't sure he could move his hands.

"I'm here to tell you what happened to your nephew was an accident," Truitt said, feeling the words come out on their own. "It was an accident, and I ran. Those men, your men, they are going to kill my mama if I don't go home. But I worried if I did go home like they asked, they'd kill her anyway. I don't know those men and have no reason to trust them. So I came here. To strike a deal."

"You trust me then?" Mr. Giordano lit up a cigar, leaned back in his chair, and shifted to face Truitt. "All right, Mr. Holt. I'm listening. What deal would you like to strike?"

Truitt pulled his notepad from his pocket. Whatever his daddy had done, it had started with greed. Truitt wasn't going to be greedy. He was going to give Mr. Giordano everything. Everything.

"I'll give you my game," Truitt said. "Every bet I ever took, every winning number I ever drew, every payout I ever made is right here. I have 8,275 dollars I will give you. That's every cent I've earned and not spent. We never wasted money, only spent it on food and the lights and such. If you want, I'll keep working the game for you or not. It's yours to do with as you like. All I care about is knowing my mama will be safe, and no one will hurt her ever. Don't even care if you have to kill me. Just not my mama."

"Just your mama?" Mr. Giordano said.

"Sir?" Truitt said, not understanding the question.

"If a man wants leverage on you, he can generally find it if he looks hard enough," Mr. Giordano said, tipping his head toward the ceiling and exhaling a cloud of smoke. "You're telling me your mama is your only soft spot?"

Truitt shrugged. He didn't know what to say so he went with Wiley's advice and said less.

"You said you'd had too much to drink when you stopped to help with the flat," Mr. Giordano said, picking up Truitt's notepad and flipping through it as he talked. "You said you drank too much, and Friday was your biggest night, and you were late heading home. All those things are the acts of a careless man. But a man who's organized, which you clearly are, he isn't careless. Unless he has a reason."

"Yes, sir."

"And your reason was a young lady, because seldom is there another reason for a man your age."

"Yes, sir," Truitt said. The blood coursing through his neck turned hot and bled into his face. His breathing turned short and shallow. Santo Giordano had picked through the little bit Truitt had told him and found his way to Addie Anne. "But she ain't—"

Mr. Giordano held up a finger, once again cutting Truitt off. He snubbed out his cigar as he stared up at the front door. He waved at the wiry man and pointed at something. Truitt shifted and he saw what Mr. Giordano saw. Charlie Wall saw too.

"Well, good goddamn." It was Charlie Wall's voice. "Here we go with another face from the past."

Wiley Bishop walked up to the table, slowly, his hands loose at his sides.

"Let's go, Truitt," he said. "You're coming with me."

CHAPTER 47

I stood at the bottom of the stairs leading up to Mama's and Daddy's room and the second telephone. My arms were numb from holding Urban. I stared down on the grate in the floor, lost in its mesh of tiny metal squares.

In the kitchen, a chair tipped over, and Aunt Jean cried out. Siebert must have pushed her. And then I heard the click of a gun being cocked. Just this morning, it had been Daddy and me, cocking the gun as we shot at tin cans. Now it was Siebert.

"One way or another," Siebert said, "Inez and I are going to find ourselves alone."

My head had emptied out. The sound of Siebert's voice was muf- fled, like it was coming from far away. The light from the kitchen and living room faded, leaving only a cone of light directly in front of me. The walls, the stairs, the banister all became fuzzy, as if slowly melting away. But the grate at my feet was so close I could count every tiny square in the metal.

Making a *shhhing* sound in Urban's ear so he'd stay quiet, I stood at the bottom of the stairs and waited. I could go upstairs and make a call, but help wouldn't arrive in time to save Mama. I had to do some- thing now.

Aunt Jean stumbled out of the kitchen just like I knew she would. She was crying. Her eyes were red. Her hair shot out in all different directions. The slender sash on her simple tan-and-white dress was torn. She grabbed me and tried to pull Urban and me up the stairs, but I didn't move. In the kitchen, another crash, maybe a chair tipping over again. Mama cried out. Aunt Jean crumpled to the stairs and pulled at me.

"I'm sorry, Addie," she said. "We have to. He has a gun."

I shook my head as I peeled Urban's arms from around my neck. He was still limp. I handed him to Aunt Jean.

This was like target practice with Daddy. He always said I was a good shot. I could wrangle my nerves, tuck away my fear, shoot with a steady hand. And that's what I needed to do. No one was going to call action or cut. There would be only one take. There was no script to tell me how it would all play out or if it would work at all. I needed to have a steady hand and to tuck away my fears.

"You go," I whispered.

Mama screamed again. The sound buckled me.

"Now," I said. "Run to the top of the stairs and scream as loud as you can."

Clinging to Urban with one arm, Aunt Jean clawed at me with her free hand, trying to get hold of some part of me.

"No," she said. "I won't leave you. You come too."

I shoved her, hard.

"Now. Go. Leave the lights out. Hide in Mama's room. Once you're in there, close the door and scream as loud as you can. And keep on screaming."

"Scream?" Aunt Jean whispered, shaking her head. "I can't. I can't do that."

"You can. Go. Go now."

As Aunt Jean started up the stairs, struggling to keep hold of Urban, I slipped from the landing into the living room. Once there, I pressed tight against the wall where no one could see me. This was me, playing the part of someone strong enough to help Mama.

A single lamp shone in the front room, throwing a glow over Mr. O'Dell's body. He looked almost peaceful. A few short hours ago, he'd

231

been sitting with Aunt Jean, the woman he thought he'd marry. Now he was dead, just like Donna Lee. It felt like once death came, it settled in to take as many lives as it could.

From the kitchen, Mama's cries continued. I pinched my eyes closed, trying to hear Aunt Jean's footsteps overhead. Only seconds passed, but it felt like hours. It felt like Aunt Jean was gone for good, and Mama and I had been left alone with Siebert.

And then Aunt Jean began to scream. One long scream that pierced the muffled sounds coming from the kitchen. And again. And again. Her screams filled the house. They filled my chest and lungs and made me want to scream too. But I couldn't. I clamped both hands over my mouth, readying myself to move. I clenched and flexed my toes, trying to force blood through my veins because I couldn't feel my legs.

At the sound of stumbling in the kitchen, I pressed tighter to the wall. Heavy footsteps hit the floor and crossed into the landing. The grate at the foot of the stairs rattled as Siebert's shoe came down hard on it. Bouncing off the walls, he ran up the steps toward Aunt Jean's screams.

First, I yanked the single lamp's plug from the wall. The living room fell dark. In the landing, I lifted the grate, exposing the hole in the floor and lunged for the first stair.

Somewhere overhead, Aunt Jean continued to scream. Siebert was yelling out for her to stop and asking what the hell. I took the stairs two at a time. My heart pounded, and my chest burned as I tried to get enough air.

At the top of the stairwell, I stopped. Straight ahead, the hallway was dark except for the moonlight spilling from my bedroom.

I crouched, trying to hide in the shadows, and looked down the hallway. Aunt Jean was behind one of the doors, still screaming. Somewhere Urban was crying. At the end of the hallway, Siebert threw open the bathroom door and slapped at the wall as if to turn on a light.

"Goddamn, Marilyn," he shouted, squinting when the bathroom lights popped on. "Stop that. Stop your screaming."

Still crouched on the ground, I crawled to my bedroom door, took hold of the knob, and waited for a break in the screams. Waited for Aunt Jean to take a breath. When she did, I slammed the door as hard as I could, and then I had to look. I had to be sure.

I turned toward the bathroom to see Siebert swing around. When he took off running toward me, I jumped down the top few stairs, grabbed the railing, and half slid, half ran the rest of the way down.

The narrow stairwell was dark, lit only by the moonlight from above and the faint glow of the kitchen light below. Aunt Jean continued screaming. Siebert's black wing tips pounded down the hallway toward the stairs. From the kitchen, Mama shouted my name.

At the bottom step, I leaped over the hole I'd uncovered when I removed the grate from the floor, dove toward the kitchen, and slapped the light switch on the wall.

The entire house fell dark.

Mama grabbed me, wrapping me up in her arms, asking what was happening over and over. Aunt Jean still screamed, sounding like she might never stop. Siebert charged down the stairwell, shouting at Aunt Jean to shut up.

I clung to Mama, not breathing, not moving, waiting for Siebert to reach the bottom of the stairs. He was moving quickly, blind in the dark. One last step.

I shoved Mama away and dove across the kitchen threshold. I had to see.

Leaping over the last stair with one long step, Siebert's foot landed in the secret cavity where Urban hid his pennies. His leg disappeared into the two-foot-deep vacant space, but the rest of him kept going. His leg snapped at the knee, and the gun fell from his waistband.

Siebert's screams stopped Aunt Jean's screams. Rolling onto his back, uncertain what had happened, he grabbed for his leg, now dangling at an unnatural angle. In the dark, he could see only shadows and seemed confused by what he saw. A silence followed what had been chaos. Behind me, the kitchen light switched on. That woke Siebert. He scrambled backward as if trying to get away from his broken leg and began to cry out.

"The gun," Mama shouted and pushed past me toward Siebert.

She and I both reached for it, but Siebert got a hand on it first.

CHAPTER 48

It surprised Truitt to see Wiley in this setting, a small, dark restaurant where people were dressed in suits and dresses. Wiley, in his button-down shirt and work boots, didn't fit in. Truitt seeing him, one familiar thing in a night chock full of seeing and doing things for the first time, was a relief. He felt he could relax for one moment, catch his breath, but that feeling quickly faded to anger when he remembered Wiley had locked him in that basement.

Truitt had been doing just fine on his own and didn't want Wiley's help. He started to stand and tell Wiley exactly that, but before he could get to his feet, another hand to his shoulder stopped him. The wiry man with the brains gave him a wink and a nod as if to say everything was all right, and he should have a seat.

"This is Mr. Giordano," the wiry man said to Wiley. "How about you have a seat. He'll have supper sent over right away."

"Yes," Mr. Giordano said. "A seat. Please. I gather you know Truitt."

"I do," Wiley said, glancing at Truitt. "You all right, Truitt?"

"We were at the end of some business, Mr. Holt and I," Mr. Giordano said.

"He's not my daddy," Truitt said, because Mr. Giordano was talking to Wiley like he was.

"But I'm guessing he's the closest thing you have to one," Mr. Giordano said. "Or he wouldn't be here. Am I right?"

Wiley waved off the steak that was offered to him. He looked different to Truitt. The lines of his face were sharper. His hair, normally neat and combed in place, hung loose across his brow. And he looked tired, but unlike Truitt, Wiley didn't look at all afraid.

"Well, here's where we are," Mr. Giordano said. "I like Truitt. He's been honest, forthright. He's willing to give up his game and pay me 8,275 dollars cash. In exchange, I promise his mama will not be harmed."

"Addie Anne too," Truitt said, flicking his eyes at Wiley.

He thought Wiley would be surprised about Addie Anne, but he didn't look it. Instead, he stared straight ahead at Mr. Giordano. He was thinking, because Wiley was always thinking. Always piecing together what someone was doing and had done and would do next.

He'd been doing the same to Truitt since he was just a kid. Truitt had grown up saying . . . he's not my daddy . . . and having said it again just now embarrassed him. Either Wiley already knew about Truitt and Addie Anne, or right now, he didn't care.

"Ah," Mr. Giordano said. "Addie Anne would be the young lady who left you drinking and staying out late. Licking some wounds, I presume."

"She has to be safe too." Truitt mirrored the way Wiley sat, feet planted flat on the ground, knees and elbows wide, making himself as big as he could.

Mr. Giordano nodded and leaned forward as if to say something else. Instead, two men appeared, blocking the table. At Mr. Giordano's signal, the men peeled apart, disappeared again into the background, and Charlie Wall stepped up to the table, hands raised as if he'd just been frisked.

"Don't mean to intrude," he said, slapping Wiley on the back. "But I never thought I'd see the day."

Wiley kept his eyes on Mr. Giordano. Truitt wanted to ask why Charlie Wall would think anything about Wiley, but the look on Wiley's face was enough to keep him quiet.

"How about you make like you ain't seeing the day," Wiley said, without looking at Charlie Wall. "Assume you ain't seeing me."

"You'll leave us to our conversation, Charlie?" Mr. Giordano said, nodding in Charlie's direction. "If you don't mind."

"Surely," Charlie Wall said. "Surely. Surely. Good to see you, Wiley. That's all I mean to say. Good to see you. Been too damn long. That's all I mean to say."

Mr. Giordano whispered to the wiry man with the brains, who always seemed to be at his side. Twice Charlie Wall glanced back as he made his way to another table and some people he seemed to know. He sat where he could see Mr. Giordano's table.

"As I was saying," Mr. Giordano said. "That deal is fine with me. All except for one thing."

"I'd say it's fine as is," Wiley said. "Truitt gives up his game, and you guarantee his mama and the young lady are unharmed."

The band no longer played, and several tables had cleared. Some voices rose above others, ladies telling their stories, men arguing over the Red Sox lineup, someone complaining their drink was watered down, but above it all was Charlie Wall.

"Tell this little lady who I am," Charlie Wall was saying. "Tell her how things were when Charlie Wall was at the wheel. And if she asks me nice, I'll tell her how goddamn good it used to be."

Mr. Giordano rubbed a thumb on the spot between his eyes, like the sound of Charlie Wall was giving him a headache. The wiry man with the brains motioned as if asking should he do something, and Mr. Giordano shook his head.

"Here's what we're forgetting," Mr. Giordano said, still rubbing the spot between his eyes, looking altogether worn out. "The game and the money guarantee Truitt's mama and his young lady are left unharmed. But what about my nephew, my sister's boy? Who will answer for his death?"

CHAPTER 49

Siebert held a gun in one hand, pointing it as best he could at Addie and Inez. They were standing right there, dead ahead. An easy shot. If only his vision would clear. He pinched his eyes closed and opened them again, trying to make the room settle around him and trying not to look at his twisted, broken leg. There had been a snap, a loud crack. Good Lord, had that been the sound of his leg snapping in two? He leaned on his one free hand and swallowed the bile that leaked into his throat.

Marilyn had been screaming. He was certain of it. Screaming like she was being split in half. Now the house was quiet.

"Marilyn," he shouted, waving the gun in Inez and Addie's direction. "Get down here. Right goddamn now. Or I start shooting."

Marilyn. He'd said it. He couldn't help that his voice was strained and probably sounded ragged, but he'd made himself clear. And if she didn't hear him saying it before, she damn sure heard him now. No more fucking around with Jean. Never again.

"Help me up," he managed to say. "You, Addie. Right fucking now."

Stretching out a hand so someone could pull him to his feet, Siebert laid his head back and closed his eyes, readying himself for the pain.

But no one grabbed his hand. Opening his eyes again he found the entryway empty. Addie and Inez were gone. The spinning wouldn't stop, and now he was shivering. Shivering so hard he struggled to hold the gun firm.

This couldn't be the end for Siebert. This was Addie's fault, and he damn sure wouldn't be one-upped by Addie Anne Buckley. He'd never been one-upped in his whole damn life.

Reaching up with his free hand, he grabbed the newel post at the bottom of the stairs and pulled. He couldn't help the groan he let out either. Like a twelve-inch knife, the pain punctured his thigh and traveled all the way up to the base of his throat. He cringed. A knife. This wasn't the time to be thinking about Donna Lee and the pain she'd felt.

One more pull, and he stood on his good foot.

"Right goddamn now, Marilyn," he shouted again, hopping toward the kitchen because that had to be where Addie and Inez made off to. "And bring that kid."

"Go." It was a whispering. Inez. She was whispering, and that was the sound of someone pushing open a window sash.

Hearing Marilyn start down the stairs, Siebert waved his gun to hurry her up and made his way to the kitchen doorway. A window had been pushed open, and its screen knocked out. Thinking she could escape, Addie had hoisted a leg to crawl through the opening. She was trying to drag Inez with her, but Inez resisted and pushed Addie to go on ahead.

"That doesn't look like a good idea," Siebert said, his gun trained on Inez.

Inez swung around, and Addie froze, one leg out the window, the other dangling in the kitchen. She eased back inside, and once she had both feet on the floor, she slid up next to Inez.

The front of Inez's dress was torn, her slip was showing, and the necklace Marilyn must have loaned her lay in pieces on the floor. As the two of them backed away from Siebert, eyes wide, hands clutched together, the tiny stones crunched under their feet.

"Sorry we got interrupted, Inez," Siebert said, his teeth clenched to fend off the throbbing that had started in his leg.

"That's enough, Siebert," Inez said, scolding him. "Look at yourself. You're not going anywhere. It's over. That's quite enough."

That's quite enough, Siebert. That's just what Inez would say when they were kids. Her being older made her think she was the boss of Siebert. Find boys your own age. Leave Norma Jean be. But there was nothing wrong with Siebert and Marilyn—Norma Jean way back then—striking up a friendship. Kids like them, they had nobody, so finding somebody meant finding a way to survive.

In the years that followed, Siebert would tell countless reporters the story about using his old Kodak to take pretend pictures of Marilyn. Already, Siebert had known that one day, he'd be a famous photographer, and Marilyn would be a star. They were a perfect fit from the beginning. It made great copy, and the press devoured every word.

But Inez, she never saw in Marilyn what Siebert saw. Inez saw only a little girl and assumed Marilyn needed protection, coddling, but Marilyn never needed either of those things. She was shrewd from the get-go. What she needed, what Siebert did for her, was to be molded. Hell, he was only a kid, and already he was closing a deal that would feed him for the rest of his life.

"You always did want to get rid of me," Siebert said, leaning in the threshold, feeling Marilyn come up behind him. "But look at me now. Look at me all these years. Me, I'm the one who made Marilyn what she is. And you and yours, you ain't nothing."

"Fine," Inez said, trapping Addie behind her as if that would stop Siebert. "I'm nothing. So just go. Why stay here and bother with nothing?"

Siebert dragged his shirtsleeve across his face again. He was shivering and sweating, and the throbbing in his leg had spread into his chest.

"Outside," he said, trying not to let on how dizzy he felt.

Getting from here to the car seemed like a near impossibility. And damn it, no one was moving. He swung the gun around, thinking he'd point it at Marilyn. Instead, he found the boy, cradled in Marilyn's arms, staring back at him.

"Mama and Daddy have a telephone in their room," the boy said and pressed a finger to his lips.

"You think I didn't remember about that?" Siebert said, though he hadn't. He tried thinking what that meant, a telephone, phone calls, but he couldn't take on one more problem. He wobbled, steadied himself in the kitchen doorway and pointed the gun at the boy. "It don't matter about no phone. Nobody's getting here in time to help you, little man. Now, go, outside, all of you."

That was the easy answer. Siebert would be long gone before help could get here. He clung to the threshold as Addie and Inez walked past him, out the screen door, and onto the porch. Marilyn went next, the boy in her arms. Once they had all walked down the stairs to the drive below, Siebert followed. He hopped to the back door and rested against the frame. A few more unsteady steps, and he reached the porch railing. He couldn't stifle the groans he let out as he half hopped, half slid down the stairs.

"Stop your whispering," Siebert said, because Inez thought she was being sneaky by whispering to Addie while Siebert suffered in pain. "You got something to say, you say it to me."

"I have nothing to say to you," Inez said, squaring up to Siebert again.

"How about you tell me where the hell the car is that you came home in?" Siebert said. Sweat dripped in his eyes. His shirt was soaked through, and he had to tip forward to keep himself from throwing up.

"Someone dropped Inez," Marilyn said, still holding the boy and using a calm, easy tone. "Remember? We were waiting for Harden. He has the car."

"Hell, yes, I remember," Siebert said, knowing Marilyn's sweet voice was for the boy and not for him. She didn't give a damn about Siebert anymore. "But Inez had to get home somehow."

Leaning against the post at the bottom of the stairs, Siebert knew he couldn't last much longer. He was struggling to hold his shoulders back and his head up.

"Tillie Harrington's oldest was kind enough to give me a ride," Inez said, still standing at Addie's side.

Siebert wanted to smack that mouth of hers. She was talking to him like she wasn't one bit afraid.

"What did you tell her?" Siebert said through clenched teeth.

"Tell her?" Inez said. "About what?"

"You said you seen my car," Siebert said. Lord almighty, she was irritating. "When you first got here, you said that. You tell her I was here?"

"She dropped me at the turnoff, and I walked the last bit," Inez said. "She had a party to get back to, and her mama needed her help. I didn't want to impose. I didn't tell her anything because I hadn't seen your car yet."

Readjusting herself, Inez clutched the neckline of her dress together. At least Siebert got that moment. Tearing the dress open, hearing Inez scream, that was a memory Siebert would hold on to for a good long time.

"And where the hell is Harden?" Siebert said. "When's he getting home?"

"She doesn't know, Siebert," Marilyn said, still talking in her sweet voice.

"He'll be home just any time," Inez said, wrapping an arm around Addie, still thinking that was enough to stop Siebert. "And you're going to wish you'd left here when you could."

"Jesus Christ," Siebert said, wanting to sit on the stairs, but afraid if he did, he'd never get back up. "I been trying to leave all fucking night."

He let the gun hang at his side and studied the pitiful scene in front of him. Just a few months ago, he'd been dining in New York City and being tended by waitresses wearing nylon stockings.

"You," he said, pointing at Addie. "Get over here and help me to the car. I'll drive on the damn rim if it means getting me out of this place."

"Let me help you, Siebert," Marilyn said, hurrying across the drive to hand the boy off to Inez. "I have an even better idea. I been thinking,

Harden probably has a tire out there in the garage. I've seen a few, in fact. Addie, you go see if your daddy has a spare that might work."

Inez propped the boy on one hip and grabbed Addie, stopping her from walking away.

"No," Inez said. "Addie's staying here. Harden doesn't keep spares. Nothing that's any good."

"Why don't you at least look, Addie?" Marilyn said, going against Inez for maybe the first time in her life. "You see what you can find, and I'll get in the trunk and get the jack."

Siebert forced his shoulders back and lifted his chest. By God, Marilyn had come up with a good idea.

"Yes, you, Addie," Siebert said, the words coming out stronger. "Go on and find a tire, one that'll fit my car. Got to be something out in that mess of a garage."

Hope was a powerful thing, and suddenly standing wasn't quite so hard. The gun wasn't quite so heavy. Same as Marilyn stood up to Inez for the first time in her life, she had a good idea for the first time too. But good as it was, it was also Siebert's last hope.

Siebert didn't like to think about last hopes. They were the end of the line. But here it was. His last hope. All he had to do was leave here before a set of headlights appeared at the end of the dark drive. And then he'd head north. He'd drive with the lights off, stick to the dirt roads. He wouldn't be able to make it far on a rim. But on a spare tire, any spare tire, he might just make it. And then he'd find a doctor, although where the hell was he going to find one of those? But still, he had a way out, and wouldn't you know, Marilyn gave it to him. She gave him the idea that would get him back to New York City or LA. Back to a nice juicy steak. A good cigar. A sweet waitress with seams running up her nylons.

Siebert was on his way back.

CHAPTER 50

I peeled Mama's hand from my shoulder and ran toward the garage. Mama was right about the tires Daddy kept being no good. Mostly he kept the odd tire so Urban could fill it with dirt and grow his own tomato plants. But I'd find something, anything, that we could put on Siebert's car, because then he'd leave, and this would all be over.

"Your daddy's all right," Mama had whispered to me as Siebert was first struggling to follow us out the back door. "He's with Truitt's mama at their house. Sheriff Bishop went to Tampa, to Ybor City, to bring Truitt home. From the Trinidad. He'll be all right. Everyone will be all right."

Hearing Mama say Truitt was going to be safe should have filled me with relief, and it did, but as I ran toward the garage, I also felt my chin buckle and tears pool in my eyes.

I didn't know how Truitt ended up at the Trinidad Café, but I knew why. The Trinidad was often written about in the newspapers alongside news of another Mafia shooting in Tampa. Truitt was there because he'd killed Santo Giordano's nephew—Santo Giordano, another name from the papers—and someone had to pay for that. Siebert said as much when he threatened to tie me to a tree. Either Truitt paid or Siebert did. I was boxed in on one side by hoping Mama was right about Truitt being safe and on the other side by being afraid she was wrong.

In the dark garage, I ran from tire to tire. Squinting in the near total darkness, I bypassed one that was tractor size and another meant for a pull cart. When I found one that looked like it would fit a regular car, I tipped it on its edge, rolled it out of the garage, and met Aunt Jean at the back of Siebert's car.

As I held the tire steady and Aunt Jean fumbled with a key to open the trunk, I looked over at Mama and forced a smile, so she wouldn't worry. Her eyes darted from me and Aunt Jean to Siebert and back again, like she was constantly weighing our safety.

When the trunk popped open, I ducked behind it so Siebert couldn't see that I had turned my head away. I couldn't bear to see Donna Lee again, but I could still feel her staring up at me with those blank eyes.

"Go do your best," Aunt Jean said, handing me the jack she pulled from the trunk. "Just leave the tire here for now."

Up near the house, Siebert still clung to the banister at the bottom of the porch stairs, yelling at Aunt Jean to hurry up. The gun dangled from one hand, his broken leg was useless and twisted, and his head bobbed as he labored to hold it up.

Letting the tire fall on its side, I took the jack from Aunt Jean. It was heavy, and I had to hold it with both hands. Truitt had swung this very tool and killed a man. Siebert told us that too. Truitt must have been scared like me. He must have had no other choice. I didn't, either, but I couldn't do it.

"I don't think I can," I said, lowering the jack. Already my arms were tired. "It's too heavy. I can't hit Siebert with it."

"You're not going to hit anyone," Aunt Jean said, motioning for me to hold open the trunk. "I want you to jack up the car. Put on that new tire. Then, we'll send Siebert on his way."

"I don't know how to change a tire," I said, propping up the trunk.

Aunt Jean brushed me off and drew in a deep breath, preparing herself for something. I still couldn't bring myself to look at Donna Lee, but seeing Aunt Jean brace herself, I knew what she was thinking.

"No," I whispered. "Aunt Jean, no."

Reaching into the trunk, Aunt Jean wrapped one hand around the knife wedged in Donna Lee's side.

I had to look. I owed it to Donna Lee. Countless times, she'd asked me if she was pretty enough to make it into the movies. Now, under the soft moonlight, if not for the dried blood on her pale-yellow dress, she'd look as if she were just waking up.

With one hand wrapped around the knife, Aunt Jean yanked, but it didn't come out. She tried again, this time using both hands to force the knife back and forth. It still didn't budge. Holding the trunk open with one hand, I reached in with my other, and on three, we pulled together.

The knife came loose. Dropping back against the bumper, Aunt Jean hugged it to her chest and then slipped it in the pocket of her simple tan-and-white dress. She didn't like to wear dresses with pockets. They ruined the line of her silhouette, but that night she'd worn a dress Mr. O'Dell would like.

"Your daddy taught you about changing a tire, didn't he?" she said. "Just do your best and holler for your mama to come help you."

"You can't stab him," I whispered, grabbing Aunt Jean before she walked away.

"It won't come to that," she said. "The knife is just a precaution. You get busy on that tire, and Siebert will be gone in no time. All we need to do is keep him happy and calm until we can put him in that car and send him on his way."

Aunt Jean's tender voice, wide eyes, and soft smile made for a nice, comfortable landing in a very uncomfortable discussion. She was an easy person to believe, and I believed her.

Using both hands, I held the jack like a sword as I walked toward the flat tire. I was ready for battle, and I called out for Mama to come help me. I wasn't sure how loudly I'd said it or if she heard. But then she was there next to me, Urban's head resting on her shoulder, her whispering to me and asking if I could do this.

Across the drive, Aunt Jean walked toward Siebert, both hands tucked in her pockets.

"Great news, Siebert," Aunt Jean called to him. "Addie found a good tire, and she's getting the old one pulled off right now. I'll help you to the car, and you and me, we'll be on our way in no time."

Squatted at the flat tire, I swung around when I heard Aunt Jean say "you and me" to Siebert. I wanted to stand and ask her why she said that, but I still had a tire to change. And that was just Aunt Jean playing a part. The quicker I fixed the tire, the quicker we'd be rid of Siebert.

Settling back on my knees, relieved that at least Siebert couldn't see me, I fumbled with the jack. I didn't know where to put it or how to make it work. I didn't even know which end was up. Mama hovered over me, Urban in her arms, her eyes still flicking from Siebert to me and back again.

"You just keep your distance," Siebert shouted at Aunt Jean. And then to me, he said, "You. Addie. You even know what you're doing over there?"

I looked up at Mama. My hands were frozen, and my heart was pounding at the base of my throat because I didn't know what I was doing at all.

"She knows full well how to change a tire, Siebert," Mama shouted. "Just let her be so she can work."

I studied the jack, not remembering how to lower it so it would fit under the side of the car or even which way it slid under. Daddy had shown me before, but I'd never done it on my own. Practice makes perfect. That's what he always said. It was what Aunt Jean always said. I closed my eyes and tried to remember what to do.

"I've seen your father put it back there," Mama whispered, nodding down at the car. She was still holding Urban, and with one hand, she cupped the back of his head and kept his face hidden in her shoulder. "There's a spot where it's meant to fit, I think."

"What are you whispering about over there?" Siebert said, his voice strained. "Marilyn, you go see what's happening."

Siebert had killed two people, and his plan to slip out of town before some mobsters could find him had collapsed. He had no money and that meant no chance of catching a train out of Florida. A good tire on the car was his only hope of escaping this mess. If I couldn't get the tire changed, I had to find a way to make Siebert believe I could. I had to keep his last hope alive, until when, I wasn't sure. Maybe until Daddy got home. Maybe until the pain and the liquor made Siebert pass out.

"Everything's just fine," I heard Aunt Jean saying, her voice light and cheerful. "That's right, isn't it, Addie Anne? She'll have us out of here in no time."

There it was again. Aunt Jean said "us" and not "you." She said . . . she'll have *us* out of here in no time. I glanced up at Mama, wondering if she'd heard the same as me. She motioned for me to keep working as she kept watch over Aunt Jean. She had heard the same thing, and like me, she was trying to decide what was real.

Again and again, I tried to make the jack fit where Mama pointed, but nothing about the tool made sense to me. Looking up at Mama again because I didn't know what else to try or do, I shrugged. She started to whisper something and stopped when Urban squirmed to the ground. Mama reached to stop him, but he was already at my side. Taking the jack from me, he released the ratchet and slid it into place.

Urban was born knowing how to rewire a lamp, that's what Mama always said. He slid the jack into place and began pumping the handle. I joined in, and the car frame rose.

"See there?" Aunt Jean said, her words sounding almost like a song. "It's working."

"We're almost done," I said, tipping my head and shouting. "It's all fine. It's working fine."

Settling back behind the car, I hugged Urban, clinging to his five-year-old little shoulders. He could change a tire. He could give Siebert what he needed. I didn't have to keep his one hope alive, because I was going to make it come true.

Not seeming to notice me, Urban continued to work. His hands moved quickly as he focused on the task before him. He slipped the handle from the jack, flipped it around, and slid it on one of the nuts holding the tire in place. Placing two hands on top, he jumped, using his weight to pop the lug nut loose.

"Should have thought of this sooner," Aunt Jean said, her voice still carrying a melody. "You and me, we'll be on our way in no time."

Aunt Jean said it again. You and me. It was no accident. Even though I knew she was playing a part, it was painful hearing Aunt Jean say that. I started to stand again, wanting to tell Aunt Jean to stop saying those things, but stopped when Urban tugged on my shirtsleeve.

I knelt on the ground, putting me at eye level with him. He leaned in to whisper in my ear. His breath was warm on my neck. As much as we'd tried to shield Urban, he knew exactly what was happening.

"That tire over there," he said, one tiny finger pointing at the tire I'd rolled out of Daddy's garage. "It ain't going to fit."

A heavy silence bubbled up and trapped me inside my own head. A long moment passed when I didn't move. I didn't know how long. The sounds of Urban popping loose another lug nut finally woke me. He looked at me, and like he was happy I'd finally come back, he smiled.

I thought that tire was the way to give Siebert his last hope. But it wasn't. It was a way to stall, and nothing more. Now, unless Daddy got home real soon, there was only one way we were getting rid of Siebert Rix, and it was tucked in the pocket of Aunt Jean's tan-and-white cotton dress.

Like Urban, Mama had seen that something was troubling me. She touched my shoulder, wanting to help. I shook my head, my way to tell her nothing was wrong, and lifted high enough to see what Aunt Jean was doing. I needed to tell her we couldn't fix the tire, but I didn't know how.

"Show me your hands," Siebert said, pointing his gun at Aunt Jean as she continued to walk closer to him.

Somewhere along the way, Siebert had stopped trusting Aunt Jean. She held up her hands, wiggled her fingers, and smiled.

"You're a silly one, Siebert Rix," she said. "How long have we known each other, and you think I'm coming to hurt you?"

Aunt Jean slid up next to Siebert, offering him a shoulder to lean on but not getting too close until he invited her. After taking in the house, the drive, and his broken-down car, he must have decided he had no other choice. He tucked his gun in his waistband and waved her closer.

Slowly, still wiggling her fingers, Aunt Jean lowered one shoulder so Siebert could drape an arm around her. With Aunt Jean's help, he took his first step, an awkward hop on his one good leg, toward his car. That one step must have been more than Mama could tolerate.

"You and Urban stay here," Mama whispered, and before I could stop her, she rounded the front of the car and started toward Aunt Jean and Siebert.

"Stay back, Inez," Aunt Jean said. Her voice was still cheerful, but it had grown a sharp edge. "I'm going with Siebert. He and I, we're both getting in that car and leaving. You just get back there and help Addie finish up."

Mama kept walking. She didn't have the cover of the car to protect her anymore. She was out in the open, an easy shot for Siebert if he wanted to pull out his gun and take it.

The new tire wasn't going to fit, but Mama didn't know that. She believed we could fix it and that Siebert could drive away. She had also heard Aunt Jean saying "we will leave" and "you and I will start a new life" and "you and I will be fine." She believed that too. She didn't understand Aunt Jean was only playing a part, doing and saying what she had to do and say to keep Siebert happy.

"Soon as the tire is fixed, we'll see Siebert on his way," Mama said. "But Jean, you're not going with him. I've heard enough of you saying 'we this' and 'we that' to him. This is your home. We are your family."

This was the version of Mama who Aunt Jean sometimes talked about. I'd listen to the stories, thinking of Mama as two different people. The one before she became my mother, and the one after. But here she was, that version Aunt Jean bragged about. Standing in a tattered red dress, the jewels ripped from her neck, her lower lip bloodied, this was the version who looked after Aunt Jean when she was a little girl, bouncing from home to home, her own mama locked up in a hospital. This was the version of Mama who, as she boarded a train bound for Florida with her new husband, hugged Aunt Jean and promised to visit. And she did. But mostly, Mama wrote letters or called on the telephone, always telling Aunt Jean she was special and loved and would have a full, wonderful life one day. Mama never forgot her.

And when Aunt Jean was old enough and she was broken for the first time, she boarded a train and came here to Hockta, to Mama. To all of us. And she had been coming back ever since. We'd been her family ever since.

"You don't understand a life like ours, Inez," Aunt Jean said as she hugged Siebert to her side and strained to hold him steady. "You never have. I'm not a little girl anymore, and I don't need you protecting me. I can't live like you, and I don't want to. I'm sorry to say it, but it's true. Now get back behind that car and help Addie."

Mama still didn't stop. Her dress hanging in tatters, she kept walking. I wanted to reach out and stop her. She was putting herself in danger, and she didn't need to. She didn't understand Aunt Jean would never leave us, and she didn't know that if Aunt Jean had to, she'd pull a knife from her pocket and kill Siebert Rix.

"Ought to listen to her, Inez," Siebert said, his words starting to slur. "She knows what she wants, and it ain't you. I've had a long damn night. Do not test me."

"I'm not letting you leave us, Jean," Mama said.

"Don't call me that anymore," Aunt Jean said. "I'm not Jean. I'm Marilyn."

I grabbed Urban up off the ground at hearing Aunt Jean say that and held him tight. Her words stung like a slap in the face. They rattled me and woke me to what was really unfolding.

I had thought Aunt Jean was playing a part, but maybe I was wrong. Maybe she really did want to leave with Siebert, because never, not once, had she been Marilyn here in Hockta.

I'd spent almost every day since Aunt Jean first came here with news of my birthday gift trying to wish away the weeks, days, and hours so my birthday would come sooner. I couldn't wait to start a whole new life, a big life, a shiny, glittery, perfume-scented life that would look nothing like Mama's. But now I wanted Aunt Jean to stay forever and be happy going on walks with me and Mama on Sunday afternoons and stitching up holes in Urban's socks and peeling potatoes for supper even though she was no good at it.

I wanted her to stay forever. I wanted to stay forever, and I didn't want forever to end in our driveway.

Siebert stopped limping forward, steadied himself, took the gun from his waistband, and pointed it at Mama. "Get that tire on. Now."

"Stop working, Addie," Mama said, continuing toward them. "Siebert is not leaving here with Jean."

Siebert cocked the gun. "I am so damn tired of your mouth, Inez. I've heard enough to last a lifetime."

"I've always known what you are, Siebert Rix," Mama said, stretching out a hand to Aunt Jean. "And you're nothing without Jean. I don't know a man on earth who could hold his head up knowing that."

"Mama," I said, clinging to Urban and crying out to her. Even knowing I was lying and knowing the tire would never fit, I still said it. "Leave him be. We're doing it. We're getting the tire fixed."

I stood, cradling Urban's head so he wouldn't see. I had thought Aunt Jean was playing a version of herself to outsmart Siebert Rix. But she wasn't. All the things she'd said before Mr. O'Dell died were true. She hated it here. She didn't need us. She didn't want us. I'd always thought she was shiny through and through, but she wasn't. This was the real Aunt Jean. The rot beneath.

"We're almost done, Mr. Rix," I said, the words spilling out though they were a lie.

Aunt Jean wasn't going to use the knife to stop Siebert. Instead, she wanted to drive away with him. She said it herself . . . she hated it here. That meant we had to find a way to make that tire fit. We'd make it stay on long enough that they could drive away. And what happened next, I didn't care.

"Let them go, Mama," I said. "Urban and me, we're almost done. Let Aunt Jean go. Let them both go."

"You going to listen to your girl, Inez?" Siebert said, looking at Mama over the barrel of his gun. "Or you got something else to say before I pull this trigger?"

CHAPTER 51

The Trinidad was filling up again but with a different crowd. A thin layer of smoke muffled the already dim lighting. The music was slow and gritty. Ice rattled in glasses. Corks popped. Truitt recognized a few men who sat at nearby tables, but they were sitting with different women.

"Well," Mr. Giordano said, still waiting for an answer. "We're dealing with two different transgressions, yes? There's Truitt's game, and there's my dead nephew. We've handled the game. But how will we appease my sister, who has lost her boy?"

"I'm the one who killed him," Truitt said. "So I'm accountable. I only care that my mama and Addie are safe. I didn't mean to kill anyone, and I'm real sorry, but—"

Wiley silenced Truitt with a hand to his forearm, the same move he made at the dinner table when a much younger Truitt would fidget during grace.

"Tell your sister you have me," Wiley said. "I'll account for her son's death."

"It's my mess," Truitt said, pulling away when Wiley tried to silence him again. "You need someone, you got me."

He liked finding reasons to dislike Wiley, especially when he was younger. He always felt Wiley was trying to backfill where his daddy had been, and even though Truitt's memories of his daddy were thin, he'd concocted a version of him by picking the opposite of everything Wiley was. Wiley was soft spoken. Truitt's daddy was bold. Wiley couldn't tell a joke. Truitt's daddy drew crowds with his stories. Wiley was a bad shot. Truitt's daddy was the best. Wiley was kind to Truitt's mama. And that's where the father Truitt tried to piece together fell apart.

As in everything else, Truitt's father was the opposite of Wiley in the way he treated Truitt's mama. He remembered her crying most of all. There were times the sound of it still echoed through the house. He'd wake some nights, thinking he heard her screams. No amount of wishing could wish that away. If he'd have been able to explain that to Addie Anne, maybe she'd have understood why Truitt could never leave his mama. He couldn't fail her like his daddy had, because that's not what a man did. Maybe he and Addie would have ended up together one day, if only Truitt had been strong enough to tell the truth.

"Is that the deal you want to strike, Mr. Holt?" Mr. Giordano said. "Your game? Your money? And you?"

"No," Wiley said before Truitt could speak. "There's no deal that ends with me leaving Truitt here. Not tonight. Not ever."

Mr. Giordano's eyes drifted toward the front of the room. He smiled, wagged a finger at Truitt to stop him from talking, and pointed toward the band. The drummer had started a slow roll that silenced the room. Truitt felt the rhythm first in his gut, and then he heard it. Mr. Giordano motioned toward a curtain near the band. It hung over a doorway. Truitt had watched the waitresses come and go, carrying trays stacked with steak dinners on their way out and empty dishes and dirty silverware on their way back in.

"Watch this," Mr. Giordano said.

The same beautiful woman who had served Mr. Giordano his dinner and draped a napkin in his lap glided out from behind the curtain. She wore a tan dress that shimmered, making her look naked except for the dark hair that fell over her shoulders. She cradled a large burlap bag in her arms, as if it were a child.

Truitt sat up tall so he could see the woman. She struck a pose in front of the band. She stood with a long, lean posture and tilted her face toward the smoky lights. Her skin sparkled as she turned slowly side to side, seeming to hypnotize the room as she showed them the bag in her arms. Truitt felt he should turn away, but he couldn't. It was as if she held his chin in her hands and wouldn't let go.

This was the bolita toss he'd read about and heard about so many times. This was Mr. Giordano's game.

Sashaying back and forth in front of the band as the drummer's beat slowly built and grew louder, the woman readjusted the bag and took hold of it with two hands. Stopping again, directly in front of the band, she began to swing the bag forward and back, her hips following the same motion. Forward and back. As she built up momentum, the drummer's beat followed her. It grew louder and faster until she let go of the bag and sent it sailing across the room.

Truitt stood, straining to see where it landed. He'd dreamed of seeing this one day. Truth be told, he had dreamed of his game being this big one day.

A man at a table near the band caught the bag. He and the woman sitting next to him stood. Positioning himself behind his date, the man wrapped his arms around her and helped her lift the bag. It held one hundred bolita balls, probably made of ivory.

As the woman worked the bag forward and back, the man moved with her. A cheer went up, and the drums fell into a slower rhythm that mimicked the motion of their bodies.

The bag sailed to another table and another. One woman swung the bag side to side instead of forward and back. Another swung it in slow circles that made her hips roll in a circle too.

When the drummer settled into a slow, steady beat—something that calmed the audience—a large man wearing a suit and tie walked from behind the curtain. The bag sailed one last time into the man's arms. Feet planted wide, he held the bag as the beautiful woman who had made the first toss walked slowly toward him. When she reached his side, she ran a hand across his shoulder, down over the burlap bag, and clutched one of the bolita balls through the rough fabric. Truitt sucked in a deep breath as cheers exploded again.

Everyone began to clap, slow and steady like the drummer's beat. As if it were a trophy, the beautiful woman held up a long knife. It glittered where the smoky lights hit it. The cheers grew louder, and with a single swipe of the knife and a final crash of the cymbals, she cut the ball free. Holding it cupped in her hand, she lifted it overhead.

"Number twenty-seven," she cried out.

Mr. Giordano slapped the table and leaned back in his chair. "Your game's drawing go anything like that?"

"No, sir," Truitt said, his face hot and his hands damp.

"Bet that little girl of yours wouldn't have left you if you had a game like this," Mr. Giordano said.

Truitt glanced at Wiley. His jaw twitched, but nothing else changed. Still, it was enough. Wiley didn't care to hear Mr. Giordano talk about Addie like that. And neither did Truitt.

"Addie's going to be famous one day," Truitt said. "And I'll be real proud of her when it happens. She don't need me or my game."

Mr. Giordano raised a hand and dipped his head as if he meant no disrespect.

"Back to the business at hand," Mr. Giordano said. "Someone needs to account for my nephew's death, and I can't insult my sister with a cheap substitute. No offense."

He was talking to Wiley. He meant Wiley was the cheap substitute.

"You can," Wiley said, starting to stand. "And you will. You'll settle for me."

With a flick of Mr. Giordano's eyes, two men appeared. They flanked Wiley, keeping him in his seat, though they didn't touch him. Truitt pressed both hands on the table, anchoring himself so he wouldn't run. Because that's what he wanted to do. He wanted to run until he was back home in Hockta.

"I will do what I want to do," Mr. Giordano said, staring at Wiley. "I'm afraid you get no say in the matter."

CHAPTER 52

I shifted Urban to my other hip and moved farther behind Siebert's broken-down car. Using the car as a shield was my best chance of protecting Urban from what was about to happen. I begged Mama to stop talking and come back. I could almost feel Siebert's finger tightening on the trigger with every step she took toward him and Aunt Jean. But no matter what I said, Mama wouldn't stop.

I closed my eyes, wishing myself back to that moment in Wilson's Market when I'd left Aunt Jean alone. If I'd stayed with her, I'd have never seen Truitt outside the swinging doors, and maybe we'd still be together. Maybe none of the rest would have happened. He'd be at home, instead of at the Trinidad Café. And now, I might never see him again because my one mistake of leaving Aunt Jean alone had led us here. If Mama didn't stop, Siebert Rix was going to pull the trigger.

"I won't let you go, Jean," Mama said, her voice quiet but stern. "Not a chance in hell."

She took another step, her hand stretched out to Aunt Jean.

Hearing Mama curse made Siebert smile. It was a satisfied look, like he figured he'd won something by dragging Mama down into the muck where he lived.

"This'll be the pleasure of my life, Inez," Siebert said, rolling his head slightly to the left, pinching one eye closed, and zeroing in on Mama as his target.

"Siebert, look at me," Aunt Jean said as Mama held her ground. "Look at me. It's me. Your Marilyn. I will go with you. Look here at me. Inez will let us go, and we'll drive until we see the Pacific. I'm done hiding out here. We'll drive until we're home again. It'll be just like it's always been, just like old times."

She punctuated her *T*s and *D*s, and her soft, breathless voice pierced the tension that had swelled between Mama and Siebert. But still, Mama didn't back down.

"I'll leave here with you," Aunt Jean said, her face shimmering in the light coming from the kitchen. Her lips sparkled. Her eyes glistened. "But if you hurt Inez, you and I will be over forever. She isn't worth that, Siebert. Inez isn't worth it. Please, don't ruin us."

It was another slap in the face, hearing Aunt Jean say those things about Mama. I wished I could shield Mama from it like I was trying to shield Urban.

Siebert lowered the gun as he leaned into Aunt Jean. She hadn't been able to make Mama back down, but she'd talked Siebert away from the ledge.

Even as small as she was, Aunt Jean wrapped one arm tightly around Siebert's waist and took on all his weight. They managed another small step toward the car. Mama stood tall, her fists clenched, not moving.

Aunt Jean continued plying Siebert with stories of the old days as he strained to take another step. She talked as if it were just the two of them. Slipping back in time, speaking in what must have been the voice she had as a little girl, she told him about looking out on that RKO tower and hoping one day, her mama would get well and come home. Hoping one day, she'd have a daddy like every other little girl. Hoping one day, she'd be in the movies.

As she kept talking about the old days and wringing out every good memory she could find there, she glanced up to see Mama still standing in her and Siebert's path. Mama shook her head, signaling she wouldn't move.

"I won't let you go," Mama whispered.

Still spinning her stories with a light touch, Aunt Jean's movements dropped back to slow motion. Her hand finding its way into her pocket was like her hand finding its way through black swampy water. And on and on she talked about Siebert taking her very first pictures, and did he remember, and didn't he want to have it all, one day?

And then her wrist twisted inside her pocket, and her hand reappeared. In it, she held the knife we'd pulled from Donna Lee's body.

Mama must have seen the knife, too, because she eased away, finally, step by step, slowly so she didn't rouse Siebert from the trance Aunt Jean had spun.

Aunt Jean was playing a part. She had been all along. She had been doing and saying whatever it took to keep Siebert happy and stop him from hurting Mama.

I should've never second-guessed myself. I'd been right from the beginning. And I shouldn't have second-guessed Aunt Jean. She would never leave us. And now Mama knew it too.

Aunt Jean had fooled even me.

That's how good Aunt Jean was. That was how brilliant.

As if Aunt Jean had rested a warm hand on his cheek, Siebert looked down on her. Smiling up at him, the knife dangling from one hand, Aunt Jean dipped out from under Siebert's arm. He wobbled, confused to be suddenly alone. He lost his balance and hopped on his good leg trying to steady himself. Wrapping a second hand around the knife, Aunt Jean drove it from low to high and caught Siebert just below the rib cage.

He crumpled to his knees and then fell face first, dropping the gun at his side.

Aunt Jean tumbled backward. I turned away, wrapping a hand over Urban's eyes. When I looked back, Mama was already in motion. Surely, she'd never seen such a thing, and yet, she knew exactly what to do.

As the dirt around Siebert's body began to turn black, Mama wrapped Aunt Jean in her arms and led her away. She called out to me quietly, as if not to wake Siebert, and told me to get inside. With

Urban bouncing in my arms, I ran in a wide arc that kept us far from Siebert. As I threw open the screen door, I heard Mama shout out that I should call for help.

She shouted, no longer worried about waking Siebert, because he was dead.

Aunt Jean had to kill Siebert, and she'd known she would from the moment she asked me to get the tire. She knew Siebert would never leave without her. And she knew Mama would never let her go. She also knew there was only one way that showdown would have ended, and she wasn't going to let that happen.

Aunt Jean knew all along that there was only one ending to Siebert's story.

Truitt's was the only number I knew by heart. I dialed, and Daddy answered. The moment I heard his voice, I remembered he was there. Mama had told me he went there to watch over Truitt's mama while Sheriff Bishop went to Tampa to bring Truitt home. Breathless and stringing words together that made no sense, I told him we needed help. We needed him to come home quick.

And like Mama, even though I had never seen such a thing, I knew exactly what to do. I told Daddy what happened, but I didn't tell him the truth.

"I killed Siebert Rix," I said, staring out at Mama and Aunt Jean as they backed slowly away from Siebert's lifeless body. "I stabbed him, and he's dead."

CHAPTER 53

I sat at the kitchen table, while Mama and Aunt Jean stood at the sink. Neither of them spoke. The water ran as they waited for it to warm. The gentle gurgle of the faucet was the only sound in the house. Urban sat on the floor at Mama's feet, his arms wrapped around her legs.

Mama tested the water, and then took Aunt Jean's hands in hers. Working soap between each of Aunt Jean's fingers, Mama scrubbed away Siebert's blood. As she worked, she whispered to Aunt Jean that it was all right. It was all over. We were safe. We were all safe. Aunt Jean smiled that smile of hers, the one she conjured when the rest of her was numb.

There was a time I would have thought about the part I was playing. What did my character want? What did she need? But that night, watching Mama love Aunt Jean the way she did made it easy to just be me.

Outside the window, a splash of light made me turn. Daddy's car jerked to a stop. The driver's door flew open, and footsteps pounded toward the house. I stood from my seat at the table in time to see Daddy jump the steps leading to the back door. Behind him, Truitt's mama hurried toward the house, too, but she stopped short.

From the kitchen window, I couldn't see the ground at Ilene Holt's feet, but I knew Siebert Rix lay there, his left leg twisted at a sickening angle. His blood had turned the dirt around him into a rectangle of black mud that cradled him like a grave. Ilene stared down at his twisted, tangled body, her hand over her mouth. I knew what she was thinking, because I was thinking the same.

We were both wondering if Truitt, down in Ybor City at the Trinidad Café, would come to the same end as Siebert Rix. Or had he already?

Bursting through the back door, Daddy swept me into his arms. He held me tight, then pulled back and checked me over, running his hands down my arms and cupping my face.

"I'm fine, Daddy," I said, aiming him toward Mama and Aunt Jean. Truitt's mama was all alone, and I needed to be with her. "I'm not hurt. I'm not hurt."

I peeled Daddy's hands from my face as he asked over and over what had happened.

Daddy always told me I was a good shot because I could rein in my nerves . . . person can think better when her nerves are in check, stay calm when trouble's barreling down. Everything Siebert had told us, the scraps of what had happened to Truitt, snapped perfectly into place. As if someone whispered it in my ear, I knew what we had to do and why.

"You have to call the Trinidad Café," I said, squeezing Daddy's hands so he'd listen. "You have to tell them Siebert Rix is dead. He said those men wanted payback for the man Truitt killed. Tell them Siebert is payback."

And then I stepped aside, giving Daddy a clear path to Mama.

By the time I reached the porch and glanced back through the kitchen window, Daddy was sweeping Mama and Aunt Jean into his arms. His sobs floated through the window screen and out into the dark night.

"That's not going to be Truitt," I said, walking down the steps. "He's not going to end up like Siebert."

Truitt's mama glanced up. Seeing me, her face crumpled. I turned and looked in the kitchen window again. Daddy had the telephone in his hand. He was making the call.

"Siebert Rix being dead means Truitt doesn't have to die," I said. "Daddy's making the call. He'll know what to say. He'll know how to make it right."

She shook her head, still not believing me. I wrapped her in my arms and said it again. Ilene was a tiny woman but forceful. I sometimes summoned her if a part called for a petite woman who defied every notion people had about her being timid and accommodating. Because Ilene was none of those things. She was opinionated, commanding, and took up far more space than people would have expected. But that night, for those few moments, she was small.

She leaned into me, her body trembling like it was getting ready to crack wide open.

"Truitt loves you," she said, staring up at me with a shallow smile. "You two thought you were so good at keeping your secret. Well, a mother knows when her boy is in love."

"Yes, ma'am," I said, thinking I didn't care anymore who knew about Truitt and me. "My mama says the same sorts of things. I love Truitt too. I think I always have. Even going back to when we were just kids."

"He didn't mean to kill anyone, couldn't have. And he sure didn't mean for any of this to happen to your family."

As if suddenly realizing she should be comforting me, not the other way around, Ilene pulled me into another hug.

"Oh, Addie," Ilene said, and like Daddy, she pulled back to inspect me for bumps and bruises. "Your daddy said you did this. To Siebert. That you had to kill him. Are you hurt? Did he hurt you?"

I didn't like lying, especially all wrapped up in Ilene's arms. We both loved Truitt, and that made us family. But I had to lie for Aunt Jean.

"I'm fine," I said. "He killed Mr. O'Dell and Donna Lee Foster. I had to do it, or he would have killed us too. I had to."

And I lied because I had to. Everyone in Hockta knew about Siebert putting Aunt Jean in a sling. And they'd see that he killed Mr. O'Dell and Donna Lee and know I had no choice. But if anyone knew

Aunt Jean had killed him, the entire world would care. Reporters and photographers would come. It would never end. Day after day, Aunt Jean would have to relive what happened. We'd all have to relive it. But if I killed Siebert Rix, no one would come. No one would care. Even as afraid as I was that I'd never see Truitt again, I pieced together something else. I had to protect Aunt Jean.

"They're going to come home," I said to Truitt's mama. "Wiley and Truitt will come home to us."

CHAPTER 54

All night, the crowd in the Trinidad Café had moved in waves, growing and dwindling with the hour. Cocktail hour. Dinner hour. And lastly, the hour when the bolita toss took place. Ever since the woman wearing the dress that shimmered had cut ball #27 from the bag, the tables had been emptying. Or maybe they'd been emptying because two of Mr. Giordano's men had taken up on either side of Wiley. The move made it clear to everyone in the place that something was about to happen. The move made it clear to Truitt that no one could stop Mr. Giordano from doing whatever he wanted to Truitt.

"I worry this moment is getting away from us," Mr. Giordano said.

Truitt's hands had gone numb from clinging to the table. He loosened them and let them slide into his lap. He'd made it all the way to Ybor City, only needing to make one thing happen when he got here. He needed to strike a deal to protect his mama and Addie. He'd done that, and now he'd do the rest of what he needed to do.

"I'm ready to make right what I did wrong," Truitt said, having to wrestle the words loose and force them out.

Wiley started to stand again, and this time, a hand on each shoulder held him in his seat.

Mr. Giordano lifted a finger, enough to make the two men back away. He turned to Truitt as if to say something but stopped when the wiry man with the brains reappeared. The man whispered in Mr.

Giordano's ear. After a few nods, Mr. Giordano dismissed him. Leaning back in his chair, he sucked on his cigar and stared at the ceiling.

"Seems another wrench has been thrown in our dealings," Mr. Giordano said after a long silence. "Though it may well be a fortunate development for our Mr. Holt."

Wiley's eyes flicked to the wiry man who still stood nearby and back to Mr. Giordano. Truitt did the same but saw nothing in either man's face to explain what had happened.

"Can I assume you know a Mr. Harden Buckley?" Mr. Giordano said.

"I do," Wiley said. Short. Simple. And he exhaled. It was a slight movement, the motion of his chest, but Truitt was certain it mattered.

Wiley was relieved.

"It would seem he's called with news that Siebert Rix is no longer Lake County's concern."

Truitt looked to Wiley, waiting for him to say something. But he didn't.

"What does that mean?" Truitt asked, irritated with himself for having not kept up. "And why would he call here saying that?"

"And would Mr. Buckley appreciate that news about Siebert Rix would hold some significance for me?" Mr. Giordano asked, ignoring Truitt's questions and speaking directly to Wiley.

"He would," Wiley said.

Truitt took a breath to ask another question. Wiley met his eyes and shook his head, warning Truitt to stay out of it.

"And he's a cautious man, this Mr. Buckley?" Mr. Giordano said. "If he was uncertain who was on the other end of the line, might he take care what he said on a phone call?"

"All true," Wiley said, relaxing into his chair, and for the first time, he took a drink of the whiskey a waitress had set before him.

"I know Mr. Buckley," Truitt said, trying to shoulder his way into the conversation. "And I don't want him mixed up—"

"I'm going to do the two of you a favor," Mr. Giordano said, giving Truitt the same look, as if to say . . . stay out of it. "We'll assume your Mr. Buckley was vague for a reason. He's cautious. But he called here, knowing what he had to say could help our young Truitt get out of trouble."

"I believe he wouldn't call unless that was precisely the reason," Wiley said.

"And there is only one outcome for Mr. Rix that would get our young Truitt out of trouble," Mr. Giordano said. "Would you agree?"

"I would," Wiley said.

"Mr. Buckley called because Siebert Rix is dead," Truitt whispered. "How? What happened?"

"Given that," Mr. Giordano said, shaking off Truitt as if it didn't matter how Siebert Rix died, "I'll let Mr. Rix account for my nephew's death, and I will consider Mr. Holt's debts satisfied."

"That'll appease your sister?" Wiley asked.

"It will, assuming I receive confirmation that Mr. Rix is, in fact, dead," Mr. Giordano said. "I'll need a body, you understand? And I damn sure don't want you calling to tell me the man has been spotted near the Florida/Georgia line. That will not suffice."

This part of the conversation, Truitt understood. Mr. Giordano was making a point. He'd known all along that Wiley had been hiding Truitt while trying to make everyone believe he'd left town.

"Agreed," Wiley said, his jaw stiff, but the subtle widening of his eyes gave him away. He understood what Mr. Giordano said, too, and he realized how badly things could have gone. "I couldn't help but notice you referred to this as a favor—you doing us a favor—accepting Mr. Rix in place of Truitt. And I'm guessing you'll now ask a favor of me in return."

Mr. Giordano smiled, impressed by Wiley. "You see Mr. Wall over there?"

Truitt and Wiley both glanced at the table where Charlie Wall was waving for the beautiful woman who cut the bolita ball from the bag to come sit on his lap. When she drifted in the other direction, he waved her off like he didn't want her anyway.

"Know what he's saying right about now?" Mr. Giordano said. "He's saying in his day, the crowd would have been twice this. In his day, the women were prettier. In his day, in his day, in his day. Every fucking night I come here, it's the same. And I think to myself, Why the hell do I have to listen to that man? Every. Fucking. Night."

"And that's the favor?" Wiley said.

As the tables around them continued to empty, Wiley kept his eyes firmly on Mr. Giordano and the two men who had flanked him since Wiley sat down.

"What are you talking about?" Truitt said. He'd tried his best to latch on to the conversation, but he had lost the thread again.

"That is what I want," Mr. Giordano said, as the woman who kicked off the bolita toss walked past. She left behind a burst of citrusy perfume. As if the scent drew him to his feet, Mr. Giordano stood and smoothed his jacket. "And here's how I want it done. I want something that will leave behind a headline. A three-inch-tall headline. I don't want simple. I don't want something that's over quick. I want dirty hands. I want details that return to the paper with every anniversary of the day. I want to relive it year after year, in excruciating detail. That . . . is the favor I'll ask in return."

Mr. Giordano waited for an answer. If he got one, it was in the form of a nod from Wiley. The deal was done, but Truitt didn't know what the deal was.

"And we'll be even?" Wiley said. "No more favors?"

Mr. Giordano nodded as he leaned over the table to snub out his cigar.

"Last thing I have for you, Mr. Holt," Mr. Giordano said. "That man over there, Charlie Wall, he's the one who killed your daddy. Probably one of the last things he managed to do before he lost the reins to me. Took him trying two times to make it happen. There was a fire, yes? That scar I see peeking out of your collar is a reminder of it, I suppose."

"Yes, sir," Truitt said, leaning in and listening hard. "All true."

Truitt had been struggling all night to keep up, and he didn't want to fall behind now. He needed to hear what Mr. Giordano was about to tell him.

"The next attempt didn't fail," Mr. Giordano said. "Because whoever shot your daddy, he was a damn good shot. Rest assured, it wasn't Charlie. The man can't shoot for shit, but it was Charlie who done it in every way that mattered."

Truitt felt another hand on his shoulder. This time it was Wiley's. Laughter broke through the crowd and landed at their table again. Charlie Wall's laughter. Truitt wanted to stand, but when he tried, the floor teetered underfoot.

"I go nowhere with my family," Mr. Giordano said, nodding at his two men and stepping from behind the table. "Don't drive to church in the same car. Don't walk down the street with them. Don't even sit on the front porch of my own damn house. And you know why?"

Truitt shook his head, but he knew. And it was a knowing so strong, it stuck in his throat and made it so he couldn't swallow.

"If I did any of those things, I'd be using my family as a shield," he said. "And I'm not a man who does that. Your daddy was, and that tells you everything you need to know about him. Big talk is a weak man's path. A strong man, he puts in the work. Your daddy was a big talker, and it got him in trouble. You saw your daddy shot that day because he was using you as a shield. Because he took the weak man's path."

"And him being killed in our driveway?" Truitt said.

"Whoever pulled the trigger," Mr. Giordano said, "he was making a statement. You and your mama stood to gain the most by your daddy being dead. That's what it means when a man is shot in front of his own home. His family is better off without him."

Mr. Giordano pulled on his hat and leaned toward Wiley.

"Just to be clear," he said. "Once this last favor is done, you, Truitt, the loved ones you share, you'll have no reason to fear me. Once this favor is done."

"I understand," Wiley said, and now Truitt understood too.

"Then I'll leave you with this," Mr. Giordano said. "Charlie Wall's wife is away on vacation. She's gone until Tuesday."

That was the last thing Mr. Giordano said before disappearing behind the curtain with the beautiful woman who brought him a steak.

CHAPTER 55

Truitt was caught between wanting to get home and wanting to go directly from Mr. Giordano's table to Charlie Wall's house so he could kill him that very night. That's what Mr. Giordano wanted. Siebert Rix was dead, so for now, Truitt's mama and Addie were safe. But keeping them safe meant killing Charlie Wall. Once Truitt had settled on that, he also settled on wanting to stay in Ybor City and kill him. Tonight. Then they could go home to Hockta, and if he never left again, he'd be a happy man.

Walking out of the Trinidad Café, Truitt said as much to Wiley. Wiley said that they would most certainly not be going to Charlie Wall's house and that Truitt should get his ass in the car.

Now, making the forty-five-minute drive from Tampa to Hockta, Truitt sat silently while echoes of the last thing he'd said to Addie bounced around inside his head . . . have a good life. Truitt slinging those words at Addie had put in motion every bad thing that had happened since.

"What's going to happen when Tuesday rolls around, Charlie Wall's wife comes home, and he ain't dead," Truitt said, breaking his long silence. "I know that's what Mr. Giordano wants. He wants Charlie Wall killed hard, killed up close. Look at what's already happened. With Mama being turned into bait. With Siebert Rix being dead. What the hell happens next if we let Charlie Wall live?"

Staring down the dark road ahead, both hands pressing against the sides of his head, Truitt was still caught between two paths. He wanted to scream at Wiley to turn around and scream at him to drive faster. The headlights cut a slender path, and it felt as if there were nothing in the world but the narrow stretch of road ahead. It felt as if he'd never see Hockta or Addie or his mama again. It felt as if that's what he deserved. To be alone the rest of his life.

"What's going to happen is that you're going home, and you're going to be safe," Wiley said. "Santo Giordano got what he wanted. Siebert Rix being dead is payback for his nephew getting killed. He'll forget about Charlie Wall. Charlie is just an annoyance."

"You don't know that," Truitt said.

"I do," Wiley said, his eyes pointed straight ahead, his hands squarely on the wheel. "Santo Giordano himself said Siebert checked the box."

"And what if Siebert Rix isn't dead?" Truitt asked, Wiley's calmness winding him up even tighter. "You just taking Harden Buckley's word for it?"

"Take Harden's word over seeing it with my own eyes," Wiley said. "Everyone's safe, and best we can do now is get ourselves home in one piece."

"For now, everyone is safe," Truitt shot back. "Are they going to keep being safe if Charlie Wall lives past Tuesday?"

Truitt was angry at himself, but he was angry at Wiley too. He'd clipped Truitt of being able to do what a man should do. Maybe he could stop Truitt from going to Charlie Wall's house tonight, but he couldn't stop Truitt from asking one simple question.

Something had been gnawing at Truitt since Charlie Wall first recognized him as being a Holt. Charlie had also recognized Wiley, and all that was adding up to be the answer to something Truitt had wondered about all his life. But like always, Wiley pieced it together first, even beating Truitt to his own question.

"You going to finally ask me what you've been working up to asking since we left Tampa?" Wiley said.

Truitt swallowed, knowing that once he asked, the answer was coming whether he liked it or not.

"How did Charlie Wall know who you were?" Truitt said.

Wiley nodded as if Truitt had asked the right question.

"The fire that nearly killed you and your mama, you probably don't remember it," Wiley said, speaking slowly. "But I sure as hell do. You spent weeks in the hospital. The burns you got, they took a long time to heal. But the infection, that's what nearly killed you. And watching it nearly killed your mama."

Truitt forced himself to sit tall and tugged on his collar to hide the scars he still had from that night. He already felt himself softening toward Wiley, and he didn't want it to be that easy. Being angry made Truitt feel powerful, like he could make his way back to Tampa and kill Charlie Wall all by himself. And that's what he needed to feel. Powerful.

"Anyone who knew your daddy knew the fire was no accident," Wiley said. "Everyone also knew it was meant to kill your daddy. And only one man could have put that in motion. Back then, that was Charlie Wall. He paid your daddy good money to bust the bars he wanted busted, haul in the bolita games he wanted off the street. But your daddy got greedy, and he liked to talk. Talked too much for his own good about taking what wasn't his to take. Charlie Wall heard, couldn't abide the stealing, and ordered your daddy killed. He made no secret of it."

"You saying you believed Charlie Wall over my daddy?" Truitt said, defending his father though he'd heard part of this same story from countless people.

"I did," Wiley said, his eyes on the road. "But that didn't really matter. What did matter . . . after the fire didn't kill your daddy, Charlie Wall would try again. And maybe he'd be just as sloppy the second time. I wasn't going to let that happen. I went to him and asked if I could finish the job. Simple as that. It was the only way I could be sure you and your mama were safe."

"Anyone ask you to do that?" Truitt said, the words so shameful they limped from his mouth.

As if Truitt had spit in his face, Wiley flinched at the question.

"No," Wiley said, taking a deep breath and righting himself. "Nobody asked me to do nothing. All on my own, I asked Charlie if I could be the one to kill your daddy."

"And Charlie Wall said yes," Truitt said.

"Actually, the man said, 'Fuck if I care,'" Wiley said, shooting a little something back Truitt's way, which was the first sign of respect Wiley had given. "And then, I killed your father to save you and your mama. But hand to God, I didn't do it so I could carry on with your mama."

Truitt had kept Wiley and his father on a scale for so long, believing first he always had to give more weight to his father. And then, as Truitt grew old enough to begin sussing out the truth, the scales corrected toward Wiley, putting the two of them in balance for a time. Now, he understood the two men never belonged side by side. There was no comparison. There was his real father, and there was Wiley. His real father had used Truitt as a shield. There was no way back from something like that. Wiley was the only one of the two who ever held any weight.

"Only one thing wrong with your story," Truitt said, lifting his chin and chest so Wiley would know he was ready to hear the rest.

The car rattled beneath Truitt, and off to the left, the orange trees sparkled with lights from Addie's house. Now, he wanted the car to slow. He was ready to believe what Harden Buckley said on that phone call. For now, everyone was safe, and this conversation between Truitt and Wiley had to play out. Truitt needed it to play out if he was ever going to put behind him what his six-year-old self saw all those years ago.

"Every word I've told you is true," Wiley said, leaning over the steering wheel as he slowed to turn onto the Buckleys' drive.

"The man who killed my daddy was a good shot," Truitt said. "Santo Giordano said the same. Sorry to say, Wiley, but you ain't a good shot. You'd have never tried to take a shot at my father, not with me in the car right alongside him."

"All true enough."

Wiley rolled the wheel hard to the left and began toward Addie's house.

"Tonight," Truitt said. "You asked Harden Buckley to watch over Mama when you came to Tampa. You went to him when you didn't know for sure you'd be coming back. Because you trust him."

Halfway down the Buckleys' drive, Wiley pulled over to the shoulder and parked, knowing the same as Truitt that this conversation had to play out. Like he was gearing up for something, Wiley drew in a deep breath, rolled his head side to side, and jostled his shoulders.

"Harden Buckley is a good shot," Truitt said when he figured Wiley was ready. "Best ever, most folks say."

"Yes, he is," Wiley said. "Shot so good, I'd trust him with my life."

"Harden Buckley shot my father." Truitt said it quick so he wouldn't have time to think about what it might mean between him and Addie.

Instead of answering, Wiley looked at something out the windshield. Truitt looked too. Someone was walking toward them. In the glare of the headlights, the figure was a long, lean silhouette. Then it stopped to hitch up its britches. It was Billy Pyke. Someone had seen to it he was let out of the basement. He held a hand up to his forehead, straining to see who was inside the car.

Wiley rolled down his window and stuck out a hand. "Just me," he shouted. "Everything all right up at the house?"

"All good," Billy said, planting his feet and crossing his arms, doing his best to cut an imposing silhouette in the headlights. "Got it all under control."

"Two things you need to understand," Wiley said after giving Billy one last wave. "First, your mama doesn't know Harden pulled the trigger. Doesn't know I asked him to either. In every way that matters, I killed your father. But your mama doesn't need to know any of that. That's for her benefit, not mine. And I'd also suggest that Addie doesn't need to know."

"I understand," Truitt said, and in that short time, he knew Harden having pulled the trigger meant nothing between him and Addie. He also knew he'd never tell Addie what her father had done. "And the second thing?"

"Your daddy chose the path he took," Wiley said. "He was a weak man, and he got himself killed."

The word stung. Weak. Truitt had been feeling weak and like a coward ever since he tried to strong-arm Addie Anne into staying with him. There was no sense hiding from it. Not anymore. Up to now, Harden Buckley had been right to keep Truitt from his daughter. Because Truitt had been weak just like his daddy.

"Addie Anne has a future in mind for herself," Truitt said, ready to put an end to his feeling like a coward. "But that future ain't here in Hockta. It's somewhere else. And wherever that is, I want to go with her. If I do that, if I leave here with Addie, will you stay with Mama?"

"I'm always telling you don't bother with the questions you know the answer to," Wiley said, grabbing Truitt by the shoulder and ruffling his hair. "Whether you stay or go, I'll stay with your mama just as long as she'll have me."

"One last thing, Wiley," Truitt said, because he was done being weak. "You did what you did to protect my mama and me. Me needing to kill Charlie Wall like Mr. Giordano said, that's my way of protecting Addie Anne and my mama. I need to do it, Wiley."

"What you need to do," Wiley said, throwing open his car door, "is trust me. Your mama and Addie will be safe. I'll see to it."

CHAPTER 56

After Wiley parked outside the Buckleys', he stood in their drive, look-ing down on Siebert Rix's broken, twisted body. Wiley hadn't slept in he didn't know how long. Hadn't eaten either. He had a hell of a mess on his hands, but he felt good. Strong. Now that Truitt knew the truth about his daddy and how he died, Wiley had space. He never realized how much room that secret took up until he let it go.

As Billy Pyke gave him a rundown of all that had happened, Wiley watched Ilene through the kitchen window. Wiley had assumed Harden killed Siebert, but that wasn't at all what happened. Reading from his notepad, Billy talked slowly, building suspense as his story got worse with every twist. Wiley had to keep reminding himself it was over, and he kept his eyes firmly on Ilene, thinking he'd likely never leave her again. Inside the kitchen, she clung to Truitt's neck, her arms so tightly wrapped around him that her feet were no doubt dangling in thin air.

He turned away for only a moment, not wanting to lose sight of Ilene, when a set of headlights flashed over him and Billy. Gerald Bigsby from the funeral home parked his truck behind Wiley's car. He'd sit and wait until Wiley was ready for him to remove the bodies. He'd take Donna Lee and Leland O'Dell first and come back for Siebert Rix. Gerald had hard-and-fast rules about who rode side by side in his truck.

"You call for a tow too?" Wiley asked Billy, the two of them wan-dering from Siebert Rix's body to the car he'd been driving since coming to town.

"Done and done," Billy said.

By the time Wiley and Truitt got back from Tampa, Billy had already taken statements from the family, untangled the whole of what had happened, pounded a piece of plywood over the Buckleys' front door, and called for the bodies to be picked up.

"You done real good, Billy," Wiley said. "Sorry I had to lock you in the basement."

Billy hitched up his pants again and gave a simple nod. He stood straight and tall, didn't slouch, and he held his head high. He'd gotten the adventure he always wanted, and it had sparked something new in him.

At Siebert's car, Wiley leaned against the open trunk and stared down on Donna Lee. Much as Wiley wished he could have changed this end for her, her life had always been barreling toward this point.

"Grab a blanket, would you?" he said to Billy. "You'll find one in the back of the patrol car."

"You figure Siebert killed her?" Billy asked when he returned with the blanket.

"That's what we're going with," Wiley said.

Given what Billy shared and what Wiley was told by the mobsters who came to town looking for Truitt, he thought it likely one of Santo Giordano's men killed Donna Lee. But he was not inviting that crowd back to his town.

Draping the blanket over Donna Lee and tucking it gently around her shoulders, Wiley leaned against the car and waited. Eventually, Truitt would tell his mama to quit fussing, and she'd come looking for Wiley. He was bracing for that moment. It would overwhelm him, no doubt, but he didn't want to cry. Three other times in his life, Wiley had cried. He figured that was enough for one lifetime.

The first day Wiley went into the basement at the sheriff's department, he cried thinking of all the people who were held down there, strung up, chained, even murdered by the previous sheriff. He'd been the big, boisterous type, and when folks grew weary of him, they elected Wiley.

He also cried the moment Harden finally agreed to take the shot that would kill Spencer Holt and save Ilene and Truitt. He'd had to beg Harden, and Wiley had never begged anything of anyone in his entire life.

And he cried the day he got the call from Harden Buckley telling him Truitt's daddy was dead. Spencer Holt is no longer Lake County's concern, Harden had said. Wiley hadn't been crying for Spencer Holt that day. The man may as well have dug his own grave. No, Wiley cried because the relief that Ilene and Truitt were safe overwhelmed him. He knew well the power of being overwhelmed.

Three times, Wiley had cried, and he didn't want this night to be a fourth. Other folks had it tougher than Wiley these past several hours, and he didn't want to wallow.

"And what of Siebert Rix?" Billy said. "Addie said she had to do it. Said he had a gun pinned on all of them, which is true enough. And she seen him kill Leland O'Dell with her own eyes."

"Then I'd say Siebert Rix may as well have dug his own grave," Wiley said.

Wiley and Billy both swung around at hearing the screen door fly open. Ilene, still looking so small in her rolled-up jeans and bare feet, ran down the porch stairs. Addie and Truitt followed, the two of them holding each other, Addie's head resting on Truitt's chest. Harden Buckley followed close behind, and if he didn't know about his daughter and Truitt Holt before, he knew now.

Wiley had thought he was ready, but taking Ilene in his arms, smelling her hair again, feeling the warmth of her body against his, he cried for the fourth time.

CHAPTER 57

Fifty years later, the groves are mostly gone. It used to be that every April ushered in the sweet scent of the orange blossoms. Up until my eighteenth birthday, I hated it. I hated the way the syrupy smell stuck in my throat and clung to my clothes. I hated a reminder that another year had come and gone, and I was still stuck.

But now, after all this time, I miss the orange blossoms. The frost that crept farther south every year eventually destroyed most of our groves. I still live in the same house, though it's only Truitt and me now. Our kids, three of them, are grown with families of their own. They're all driving in today so they can be here for the celebration.

I throw open the kitchen window, thinking of Mama and hoping for the slightest hint of the sweet blossoms. I've made her three-egg cake. Truitt doesn't like that I make my own birthday cake, but I don't mind. Not that it's easy. Mixing it up, setting it out to cool by the window, it makes me ache in my gut. I always make sure to do the baking when Truitt's not around to see how much it still hurts.

Five years since Mama passed. Daddy, almost ten years. I miss them every day.

In the living room, I tidy up. Things don't get so messy anymore. When the kids were young, it was a battle I lost every day. Mama would say the same when Urban and I were young, but the house was always neat and tidy when Mama was at the helm.

We're going to have a full house today and then some. Truitt's dealing with the outside, which is the way it always goes, and I'll handle the inside. Our kids are bringing their families. Between our three children and their spouses, we have seven grandchildren and one great-grandbaby on the way. Urban flew in from LA last night and will be driving down this morning. He's the only one who made it to Hollywood, having worked as a screenwriter for years now.

Everyone from the Lake County Theater will be coming too. April 30 will mark the fiftieth anniversary of the program that Aunt Jean founded, and today we will celebrate the occasion.

I've spent at least some part of every day of the last five decades working with the theater in one way or another. Between my work and Truitt's, I like to think that's why my house was never as clean as Mama's. I have no idea how many from the program will come. They'll range from children who are involved now, all the way up to retirees who are coming back to mark the occasion. We even expect a few who were there for the inaugural performance of *The Glass Menagerie*.

We're expecting reporters, too, but how many, I don't know.

Fifty years ago, we had plenty of reporters who came to town looking for Marilyn Monroe. They were racing to break the story that explained what had become of her and why she'd abandoned a career at its peak. People called the house. Letters came in the mail. We even got a call once from Dean Martin. Mama tried to hide her excitement from Daddy and was polite to Mr. Martin as she told him no one named Marilyn lived at our house.

A few of those reporters stumbled on news of Siebert Rix's death. He had been well known in Hollywood as Marilyn's first photographer, but when they learned he died attacking a young local woman, the news withered and died with him. Had they known he died at the hand of Marilyn Monroe, the news would have traveled the world and been regurgitated with every story written about Aunt Jean.

We still get the occasional reporter in town. When they do show up, Billy Pyke, who is the sheriff, tracks them down and tells them he'd be happy to give them directions to the onetime home of Marilyn Monroe.

"Take a right at the Baptist church outside of town," he says to them. "Can't miss it. Next right'll land you at the place. It's a ways back in there, so just keep driving."

Easy to get lost on those roads—that's what everyone in Hockta knows.

Straightening a few pillows, I pick up the newspaper Truitt left strewn across the couch. Tucking one section inside another so I can read it later, I fold it over. The three-inch headline shouldn't surprise me. Something similar shows up in the paper every year on the anniversary of the day Charlie Wall was murdered. When the anniversary is a nice round number, like fifteen, twenty, or twenty-five, the headline is larger. For this anniversary, the type is three inches tall.

50 YEARS LATER—MURDER OF TAMPA'S FIRST GANGSTER REMAINS UNSOLVED.

Each time an article runs, the speculations as to who killed Charlie Wall are largely the same. For a time, his bodyguard was a suspect, but most theories still point to Santo Giordano having ordered the hit. The reporters recycle the same facts about Charlie Wall's life, his ties to Tampa's wealthiest families, and his claim to fame as the grandfather of Tampa's organized crime. The articles also detail the brutal way in which he was murdered. After apparently inviting his assailant into his home, Charlie Wall was beaten with a blackjack and then with a baseball bat, and lastly, his throat was slit ear to ear.

It's been fifty years since the night Charlie Wall died, and still, no one knows who killed him.

◆ ◆ ◆

A few days after Wiley saw to it that the last body was loaded up and removed from the Buckleys' house, he woke, happy it was Wednesday.

He dressed in his uniform and quietly left the house, not wanting to wake Ilene or Truitt. After everything that had happened in Tampa and all the trouble Siebert Rix had caused, there had been no discussion about Wiley moving in with Ilene and Truitt. It just happened, like it had been that way all along.

Having Tuesday safely behind them would mean nothing to Ilene, but it would mean something to Truitt. He knew, same as Wiley, that Tuesday was the day Charlie Wall's wife returned from her vacation. It was the deadline Santo Giordano had set for killing Charlie Wall. Every day since they drove back from Tampa, Truitt had been pestering Wiley about the danger they were in if Charlie Wall lived past Tuesday. And every day, Wiley had asked that Truitt trust him to do what needed to be done.

Wiley drove out to the Buckleys' house first. As had been the case for the last few days, Harden was outside, alone, and a shotgun was propped near the back door. Wiley had come by every morning since he'd overseen Siebert Rix's broken body loaded up and toted away. And every morning, Harden had been outside, passing his time with one chore or another. This morning, though the sun was barely up, he was scraping the porch for a fresh coat of paint. Like Wiley, Harden had been keeping watch, neither of them getting much sleep, both of them needing to make sure things had settled and their families were safe.

"You sticking with a white paint?" Wiley said, stepping from his patrol car.

"That'll be for Inez to decide." Harden pushed off the ground where he had been using a putty knife to scrape loose paint.

"Everyone doing as well as can be expected?" Wiley said, glancing up at the quiet house.

"Guessing you already know the answer to that," Harden said, his voice edged with sarcasm.

Truitt had spent almost every minute of the last few days on the Buckleys' porch, he and Addie Anne sitting side by side, not room enough for a sliver of light between them.

"Truitt's kept me updated," Wiley said, surveying the spot where Siebert Rix's body had been. Someone dug out all the bloody mud, and there was no sign of the man left. "You telling me you really didn't know about Addie and Truitt?"

Harden grunted and went back to scraping. "Apparently Inez knew as much."

"He's not his daddy," Wiley said. "He's a good man. He'll give her a good life."

"Inez tells me the same," Harden said, pausing to glance up at the open kitchen window as if speaking more to Inez than to Wiley. "And she's proven herself generally right on all matters."

"True enough," Wiley said, giving a wave toward the kitchen window because he figured Inez was there. "One last thing. Not sure you'll take me at my word but wanted you to know there's no need of your shotgun anymore. And get yourself some rest. Things are settled now. For good."

Wiley's last stop before hustling back home for a late breakfast was Merle Gaffney's place. He didn't trouble Merle, but instead walked the property, following the cut grass to the seam where it met the overgrown grass. There, he found Merle's lawn mower. He pushed it back to the garage. He tried the side door first. It was still locked, something Wiley asked Merle to do several days earlier so no one could get inside to see Merle's car right where it belonged. Glancing around, Wiley settled on leaving the mower outside the locked door where Merle couldn't miss it.

Pulling up the drive at Ilene's place, Wiley's place now, too, he threw the car in park and let the feeling of coming home sink in. He hoped the sweetness never faded.

Up on the porch, Wiley reached for the screen door. The smell of bacon frying on the stove drifted through an open window, and that meant bacon-and-egg sandwiches for breakfast. He dropped the door, letting it slap closed, when one of the rocking chairs creaked and startled him. Truitt sat in the rocker, his weight pitched forward, elbows resting on his knees, a newspaper in hand.

"You seen this?" Truitt said.

He unfolded the paper so Wiley could get a look at the front page.

In the days after the fire that many years earlier almost killed Truitt and Ilene, Wiley had made a trip to Charlie Wall's house to ask if he would allow Wiley to finish the job on Spencer Holt.

So, when Wiley needed to return to Charlie's house, he already knew the way.

Long after dusk, on the day before Charlie's wife was to return home from vacation, Wiley parked outside Charlie's house, walked up the stone path, and knocked on the door.

Wearing slippers and a robe, Charlie answered.

"I'll be damned," he said.

Charlie had smiled at seeing Wiley again so soon after having seen him at the Trinidad Café, and, like the two of them were old friends, he had invited Wiley inside.

That had been the last time anyone saw Charlie Wall alive.

Now, as Wiley stood on the porch, his stomach growling for one of Ilene's bacon-and-egg sandwiches, he glanced down at the newspaper Truitt held. Reading the headline splashed across the front page, Wiley shrugged.

"Looks like someone got to Charlie Wall before his wife came home after all," he said. "Just like Mr. Giordano wanted."

The headline read . . . CHARLIE WALL FOUND SLAIN.

I fold the newspaper in half, closing it on the fifty-year-old headline about an unsolved murder, and tuck it away as Truitt walks in from outside. I still see the man I married at eighteen when he walks through the door. He tells people his construction business runs itself and that he's mostly retired. But we both know he'll work as long as his body will let him.

Truitt lost his mama seven years ago. Wiley passed thirty days later.

We meet at the bottom of the stairs, each of us taking care not to step on the grate in the floor. Even now, we still step over it so we don't conjure memories of that night. And we do it out of respect for Leland O'Dell and Donna Lee Foster.

Back then, the night the two of them died, Wiley had asked me, Aunt Jean, and Mama a few questions and then reassured Daddy there would be no consequences for me. Or for whoever killed Siebert Rix, because even before I shared the truth with the family who didn't already know, Wiley suspected Aunt Jean really killed Siebert.

Leland O'Dell was buried first. The entire town and most of Lake County turned out for him. A lovely service was also held for Donna Lee, and while not everyone treated her kindly in life, they did so in death. Siebert Rix was alone on his burial day; only the two men who dug his grave had been there to send him off.

"Tables are all set up," Truitt says, brushing a kiss past my cheek. "Chairs too. Don't know where you want me to put the reporters and such."

"They can sit with everyone else," I say. "We might have one show up. Might have a hundred. I just don't know how many will care to come."

Wallace Oehme is the first to arrive. He pulls his smoker in and parks it downwind of the tables. His wife, Debi, pulls in next with the rest of the food and the drinks. By two o'clock, our guests are arriving, and the kids from the high school have shown up to help serve and clear.

My three children arrive, and they sit with their families. Altogether, they take up an entire table, and seeing that makes me happy. Next to them, filling another table, is Aunt Jean's family—two sons and seven grandchildren. She has a daughter, too, who has yet to arrive.

Between the two tables, there's a flurry of passing food and throwing back drinks. They're laughing and telling stories, and seeing it makes me ache with joy, though I wish Aunt Jean's daughter were here to join in. And just as I think it, a car rolls up.

Everyone else sees the car as well, and every person at every table leaps to his or her feet and begins to cheer and clap.

Rossie is Aunt Jean's youngest, and she was a late-in-life surprise. Jean's husband, Walter, had always wanted a little girl. As Rossie steps from the car, I get a glimpse of her as I continue to weave through the cheering crowd. It's like getting a glimpse back in time. Rossie has Aunt Jean's heart-shaped face and delicate chin, and the color of her eyes shifts with the changing light, just like Jean's. Rossie's hair is the same soft shade of blonde, too, but mostly, Rossie shines like her mama always did.

Truitt sweeps up behind me, takes my hand, and as we reach the car together, the passenger-side door opens. Anticipation always preceded Aunt Jean. It was as if she set off sparks that made the air around her crackle. Her nearness was enough to make a person suck in a deep breath, hold it, and ready themselves to see something they would never see again.

The cheers grow louder when Aunt Jean appears. She's smiling, and her cheeks are flushed. Embarrassed by the attention, she waves for people to stop cheering.

Though her hair is now silver, and her eyes a watery blend of blues, greens, and browns, Aunt Jean still has the innocence and elegance she's always had. She's slowed the last few years, but only in the pace she walks. She'll still call me late at night or near dawn with an idea for a costume or next season's play. Long ago, she donated most of her dresses from her life before to the thrift shop over in Mount Dora. Every once in a while, one of them no doubt shows up in a prom picture, the young lady having no idea she's wearing a dress that once belonged to the great Marilyn Monroe.

Kissing Aunt Jean on the cheek, I give Rossie a hug and send her off to join her family.

"You look beautiful," I say, taking Aunt Jean's warm hand.

All these years later, she still smells of her sweet lotions and powders like she did the first time she came to Hockta. She had yet to change her name back then, and her hair had been soft brown with an amber sheen. She was nineteen. I was just a child. In a way, we grew up together.

Aunt Jean will be seventy-nine years old in a few months. She and I never went on our trip to California, though I did walk the red carpet with her at *The Seven Year Itch*. It was the shiniest night of my life. I even met Joe DiMaggio, who was there to escort Aunt Jean, though they weren't married anymore.

That was Marilyn Monroe's last public appearance.

Truitt and I each take one of Aunt Jean's hands and lead her through the crowd as the thunderous cheers continue.

At her family's table, Aunt Jean sits. Pulling her youngest grand-child into her lap, a plump little girl with red cheeks and a whisp of white hair, she lifts her chin ever so slightly to catch the light and smiles for the cameras pointed at her. Wearing a simple white cotton dress, always her best color, she looks to me like she did in that very first *LIFE* magazine. Like she's soaking up a sunny Sunday afternoon.

"People once knew me by Marilyn Monroe," she says, addressing the reporters gathered around the table. "I had a career in the movies for a time. My Addie Anne has shown me on the computer where you can see all the ones I was in if you're interested. I think about anything you want to know about Marilyn Monroe is out on that computer, if you'd like to look."

The reporters smile and laugh, already charmed by Aunt Jean. They're also surprised she doesn't realize they already know every detail of Marilyn Monroe's life. The entire world does.

"We have a marvelous theater program here," Aunt Jean says. "I hope all of you will spread the word and help us raise enough money to keep it going for another fifty years."

Making one last public appearance had been Aunt Jean's idea. She saw it as a way to bring in more donations, enough to support the the-ater long past her days. That's how she put it when she posed the idea.

"Invite the press," she said. "Invite them all, and let's hope a few still remember Marilyn."

For a half hour, Aunt Jean answers questions about her theater and the things she remembers from her long-ago career in acting. She recounts her favorite leading men, the feuds the newspapers wrote about that never were, the unhappiness she battled for so long.

"This town saved me, if you want to know the truth," Aunt Jean says. "Starting when I was barely more than a child, before I'd even invented Marilyn, they took me in. They tried to soothe what troubled me. I didn't make it easy on them."

There is more laughter.

"Tell us, Mar . . . Jean," a young reporter says. Her long hair has gone limp in our humidity. She brushes it from her eyes only to have it fall again. She reminds me of myself. "Why did you stay here in Hockta? I know you were married. My condolences. Did you quit your career for the love of your life?"

Aunt Jean smiles, and that faraway look settles in her eyes.

"I quit the movies and settled here in Hockta some years before meeting my Walter. I chose this life because I started something new. I've always been happiest when I was working. I simply changed my work. But to answer your question, yes, I stayed here for the love of my life. The *loves* of my life, actually. My family. Addie Anne. Urban."

She pauses, looking for Urban. Spotting him, she takes his hand and pulls him to her. He looks like Daddy. His blond hair has faded to silver, but he holds his head like Daddy always did. High. Strong. I'm still the better shot, though.

"And their mother, Inez, and their father, Harden," Aunt Jean says, finding me in the crowd and smiling.

Her smile is soft and measured, perfect for the mixture of sadness and joy that comes with remembering Mama and Daddy.

"All of my family," Aunt Jean says. "They're the reason I stayed. Something happened to me fifty years ago, on one terrible night, that made me think about how I wanted to spend the one life I had. You ask me why I left because you assume I lost something. But I didn't. I lost nothing, and I gained everything."

As I listen, I realize I stayed here in Hockta for many of the same reasons. I didn't stay because I was afraid to go. I didn't stay because I was afraid to lose Truitt. I never truly dreamed of becoming an actress. Instead, I dreamed of the glittery, perfect life I thought Aunt Jean had as Marilyn Monroe. I thought it was an easy path to happiness, but I was wrong.

I stayed here in Hockta because I found a new dream. Many new dreams. The one we celebrate today is the dream Aunt Jean and I shared and have brought to life over these past fifty years.

Pushing to her feet, Aunt Jean makes a sweeping gesture across all the people gathered around her. Some of them found their way to her theater program because they were somehow damaged. Aunt Jean told them to take what had hurt them and use it in their work. Pain will pave your way, not beauty.

A few others who found Aunt Jean were people who stuttered, and she taught them the breathy whisper that helped her overcome her own stutter. And many others who found her were lonely. Her contagious joy swept them up and healed them. Once they were joyful, too, they swept up someone else who was lonely. And so on and so on.

Over a span of fifty years, Aunt Jean has built a community where people who never belonged found a home.

"Look at all that's come since I chose a new path," Aunt Jean says. "We've built something here. All of us together, and it's been the greatest pleasure of my life."

Daddy once warned me to take care around shiny things. Most folks are too easily fooled. It takes strength to look at what's underneath, what's at the heart of it. Aunt Jean and I both, all of us, we've found a life here that shines through and through.

"Those years I spent as Marilyn," Aunt Jean says, "they were only a sliver of who I am. You'll find the rest right here in Hockta, Florida."

ACKNOWLEDGMENTS

Many thanks to everyone at Thomas & Mercer and Amazon Publishing for embracing this book and taking amazing care of it as it made its way to readers. I owe tremendous thanks to Liz Pearsons for her interest in my work, her editorial guidance, and her enthusiasm for this story. And a big thank you for asking . . . what else are you working on? My thanks also to Charlotte Herscher for the tremendous care she showed my characters. And thanks to Jenny Bent and all the fine folks at the Bent Agency for their professionalism and commitment.

Writing about organized crime and Ybor City in the 1950s was a little beyond my comfort zone as I struck out on this project. I owe great thanks to Ace Atkins for all the writing he's done—be it fiction or nonfiction—on the subject. His attention to detail and skills as a writer, both of which brought this world to life, gave me the confidence to tackle it as well. I also owe tremendous thanks to Gilbert King for the extraordinary and enlightening research and writing he's done regarding the history of Lake County in Central Florida. Though my Lake County is a fictionalized version, Gilbert's work inspired me to spend some time in this part of the country to see what I might find.

Thanks to William and Karina, my early readers. And to Andrew and Sam, thanks for talking over storylines and drumming up crowds. And lastly, this is a novel that examines the difference between power and strength, with particular emphasis on the strength of women. My thanks to the first strong woman in my life, Dr. Jeanette Harold.

ABOUT THE AUTHOR

Photo © 2019 Val Ritter

Lori Roy's debut novel, *Bent Road*, was awarded the Edgar Allan Poe Award for Best First Novel by an American Author. Her work has been twice named a *New York Times* Notable Crime Book and has been included on various "best of" and summer reading lists. *Until She Comes Home* was a *New York Times* Editors' Choice and a finalist for the Edgar Allan Poe Award for Best Novel.

    Let Me Die in His Footsteps was included among the top fiction of 2015 by Books-A-Million and named one of the best fifteen mystery novels of 2015 by Oline Cogdill. The novel also received the 2016 Edgar Allan Poe Award for Best Novel, making Roy the first woman to receive an Edgar Award for both Best First Novel and Best Novel—and only the third person ever to have done so. *Gone Too Long* was named a *People* Magazine Book of the Week, was named one of the Best Books of Summer 2019, and was excerpted by *O, The Oprah Magazine*.

    Roy lives with her family in West Central Florida.